Shakespeare's Playhouses

AMS Studies in the Renaissance: No. 19

ISSN: 0195-8011

The Theatre 1576-1599

The Blackfriars (after Hollar) 1608-1655

NON SANS DROICT

STRUCTOR

CONSILIARIUS

SHAKESPEARE'S PLAYHOUSES

by

Herbert Berry

With illustrations by C. Walter Hodges

AMS

The Globe 1599-1613

1614-1644

1613

Library of Congress Cataloging-in-Publication Data

Berry, Herbert.
    Shakespeare's playhouses.

    (AMS studies in the Renaissance, ISSN
0195-8011; no. 19)
    Bibliography: p.
    Includes index.
    1. Theaters—England—London—
History—16th century. 2. Theaters—
England—London—History—17th century.
3. Shakespeare, William, 1564-1616—
Stage history—To 1625. 4. Theatre, The
(London, England) 5. Blackfriars Theatre
(London, England) 6. Globe Theatre
(Southwark, London, England) 7. London
(England)—Buildings, structures, etc. I.
Title. II. Series.
PN2596.L6B47   1987   792'.09421   85-48061
ISBN 0-404-62289-5

AMS PRESS, INC.
56 East 13th Street
New York, N.Y. 10003

Manufactured in the United States of America

Contents

Preface

One can describe all the playhouses of Elizabethan, Jacobean, and Caroline times as Shakespeare's because one thinks first of him when one considers the theatrical industry of those times. But four playhouses were literally his because he was (or became) a shareholder in the enterprises that controlled them, and it is with these four playhouses that this book has to do. They are the Theatre in Shoreditch, the Blackfriars of 1596, the Globe of 1599, and the Globe of 1614.

Apart from the fascination they have because Shakespeare was associated with them, these places are important because they embrace and virtually define the whole of the most remarkable period in English theatrical history. The Theatre opened at the very outset of the period, in 1576, and in size and shape was the archetype for later playhouses. Blackfriars was refurbished into its final form in 1596, at what one might call the beginning of the apogee of the period. Three years later the Globe opened, having been built partly of materials taken from the Theatre when it was pulled down during the Christmas season of 1598-99. The Globe burned to the ground in 1613, at the end of that apogee, and a new and better Globe opened the following year. This new Globe and the refurbished Blackfriars were the homes for many years of the most celebrated company of players of the time, the King's Men, and playhouses and men fell silent only when Parliament put an end to the whole period in 1642.

This book consists of the six essays I have written about these playhouses, two concerning the Theatre, one Blackfriars, and three the first and second Globes. All the essays are based on studies of the documents of the time. Five essays have been published before. The sixth, which is the longest, has not. It concerns mainly the second Globe but has implications for the other playhouses discussed here.

I have left three of the published essays as they were, except for a few corrections and clarifications. The essay about Blackfriars is twenty years old, and the world of theatre history has moved on. I have reshaped my argument and sought out more ancient documents, but I have not changed my point, which I still think right. In the essay called "The Globe: Documents and Ownership," I have reresearched and rewritten the section about tilting and other martial games, including the appendix that goes with it. I have also dropped the section at the end in which I reported my earliest findings of the matter treated here in the essay that has not been published before. My new remarks about martial games are largely the result of generous suggestions by Professor Alan Young of Acadia University in Wolfville, Nova Scotia.

I am indebted to the McGill-Queen's University Press, Wayne State University Press, and to the editors of *Studies in Philology*, *Shakespeare Quarterly*, and *Medieval & Renaissance Drama in England* for permission to republish material here. I am also indebted to Prof. P. M. Swan of the University of Saskatchewan for going over my expansions of abbreviated Latin, to Mr. C. Walter Hodges for illustrating another work of mine, and to my wife, Elizabeth, for a great deal of editorial assistance. I am indebted, finally, to the University of Saskatchewan for a generous grant toward the preparation of this book.

In referring to dates given in old documents, I modernize those from January 1 to March 24. In transcribing old documents, I also modernize "I" and "J" and the sign at the ends of words by which writers usually meant an "s" but sometimes an "es." I expand abbreviations in italics when an abbreviation sign is present, in square brackets when one is not. I do not expand abbreviations signified by superlinear letters. I transcribe significant crossings out in square brackets and use "CO" to mean crossed out. I cite documents at the Public Record Office by giving only the call number. When I cite documents in other collections, I give the name of the collection and then the call number. I abbreviate the more familiar of these collections as B.L., G.L.C., Guildhall, and Corporation of London, meaning the British Library in Bloomsbury, the Library of the Greater London Council in Clerkenwell, the Guildhall Library at Guildhall, and the record office of the Corporation of London also at Guildhall. I cite a series of documents belonging to the same class by giving the first call number fully and the others by a slash and the part that is different: for example, I cite C.54/450/m.50 and C.54/462/m.36 as C.54/450/m.50, /462/m.36.

I use the customary abbreviations for well known published works: H.M.C. for the volumes of the Historical Manuscripts Commission, V.C.H. for the Victoria County Histories, and C.S.P. for the Calendars of State Papers (Dom. for the Domestic series, Ven. for the Venetian one). By "Chambers" I mean E. K. Chambers' *Elizabethan Stage* unless I give another title.

Transcriptions of documents at the Public Record Office appear here by permission of the Controller of Her Majesty's Stationery Office.

The Theatre

Aspects of the Design and Use of the Theatre in Shoreditch[*]

Much of what we know about Elizabethan and Jacobean playhouses as buildings comes at random from documents about something else. Seeking information about these buildings is a frustrating business, and never more frustrating than when the building in question is the Theatre in Shoreditch, because while many documents have been found about the place, they seem to say particularly little about the building itself, its equipment, and its use. They retail the misunderstandings, miscalculations, probably the chicanery of the Burbages, the Braynes, the Miles, the Allens, the Peckhams, and Thomas Screven with peculiar and depressing persistence. Here and there, however, even these documents allude to the building, and thanks to the sheer quantity of the documents, these allusions are more numerous than one might think. Virtually all these allusions have been known at least since 1913, and most have appeared often enough in histories of the

1

playhouses. Nobody, however, has listed them in one place, and, more important, nobody has pointed out some of the conclusions about the place that such a listing might suggest. If the resulting image of the Theatre is very incomplete indeed, it is worth considering. Some of it reminds us of what we know of other playhouses, but some does not.

I discuss here various aspects of the building and its use, drawing upon every detail about it that I have found in the documents mentioned below in my "Handlist of Documents about the Theatre in Shoreditch." First of all, the Theatre was a timber building, as all the litigants and several deponents who mentioned the building said,[1] and it was built among other timber buildings that had existed for a long time and many of which continued to exist. The Theatre depended on these other buildings in many ways. The same phrases were sometimes used to describe physical aspects of them all.[2] At least two workmen worked on them all.[3] At the beginning of the Theatre's history it could incorporate building materials from the other buildings, and at the end of its history building materials from the Theatre could be used in the other buildings.

In addition to timber, the Theatre had in it wainscoting, tile, brick, sand, lime, lead (for gutters and flashings?), and at least £40 worth of iron.[4] Possibly 10% of its cost was in iron. It was built mainly by carpenters and plasterers, but also by "wo'kmen of all sortes for that purpose."[5] In 1582, a painter, Randolph May, was a regular employee in it, "A servant," as he put it, "in the house Called the Theater."[6] It was eventually taken down by a carpenter and his workmen. Nobody mentioned thatchers or stonemasons in connection with its erection, repairing, or taking down. Hence the tile was presumably for the roof, and it must be a nice question why when they re-erected the place as the Globe in 1599 the Burbages should have used thatch. Hence, too, the brick must have been at least partly for the foundations. A bricklayer who worked for James Burbage said that he built chimneys, but he mentioned only Burbage's other buildings on the property, not the Theatre.[7]

The timber buildings around the Theatre were also part of James Burbage's leasehold. In 1576, when he acquired them, these (according to a carpenter who eventually worked on them and a painter) were "very symple buyldinges but of twoe storyes hye of the ould fashion and rotten."[8] Burbage had the right to pull these down and use their materials for other buildings. These materials were "timber tile bricke yron lead and all other stuffe whatsoeuer of the said ould howses or buildinges."[9] The nature of their roofs and siding appears in a remark of the Burbages: in 1576 the buildings were open to the weather because they lacked "tyling" and "dawbing."[10] They were, that is, timber-framed ("half-timbered") buildings with tile roofs. At least some of them, as we have seen, had chimneys. James Burbage supplied for the Theatre about £50 worth of "od peces of Tymber waynescott & suche like thing*es*," which very likely came from these older buildings.[11] It must be, therefore, a fair guess that the Theatre was also a timber-framed building with tile roofs.

The Theatre was, as Elizabethan playhouses went, expensive to build. When finished, it was worth, according to the landlord, Giles Allen, £700, and the Burbages more or less agreed with him. According to Henry Lanman, who had built the Curtain nearby, and Allen on another occasion, it was worth a thousand marks (£666.13s.4d).[12] One might fairly say, therefore, that it was worth £683 plus or minus 2.5%.

Like other playhouses of the time, or maybe of any time, the original estimates were much less than the eventual cost. In this case they were about £200 less.[13] Even so, there may be a hint that the finished Theatre was not fully the building originally planned. For a fragment of a lawsuit of 1588 has James Burbage saying that his partner, John Brayne, did not have money enough "to redeeme the said Lease nor had wherw[th] to *pr*ocied in those manner of building*es* wherein he had procured" Burbage "to enter into." Curiously, however, great quantities of timber, lead, brick, tile, lime, and sand were left over, unused, when the place was finished, worth something like a hundred marks (£66.13s.4d.) or £100.[14]

The Theatre was large and solid. After it had been taken down it was called "the late greate howse called the Theatre."[15] One of the old buildings near it was (according to the landlord, Allen) "one great tiled Timber barne...verie substantiallye builte." This barn was eighty feet long and twenty feet wide, and it was only a few feet from the Theatre. But though Allen thought the barn impressive, in 1576 it was "Ruynous and decayed," and, as a tenant said, "soe weake as when A greate wynd had Come the tenan*tes* for feare haue bene fayne to goe out of yte.'' When the Theatre was up, Burbage shored this barn in two or three places against the Theatre, and these ''shores'' remained until the taking down of the Theatre in the winter of 1598-99, when, because they were still necessary, they were fixed against the ground.[16] One may speculate about the shape of a building shored in two or three places against a long rectangular one (in 1596 De Witt wrote that the Theatre was one of the four ''amphitheatra Londinij''). Whatever its shape, the Theatre was clearly a solid affair. Burbage presently had the barn, as well as shored up, ''grouncelled, Crosse beamed, dogged togeather,'' and cut up into flats.[17] At one point, towards its end, Allen and Cuthbert Burbage spoke about using the Theatre as a playhouse for only five more years and then converting ''the same to tenem[tes] or vppon rep*aracio*ns of the oth*er* houses there.''[18] So the Theatre was suitable for cutting up into small holdings—flats, no doubt, like the great tiled barn—and if the houses near it could contribute to the Theatre in 1576, the Theatre could contribute to them at the end of the century.

The Theatre needed repairs fairly often, including extensive repairs and ''further building'' in January and February 1592, at about the same time Henslowe was extensively refurbishing the Rose. On February 25, 1592, James Burbage had spent from £30 to £40 ''w*t*in this vj or vij weekes passed,'' as a carpenter said who had probably worked on the project.[19]

The Theatre was designed so that it could be taken down and carried away, for in their lease of April 13, 1576, before the first timbers rose, James Burbage and Allen had agreed that if Burbage carried out various aspects of the lease, he could ''take downe and Carrie awaie...all such buildinges and other thinges as should be builded erected or sett vpp...either for a Theatre or playinge place.'' Burbage included the same clause in a renewal that he had drawn up in 1585 (and Allen refused to sign).[20] In a sense, Burbage's heirs eventually did take down the Theatre and carry it away to Southwark where they re-erected it as the Globe. Allen said some eight times in three lawsuits that the Burbages pulled the playhouse down and took it away, and two of his witnesses who actually saw the building coming down and being removed said the same thing once each, as did the Burbages once.[21] The matter, however, was not that simple. The building was such that once it was down neither the Burbages nor others would have wanted it all. The Burbages spoke once of having taken away just the "tymber" and once of having exercised their right to take away the "tymber and building*es*." They also spoke once of having taken down and carried away "parte" of the playhouse, and in the same sentence and some four others identified that part as "certayne tymber and other stuffe wch weare ymploied in makinge and errectinge the saide Theator." Their friend who helped in the work, William Smyth, said as much once, and their antagonist, Robert Miles, said once that the place was good for its "tymber and other thinges."[22] Eventually, both the Burbages and Allen became more precise, and then they said the same thing, the Burbages twice and Allen twice. The Burbages spoke of their "pullinge downe, vsinge and Disposinge of the woodde and tymber of the saide Playe house," and Allen said that the Burbages, having pulled the Theatre down, "did then...take and carrye awaye from thence all the wood and timber therof vnto the Banckside in the p*a*rishe of St Marye Overyes and there erected a newe playe howse wth the sayd Timber and wood."[23] Evidently the building was valuable for its main members (timbers) and its facings, doors, wainscoting, and the like (wood) and little else. In his original lawsuit, Allen said that in pulling down the building, the Burbages trampled and wore out his grass to the value of 40s.[24] Could he have had in mind great piles of rubble that the Burbages had left behind in the open places around the Theatre and that (since Allen did not complain of having to do so himself) they eventually carted away?

Allen said that sixteen people pulled the Theatre down and took away its timber and wood: Cuthbert and Richard Burbage, their builder (Peter Street, "the Cheefe carpenter"), their friend of some fourteen years (William Smyth), and twelve workmen, with the Burbages' mother, Ellen, the ostensible owner, looking on. Nobody challenged Allen here, and Street and Smyth, when given the chance, did not deny their parts in the work.[25] How long these people spent pulling the Theatre down and when they did so have long been moot points. On February 4, 1600, Allen said they pulled it down "aboute the feast of the Natiuitie of our Lord God" in 1598. On April 26 of the same year, two of his witnesses who saw the work being done said it was done at Christmas, 1598. Another, who did not see the work being done, gave the date as "about A yeare or better as he remembrythe sythence." Then on November 23, 1601, Allen said the Theatre was pulled down "aboute the eight and twentyth daye of December" in 1598.[26] There would be little problem about the business, except that in the official summary of Allen's first lawsuit about it the people who pulled the Theatre down are said to have entered Allen's premises for the purpose on January 20, 1599. Allen is said to have gone before the court in the Easter Term following, and the lawsuit is said to belong to the Trinity Term following that. In another lawsuit of 1601, however, Allen said that he had filed this first lawsuit in Hilary Term, 1599, and the Burbages agreed with him.[27] Moreover, in 1599, January 20 was one of the four days on which preliminary business could be conducted in the law courts before the formal sittings of Hilary Term began. It was, that is, one of the first days on which Allen could have filed his lawsuit. It is likely, therefore, that the clerk who drew up the summary used the date of filing for the date of the offence, and that the date of the offence does not appear in the summary.

Two of Allen's friends and tenants went to see the Theatre coming down, and their remarks in April, 1600, also may suggest when the removal took place. One of them, John Goburne, a merchant tailor, put his experience this way: he heard "that the Theatre was in pullinge downe. And having A *lettre* of Attorney from the defendt [Allen] to forbid them: did repayre thyther" where he found the men pulling the place down. The other, Henry Johnson, a silk weaver, said he went to the Theatre "when yt was in pullinge downe to charge" the Burbages *et al.* "not to pull the same downe" because they had no contractual justification to do so. They assured him that they were taking it down only to put it back up in the same place "in another forme," and they showed him "decayes" that prompted them to do so. Yet despite all their speeches, "they pulled yt downe and Carried it Awaye."

Allen seems not to have anticipated the removal of the Theatre, hence would not have equipped his friends in advance with a letter of attorney to forbid it. His friends' accounts, therefore, are probably abbreviated and perhaps may be expanded roughly as follows. When one or both of them heard about what was going on at the Theatre, he or they sent word to Allen, who was "then in the Countrie," as Allen said, presumably at his house at Hazeleigh in Essex. Being sixty-five or sixty-six years old and approaching the state he described three years later as "verye aged and vnfitt to travell, Allen supposed his letter of attorney would get to Shoreditch more quickly than he could.[28] He sent the letter, therefore, to Goburne and Johnson, and a day or two after the work had begun they went, apparently separately, to the site in Allen's name. The work was still going on, and most of the materials of the Theatre were still there. The Burbages and their associates thought it wiser to deceive Allen's emissaries than to push them aside. So they placated at least one of them with a playlet about rebuilding the Theatre in the same place and got on with the work. If the Theatre would not have been removed on a single day, December 28, as Allen said, the process of removing it may well have begun on that day. It was a Saturday, which especially in the midst of the Christmas holiday was a good day to begin such an enterprise, because people like and his lawyers could be expected to be in places like Hazeleigh. The removal, therefore, may have gone on over a weekend and into the following week, when after the first day or two, the Theatre trickled in wagons along Shoreditch and Bishopsgate, into Gracious Street, down Fish Hill, across London Bridge, then west along the River, and into Maid Lane.

The main question for us is what sort of building could be designed to be removable, could be pulled down and its valuable parts taken away by some sixteen people in two to four days, and its valuable (and visible) parts identified as timber and wood. The answer must be what the other evidence suggests, a timber-framed building. In view of all the iron in it, perhaps some of its timbers were held together with ironmongery rather than the usual and preferable mortises and tenons cut into the timbers so that the timbers could be fitted together and hold themselves in place. In 1620 the authorities tried to stop builders in London from "knitting and fastening" timbers together with "barres and crampes of Iron, and other like deuices" because the practice contributed to deformities in buildings.[29] To James Burbage forty-five years before, however, it might have seemed appropriate because of the unusual shape of the building or his need to make it removable. Those parts of the Theatre the Burbages did not immediately take away and did not use in the Globe must have been piles of daubing and plaster, much lath, perhaps numerous broken tiles, and the brick foundation.

Because they used the timbers of the Theatre in the Globe, the new building must have been of much the same size and shape as the old one. Otherwise the timbers would not have fit with one another whether held together with mortises and tenons or ironmongery. The Burbages and associates could have cut the timbers, of course—made new mortises and tenons, drilled new holes for ironmongery—but to do that was to build a playhouse smaller in all its dimensions than the Theatre was. There seems little sense in cutting timbers to achieve a smaller playhouse. In the first Globe, therefore, the Theatre seems to have been substantially reborn.

Once he had secured his lease on April 13, 1576, James Burbage and his partner, John Brayne, set about getting the Theatre up and open to the public as soon as possible. They put off doing much about the buildings already there on which Burbage had engaged himself to spend £200 within ten years. They seem to have opened the playhouse to the public within a few months and long before the place was fully finished. Perhaps they opened as soon as they had their main members together, gallery floors in place, and walls up around the tiring house. They then set about less necessary tasks, in the mornings no doubt, and paid for them with the takings of plays performed in the afternoons. By this time even Brayne's wife was at work on the building. They did not seriously turn to the other buildings until 1582 and after.[30] Obviously they thought there was more money to be made in plays than in a housing estate.

The Theatre had a "Theater yard," as an actor, John Allein (Edward Alleyn's brother), said, and, as he also said, "the Attyring housse or place where the players make them readye."[31] It may also have had at least one window, out of which James Burbage called his dead partner's widow a "murdring ho^r," but the window is mentioned only as on the Burbages' "grounde" and could have been in their dwelling near the Theatre rather than in the playhouse.[32] The Theatre also had galleries in which people sat and stood to watch plays, and parts of the galleries were called rooms. It was written into the draft lease of 1585 that the landlord, Giles Allen, his wife, and family had the right to watch plays *gratis* there, or as the lease ran, "vpon lawfull request," they could "enter or come into the premisses & their in some one of the vpper romes...have such convenient place to sett or stande to se such playes as shalbe ther played freely wthout any thinge therefore payeinge soe that the sayde Gyles hys wyfe and familie doe come & take ther places before they shalbe taken vpp by any others." There was a door where a gatherer stood at the bottom of stairs (presumably) going up to the galleries. A witness said that he was "to stand at the do^r that goeth vppe to the gallaries of the said Theater to take...money that shuld be gyven to come vppe into the said Gallaries at that do^r." He spoke a few sentences later of "the said do^r going vppe to the said Gallaries."[33] James Burbage should have been alluding to this portal when he mentioned "doares" and "Gates," but he probably meant the main entrance to the playhouse, which, therefore, was sizable.[34] Two of the gatherers at the Theatre are named: during the first ten years of the place a literate man named Henry Johnson, who was or became a silkweaver and was both a tenant and agent of Giles Allen; and after 1586 the widow, Margaret, of Burbage's partner, Brayne, who was also Burbage's wife's sister and therefore aunt to Cuthbert and Richard.[35]

It seems that the scheme for dividing the profits at the Theatre was the same as that at other early playhouses. The players apparently received the money of people who went into the yard and the house-keepers, that is, the owners, Burbage and Brayne, received the money of those that went into the galleries. Burbage and Brayne, and after Brayne his widow, and after her her executor (Robert Miles) argued throughout virtually the whole life of the Theatre about the division of the housekeepers' takings. The notary public whom Burbage and Brayne hired in 1577 and later as an arbitrator said that the arguments about takings concerned "the yndifferent dealing and collecting of the money for the gallories in the said Theatre for that...John Brayne did thinck him self much agreyved by the indyrect dealing of the said James Burbage therein." After Brayne's death in 1586, Burbage allowed the widow for "A certen tyme to take & Receyve the one half of the profittes of the Gallaries of the said Theater." When, finally, the widow Brayne with the help of a court order tried to compel Burbage to share the housekeepers' profits with her, she sent a man to collect "half the money that shuld be gyven to come vppe into the said Gallaries."[36]

If James Burbage shared profits of the galleries with his fellow housekeeper, Brayne, he also shared money with players. The player, John Allein, said that he went to Burbage in November 1590 for "certen money" which Burbage had "deteyned" from Allein "and his fellowes [out] of the Dyvydent money betweene him and them growing also by the vse of the said Theater." Allein identified himself and his fellows as the Lord Admiral's Men. Moreover, Brayne's successor, Robert Miles, said that Burbage gathered money which was "Devident betwene him & his said ffelowes," some of which he would often "thrust…in his bosome or other where about his bodye Disceyving his fellowes of ther due Devydent wch was equally to haue bene devyded betwene them." These sums shared with players evidently had nothing to do with Brayne or his successors, who did not claim them. Hence they arose in the yard rather than the galleries and belonged to players, and hence Burbage shared them not as house-keeper but as leader of a company of players who used the Theatre. Perhaps the Lord Admiral's Men shared the Theatre with Burbage's company for a time in 1591 as they did the playhouse at Newington Butts for a time in 1594.[37]

Burbage and Brayne put the money from the galleries into "the Commen box," which neither was supposed to be able to open by himself. There may have been one lock, to which somebody else had the key—or perhaps two, to one of which Burbage had the key and to the other of which Brayne had the key. When it came time to share profits, the two men would together open the box or have it opened. But as Brayne's successors remembered him saying, Burbage had "A secret key wch he caused one Braye A Smyth in Shordiche to make for him," with which he "did by the space of about ij° yeres purloyne & filche therof to him self moch of the same money."[38]

Other than the remarks about James Burbage's sharing money with John Allein and other players, there is only one episode mentioned in these documents in which players figured significantly. Two people who worked at the Theatre in 1582, a painter and a yeoman, described the way in which Edmund Peckham had then tried to wrest Giles Allen's property from him (see "Handlist," Category A). Allen's property included that which Burbage had rented and on which he had built the Theatre. Peckham sent people to harass the Theatre, and Burbage had to hire people to protect it. Burbage kept his playhouse, but "the players for sooke the said Theater to his great losse." He seems to have estimated his loss at £30 and to have refused to pay that much rent to Allen.[39]

Because eight people connected with the property in Shoreditch spoke about how much money the Burbages had made or were making with the Theatre, it has been tempting to guess what the place might have been worth annually to its owners. Wallace tried it, for example, and by misquoting or inadequately quoting four of the people he arrived at £80 a year (p. 21). Chambers (II, 391 and note) also tried it, and he arrived at a generous tolerance: £100 to £200 a year. The eight people, however, seem to raise more questions than they answer. Most included properties other than the Theatre in their computations and did not distinguish money gained in the Theatre from that gained in the other properties. Only one made it clear whether he thought of the Burbages as whole owners or half-owners, and only one (another) distinguished the Burbages' role as housekeepers, that is, owners, from their other roles as managers of a company and players in it.

Four people spoke in 1592 about James Burbage's profits in recent years. Two of these four are the most reliable of all the witnesses. One, the actor John Allein, who belonged to a company at the Theatre, said that Burbage had received for the last five years "of the proffittes of the said Theater & other the premisses to the same belonging an hundreth poundes or CC markes [£133.6s.8d.] by yere for his owne share." The other, Henry Lanman, owner of the Curtain, said that since August 1586, Burbage had received "for his parte of the proffittes" of both the Theatre and Curtain, "one yere w^t another to this daye the some of one hundreth markes [£66.13s.4d] or fourscore poundes by the yere." Raphe Miles, considerably less reliable than these two, said that Burbage had received for the same period "seaven or eight hundreth poundes of Rentes and proffites growing of the said Theater and the appurtynances longing & adioyning to the same." And his father, Robert Miles, perhaps even less reliable, said that for the "viij or ix yeres past" James and Cuthbert Burbage had received "for the proffittes & Rentes of the Theater & the howses & tenem^{tes} there...two thowsand markes [£1,333.6s.8d.] at the least for his owne [presumably James's] parte/ And so moche shuld the said Braynes" and his successors "haue had for ther partes of the said proffittes and Rentes."[40] The two Miles certainly meant to distinguish the Burbages' share from Brayne's, and Allein and Lanman may have. All four probably meant the Burbages' share as housekeepers only. Three of them, however, combined the Theatre with the other properties; and they ignored the deal Burbage and Brayne had made with Lanman in the winter of 1585-86 providing that the owners of the Theatre and Curtain would share the profits of the two houses for seven years. Lanman, finally, combined the profits of those two houses.

Eight years later, in 1600, Giles Allen and two of his witnesses, the two Miles, spoke of how much the Burbages had made with the Theatre, presumably for all twenty-two years or so of its existence. They gave, however, figures that are grossly low and bear no relation to the figures of 1592, yet all three meant these figures to be impressively high. Had they forgotten how long the Theatre had existed? The two Miles said that "James Burbadge and Cuthberte Burbadge in ther seuerall lyfes tymes haue gayned by the Theater aboue A thousand markes [£666.13s.4d.]. Allen had "Crediblie hard" that the two Burbages "in their seuerall times haue made" of the Theatre "the somme of twoe thousand powndes at the least." Another of Allen's witnesses said that the Burbages "haue gayned muche," and yet another, "greate somes of money," from the Theatre. Cuthbert Burbage said that Allen's figure was wrong,[41] and he must have been right to say so, not, as Allen probably thought, because it was too high, but because it was too low. None of these people said how much Brayne had or should have made, nor how much of the money was for housekeeping and how much, if any, was for managing and acting.

When we use these statements, we are comparing not just apples and oranges, but pears, peaches, and pineapples as well, and hence we are unlikely to arrive at really reliable figures. It is possible, however, to blend all these fruits and so to see at least what some of the limits of the figures might be. Let us suppose that all the figures refer to the profits deriving from the playhouse only and owing to the housekeepers only. Let us also suppose that John Allein, Lanman, and the two Miles meant only half the profits of the housekeepers and assumed that Brayne had or should have received a like amount. Let us suppose, finally, that the Curtain yielded exactly what the Theatre did, so that the deal between James Burbage, Brayne, and Lanman made no difference in the profits due each housekeeper. Then, if we take mean figures when people mentioned two, and divide when they mentioned sums for several years, we should arrive at this table of the figures given in 1592:

Source	Housekeepers' profits per year	Half share
John Allein	£233.6s.8d.	£116.13s.4d.
Henry Lanman	£146.13s.4d	£73.6s.8d.
Raphe Miles	£250.0s.0d.	£125.0s.0d.
Robert Miles	£313.14s.6d.	£156.17s.3d.

The figures given in 1600 produce these results if one divides them by twenty-two: Giles Allen, £99.18s. a year, and the two Miles, £30.6s. Allen's figure could be useful if he was thinking only of the owners' share of the Theatre and only of the Burbages as half-owners. The figures of the two Miles make no sense unless they were thinking as Allen may have been and, as well, meant the profits only for the years from 1592 onward. Should these guesses be right, one could add the three men to the table above as follows:

Source	Housekeepers' profits per year	Half share
Giles Allen	£181.16s.0d.	£90.18s.0d.
Robert and Raphe Miles (1600)	£190.9s.6d.	£95.4s.9d.

Even so, their figures are rather lower than the others.

Because of our first assumption at least, all these figures could be higher than the true figure, but the true figure probably cannot be higher than they are. The average of the two most reliable figures is £189.10s. a year for the housekeepers. The average of all the figures is £219.6s.8d. a year and the average of all but those of 1600 is £235.18s.5d. The range, then, lies between £190 and £235 profits a year for the housekeepers from about 1584 to 1592, with two conditions: 1) any number is likely to be higher than the true figure, and concomitantly 2) the reliability of the figures diminishes as they increase. A reasonable guess, which might be high, would be £190.

If all the figures behind these calculations are imprecise to say the least, one additional figure seems more precise, and it leads to further calculations. In 1578 Burbage and Brayne tried to settle their differences by submitting them to arbitrators. These arbitrators proposed, among other things, that Brayne "shuld haue x^s by the weeke for & towardes his house keeping and the said Burbage to haue viijs...for & towardes his house keping of the profittes of such playes as shuld be playd there vpon sundaies."[42] In other words, in 1578 the galleries of the Theatre were expected to yield profits of at least 18s. on Sundays.

How often were the players likely to use the place in a year? Between 1594 and 1600, Henslowe's players used the Rose six days a week and, on average, 236 days, or forty weeks, a year.[43] If the players at the Theatre worked similarly, if 18s. represents the housekeepers' profits from a relatively full house, and if there were nothing but relatively full houses, the housekeepers' profits would have been £212.13s.5d. a year. At least part of this reckoning is about right, for when in 1582 the mortgageholder, John Hyde, collected the housekeepers' profits towards the money owing him, he received £5 a week.[44] If forty weeks a year is a reasonable figure for the Theatre as well as for the Rose, the Theatre would have been worth £200 a year to the housekeepers. So the reasonable guess above, however awkwardly derived, is obviously worth considering.

One may, then, suggest a few things about the profits of the Theatre with confidence and some others, if not with confidence, with reason. With confidence: during at least the first half of its history, the galleries (the takings of which provided the profits of the housekeepers) yielded about 18s. on Sundays and almost as much on other days, so that the weekly amount was about £5. With reason: such sums persisted through the whole history of the place, so that the housekeepers could count on profits of about £190 to £200 a year in the 1590s and also in the 1570s and early 1580s. Such sums, finally, would explain why Burbage and Brayne were willing to let the cost of the Theatre rise to some £683, why Brayne was willing to sell his assets to join in building it, and why moneylenders were willing to lend money on it. It was worth about three and a half years' purchase, 29% of capital a year. Yet, attractive as such a venture may seem, it may have been considerably less attractive than Burbage and Brayne at first thought it might be. At one point when Brayne was worried about their rising costs, Burbage is said to have assured him, "it was no matter[,] praying him to be contented[;] it wold shortlie quyte the cost vnto them bothe."[45]

NOTES

* Originally published in *The First Public Playhouse*, ed. H. Berry (Montreal, 1979), pp. 29-45.

   I give below the place in C. W. Wallace's *The First London Theatre* (Lincoln, Nebraska, 1913) where one may find a transcription of a relevant allusion, page first, then a colon, then the lines or item number, then, in brackets, the number of the document as listed in "A Handlist of Documents" below. The "Handlist" gives information about the document, including the modern citation under which one may find it.

1. The building is described as a timber one some twenty times. See the allusions quoted and cited below.

2. P. 189: 9-14, 29-31 [D-2].

3. Three carpenters (Richard Hudson, Thomas Osborne, Bryan Ellam), a bricklayer (Thomas Bromfield), and a laborer (William Furnis) said they had worked on the old buildings, and two of the carpenters (Hudson and Ellam) said they had also worked on the Theatre: pp. 76, 77 [both C-17], 226-29, 229-31, 231-34, 234-36 [all D-7].

4. Pp. 142: 9-13; 147: 15-18; 137: 19-21 [all C-23].

5. Pp. 141: 6-7; 137: 9 [both C-23]. Three carpenters specifically worked on the place: Richard Hudson, also called a bricklayer and plasterer; Bryan Ellam, also called a plasterer; and James Burbage. See pp. 71: 14-15; 76, 77 [all C-17]; 141: last line; 142: 13 [both C-23]; 226-29 [D-7].

6. P. 240: 2, 21-22 [D-7]; he made the remark and identified himself as a painter in May 1600, when he was sixty years old.

7. P. 230: 11-25 [D-7].

8. P. 241: 1-6 [D-7].

9. Pp. 188: 29 to 189: 2; 189: 9-14, 29-31 [all D-2].

10. P. 273: 26-34 [D-16].

11. Pp. 142: 10-13 [C-23]; 189: 9-14 [D-2].

12. Pp. 148: #5 [C-23]; 164: 21 [D-1]; 185: 12-13 [D-2]; 277: 19-21 [D-17].

13. P. 140: 1-2 [C-23].

14. Pp. 41: 2-4 [C-3]; 147: 15-18 [C-23].

15. E.134/44-45 Eliz./Interrogatory #9 and the answers to it.

16. Pp. 193: 14-17 [D-2]; 225: #10; 227-28: #10; 231: #10; 233: #10; 236: #10; 241: #10; 243: #10 [all D-7].

17. Pp. 201: 29 to 202: 8 [D-2]; 233: #10 [D-7].

18. Pp. 216: 18-23; 221: 9-13 [both D-7].

19. Pp. 69-70: #5; 70: #6; 76: 20-24 [all C-17]; 104: bottom to 105: 4 [C-21]; 119: 26 [C-22]. See Glynne Wickham, "'Heavens,' Machinery, and Pillars in the Theatre and Other Early Playhouses," in *The First Public Playhouse*, pp. 1-15.

20. Lease of 1576: pp. 191: 1-15 [D-2]; see also pp. 159: 8-15 [C-28]; 167: 29 to 168: 11 [D-1]; 182: 34 to 183: 14; 184: 30-36; 185: 22-24; 197: 17-22 [all D-2];

277: 11-17 [D-17]. Draft renewal of 1585: pp. 176: 34 to 177: 14 [D-1].

21. Allen: pp. 164: 19-22; 165: 1-2, 6-7, 33-35; 179: 11-14 [all D-1]; 197: 7-11, 22-25 [D-2]; 279: 12-13 [D-17]. Witnesses: pp. 216: 33-34; 222: #10 [both D-7]. Cuthbert Burbage: p. 285: 8-9 [D-17].

22. Pp. 285: 25-27 [D-17]; 185: 22-23; 184: 17-24, 9, 35 [both D-2]; 224: #5; 238: #5 [both D-7]; 160: 33 [C-28].

23. Pp. 284: 6-8, 19-20; 277: 36 to 278: 3; 278: 35 to 279: 8 [all D-17].

24. P. 164: 17-19 [D-1].

25. P. 278: 14-28 [D-17]; see also pp. 217-18: #10; 222: #10 (in both of which Smyth's Christian name is Thomas); 238: #5 [all D-7]; 283-86 [D-17].

26. Pp. 197: 8-10 (where he gave the year as "the fourtith yeare" of Elizabeth, surely a slip for the one and fortieth year—1598) [D-2]; 216: 32-34; 221: 20-23; 212: 29-31 [all D-7]; 278: 20-21 [D-17].

27. Pp. 164: 1-17 [D-1]; 279: 8-13; 284: 12-15 [both D-17].

28. Pp. 217-18, 222: #10 [D-7]; 197: 5-12 [D-2]; 74: 15-17 [C-17]; 280: 26-27 [D-17].

29. See the royal proclamation "for explaining and enlarging...former orders for Buildings, in and about London," issued July 17, 1620 (S.T.C. 8639).

30. Pp. 141: 20-27; 135: 4-5 [both C-23]; 233: 28-32; 236: 1-13 [both D-7]. The Theatre is first mentioned as open for business in a Privy Council inhibition of August 1, 1577: E. K. Chambers, *The Elizabethan Stage* (Oxford, 1923), II, 388; IV, 276.

31. Pp. 126: 33; 127: 5-6 [both C-22].

32. After an order of Nov. 13, 1590 (p. 48), Margaret Brayne's people appeared several times at Holywell (pp. 95: 19-20; 97: 20-21; 100: 19-20; 105: 17-18 [all C-21]), two or three of which are mentioned particularly, one on Nov. 16, when they went to the Burbages' "dwellings howse" near the Theatre (pp. 57: #2; 62: 2-3 [both C-12]), and another presumably later, when they tried to collect money from people going up to the galleries at the Theatre (pp. 97: #13; 100: #13 [both C-21]; 114: #2; 125: #2 [both C-22]). Raphe Miles made the remark about the window as an eye witness (p. 121: 13-17 [C-22]), but he added that he was not present when they tried to collect money for the galleries (pp. 119: #9; 122: #9 [both C-22]).

33. Pp. 177: 34 to 178: 5 [D-1]; 97-98: #13 [C-21]; 114: 16-20, 31-32 [C-22]. Referring to a remark by Samuel Kiechel (a visitor to London in 1585), Chambers added that the Theatre had three galleries, and he may well have been right. Kiechel, however, did not specifically mention the Theatre. He wrote, "There are some peculiar houses, which are so made as to have about three galleries over one another." See Chambers, II, 393, 358.

34. Pp. 112: 19-21; 117: 28-29; 119: 3-4; 123: 11-12; 124: 26 [all C-22].

35. Pp. 105: 6-8 [C-2]; 222: 3-4 [D-7].

36. Pp. 152: 1-6 [C-23]; 105: 1-2 [C-21]; 114: 15-20 [C-22]. Moreover, in "The Sharers Papers" of 1635, Cuthbert and Richard Burbage said as much: Chambers, II, 384, 393.

37. Pp. 101: 14-17, 21 [C-21]; 129: #7; 142: 28-34 [both C-23]; Chambers, II, 140-41.

38. In a question, Margaret Brayne implied that the money in the box was to be shared with both the players and her husband. In his answer to it, however, Robert Miles seems to distinguish between money in the box, which belonged to Burbage and Brayne, and other money not in the box, which belonged to Burbage and the players: pp. 129: #7; 142-43: #7 [both C-23].

39. Pp. 201: 5-18 [D-2]; 224-25: #6; 240: #6; 242: #6 [all D-7]. Cuthbert Burbage's and his witnesses' remarks about the Peckham episode seem to be a response to Allen's claim that the Burbages still owed him £30 in rent (pp. 193: 3-5 [D-2]; 207: #3 [D-7]).

40. Pp. 102: #14 [C-21]; 150: #19 [C-23]; 106: 1-6 [C-21]; 146: 32 to 147: 6 [C-23].

41. Pp. 263: #6; 266: #6 [both D-7]; 198: 18-19 [D-2]; 217: #9; 222: #9 [both D-7]; 205: 3-5 [D-2].

42. Pp. 116: #2; 119: 29 to 120: 3 [both C-22].

43. So Chambers worked out the figures in Henslowe's Diary, except that he divided the six years into two periods of three years each, 1594-97 (126 weeks, 728 playing days), 1597-1600 (115 weeks, fewer than 690 playing days): II, 141-42, 159-60.

44. Pp. 52: #7; 55: #7 [both C-10].

45. P. 140: 1-12 [C-23].

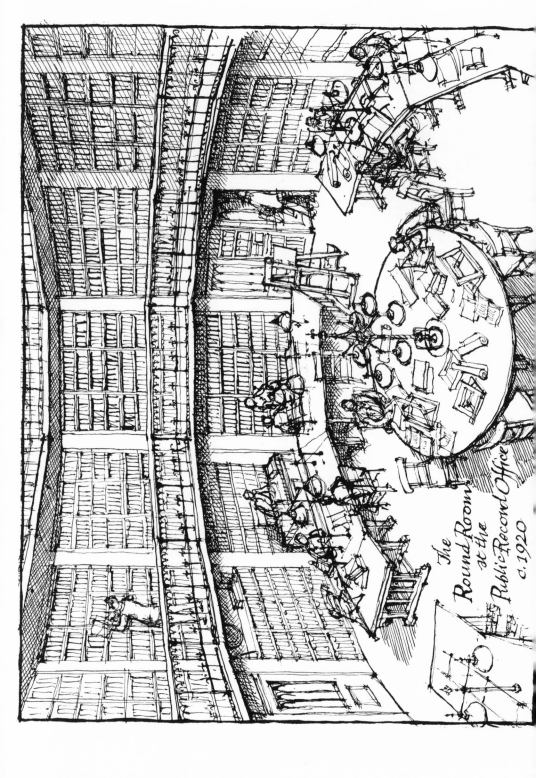

The
Round Room
at the
Public Record Office
c. 1920

A Handlist of Documents about the
Theatre in Shoreditch*

For more than 130 years we have been alluding to and arguing over the documentation for the Theatre, the playhouse James Burbage and his brother in law, John Brayne, built in Shoreditch more than 400 years ago. More documentation has been found for the Theatre than, with the possible exception of the Boar's Head, any other public playhouse, and since 1913 most of this documentation has been available in printed form, unlike the documentation for any other playhouse, even now. Yet no one seems to have looked at the originals for some sixty years. No one seems to have wondered if the printed transcriptions are accurate, no one seems to have asked if one could find yet more, and no one seems even to have asked whether many of the citations used so long ago would, if written on tickets today, cause the proper documents to be produced. I propose here to survey the documents, assess the printed transcriptions, announce a new docu-

19

ment or two, and give the current citations for them all. For since 1913 many of the numbers have been changed, and in some cases the new ones (now themselves sixty or more years old) are by no means easy to establish.

J. P. Collier published the first notices of documents about the Theatre, in his *Memoirs of the Principal Actors in the Plays of Shakespeare* of 1846 and more three years later in his article, "Original History of 'The Theatre,' in Shoreditch, and Connexion of the Burbadge Family with it."[1] Perhaps luckily, Collier had not found them himself. A Mr. Monro, one of the registrars of Chancery, had found those Collier used in the book, and F. Devon of the Chapter House, Westminster, those he used in the article. Before the Public Record Office opened in 1866, such public records were kept in, among other places, the Roll's Chapel in Chancery Lane, the Chapter House, and the Tower. Collier misunderstood the documents and did not pursue them. Indeed, he thought those in the book referred to Blackfriars. He corrected himself in the article, but in reprintings of the book as late as 1879,[2] the documents there were still said to concern Blackfriars. It was his younger contemporary, J.O. Halliwell-Phillipps, who fully realized what Collier had been given and who set out to find more of the same. He found some of the better things, which he used discriminatingly, beginning in the second edition of his *Outlines of the Life of Shakespeare* (1882). Document work was still in its infancy, however, so that Halliwell-Phillipps missed some citations completely, gave others inadequately, and used the documents less fully than he could have done. Moreover, he by no means exhausted the hoard, and without some of the documents he could have found but did not, his understanding of those he did find was necessarily imperfect.

The documents about the Theatre then became much of the fuel of the competition in the Round Room of the Public Record Office between the American, C. W. Wallace, and the redoubtable Scottish lady, Mrs. C. C. Stopes (mother of the even more redoubtable Marie Stopes) in the years before the first World War. Wallace and his energetic wife, Hulda, worked across the room from Mrs. Stopes, both parties striving to obscure their work from the other and at the same time to find what the other was doing. Needless to say, both parties ransacked the classes of documents from which Collier's and Halliwell-Phillipps' documents had come. Between them, they found everything there that their predecessors had used and much more. They also pressed into other classes of documents and found yet more. Both parties published books in 1913 about their work, in which they revealed what they had been doing in the Round Room and, inevitably, altered dramatically the case at the Theatre.[3] All too often they revealed that they had been at work on the same documents, but, fortunately, they also revealed that the Wallaces had spent a good deal of their time among matters of which Mrs. Stopes had not known, and that Mrs. Stopes had spent some of hers among a few unknown to the Wallaces. The Wallaces quite clearly had the better of everything to which both they and Mrs. Stopes had put their hands, but because Mrs. Stopes had dealt with some documents unknown to the Wallaces, her book is still useful, though these documents are much less important than the others.

W. W. Braines then set out to locate in the London of his day exactly where the Theatre had stood. He was "a principal officer" in the Department of the Clerk of the London County Council, and his work was the result of a suggestion made in the council in 1914. (As the result of another suggestion made in the council in 1921, he was also to locate the site of the Globe.) Braines reviewed the Wallaces' work carefully but could not extend it. He reviewed those parts of Mrs. Stopes's work of which the Wallaces had not known and managed to find considerably more than she had done. The London County Council issued his work as a pamphlet in the series, *Indication of Houses of Historical Interest in London*, in 1915, but Braines continued to think about the matter and to go back to the documents. He issued his work himself with significant revisions in 1917,[4] and the London County Council issued it again, with more significant revisions, in the section of the *Survey of London* dealing with Shoreditch, for which Braines was responsible (vol. VIII, 1922). The London County Council reissued the work as a pamphlet in 1923, in the same series as the original one (part xliii) but with the revisions of 1922 and a few more. This version appeared without further change in 1930. Braines thought of this version of 1923 (p. 9) as a somewhat abbreviated form of that of 1922, so that the final version must be a conflation of the two. Though neither a literary man nor a historian by profession, he became one of the most astute and successful of workers among documents, and only partly because he severely limited his objectives. He seems to have been the last person who fingered, at least for publication, the documents about the Theatre.

Collier, Halliwell-Phillipps, and Braines used documents as most writers do, to substantiate assertions. So they merely quoted these documents here and there, alluded to them, paraphrased them. Thanks to their warfare in the Round Room, however, Wallace and Mrs. Stopes apparently strove to get their findings into print before the other did. They probably felt they could not afford the time an elaborate study of their documents would require. Both their books are, therefore, mainly a succession of transcriptions, especially Wallace's. Between them, they printed transcriptions of all the really important documents. All Braines's documents extend the lines of inquiry in which Mrs. Stopes had worked and Wallace had not. Braines's documents, therefore, are not the crucial ones. They have to do with a then ancient argument about the land on which the Theatre stood and a then new one about a neighbouring site, both very useful for his purpose but not for ours, if ours concerns the playhouse itself. Chambers reviewed all these matters in his *Elizabethan Stage* of 1923. He pointed out that the documents concern four separate legal quarrels, each quarrel consisting of numerous lawsuits and other legal ploys, and none of the quarrels materially overlapping any of the others. He put each document, therefore, into one of four categories, which he called A, B, C, and D.

Category A is a long series of lawsuits beginning in the early 1580s and not ending from our point of view until 1612. They concern the ownership of the land on which the Theatre stood. Mrs. Stopes and Braines found all these documents, except for a few I have found.[5] The litigation was extensive, and almost certainly more documents remain to be found. Category B is a series of lawsuits from 1596 to 1604 about the ownership of an adjoining piece of property once leased by the Burbages. It has little to do with the playhouse. Mrs. Stopes and Braines found all these documents, too, except for those I have found. Probably more of these also remain to be found. Category C is a series of lawsuits from 1586 to 1597 between the Burbages and their partner in building the playhouse, John Brayne, and his successors. Mrs. Stopes and Wallace competed fiercely for these documents in Category C, and Wallace conspicuously had the better of the competition. Category D is a series of lawsuits from 1599 to 1602 between the Burbages and their landlord in Shoreditch, Giles Allen, over the pulling down and taking away of the Theatre in the Christmas season of 1598-99. Mrs. Stopes and Wallace competed here, too, and once again Wallace had vastly the better of the competition. Perhaps the best general discussion of all these lawsuits has been that by J. Q. Adams in his *Shakespearean Playhouses* (1917).

Wallace is among the great figures of the P.R.0., and his work about the Theatre is among his most thorough, sensible, and practised. He went through vast piles of paper and parchment, pursuing not only the main documents of a case, but also the supporting and arcane ones. If we are to find significant new documents in the matters Wallace studied, we must do so by strokes of luck and not by systematically carrying the work farther than he did. Mrs. Stopes was not nearly so thorough or patient.

Moreover, the Wallaces' transcribing is systematically rigorous, and it is generally accurate, especially in the really major documents, such as the bills and answers and the depositions. On page after page of theirs, one can find relatively little to which he might seriously object. They are less accurate, however, in the supporting documents, such as the decrees and orders of the various courts. I have looked letter for letter at more than 2,000 lines of the Wallaces (as they printed them), including at least part of every numbered item below. I reckon that they made a mistake in only one line out of nine or ten among the most important documents in English, the bills and answers and depositions, but one line out of just over five among the decrees and orders, at all of which I looked. They made one mistake in about four lines of Latin, but there the work is much more difficult, and the Wallaces' reconstruction of so much abbreviated Latin must remain a tour de force of its kind. It is one thing to go over transcriptions of such difficult material; it is quite another to read it with nothing before one but the text. Wallace must have done the Latin himself. Could he also have done the important things in English himself and passed the others to his wife? Or vice versa?

In any event, even where they are not perfect, they missed spellings and sometimes punctuation, but rarely the sense. For example, in one order of the Court of Chancery, the Wallaces made seven mistakes in the thirteen lines of the document as they printed it (C.33/81/f.493^v, Wallaces' pp. 64-65):

Lines	The Wallaces	The Document
3-4	"hathe in"	"haue put in"
4-5	"Insuffycynt"	"Insuffycyent"
5	"showinge"	"shewinge"
5	"cause"	"causes"
9	"demurrer"	"demorrer"
9	"suffycynt"	"suffycyent"

and in the marginal entry they left out "Myles" after "Robte" (they seem to have added it by mistake to the marginal entry at f. 720[v], their p. 65). This is their worst patch of transcription that I have noticed. In an order of the Court of Requests, they did nearly as badly, eleven mistakes in twenty-three lines as they printed the document (Req.1/49/22 Apr. 42 Eliz., their pp. 205-6):

Lines	The Wallaces	The Document
1	"Cuthbert"	"Cuthberte"
5	"Iniunccion"	"Iniunction"
6	"one"	"m[r]"
6	"seuerallye"	"seuerally"
7-8	"Accordingly"	"Accordingely"
9	"is"	"ys"
9	"counsail"	"counsaill"
10	"furthw[th]"	"furthew[th]"
19	"therof"	"thereof"
21	"is"	"ys"
23	"heard"	"hearde"

Rather hasty transcribing as the bells were ringing at the end of the day? In transcribing their other nineteen orders of Chancery and Requests, they made some forty-five mistakes in 289 lines, or one in about six and a half lines, but only one mistake is important (see C-26 below).[6]

Mrs. Stopes could do much worse. For a start, she was not systematic. She often modernized spelling, capitalization, and punctuation, but by no means always, and when she has an old spelling it not infrequently is an invention of her own. She too often abstracted documents when she seems to be transcribing them, reading, for example, "at lardge" where the document reads "more at lardge," and "on behalf" for "on the behalf," and "that the said" for "that then the said" (E.123/27/f.110[v], her p. 189). Moreover, she usually wrote the abbreviation for page when she meant that for folio, and sometimes got dates wrong by a year or so, or left them so vague that the reader can get them right only by luck. In another document, for example, she has "enformed" where the document has "informed," "defts." where the document has no abbreviation, "unpublisht" where the document has "vnpublished," "each parties" for "each partie," "shalle" for "shalbe"—all perhaps rather unimportant. But in the same document she read "he could not have his commission readie" where the document reads "he could not haue his Commissioners readie," and "not concerned in the bill" where the document reads "not conteyned in the bill" (E.123/28/f.270ᵛ, her p. 194).

In one list of names, she read "Philip," "Gobourne," and "Brymefield" where the document reads "Phillipp," "Goborne," and "Bromefeyld," and she omitted a name after Bromefeyld, "William Furnis." In another list of the same kind, she read "Oliver Lilt" for "Oliver Talte" and "Maye" for "May"; and in yet another list in the same series, she read "Robert Myles, gent." and "Raff Myles, gent." for "Roberte Myles gent" and "Raffe Myles gent" (Req.1/188/Easter 42 Eliz./9 Apr. 42 Eliz. [1600]; /Trin. 42 Eliz./23 May 42 Eliz.; her pp. 216-17). In one document that she shared with the Wallaces, she got the folio right (454) when the Wallaces bungled it (485), a triumph, perhaps. But she got the date wrong, 22 February for 17 February (C.33/77/f.454, Wallace's p. 46, Stopes's pp. 159-60).

Although Mrs. Stopes's imperfections are more persistent and more serious than the Wallaces', they do not render her book useless. For her transcriptions almost always get the matter generally right if not right in detail. Her practices with spelling, capitalization, and punctuation, not to say omission, are so capricious, that it is probably safer to paraphrase rather than to quote her transcriptons. In longer and more arduous documents, she regularly left out the *pro forma* things and added words of her own for clarity, and in these places she clearly meant her work not as transcription, but sensible abstracting (for example, Ward 13/B.29/16-19 from the end, her pp. 166-70). This particular document is so trying, that one should probably be more grateful than censorious. Her work in general is simply on a lower order of rigor and accuracy than the Wallaces', and it is not surprising that Braines could carry her work farther than she did.

In the Handlist, I have grouped the documents about the Theatre into Chambers's four categories, summarizing the quarrel a category records, then listing the documents in that category, call number by call number, in chronological order, as though each call number represents one document. Following each call number the places are cited where Collier, Halliwell-Phillipps, Wallace, Stopes, and Braines transcribed or quoted the matters included in the call number. Then there is a summary of those matters. Where a call number includes more than one document, I use the document with the earliest date for the chronological scheme and list the documents included. One call number can include as many as eighteen or more documents dated over many months (see D-7). All call numbers are the current ones, rather than those Wallace and others used. I cite the first editions of Collier's book and article, the seventh of Halliwell-Phillipps's book (1887), and the version of 1923 of Braines's work. Except for a photographic reprint by Blom in 1969, Wallace's book has not been reissued, nor, except for a reprint by Haskell House in 1970 has Mrs. Stopes's book.

Where a significant document is missing but its contents are clear from remarks in other documents, I cite the document as though it exists, giving the word "Missing" in lieu of a call number and adding in parentheses the documents which describe this one. For documents not previously reported, the phrase "not yet used" appears in lieu of the works by Wallace and the rest. I modernize people's Christian names but spell their surnames as they usually appear in the documentation, preferring the spelling of a signature if there is one.[7] Exceptions are the Burbages, Richard and Cuthbert, who signed themselves "Burbadge"; and Giles Allen, who signed himself "Gyles Aleyn" and whom Wallace called "Gyles Allen" and Mrs. Stopes "Giles Alleyn." Where I have noticed a mistake in the Wallaces' transcribing that materially affects meaning, I mention it in the remarks about the document. But I have not looked letter by letter at the whole of every document, hence have by no means caught every mistake.

My remarks about some aspects especially of Categories A and B, but also C and D, reflect, often silently, a reading of the documents different from that of previous writers.

Category A

In this legal quarrel a family named Peckham challenged Giles Allen's ownership of the land on which the Theatre stood. A family named Webb had acquired it from the Crown in 1544 and made it part of a marriage contract with the Peckhams in 1554. The marriage took place and the property passed to the Peckhams. In 1555 they sold it to a family named Bumpsted, who in the same year mortgaged it for £300 to a family named Allen. In the next year the Bumpsteds took another £300 from the Allens and let them have it. Now Giles Allen owned the property, or thought he did, and in 1576 he became the Burbages' landlord there. In 1582 the Peckhams began a long legal fight to regain the property, arguing mainly that though the marriage had taken place in 1554, it had not taken place before Michaelmas in that year as it was supposed to do in the marriage contract. Therefore the Peckhams could not sell it to the Bumpsteds, who could not sell it to the Allens. Allen fought valiantly, but, as Braines found, the Peckhams actually won. For while Allen still had it when he died, on March 27, 1608 (A-15), the Peckhams sold the place with an apparently good title in March 1612. Braines thought this turn of events incredible, but one of his own documents explains how it happened. Braines must not have read the document very carefully. It is a sheet on which in about 1582 the Peckhams summarized their case for their own purposes. In the last lines they explained how they really expected to get the land back. They offered to buy it for as much as the Allens had paid the Bumpsteds. Or as the document concludes: "Note that this p*laintiff* [the Peckhams] offereth the defendant [Giles Allen] for the discharge of his fathers Couenante wth Bumsted asmuche mony as he receaued for the land so that consideringe the meane proffits wch he hath receaued now xxvi yeres, the defendant can be no loser by it" (see A-11). The lawsuits were only ways of putting pressure on Allen and keeping the price down. Eventually Allen's widow must have made some deal with the Peckhams and quietly passed the property to them.

A-1. B.L., Cotton, Vesp., F, III, no. 38 (Braines, p.8): A letter of July 23, 1544, from Queen Katherine Parr to an unnamed recipient. The King had meant to grant all of Holywell Priory to Henry Webb, gentleman usher of her privy chamber, but Webb got only part. She desired the recipient's favor in Webb's behalf. (Braines used this letter as it appears in Sir William Dugdale's *Monasticon*, [1846], IV, 392; the original is abstracted in *Letters and Papers, Foreign and Domestic,...Henry VIII*, XIX, i, #967.)

A-2. C.66/747/m.41-42 (not yet used): A patent by which the Webbs acquired for £81 part of the land in Holywell Priory on which the Theatre eventually stood: August 5, 1544. (Noted in *Letters and Papers, Foreign and Domestic,....Henry VIII*, XIX, ii, #166[7].)

A-3. C.66/740/m.4-5 (not yet used): A patent by which the Webbs acquired for £55 the rest of the land (see A-2) in Holywell Priory on which the Theatre eventually stood: September 23, 1544. (Noted in *Letters and Papers, Foreign and Domestic,...Henry VIII*, XIX, ii, #340[33]; see also #586.)

A-4. E.371/324/#70 (Braines, p. 9): A copy of the patent of September 23, 1544 (A-3), kept in the Exchequer.

A-5. C.54/516/m.8-9 (Braines, p. 9): The entry on the close roll of the contract, dated August 16, 1555, by which the Peckhams sold to Christopher Bumpsted for £533.6s.8d. the land in Holywell Priory on which the Theatre eventually stood.

A-6. C.P.25(2)/74/629/2-3 P&M/Mich./no.50 (not yet used): A fine of 1555 by which the Peckhams acknowledged that they had sold to Christopher Bumpsted the land on which the Theatre eventually stood.

A-7. C.54/521/m.12-13 (Braines, p. 9): The entry on the close roll of the contract, dated November 1, 1555, by which Christopher Bumpsted mortgaged to Christopher Allen and his son, Giles, the land in Holywell Priory on which the Theatre eventually stood. The Allens had paid £300 and would pay £300 more on April 4, 1556, if they wanted to buy the property, if Bumpsted wanted to sell it, and if Bumpsted could give them a good title.

A-8. C.54/521/m.13 (not yet used): A bond of £700 of November 1, 1555, by which Christopher Bumpsted guaranteed performance of his part of the contract of the same date (A-7).

A-9. C.3/9/82 (Braines, p. 9): A lawsuit in Chancery in which Christopher Bumpsted sued Giles Allen so as to stop a lawsuit of Allen's at common law against Bumpsted. The Allens had, apparently, advanced Bumpsted the second £300 on the land in Holywell Priory on which the Theatre eventually stood (A-7, 8; B-5), but found that it was not worth what Bumpsted had claimed, that Bumpsted was unwilling to draw a second contract conveying the property to the Allens, and that Bumpsted would not give the Allens the documents that would guarantee their title. Bumpsted denied all these claims. Documents: the bill (October 9, 1562), and Allen's answer and Bumpsted's replication (both undated).

A-10. E.13/344/25 (Braines, p. 23): A summary of the Peckhams' first lawsuit against Giles Allen, in the Court of Exchequer of Pleas, Easter 1582.

A-11. B.L., Lansdowne, III, f.101 (or, in another series of foliation, f.110) (Braines, p. 23): A summary of their case (A-10) drawn up by the Peckhams for their own use, c. 1582.

A-12. Ward 13/B.29 [16-19 from the end] (Stopes, pp. 166-70): The Peckhams' second lawsuit against Giles Allen, in the Court of Wards because the elder Peckham (Edmund) had died and his son (George) was a royal ward. Documents: the bill (June 9, 1589), Allen's reply (October 20, 1589), Edmund Peckham's replication (October 31, 1589), and Allen's rejoinder (November 28, 1589).

A-13. Ward 9/86/f.159-60 (Braines, p. 23): A summary of the Peckhams' lawsuit against Giles Allen in the Court of Wards (A-12), and the Court's decision to dismiss it: Michaelmas 1591 (after November 16).

A-14. K.B.27/1377/m.253 (Braines, p. 23): A summary dated Hilary 1603 of a lawsuit in the King's Bench that may constitute the Peckhams' third against Giles Allen. The Peckhams had leased several houses in Shoreditch to John Hollingworth on November 10, 1602, and now Hollingworth sued three men (John Goodgame, William Rowe, and James Kelley) for trespass on the premises. Braines identified the men as Allen's tenants, though the document does not, and presumed, therefore, that the houses were part of Allen's domain in Holywell. In a companion lawsuit (summarized on the next membrane), Hollingworth also sued Cuthbert Burbage at the same time and on the same occasion, yet Burbage does not seem to have been a tenant of Allen's after the winter of 1598-99.

A-15. C.142/309/#163 (Stopes, *Notes & Queries*, Oct. 30, 1909, p. 343; Braines, *Survey of London*, VIII, 171): The inquisition post mortem taken July 16, 1608, on Giles Allen, showing that when he died he still owned the property in Holywell on which the Theatre had stood. (Braines, oddly, got the date of Allen's death wrong by a year.

According to this document, he died on March 27, 1608; his widow took administration of his goods on April 21, 1608: PROB.6/7/f.111ᵛ.)

A-16. C.54/2128/m.20 (Braines, p. 23): The entry on the close roll of the contract of March 10, 1612, by which the Peckhams sold the property in Holywell on which the Theatre had stood.

Note. Braines, in *Survey of London*, VIII, 171, offered a fine of 1610 to show that the Peckhams by then owned the property in Holywell on which the Theatre had stood; but while the fine mentions George Peckham, it does not mention property specifically in Holywell and so cannot be taken as necessarily referring to that on which the Theatre had stood: C.P.25(2)/323/7 Jas.I/Hil./4.

Category B

This quarrel is about whether Giles Allen or the Earls of Rutland owned a part of Holywell Priory consisting of two buildings and an open space at the sides of which they lay. The buildings were a barn (anciently, but no longer, called the oat barn) and a stable. The open space was the "void ground or yard," as it is called in one lawsuit (B-5, 10), or the inner court of the Priory, as it is called in another (B-8, 9). A great barn undeniably Allen's was on the north side of this void ground, the stable was on the east side, the oat barn was on the south side, and the Priory wall was on the west side. The oat barn, stable, and void ground should have belonged to Allen, because they had belonged to his predecessors, being specifically mentioned in Henry Webb's patent of 1544 (A-3) and not mentioned in any of the Earls' leases (see B-1).

In 1539, however, before the Priory had been dissolved, the prioress and convent had leased the oat barn and stable to Richard Manners for twenty years. He became Sir Richard, and he must have been a relative of the Earls of Rutland. Along with the oat barn and stable, Manners had got "convenient rome betwene" and ingress, egress, and regress—the use, that is, of the void ground. This lease is mentioned in Webb's patent as an encumbrance on his property. Though it expired in 1559, four years after the Allens had acquired their part of Holywell, the Earls of Rutland evidently continued to occupy the buildings and use the ground, and they came to assume that the buildings and, eventually, even the ground belonged to their part of Holywell.

Allen suffered this state of affairs for many years, resigning himself, it seems, to the loss of his buildings but not to the loss of his void ground. At least once he rented part of the void ground to a tenant of his in the great barn, and he included the whole of the void ground with the premises he leased to the Burbages for, among other things, the building of the Theatre. In his lease to the Burbages (see B-2 and Wallace, pp. 170-71), however, he mentioned the oat barn and stable as occupied by the Rutlands and he did not include them among the leased premises; in a lawsuit of 1601 (B-8) he mentioned those buildings as "by some of the Earles of Rutland...wᵗʰ houlden from" him.

During all these years the void ground lay for the most part open and used by anyone having business in that part of Holywell. The Burbages built their playhouse not on the void ground, but immediately north of the great barn, the north side of which they shored against the playhouse. Then, the Rutlands having ceased to live in

Holywell, the current Earl leased his part of it to his steward, Thomas Screven, who set about capitalizing the void ground. He rented the two buildings and the ground for a short term to John Powell and Richard Robinson (two saltpetremen who were making the stuff in the oat barn), who with a labourer, Roger Amyes, seized (that is, no doubt, fenced off) part of the void ground on May 1, 1596, and kept it until June 27.

Allen decided at last to act, and the Burbages decided to help him. Urged on by Allen, the Burbages sued Powell, Robinson, and Aymes at once in the King's Bench for trespass in the barn and on the ground. Screven hastened in the Earl's name to sue the Burbages in the Court of Wards (the current Earl being a minor) in an effort, which was successful, to get the lawsuit in the King's Bench stopped. On July 20 Screven leased the ground and both buildings to John Knapp for twenty years for a fee of £50 and £14.14s.8d. a year, and Powell and Robinson continued making saltpetre in the barn. When the Earl came of age on October 6, 1597, the lawsuit in Wards perforce ceased. The Burbages and Allen then pressed the lawsuit in King's Bench. Screven did his best to delay it, but first he gave the Burbages and Allen something more to sue him about. On November 2 Powell and Robinson, now joined by Knapp, once again seized part of the void ground, this time building a mudwall around that part and keeping it. The Burbages and Allen managed to bring the lawsuit in King's Bench to the point of a decisive hearing early in the winter of 1598-99, but just as they did so, Screven (using the Earl's name) sued them again, this time in the Court of Exchequer King's Remembrancer, and again got the lawsuit in King's Bench stopped. He took his business to that court, he said, because the disputed premises were part of the Queen's inheritance and so a concern of the Exchequer. Unlike Webb, that is, the Rutlands had not negotiated a grant of their part of Holywell from the the Crown but had been content with a series of leases, first from the Priory and then from the Crown. So the place had belonged to Henry VIII on the dissolution of the Priory and had descended to Elizabeth. Coincidently, or perhaps mainly, the point enabled Screven to argue that the Burbages and Allen were trying to deny the Queen a part of her inheritance.

Allen delayed answering this newest lawsuit for almost two years, perhaps because from the Christmas season of 1598-99 he had his hands full with the Burbages, who had dismantled the Theatre, carried it across the river, and rebuilt it as the Globe. Allen had to be arrested, on October 22, 1600, to bring him to answer the lawsuit in the Exchequer. He and Screven then went expeditiously through the preliminary steps, but no further. At the end of January 1601 Allen futilely asked the court to dismiss Screven's lawsuit. To more purpose, Screven and Knapp were presiding over a process of subleasing that made Allen's task more difficult. Knapp leased the two buildings and the void ground to John Lewis on February 17, 1598. The two of them then leased the oat barn and part of the void ground to Richard Hill for £3 a year, and on April 23, 1601, Hill leased his barn and ground to Francis Langley for thirteen or fourteen years (Langley could not remember which) and £3 "& odd monie" a year. (Langley also could not remember the first name of Cuthbert Burbage.) Langley was the builder of the Swan, and he was fresh from a similar, but much grander venture in disputed property at the Boar's Head. On May 16, having brought along his man, John Johnson, and hired Amyes and Lewis, Langley set about building a mudwall around his part of the void ground, which, with the other walled part, completely blocked that ground. Amyes left on other business, and Allen and some tenants arrived to chase the rest away, but soon Langley returned and effectually fenced off his part of the ground.

Protesting that he already had legal fees "farre exceedinge the value of the said grounde," Allen now took the lot of them to the Star Chamber, as Richard Samwell had done at the Boar's Head the year before. But after most of the preliminaries were finished in November 1601, Allen seems to have lost interest in this lawsuit, too, and the Court seems to have given him no comfort.[8] In the summer and fall of 1602 Screven was pushing on with the case in the Exchequer, and Allen was ignoring it. In October he took momentary interest, but after that neither he nor Screven did anything for a year and a half. On April 30, 1604, finally, Allen asked the Court of Exchequer to dismiss the matter so that he could get on with his eight-year-old lawsuit in the King's Bench. The court decided a few days later that the matter should be heard during the first sitting of the next term. Whether it was heard or not (the documents are missing for that term), Allen gained nothing by it. He did not renew his lawsuit in the King's Bench, nor did he, it seems, repossess his two buildings and void ground, though his successor in Holywell was interested in them as late as 1615 (B-14).

The Burbages helped Allen against Screven even though at the same time they were arguing strenuously with Allen about the terms on which they might renew their lease. It expired in April 1597, and thereafter the Burbages rented the place without a lease. They must have thought that by helping Allen against Screven they might get a renewal on relatively favorable terms—provided, presumably, that the whole place did not prove to belong to the Peckhams.

B-1. E.303/11/Middx./no.5 (Braines, pp. 8, 14): A lease of April 1, 1539, in which Holywell Priory leased to Richard Manners (evidently a relative of the Earls of Rutland) for twenty years an oat barn and a stable with the use of the yard at the sides of which they lay. The Burbages and Giles Allen eventually quarrelled with Thomas Screven and the Earl of Rutland about the ownership of these premises. Allen thought he owned them because his property in Holywell had specifically included them when his predecessor, Webb, had acquired it from the Crown in 1544, and this lease was then cited as an encumbrance on it (see Webb's patent, A-3). Moreover, they are not mentioned in the leases by which the Earls of Rutland held their part of Holywell: two from the Priory, November 8, 1537, and January 1, 1538 (L.R.1/47/f.205, 202), and a renewal from the Crown, December 18, 1584 (C.66/1267/m.29-30).

B-2. Missing (see B-3, 4, 5, 6; D-1): The lease of April 13, 1576, by which the Burbages leased parts of Holywell from Giles Allen as, among other things, a site for the Theatre. Included was the ground at the sides of which lay (not included) an oat barn and a stable; the ownership of these premises was eventually claimed by both Allen and the Earl of Rutland and their tenants. A draft renewal of the lease (November 1, 1585) is quoted, apparently completely, in D-1 (transcribed by Wallace, pp. 169-78), where at least the description of the property should be the same as in the original lease.

B-3. K.B.27/1353/m.320 (Halliwell-Phillipps, I, 351; Stopes, pp. 184-85): A summary of a lawsuit in the King's Bench in which Cuthbert Burbage sued three of Thomas Screven's tenants (John Powell, Richard Robinson, Roger Amyes) for trespass between May 1 and June 27, 1596, in the oat barn and on the ground beside which it lay. The ground was included among the parts of Holywell that the Burbages rented from Giles Allen. It and two adjoining buildings, the oat barn and a stable, were claimed by both Allen and the Earl of Rutland, who had leased them all to his steward, Screven. Burbage began the lawsuit in Trinity Term 1596, and the summary is dated January 15, 1599, by which time Powell et al. had pleaded not guilty and demanded trial, but the lawsuit had been postponed and no date set for trial.

B-4. Missing (see B-5, 8): A lawsuit in the Court of Wards in which Thomas Screven (in the name of the Earl of Rutland) sued Cuthbert Burbage and Giles Allen in a successful attempt to stop Burbage's lawsuit in the King's Bench (B-3). The lawsuit was filed in the summer of 1596 and, according to Allen, was the same as B-5. It was filed in Wards because the Earl was still a minor.

B-5. E.112/28/369 (Halliwell-Phillipps, I, 350; Stopes, pp. 185-89; Braines, pp. 9, 26n): A lawsuit in the Court of Exchequer King's Remembrancer in which Thomas Screven (in the name of the Earl of Rutland) sued Cuthbert Burbage and Giles (misnamed Richard) Allen in a successful attempt to stop Burbage's lawsuit in the King's Bench (B-3). The Court of Wards (B-4) could no longer stop the King's Bench lawsuit after the winter of 1597-98, when the Earl came of age (October 6, 1597) and sued livery. Documents: the bill (dated only Michaelmas 41 Elizabeth, evidently the winter of 1598-99), Allen's reply (after October 22, 1600), the Earl's replication (Michaelmas 1600), and Allen's rejoinder (Michaelmas 1600). In his reply, Allen gave the chronology of the events in Category B from 1596 to 1600 and also the history of how he and his father had come to own their part of Holywell (see Category A).

B-6. E.123/26/f.165^v (not yet used): An order of the Court of Exchequer King's Remembrancer of November 19, 1600. Giles Allen pointed out that Cuthbert Burbage's lease (B-2) had now run out so that the Earl of Rutland should proceed against Allen only (B-5). The court agreed. It had already stopped Burbage's lawsuit in the King's Bench (B-3).

B-7. E.123/27/f.110^v (Stopes, p. 189): An order of the Court of Exchequer King's Remembrancer of January 30, 1601. The Earl of Rutland had not proceeded in his lawsuit (B-5), so Giles Allen asked the court to dismiss it. The court gave Rutland until the end of the term (Hilary).

B-8. St.Ch.5/A.33/37 (Braines, p. 14n): A lawsuit in the Star Chamber of Trinity Term 1601 in which Giles Allen sued Thomas Screven, John Knapp, Francis Langley, and their associates for three trespasses on what he took to be his properties in Holywell. Screven's associates (John Powell, Richard Robinson, and Roger Amyes) had seized one piece of property in May 1596, and the first two and Knapp the same piece for a second time on November 2, 1597 (see B-3, 5); Langley and his associates (Amyes, John Lewis, and John Johnson) had seized another piece on May 16, 1601. Allen's lawyer supposed that the seizure of November 1597 was the first, so he described the three lawsuits earlier than this one as coming after that seizure rather than two before (B-3, 4) and one after (B-5). Allen, of course, would have known better. The lawyer also got the date of a lease between Screven and Knapp wrong (he gave it as November 1, 1597, rather than July 20, 1596), but that was probably Allen's ignorance, who had learned the right date by the time he drew up his interrogatories (B-9) for this lawsuit. Documents: bill (June 27, 1601), the reply (a demurrer) of Langley, Amyes, Knapp, and Lewis (October 17, 1601), the reply of Screven (October 20, 1601), the replication of Allen (November 29, 1602), a synopsis of Allen's replication (November 29, 1602).

B-9. St.Ch. 5/A.26/1 (Braines, pp. 14, 26n): Interrogatories and depositions belonging to the lawsuit in the Star Chamber (B-8), all on Giles Allen's behalf. Allen sought to establish mainly the process by which Thomas Screven and his tenants had sublet the disputed properties. Documents: interrogatories for John Knapp, Roger Amyes, John Lewis, and Francis Langley (October 1, 1601); interrogatories for Screven (October 23, 1601), depositions of Knapp, et al. (October 26, 1601), deposition of Screven (November 10, 1601).

B-10. E.134/44-45 Eliz./Mich./18 (Halliwell-Phillipps, I, 350, 352, etc.; Stopes, pp. 189-93; Braines, pp. 5n, 13n, 14n, 16, 26n, 27): The interrogatories and depositions ostensibly for both Giles Allen and the Earl of Rutland, but actually only for Rutland (see B-11), in the lawsuit in the Court of Exchequer King's Remembrancer (B-5). Thomas Screven (in the Earl's name) tried to show, among other things, that what in Richard Manners's lease (B-1) and Webb's patent (A-3) was called the oat barn was not the barn giving onto the void ground of the 1590s, but Allen's great barn or brewhouse. Hence, presumably, the premises the old documents gave to Allen were not the ones about which Allen was now complaining, but others to the north that were part of Allen's acknowledged domain in Holywell. Screven's witnesses, however, could not bear him out, though all had known Holywell for at least forty years and one for sixty. Documents: interrogatories (undated), a commission appointing examiners (June 23, 1602), depositions of Mary Askew,[9] Anne Thornes, Nicholas Sutton, Mary Hebblethwayte, John Rowse, and Leonard Jackson (all taken on October 12, 1602).

B-11. E.123/28/f.270ᵛ (Stopes, p. 194): An order of the Court of Exchequer King's Remembrancer of October 18, 1602. Giles Allen protested that he had not been ready when the court had taken depositions six days before (B-10), and that the Earl of Rutland had introduced irrelevances in his interrogatories. The court gave both sides until the end of the month to finish the depositions and ordered any irrelevances suppressed.

B-12. E.128/17/Easter 2 Jas. I/[52 from bottom] (not yet used): An order of the Court of Exchequer King's Remembrancer of April 30, 1604. Giles Allen asked the court to dissolve the injunction (see B-5) that prevented him from getting at the Earl of Rutland in the King's Bench (B-3). The court gave the Earl a week to show cause to the contrary.

B-13. E.128/17/Easter 2 Jas. I/[102 from bottom] Braines, p. 23):[10] An order of the Court of Exchequer King's Remembrancer of May 4, 1604. On the appearance of the Earl of Rutland's lawyer (see B-12), the court ordered that the Earl's lawsuit against Giles Allen (B-5) be heard during the first sitting of the next term and in the meantime the Earl's injunction was to remain in force. (The orders for the next term are missing, and there is no order in the case in the term after that: E.128/18/Mich. 2 Jas. I.)

B-14. E.13/472/m.1 (Braines, p. 15): An entry on the Exchequer plea roll of an indenture of June 20, 1615, by which Thomas Screven's executor, Francis Gofton, sold his property in Holywell. Among the pieces sold were the disputed ones of Category B, which Gofton had had trouble selling "by reason of a title or question therevnto made by" Giles Allen's successor, Sir Thomas Dacres. So the argument went on, but Screven and then his successor seem to have had possession. Screven had died in 1613, Allen in 1608.

Category C

This quarrel took place between James Burbage and his family on the one hand and his financier's financiers and widow on the other. When Burbage took his lease on the site of the Theatre, he had nothing like enough money to build the playhouse and not even enough to build or renovate the other, lesser structures on which he had engaged himself to spend £200. He therefore took in his childless brother-in-law, John Brayne, an apparently successful grocer. The general understanding was that Burbage and Brayne would own the place jointly and finance it jointly; and inasmuch as Brayne was childless, he spoke of leaving his half to Burbage's children in his will. It was obviously a good bargain for Burbage, and it provided Brayne a rather exotic venture in his declining years. They got the place built, but the cost was much greater than they had thought it would be. Brayne bankrupted himself, and the two men fell to arguing (sometimes violently). Neither carried out the legal steps he had promised. Burbage kept the lease entirely in his own name, and Brayne did not draw a new will. Brayne's only documentary rewards for his investment were two bonds that he extracted from Burbage for performance of various parts of their arrangement. There was an arbitrament in 1578 by which the two men proposed to regularize their affairs, but they could not carry out some of its requirements.

Brayne died in 1586, and soon his widow, Margaret, and his creditors, mainly Robert Miles, began trying in one of the courts of common law to collect the value of Brayne's two bonds from Burbage or (alternatively) to get title to half the Theatre and so collect half its profits. In the fall of 1588 Burbage sued them in Chancery to get the bonds cancelled and to stop them from making claims on the playhouse. Margaret Brayne soon counter-sued in Chancery. The two lawsuits in Chancery jogged on side by side for seven years. Then, with Margaret Brayne dead and Miles carrying on by himself, Chancery returned the case to the point at which it had begun, when, at the Burbages' suggestion, the court told Miles to try to collect his bonds at common law. Seven years before, the Burbages must have feared that he and Brayne's widow might collect them, but now, evidently, they felt safe enough. Perhaps it was one thing for the widow Brayne to sue them and another for one of her husband's creditors to do so. In any event, Miles did not collect the value of the bonds, and after James Burbage died in February 1597, and the lease fell in two months later, Miles sued Cuthbert Burbage in the Court of Requests. It was fundamentally the same matter as that of the two lawsuits in Chancery, but because Burbage was dead and the lease at an end, Miles could introduce enough new matter to qualify the old matter for another court. This lawsuit disappears possibly because the documents among which it could have been chronicled are missing. Cuthbert, the son, might actually have done what James, the father, had stoutly and sometimes violently refused to do, pay Miles something for peace. Wallace, however, an ardent partisan of the Burbages, allowed no such possibility. He may have underestimated the force of the widow Brayne's case as a matter of equity, if not as one of common law (pp. 157, 158, 163).

C-1. Missing (see C-2): A lawsuit in the Court of Chancery of 1586-87 in which John Brayne's widow, Margaret, sued one of his creditors, Robert Miles. Miles was probably trying to sue her at common law for money lent her husband toward the Theatre and another of her husband's enterprises, the George Inn, Whitechapel; and she probably sued Miles in Chancery to head off the lawsuit at common law. (In any event, the widow Brayne and Miles soon gave up suing one another and joined in attacking one of the sources of John Brayne's financial troubles, his dealings with James Burbage. See Stopes, pp. 48-49.)

C-2. C.33/73/f.384^v (A book) and /74/f.372 (B book) (Stopes, p. 159): An order of the Court of Chancery of May 6, 1587, in Margaret Brayne's lawsuit against Robert Miles (C-1). Miles was given a week to answer.

C-3. C.3/222/83 (Wallace, pp. 39-45; Stopes, pp. 154-59): A lawsuit in the Court of Chancery of Michaelmas term 1588 in which James Burbage sued John Brayne's widow, Margaret, and her confidant and Brayne's former associate, Robert Miles. Brayne's widow and creditors, including Miles, had been suing James Burbage at common law for two bonds that Burbage had given Brayne for performance, and (which was much the same thing) they had been publicly claiming half the Theatre. The Burbages wanted the bonds cancelled and the claims on the Theatre stopped. Documents: the bill and answer (a demurrer), both undated except that the bill has an 8 at the top as the last digit of a date, evidently 1588.

C-4. C.33/77/f.454 (A book) and /78/f.449 (B book) (Wallace, p. 46; Stopes, pp. 159-60): An order of the Court of Chancery of February 17, 1589, in James Burbage's lawsuit against Robert Miles and others (C-3). Burbage urged that Miles and the others should reply fully rather than merely demur, and the court appointed one of the Masters in Chancery, Dr. Matthew Carew, to look into the matter.

C-5. Missing (see C-6 ff.): A lawsuit in the Court of Chancery of 1589-90 in which Margaret Brayne responded to James Burbage's lawsuit of 1588 (C-3, 4) by counter-suing the Burbages (James and his two sons, Cuthbert and Richard). Documents: the bill and answer (a demurrer). (See Wallace, p. 46.)

C-6. C.33/79/f.610 (A book) and /80/f.597^v (B book) (Wallace, pp. 46-47; Stopes, p. 160): An order of the Court of Chancery of May 21, 1590, in Margaret Brayne's lawsuit against the Burbages (C-5). She urged that the Burbages should reply fully rather than merely demur, and the court appointed one of the Masters in Chancery, Dr. Julius Caesar, to look into the matter.

C-7. C.33/81/f.109 (A book) and /82/f.113^v (B book) (Collier, *Memoirs*, pp. 8-9; Halliwell-Phillipps, I, 371; Wallace, pp. 47-48; Stopes, pp. 160-61): An order of the Court of Chancery of November 4, 1590, in Margaret Brayne's lawsuit against the Burbages (C-5). Caesar ruled that the Burbages should answer (see C-6), and Margaret Brayne then demanded that the court collect half the profits of the Theatre and other premises on the site. The court gave the Burbages a week to argue why it should not.

C-8. C.33/81/f.145 (A book) and /82/f.150 (B book) (Wallace, pp. 48-49, Stopes, p. 161): An order of the Court of Chancery of November 13, 1590, in Margaret Brayne's lawsuit against the Burbages (C-5). The Burbages gave reasons why the court should not collect half the profits of the property (see C-7), and the court ordered rather oracularly that both sides observe an arbitrament of July 1578. That arbitrament provided that John Brayne and James Burbage each owned half of the Theatre and other buildings, and required that the profits of the place go to pay the joint debts of Brayne and the Burbages, and after those debts were paid, go wholly to Brayne until he had been paid what he had spent above what the Burbages had spent. One of the troubles with the arbitrament now was that how much each of the parties had spent was one of the questions to be decided. Margaret Brayne regarded this order, therefore, as a victory for her, but the Burbages thought otherwise and violently defied her attempts to enforce it (see Wallace, pp. 7-8, 17-19).

C-9. C.33/81/f.270 (A book) and /82/f.280^v (B book) (Wallace, p. 49; Stopes, p. 161):

An order of the Court of Chancery of November 28, 1590, in Margaret Brayne's lawsuit against the Burbages (C-5). Robert Miles (Margaret Brayne's backer) swore that James and Cuthbert Burbage had defied the order of November 13 (C-8); the Court ordered the Sheriff of Middlesex to attach the Burbages.

C-10. C.24/218/93 [pt. 2, halfway through the box] (Wallace, pp. 50-57): Interrogatories and depositions in the Court of Chancery on behalf of the Burbages as part of Margaret Brayne's lawsuit against the Burbages (C-5). Documents: interrogatories (undated); the depositions of John Hyde, grocer, and George Cloughe, clothworker (both December 8, 1590). The Burbages sought to discredit her husband and to establish that he had invested much less in the Theatre than she said, and hence that neither he nor she should own half the place. (On Wallace's p. 57, line 4, "Js." should be "Jo.")

C-11. C.33/81/f.317^v (A book) and /82/f.327^v (B book) (Wallace, p. 49; Stopes, p. 161): An order of the Court of Chancery of January 30, 1591, in Margaret Brayne's lawsuit against the Burbages (C-5). Cuthbert Burbage had freed himself (and presumably his father, James) from the Sheriff of London (rather than Middlesex—see C-9) by bonding himself to appear in court on this day;[11] he duly appeared and so saved his bond.

C-12. C.24/221/12 [first in the box] (Wallace, pp. 57-63): Interrogatories and depositions in the Court of Chancery on behalf of Margaret Brayne as part of her lawsuit against the Burbages (C-5). Documents: interrogatories (undated); the depositions of Cuthbert and James Burbage (both February 16, 1591). She inquired into the Burbages' defying the order of November 13, 1590 (see C-8, 9).

C-13. C.33/81/f.456^v (A book) and /82/f.455^v (B book) (Collier, *Memoirs*, p. 9; Wallace, p. 64; Stopes, pp. 161-62): An order of the Court of Chancery of March 23, 1591, in Margaret Brayne's lawsuit against the Burbages (C-5). The Master of the Rolls ordered the depositions of Cuthbert and James Burbage (C-12) referred to Dr. Julius Caesar, one of the Masters in Chancery, who was to report whether the Burbages had committed a contempt of court (see C-8, 9).

C-14. C.33/81/f.493^v (A book) and /82/f.497 (B book) (Collier, *Memoirs*, p. 9; Wallace, pp. 64-65; Stopes, p. 162): An order of the Court of Chancery of April 24, 1591, in James Burbage's lawsuit against Margaret Brayne and Robert Miles (C-3). The Burbages diverted attention from Margaret Brayne's lawsuit against them by pointing out that she and Miles had not yet answered James Burbage's lawsuit of Michaelmas 1588; the court again referred the matter to Dr. Carew (see C-4). (For a list of mistakes in Wallace's transcription, see p. 24 above.)

C-15. C.33/81/f.720^v (A book) and /82/f.725^v (B book) (Wallace, p. 65; Stopes, p. 162): An order of the Court of Chancery of June 15, 1591, in James Burbage's lawsuit against Margaret Brayne and Robert Miles (C-3). Evidently Dr. Carew had not carried out the order of April 24, 1591 (C-14); so Burbage got the court to repeat it.

C-16. C.33/81/f.818 (A book) and /82/f.831^v (B book) (Collier, *Memoirs*, p. 10; Wallace, p. 66, Stopes, p. 162): An order of the Court of Chancery of July 20, 1591, in Margaret Brayne's lawsuit against the Burbages (C-5). Dr. Caesar had not been able to carry out the order of March 23, 1591 (C-13). So the Master of the Rolls appointed another of the Masters in Chancery, Dr. John Hone, to carry it out and also, if possible, to end the lawsuit, and, if not possible, to report to the court his opinion of the lawsuit and whose fault it was that he could not end it.

C-17. C.24/226/9 [pt. 2, second in the box] (Wallace, pp. 68-78): Interrogatories and depositions in the Court of Chancery on behalf of the Burbages as part of Margaret Brayne's lawsuit against them (C-5). Documents: interrogatories (undated); the depositions of Henry Bett (September 30, 1591), Giles Allen (November 3, 1591), and Bryan Ellam, Richard Hudson, and William Clerke (all February 25, 1592). The Burbages continued trying to establish that Margaret Brayne's husband had not invested as much money in the Theatre as she said (see C-10), and hence that she should not own half the place. (On Wallace's p. 72, line 8, "buildinge" should be "buildinges" and, line 20, "it" should be "is.")

C-18. C.24/226/10 [pt. 1, last in the box] (Wallace, pp. 78-92): Interrogatories and depositions in the Court Chancery on behalf of James Burbage as part of his lawsuit against Margaret Brayne and Robert Miles (C-3). Documents: two sets of undated interrogatories, one for Gascoyne, Bett, and James, the other for Hynd, depositions of Henry Bett (September 30, 1591), Ellen Gascoyne (May 8, 1592), and John Hynd and William James (both July 24, 1592). Burbage tried to make the same case in this lawsuit as in Margaret Brayne's lawsuit against him and his sons (C-5), that Brayne had not invested as much in the Theatre as his widow said, and hence that she should not own half the place. He added here that if Brayne had ruined himself, he had done so not because of his interest in the Theatre, but because of his and Robert Miles's interest in an inn, the George in Whitechapel.

C-19. C.33/83/f.16ᵛ-17 (A book) and /84/f.18ᵛ (B book) (Wallace, pp. 66-67; Stopes, pp. 162-63): An order of the Court of Chancery of October 12, 1591, in Margaret Brayne's lawsuit against the Burbages (C-5). Dr. Hone reported that the Burbages should be arrested for contempt (see C-9, 13, 16). The Burbages protested and the court ordered that two other Masters in Chancery, Drs. Edward Stanhope and Thomas Legg, consider further whether the Burbages had committed a contempt, and in the meantime Margaret Brayne was not to take advantage of Hone's report.

C-20. C.33/83/f.151-51ᵛ (A book) and /84/f.163-63ᵛ (B book) (Wallace, pp. 67-68, Stopes, p. 163): An order of the Court of Chancery of November 13, 1591, in Margaret Brayne's lawsuit against the Burbages (C-5). Drs. Stanhope and Legg had heard both sides and recommended (with the consent of both sides) that they seek authority to put to John Hyde, Raphe Miles, Nicholas Byshop, and John Allein (all witnesses for Margaret Brayne) such questions as both sides might propose (see C-19). The court gave authority. (In his note on p. 68, Wallace is oversimple and so misapplies three of the five sheaves of interrogatories and depositions he mentions— C-17, 18, 21, 22, 23.)

C-21. C.24/228/11 (Wallace, pp. 92-109): Interrogatories and depositions in the Court of Chancery as part of Margaret Brayne's lawsuit against the Burbages (C-5). These are the interrogatories (undated) that Margaret Brayne drew up because of the order of November 13, 1591 (C-20), and the depositions of Nicholas Byshop (January 29, 1592), John Allein (February 6, 1592), Raphe Miles (February 10, 1592), and John Hyde (February 12, 1592). She continued to argue that she owned half the Theatre and other buildings on the site. James Burbage was wrong, therefore, to deny her half the profits and had committed a contempt in defying the order of November 13, 1590 (C-8; see also C-9, 11-13, 16, 19). (On Wallace's p. 98, line 4, "his" should be "him.")

C-22. C.24/228/10 (Wallace, pp. 109-27): Interrogatories and depositions in the Court of Chancery as part of Margaret Brayne's lawsuit against the Burbages (C-5). These are four sets of undated interrogatories (one for each witness) that the Burbages drew up because of the order of November 13, 1591 (C-20), and the depositions of John Hyde (February 21, 1592), Nicholas Byshop (April 6, 1592), Raphe Miles (April 26, 1592), John Allein (May 6, 1592). The Burbages tried to discredit the deponents and to show that Robert Miles was financing Margaret Brayne's lawsuit and in return he hoped to own a share of the Theatre; they suggested that the Braynes' right to half the Theatre ended when the lease was mortgaged and the mortgage was not promptly paid off, so that the lease technically passed for a time to the mortgagor.

C-23. C.24/226/11 [pt. 1, first in the box] (Wallace, pp. 127-53): Interrogatories and depositions in the Court of Chancery on behalf of Margaret Brayne, part of her lawsuit against the Burbages (C-5). Documents: interrogatories (undated); the depositions of John Griggs, Edward Collyns (both July 29, 1592), Robert Miles, Henry Lanman (both July 30, 1592), and William Nicoll (July 31, 1592). She tried to establish that up to the time of his death, her husband was indeed half-owner of the Theatre and had expended great sums on it.

C-24. Guildhall, MS.9172/16/26^v (the original), MS.9171/18/26^v (the register copy) (Wallace, pp. 153-54): Margaret Brayne's will, made on April 8, and proved on May 3, 1593, in the London Commissary Court. She left all her possessions to Robert Miles, including her interest in the Theatre, hence her lawsuit (C-5).

C-25. C.33/85/f.758 (A book) and /86/f.785 (B book) (Wallace, p. 155): An order of the Court of Chancery of February 11, 1594, in Margaret Brayne's former lawsuit, now Robert Miles's, against the Burbages (C-5). Drs. Stanhope and Legg had been about to make their report about the lawsuit when she died and the lawsuit ended. Since then Miles had revived the lawsuit in his name (see C-24). The court therefore ordered that Stanhope and Legg make the report that they would have made had Margaret Brayne not died. (Wallace's text follows that of the B book, unlike his usual practice; apparently he had not found the entry in the A book.)

C-26. C.33/87/f.857^v (A book) and /88/f.862 (B book, perished) (Wallace, pp. 155-56; Stopes, p. 163): An order in the Court of Chancery of March 14, 1595, in James Burbage's lawsuit against Margaret Brayne and Robert Miles, now Miles alone (C-3). The Burbages pointed out that this lawsuit and the other (C-5) in which Miles was suing them were essentially the same matter, and they proposed that because Miles's lawsuit was due for hearing on May 28 and theirs ready for hearing, though unscheduled, the two should be heard together on the 28th. The court agreed with them, unless Miles could show good cause to the contrary. (For ''28,'' Wallace misread ''23.'')

C-27. C.33/89/f.130 (A book) and /90/f.140^v-41 (B book) (Collier, *Memoirs*, pp. 10-11; Wallace, pp. 156-57; Stopes, p. 164): An order in the Court of Chancery of May 28, 1595, technically in Robert Miles's lawsuit against the Burbages (C-5), but actually also in James Burbage's lawsuit against Miles (C-3; see also C-26). The court heard the case and agreed with the Burbages, that Miles should try at common law to collect from the Burbages the value of the two bonds James Burbage had given John Brayne for performance, and if he could not succeed there, then Chancery would take up the case again. (The two lawsuits in Chancery ended here, where they had begun. Miles did not collect the value of the bonds at common law, nor did he return to Chancery.)

C-28. Req.2/241/14 (Wallace, pp. 158-62): A lawsuit in the Court of Requests of between April 13 and May 9, 1597, in which Robert Miles sued Cuthbert Burbage and Giles Allen. James Burbage having died in February 1597, and the lease on the site of the Theatre having expired on April 13, 1597, Miles sued Burbage's son and heir, Cuthbert, and the owner of the property, Allen. He argued as Margaret Brayne and he had in Chancery (C-5), except that he now involved Allen, mainly because he needed to make the lawsuit different from the other in order to qualify it for another court. He urged that Allen should renew the lease, and he said that he had asked the Burbages to pull down the Theatre (as the lease entitled them to do while it was still in force) so that he and they might sell the materials and divide the money. Document: the bill only, undated.

C-29. Req.1/48/9 May 39 Eliz. (Wallace, p. 162): An order of the Court of Requests of May 9, 1597, in Robert Miles's lawsuit against Cuthbert Burbage and Giles Allen (C-28). Burbage and Allen declined to reply, arguing that this lawsuit was the same as Margaret Brayne's and Miles' lawsuit in Chancery (C-5). The court ordered that the attorneys on both sides compare the two bills and make a report.

C-30. Req.1/48/27 May 39 Eliz. (Wallace, p. 163): An order of the Court of Requests of May 27, 1597, in Robert Miles's lawsuit against Cuthbert Burbage and Giles Allen (C-28). Miles argued that this lawsuit involved different people from those in the lawsuit in Chancery (C-5, see C-29); the court agreed and ordered Burbage and Allen to reply to the lawsuit without delay. (The lawsuit disappears now, possibly because the decree and order books of the Court of Requests are missing from December 7, 1597, to April 24, 1599.)

Note. Mrs. Stopes (pp. 163-64, 164-65) noted two additional documents, an order in Chancery of June 7, 1594, and a lawsuit in Chancery, the bill dated November 13, 1594, but neither concerns the Theatre. The order is part of a lawsuit in which James Burbage sued one Gregory More: C.33/87/f.274-74ᵛ (A book) and /88/f.277ᵛ (B book). In the lawsuit, Robert Miles sued his son, Raphe, and Nicholas Byshop about the George Inn in Whitechapel: C.3/245/85.

Category D

This legal quarrel arose because the Burbages and their associates dismantled and took the Theatre away from the site in Shoreditch so that they could use much of it in building the Globe in Southwark.

The Burbages' lease on Giles Allen's property at Holywell began in April 1576 and ran for twenty-one years. The lease contained a clause stating that if James Burbage spent £200 on various structures other than the Theatre within ten years, Allen would renew the lease for another twenty-one years, to begin when the renewal was signed. Burbage thought he had spent the money, and he presented a new lease for Allen to sign in 1585. Allen refused to do so on several pretexts, mainly that the new lease was not word-for-word like the original one and that Burbage had not spent the money. Toward the end of the original lease, the Burbages offered to take another lease for twenty-one years at a higher rent and with a cash payment of £30 (which Allen said James Burbage owed for rent). Allen demanded another cash payment of £100 for repairs to the various structures other than the Theatre, which the Burbages may or may not have been willing to pay. But he also demanded that the Burbages use the Theatre as a playhouse for only five more years, after which they were to use it for some more decent purpose and eventually to pass it to Allen when the lease should run out. To this condition the Burbages and their company could not agree. So from April 1597, when the original lease ran out, until Christmas 1598, Allen suffered them to keep the property without a lease. Then in that Christmas season, they had the Theatre dismantled and carried away, as a clause in the original lease allowed them to do while the lease was in effect.

Allen, of course, by this time thought he owned a playhouse. When he found that he owned a vacant piece of ground instead, he went smartly to law, and the Burbages and company (who must have worked it all out in advance) set about very skillfully defending themselves. Allen sued them in the King's Bench for trespass and damage. The Burbages counter-sued Allen almost a year later in the Court of Requests, a court known for swift judgments, arguing mainly that Allen should have renewed the original lease, hence that the Burbages still had the right to take away their playhouse, and hence that the lawsuit in the King's Bench should be stopped. The Court of Requests stopped the lawsuit in the King's Bench in April 1600, heard the case on October 18, 1600, and found for the Burbages. Allen promptly (in January 1601) tried another lawsuit in the King's Bench, accusing the Burbages not of taking away the Theatre, but of having failed to keep the terms of the original lease. Then in the November following he took the Burbages to the Star Chamber, charging them with having got their verdict in Requests by various frauds. That court was looking into one of these alleged frauds in May 1602—ironically, one that even if it was a fraud would not have affected the verdict in Requests—but evidently Allen got as little comfort from the Star Chamber as he had got from Requests.[12] In 1602, therefore, three years after it had opened, the Globe was free at last of Giles Allen.

D-1. K.B.27/1362/m.587 (Halliwell-Phillipps, I, 348-49, 359-60, 361, 362; Wallace, pp. 163-80; Stopes, pp. 198-200): A summary (dated Trinity Term 1600) of a lawsuit in the King's Bench in which Giles Allen sued the Burbages' builder, Peter Street, for entering "the Jnner Courte yarde" of Holywell Priory with force and arms and taking down and carrying away a building called "the Theater," worth £700. The summary reads that the offence occurred on January 20, 1599, and that Allen filed the lawsuit in Easter Term following. The offence, however, is more likely to have occurred shortly after Christmas 1598 and Allen to have filed the lawsuit on January 20, 1599 (see above, pp. 5-7. (On Wallace's p. 177, three lines from the bottom, "may lawfull" should be "maye be lawfull.")

D-2. Req.2/87/74 (Collier, "Original History," p. 64; Halliwell-Phillipps, I, 348-49, 358-59, 360, 361, 362, 371-72; Wallace, pp. 180-205, 253-58; Stopes, pp. 200-16): A lawsuit in the Court of Requests in which Cuthbert Burbage sought to stop Giles Allen's lawsuit in the King's Bench (D-1). Documents: Burbage's bill (January 26, 1600), Allen's reply (February 4, 1600), Burbage's replication (April 27, 1600). Attached to these documents are interrogatories (June 5, 1600) for two of Allen's witnesses, Robert Vigerous and Thomas Nevill, their depositions (both of August 14, 1600), and a commission to examine them in the country (June 5, 1600): separated from the other documents of the kind (D-7), probably because unlike the other witnesses, these were examined in the country.

D-3. Req.1/198/Easter 42 Eliz./9 April (Stopes, p. 216): A list of witnesses of April 9, 1600, in the Burbages' lawsuit against Giles Allen in the Court of Requests (D-2), for both sides: Philip Baker, Henry Johnson, John Goburne, William Smyth, Richard Hudson, Thomas Osborne, Thomas Bromfield, William Furnis.

D-4. Req.1/49/10 Apr. 42 Eliz. (Wallace, p. 205): An order of the Court of Requests of April 10, 1600, in the Burbages' lawsuit against Giles Allen (D-2). The court ordered Allen's lawsuit in King's Bench (D-1) stopped if on April 17 Allen could not "shewe good matter" to the contrary.

D-5. Missing (see D-6): An order of the Court of Requests of April 17, 1600, in the Burbages' lawsuit against Giles Allen (D-2). The court declared that it would hear both sides on April 22 about whether Allen should stop his lawsuit in the King's Bench (D-1). This document is missing probably because Allen challenged the stopping of that lawsuit twice, in Requests and then in the Star Chamber (D-14, 16, 17, 18).

D-6. Req.1/49/22 Apr. 42 Eliz. (Wallace, pp. 205-6): An order of the Court of Requests of April 22, 1600, in the Burbages' lawsuit against Giles Allen (D-2). As it had appointed on April 17 (D-5), the court heard arguments on this day about whether Allen should stop his lawsuit in King's Bench. The court decided that both sides should examine their witnesses by the second day of the next term (May 19) and that the whole matter should be heard on the eleventh day of the next term (May 31) "*per*emptorilie." In the meantime the court ordered that the Burbages reply to Allen's lawsuit in the King's Bench before Monday next (April 28), but that Allen not proceed with it himself. (For a list of Wallace's mistakes in transcription, see p. 24 above.)

D-7. Req.2/184/45 (Wallace, pp. 206-50; 259-66): Interrogatories and depositions for both sides in the Burbages' lawsuit against Giles Allen in the Court of Requests (D-2). Allen tried to show that he did not have to renew the Burbages' original lease because they had not kept its terms, and that the Burbages had agreed to a lease recently that, among other things, raised their rent, cost them £100 in repairs, and precluded their taking away the Theatre. The Burbages tried to show that they had kept the terms of the original lease and had not agreed to the recent one. Documents: Allen's interrogatories (Easter 1600); the depositions of his witnesses, Philip Baker, John Goburne, and Henry Johnson (all on April 26, 1600); the Burbages' interrogatories (Trinity 1600); the depositions of their witnesses, Richard Hudson, Thomas Bromfield, Thomas Osborne, William Furnis, William Smyth, Randolph May, and Oliver Tylte (all on May 15, 1600); the Burbages' interrogatories (Trinity 1600) for Allen's witnesses, Johnson and Goburne, and their second depositions (both on May 23, 1600); Allen's interrogatories (June 5, 1600) for two later witnesses, Robert Miles and his son Raphe, and their depositions (both on October 1, 1600). See also D-2.

D-8. Req.1/198/Trin. 42 Eliz./23 May (Stopes, p. 216): A list of witnesses of May 23, 1600, in the Burbages' lawsuit against Giles Allen in the Court of Requests (D-2), for both sides: Oliver Tylte, Randolph May, John Goburne, Henry Johnson.

D-9. Missing (see D-11, 16-18): An order of the Court of Requests of May 31, 1600, in the Burbages' lawsuit against Giles Allen (D-2). The court did not hear the case on this day as it had appointed on April 22 (D-6), but ordered that the case be heard on the eleventh day of the next term (October 18), and, probably, that the examining of witnesses be completed early in October. In the meantime, court ordered Allen not to proceed with his lawsuit in the King's the Bench (D-1). This document is missing probably for the same reason as D-5.

D-10. Req.1/121/2 June 42 Eliz. (Affidavit Register) and /122 [uncovered volume] /2 June 42 Eliz. (Affidavit Entry Book) (Wallace, p. 251): An affidavit of June 2, 1600, by Giles Allen in the Burbages' lawsuit against him in the Court of Requests (D-2). Allen swore that he knew nothing of the depositions so far taken and that he wanted others examined on his behalf: Richard Parramore, Robert Vigerous, Thomas Nevill, Robert Miles, Raphe Miles, John Hyde, and William Gall. (Wallace's text follows /122.)

D-11. Req.1/121/11 June 42 Eliz. (Affidavit Register) and /122 [uncovered volume] /11 June 42 Eliz. (Affidavit Entry Book) (Wallace p. 252): An affidavit of June 11, 1600, by Cuthbert Burbage in the Burbages' lawsuit against Giles Allen in the Court of Requests (D-2). Burbage swore that Allen was pressing the lawsuit in the King's Bench (D-1) contrary to the order of the Court of Requests on May 31, 1600 (D-9). (Wallace's text follows /122. On his p. 252, line 3, "Counsailo^r" should be "Counsailo^{rs}"; hence the two abbreviated nouns following should be expanded as plurals.)

D-12. Req.2/372/pt.I [bottom of the box] (Wallace, pp. 252-53; Stopes, p. 216): An order of the Court of Requests of June 11, 1600, for the arrest of Giles Allen because he had defied an order of May 31, 1600 (see D-9, 11), part of the Burbages' lawsuit against him (D-2).

D-13. Req.1/109/f.8 (Wallace, p. 266): A note in the Appearance Book of the Court of Requests that Giles Allen appeared in court on October 9, 1600, by virtue of the order of the court that he be arrested (D-12), part of the Burbages' lawsuit against him in that court (D-2).

D-14. Missing (see D-16, 17): An order in the Court of Requests of October 18, 1600, in the Burbages' lawsuit against Giles Allen (D-2). The court heard the case on this day and decreed that Allen should have renewed the original lease for ten years, and hence that the Burbages were right to take the Theatre down and carry it away. The court ordered that Allen stop his lawsuit in the King's Bench (D-1) permanently and not sue the Burbages about the matter again. The court also ordered that the Burbages could, if they liked, sue Allen for not renewing the original lease. The court allowed Allen just one crumb. He charged that the Burbages had fraudulently secured the order of May 31 (D-9), which had caused him to be arrested (D-11, 12), and he was allowed now to pursue the matter—but the matter had nothing to do with the dismantling and taking away of the Theatre. The book is missing in which this order would have been entered, if it was not omitted, as D-5, 9 may have been, because Allen challenged the matter in the Star Chamber (D-17).

D-15. Missing (see D-18 and Wallace, p. 294): An order of the Court of Requests of November 1, 1600, in the Burbages' lawsuit against Giles Allen (D-2). The court ordered that the verdict of October 18 (D-14) not be signed until the court had considered further Allen's assertion that the order of May 31 (D-9) was fraudulently incomplete (see D-17). This document is missing probably for the same reason as D-5, 9, 14.

D-16. K.B.27/1373/m.257 (Halliwell-Phillipps, I, 349, 358; Wallace, pp. 267-75; Stopes, pp. 217-19, Braines, pp. 11-12): A summary of a lawsuit in the King's Bench, begun in Hilary Term 1601, in which Giles Allen (having just lost the lawsuit in the Court of Requests—see D-14) sued the Burbages not for having taken away the Theatre, but for having failed to keep the terms of the lease on the property on which the Theatre had stood. The summary is dated Easter 1602. (On Wallace's p. 268, line 2, "ascensu" should be "assensu"; and five lines from the bottom and on p. 269, line 1, "Daridge" should be "Dotridge.")

D-17. St.Ch.5/A.12/35 (Collier, "Original History," p. 69; Halliwell-Phillipps, I, 360-61, 372; Wallace, pp. 275-90; Stopes, pp. 220-27): A lawsuit in the Star Chamber, in which Giles Allen (having lost his case in the Court of Requests [D-2] on October 18, 1600) sued the Burbages for removing the Theatre from Holywell. Allen charged that the Burbages had got the verdict in Requests (D-14) by a number of frauds, and that the order of May 31, 1600 (for violating which he was arrested), was fraudulently incomplete and hence that he did not violate it (see D-9, 11, 12). Documents: Allen's bill (November 23, 1601), the demurrer of the Burbages, their builder (Peter Street), and others (April 28, 1602), the reply of Richard Lane, the clerk who entered the order of May 31, 1600 (April 28, 1602), and the demurrer of Richard Hudson and Thomas Osborne, two of the Burbages' witnesses (June 12, 1602). (On Wallace's p. 287, line 20, "ther" should be "then.")

D-18. St.Ch.5/A.33/32 (Wallace, pp. 290-97): The interrogatories (May 1, 1602) for Richard Lane and his deposition (May 11, 1602), part of Giles Allen's lawsuit in the Star Chamber against the Burbages (D-17)

Note. Mrs. Stopes (p. 219) included an additional document, K.B.27/1373/m.260, a summary of a lawsuit in the King's Bench in which Giles Allen sued John Knapp for trespassing apparently on the property in Holywell. The summary follows immediately that of D-16 on the King's Bench roll, but the matter does not concern the Theatre, because the trespass occurred in January 1602, three years after the removal of the Theatre from Holywell. A John Knapp was one of Screven's associates against Allen in 1601 (B-6).

NOTES

* Originally published in *The First Public Playhouse*, ed. H. Berry (Montreal, 1979), pp. 97-133.

1. Published among *The Shakespeare Society Papers*, IV (1849), 63-70.

2. See *History of English Dramatic Poetry to the Time of Shakespeare* (London, 1879), III, 257 ff.

3. Wallace, *The First London Theatre*, and Stopes, *Burbage and Shakespeare's Stage* (London, 1913). See his waspish notes about her (pp. 45, 276) and her pained notes about him (pp. ix-x, xii-xiii&n.).

4. "The Site of 'the Theatre,' Shoreditch," *London Topographical Record*, XI (1917), 1.

5. Wallace wrote a footnote (p. 31) to show that he knew about Category B and did not think it very important. Unintentionally, he also showed that he had not given it much attention. He alluded to a series of matters belonging to it, all but three of which Halliwell-Phillipps had found, especially in one document (B-10), and quoted extensively without giving a citation. Wallace mentioned the document but cited only Halliwell-Phillipps. The other three matters (Francis Langley and lawsuits in Wards and Star Chamber) can most conveniently be found in either of two documents, B-8 or its dependent, B-9, an important part of Category B that Halliwell-Phillipps had not found. Evidently Wallace had found one of these documents or both and little else. He cited neither, but he assured his readers that the important parts of Category B would take "their due place in the final presentation," a work he did not live to write.

6. I count only clear mistakes. One could find many more if he were to insist on absolute rigor. Many of the Wallaces' mistakes were probably the result not of transcription but of proofreading, which somebody in Lincoln did while they were in Europe (p. 39), and which must have been a nightmare to do. For all 2,050-odd lines at which I looked, the Wallaces made one mistake in seven or eight as they printed them.

7. The Wallaces were strangely prone to mistranscribing signatures, as those of James Burbage (p. 63), John Goburne (p. 218), Richard Hudson (p. 229; he spelled his name "Hudsone" here but later in his life left off the "e"), and William Smyth (p. 239).

8. No one was fined as a result of the lawsuit, for there is no estreat of fine in E.159 for any of the people in it.

9. Her name at the beginning of her deposition is not easily legible. In answer #2, she said she was once the wife of "Roberte Farrer." So Mrs. Stopes called her "Mrs. Farrar." Braines (p. 16), however, read her name at the beginning of her deposition correctly as "Marie Askew."

10. Braines used the document correctly in his article in the *London Topographical Record*, p. 10n., but he left it out of his part of the *Survey of London*, VIII, and misread and misapplied it in 1923.

11. Confusion about sheriffs of London and Middlesex occurred because the two sheriffs of London served jointly as sheriff of Middlesex.

12. There is no estreat of fine in E.159 for the Burbages or Richard Lane; hence they were probably not fined in Star Chamber.

The Stage and Boxes
at Blackfriars*

Though much remains to be learned about theatres in the times of Elizabeth and her two successors, few aspects of them are less well served by the available evidence than the most important, the stages. Such evidence as there is, moreover, happens to concern almost entirely the stages of the public playhouses. Virtually nothing is known for certain about the equally important stages of the private playhouses, those indoor theatres that, after all, existed side by side with the public ones throughout the period, housing players and plays that were in many cases the same as those of the public theatres and otherwise were scarcely inferior.

I have found a document at the Public Record Office alluding specifically to the stage of the principal private playhouse, Blackfriars. Though at first glance the episode it reports may not seem remarkable, ultimately its words lead one into many aspects of the Shakespearean stage, public as well as private. It is in any case sufficiently dramatic in another sense. It concerns a public brawl that proceeded to a hearing in the Star Chamber and involved some curiously related people, two of whom were eventually to be numbered among the most considerable men in the kingdom.

As with so many other documents alluding to Shakespearean playhouses, the writer of this one was mainly concerned with something other than the playhouse. The document refers, moreover, to a relatively late time, the winter season of 1631-32. But the main inferences about the stage are quite clear, and it seems that Blackfriars was not seriously altered from its expensive rebuilding by the Burbages in 1596, and its occupancy by Shakespeare's company, the King's men, some twelve or thirteen years later, to its closing in 1642.[1]

The document is one of a bundle of newsletters written from London by a professional writer of such letters, John Pory, to his client, the Viscount Scudamore, at Craddock in Herefordshire during a year beginning in December, 1631.[2] Pory dated this newsletter February 4, 1632. He spent most of the first two pages reporting recent cases in the Star Chamber. The lords of that court had just fined "Sir Richard Greenvill of the west" £8,000 for calling the Earl of Suffolk a "base lorde" (the King to have £4,000 and Suffolk £4,000). They had fined Dr. Carrier £500 (which Pory thought exceedingly "cheap," the result of mismanagement by the court) for preaching Papistry. The lords of the court had, besides, just compelled Mr. Walter Steward to give Sir Miles Fleetwood, treasurer of the Court of Wards, "suche satisfaction" in their presence as "they thought reasonable." Steward had observed that Fleetwood was "a briber...yea more, that he was a base knave, and that hee went to twoe sermons on a Sunday, and that on Monday morning hee would sell his friend for twoe shillings."

Pory's remarks about Blackfriars follow immediately. "Their lo:Ps," he wrote, "made my lord Thurles of Irland also to doe the like satisfaction to Captaine Essex. The occasion was this. This Captaine attending and accompanying my Lady of Essex in a boxe in the playhouse at the blackfryers, the said lord coming upon the stage, stood before them and hindred their sight. Captain Essex told his lo:P, they had payd for their places as well as hee, and therfore intreated him not to depriue them of the benefitt of it. Wherevpon the lord

stood vp yet higher and hindred more their sight. Then Capt. Essex
with his hand putt him a little by. The lord then drewe his sword and
ran full butt at him, though hee missed him, and might have slaine the
Countesse as well as him." The Star Chamber heard the matter
sometime "Within the compasse of this week" ending February 4.
The countess's theatrical outing, therefore, probably occurred toward
the end of January, 1632.

The countess was the new wife of the Earl of Essex,[3] son of the
Elizabethan earl. He had already achieved much fame as husband of
the notorious Frances Howard and was to achieve more as Parliamentary commander in chief. The captain was Charles Essex, a professional soldier who was a follower of the Earl of Essex. As Clarendon
eventually explained, he "had been bred up a page under the earl of
Essex, who afterwards, at his charge, preferred him to a command in
Holland; where he lived with very good reputation, and preserved the
credit of his decayed family."[4] The captain was probably on leave in
England, since the Dutch wars did not extend into the winter, when
both sides partly disbanded their forces. Thurles was a dashing young
man in more ways than one. He was about twenty-one years old, heir
of one of the most powerful families in Ireland, and the future "loyal"
Duke of Ormond, King's commander and then Lord Deputy in
Ireland for many years. He had just arrived in London from Ireland
via Scotland "to sollicit the Court in a matter of confiscations due to
his Majesty...which might have turned to his own advantage, had it
succeeded." He had ridden from Edinburgh to Ware in three days
and might easily have reached London on the third day if he had
wished.[5]

What happened to the play in progress does not appear. As to
Thurles, it was routine that his case should be filed in the Star
Chamber, for that court had always dealt especially with notorious
breaches of the peace. It is probably significant of the place and
occasion that the matter was actually heard in the court (unlike the
vast majority of cases filed there). It is probably also significant that
Thurles had to give Captain Essex what one supposes was merely a
verbal apology. As the Venetian ambassador had remarked some
years earlier, the Earl of Essex and his family were not "in much
favour at" Whitehall.[6]

Pory's remarks contain two pieces of information about the stage at Blackfriars. First and less important, they demonstrate for the first time that gallants sometimes stood there, at least in 1632. While interesting, this information is not crucial since it is a reasonable extension of information long available about spectators sitting, even reclining, on that stage. Second and much more important, they clearly imply that boxes were a) contiguous to the stage and b) on a level with it. That is an unusual and significant arrangement.[7] No other conclusion is possible if a person standing on the stage could block the view of those sitting in a box, if the box-holders could converse with and then reach out to touch the person on stage, if that person could block the view even more by standing higher, and, finally, attempt (with a good chance of success) to run his sword through one of the box-holders. Moreover, Pory's phraseology suggests that the captain's and countess's box related to the stage like other boxes, that boxes in general at Blackfriars, not just one of them, were contiguous to and level with the stage.

Was Thurles standing in defiance of accepted practice? Should he, that is, have been sitting on one of the usual three-legged stools on stage or reclining on rushes there, as gallants had been doing for some thirty years, especially at Blackfriars (the renting of the stools had brought the lessee, Henry Evans, as much as 30s. per week, "or thereabouts," in 1603-4)?[8] Pory's remarks suggest that the managers at Blackfriars allowed occasional standing on the stage, expecting, or hoping, that the stander would place himself where he would not obstruct the box-holder's view: before vacant boxes, for example, perhaps before partitions and stage doors as well. For Pory seems to say that Thurles should have lowered himself when Captain Essex first objected. When instead he did the reverse, "stood vp yet higher," Essex accepted Thurles's upright posture so long as it did not obstruct the view, as, since he has no special remark about it, Pory seems to do. The managers could not have allowed the stander as a matter of course to interfere with the view from the boxes. If they had, Pory's remark would hardly be the only one yet found describing such a situation. They would have found it difficult to be very firm about the matter in any case, considering the rank and importance of at least one of those who stood.

It has long been apparent that there were boxes at Blackfriars.

Leonard Digges says as much in his commendatory lines for Shakespeare's *Poems* (1640):

> let but *Beatrice*
> And *Benedicke* be seene, loe in a trice
> The Cockpit Galleries, Boxes, all are full
> To hear *Malvoglio*, that crosse garter'd Gull.
>
> (ll. 57-60)

Much Ado and *Twelfth Night* belonged, of course, to the King's Men, and the only playhouse of theirs with a "Cockpit" was Blackfriars. When the Reverend George Garrard described another quarrel at the Blackfriars almost exactly four years after the one Pory described, he, too, mentioned boxes. Garrard reported this second affair to his regular correspondent in Ireland, Wentworth, the Lord Deputy, on January 25, 1636. There had been "A little Pique...betwixt the Duke of *Lenox* and the Lord Chamberlain about a Box at a new Play in the *Black Fryars*, of which the Duke had got the Key: Which if it had come to be debated betwixt them, as it was once intended, some Heat or perhaps other Inconvenience might have happen'd. His Majesty hearing of it, sent the Earl of *Holland* to command them both not to dispute it, but before him, so he heard it and made them Friends."[9]

That the boxes were contiguous to and level with the stage should be no surprise. Thomas Dekker suggested as much certainly once and probably twice, though without the evidence from Pory no one has realized what he meant. In *Satiromastix* (1602) Dekker had Sir Vaughan tell Jonson, then the Blackfriars poet, that "you must forsweare to venter on the stage, when your Play is ended, and to exchange curtezies, and complements with Gallants in the Lordes roomes."[10] Surely the stage Dekker meant was that at Blackfriars. Surely, too, Dekker implied contiguousness and a common level. And in the "*proemium*" of his *Gull's Hornbook* (1609) Dekker wrote the familiar remark about "the twelue-penny roome next the stage" where the gull might mingle with lords. By *next*, I suggest that Dekker meant what we mean by the word: *nearest*, hence in the case of structures, *adjacent* and on the same level. Otherwise he probably would have used the less exact word, *near*. One cannot be certain, however, that Dekker meant the stage at Blackfriars here, though it is better than a fair guess that he did (along with, perhaps, other private stages), since there was no such place "next" the stages of the public playhouses for which there is evidence, and, thanks to Pory, it is clear that there was indeed such a place "next the stage" at Blackfriars—and lords really sat there.

Writers have invariably assigned these remarks of Dekker's to the public playhouses despite Dekker's allusion in one of them to Jonson's theatre. The lords' and twelve penny rooms have usually been equated, therefore, with the portion of the lower gallery called the "orchestra" in the Swan drawing. So Jonson has had to exchange courtesies with gallants over the heads of groundlings in the yard and the gull to mingle with lords in the same curious way. Pory's account now strips the public playhouses of at least one of these bedeviling pieces of evidence and probably both. I shall return to these and other of Dekker's remarks later.

Were Pory's boxes along the sides of the stage? or along the back? or even along both sides and back, where Milton says "all the Lords and each degree / Of sort" had seats in the theatre Samson pulled down?[11] One is concerned not merely with where a patron might sit at Blackfriars if he cared to pay enough, but also with the idea of stage that prevailed in a very important theatre.

If the boxes were contiguous to and on a level with the stage at its sides, there are two possibilities about how the boxes would have fitted into the design of the house. They might have been a part of the stage itself, or part of galleries running at stage level the whole length of the room. Either way, those boxes would have rendered the stage essentially different from the customary Shakespearean conception. The stage would have gone completely across the house, in effect, and the mass of the audience would have been out front peering directly at and through a more-or-less enclosed room. Blackfriars would have constituted a crucial step in the direction of the proscenium-arch stage, and the arrangements there would have been similar to those in the Restoration theatres, where boxes were indeed contiguous to and on a level with the sides of the stage. Blackfriars would have lacked only the devices behind the stage meant to promote realism.

If, on the other hand, the boxes were at the back of the stage, Blackfriars could have possessed the essential elements of the common Shakespearean stage. The pit could have extended along the sides of the stage. The galleries could have run along the sides of the room, over the heads of people in the pit, directly to the wall behind the stage. (That Blackfriars had galleries of some kind, several contemporaries have assured us, among them Digges in lines quoted above.) Back to front, the stage could have extended about half way across the pit. The stage would have been a relatively open platform and realism impossible on it.[12] This is the crucial fact of what we have come to think of as the Shakespearean stage. The implications for plays and stagecraft are great. On the Shakespearean stage, rhetoric, symbol, and pageantry are in their element. The Restoration and similar stages were specifically introduced to facilitate realism, and on them realism commenced its long domination of English drama.

Because of the lack of evidence about the stage at Blackfriars, the arguments for boxes at the sides or back must be circumstantial and speculative, so that neither case can be really proved. Writers have almost always put the Blackfriars stage completely across one of the narrow ends of the rectangular room, hence begun there the history of the proscenium-arch stage in professional English playhouses. The tendency now, therefore, will be to put Pory's boxes along the sides of the stage. There is good reason, however, to put them at the back, hence to associate Blackfriars with its great contemporaries rather than with centuries of later places. I do not deal with the third possibility, boxes at sides and back, because I suppose that arguments militating against sides alone militate also against sides and back.

Two things are certain. The stage and thus the boxes at Blackfriars were raised above the crowd, for that house had a pit, an area, that is, below the stage accommodating, one supposes, much of the audience. Among others, Shirley mentioned such a place in the prologue to his *Doubtful Heir* (1640), as did Digges in the above passage. And next, wherever the boxes were, they could not have been where C. W. Wallace put them in his plan of Blackfriars (1908), which has remained the usual conception of that house. He described Blackfriars as "the model of the modern theatre."[13] He had the stage level extending completely across one end of the room and galleries running at stage level from the back of the room along the sides up to the front of the stage, where they stopped. He put his boxes in the portions of these galleries nearest the stage, roughly where they would be in modern theatres. He put his stage sitters along the sides of the stage, occupying a strip as wide as the galleries, so that the stage sitters were, in effect, a continuation of these galleries. In this arrangement, it is very unlikely that Thurles could have blocked the view of the captain and countess, for that pair would have watched the play over the front of the stage and Thurles over the side.

An objection to putting the boxes at the sides of the stage at Blackfriars is that the historical arguments one must make do not bear much thinking about. The argument that the Burbages would have built their playhouse under the influence of proscenium-arch stages on the Continent must be unconvincing as must the argument backwards from the stages of Restoration times.

The strict proscenium-arch design does not allow boxes, much less sitters and recliners, at either the sides or back of the stage. Neither the Continental originators nor their English imitators, Inigo Jones and his associate, John Webb, show such things in their plans and drawings. If the Burbages built a first step toward the proscenium-arch stage rather than the full design, it is a step unrecorded not only in these plans and drawings but in all the other specific, contemporary evidence about stages, whether for regular professional or other use. The Jones-Webb scheme that may or may not have been meant for the private playhouse in Drury Lane, the Phoenix, ca. 1616, does set out a theatre which, with some rebuilding, could have had boxes at the sides of the stage. The arrangement of stage and spectators and the general effect thus created, however, would be quite different from what the drawings show, which is more than a little reminiscent of the ordinary Shakespearean arrangement. In any event, this and all their other theatrical schemes for which evidence exists belong to a time well after 1596, when the Burbages built their playhouse in Blackfriars.

As for Restoration theatres, one might argue that, like Blackfriars, they were indoors and intended for select audiences. In some ways they were successors to Blackfriars: the King's company, for example, might be said to have moved out of the one and into one of the others. Ultimately, however, one would have to admit that twenty years intervened in the succession and well over sixty in the construction, and that what one knows of Restoration theatres and Shakespearean playhouses is more a matter of differences than similarities.

One might argue that expensive places for spectators were at the sides of the stages in some of the public playhouses and produce the

picture of the Swan and the contract for that theatre modeled on the
Swan, the Hope. One would call attention to the "orchestra" in the
picture, which is beside the stage in a sense and perhaps level with it.
One would have to admit, however, that the "orchestra" is by no
means contiguous to the stage but separated from it by a portion of the
yard. Contiguousness here is the whole point. The lack of it renders
the stages at the Swan and Hope thoroughly Shakespearean and no
progenitors of the proscenium-arch stage. Besides, so far as one knows
for certain, an "orchestra" in this position existed only in two public
playhouses, both quite separate from the line of playhouses built by
the Burbages and their associates.

The argument to put Pory's boxes contiguous to and level with
the stage at the back is more congenial. Literally all the best evidence
about the walls behind Shakespearean stages, for example, has expensive seats in those walls, not level with the stages but above the stage
doors. Hence, one might argue, expensive seats were conventionally
behind the stage, and the curiosity about Blackfriars is not that they
were there but that they were level with the stage. This evidence
includes all four early pictures of professional Shakespearean stages,
and even the Jones-Webb scheme meant perhaps for the Phoenix.[14]
Seats behind and above the stage, indeed, together with the general
idea of the thrust stage, are almost the only ways in which these things
(which date from 1596 to Restoration times) do agree. In addition,
Edward Guilpin confirmed the presence of such seats there in 1598,
Ben Jonson did as much in 1599, and so did Dekker and George
Wilkins in 1607.[15] That arrangement clearly existed also in the playhouse inexpensively built in the yard of the Boar's Head, Whitechapel,
in 1598 and expensively rebuilt there in 1599. In 1603, three people
said some nineteen times that there was a gallery over the stage, and
one of them added that it was also over the tiring house. They should
have known, for one was the player who led the company of players at
the Boar's Head, another was the contractor who had rebuilt the
playhouse in 1599, and the third was a carpenter who had worked in
the rebuilding. That the gallery was for spectators, several lawsuits
about the income from it make quite clear.[16] Except, perhaps, for the
picture in the frontispiece of Francis Kirkman's *The Wits* (1662), most
of this evidence obviously concerns public, not private, playhouses.
But when the Burbages and their associates designed and carried out

the rebuilding of Blackfriars in 1596 for their own use, their experience lay in public playhouses.

Another kind of evidence is also equally persuasive. As a contemporary observed, people like Thurles, "Knights of the Order," had in King Henry's time sought honor and praise,

> But now they adventure
> A Tavern to enter,
> And sit in the Center
> Of common stage Playes.[17]

If they were directly in front of the boxes, as at least one of them clearly was in this incident of 1632, those boxes must have been at the back. Jonson described the same situation in *Cynthia's Revels* (1601), alluding surely to Blackfriars. The boys of the Blackfriars company tell their comrade imitating the foolish gentlemen to "throne" himself "in state on the stage, as other gentlemen vse" (induction, ll. 144-46). Such quite clearly is the scheme Dekker had in mind in the sixth chapter of *The Gull's Hornbook*. There the gulls on stage sit as justices "in examining of plaies," in "the Throne of the Stage," "vnder the state of *Cambises* himselfe," while since the gulls have moved out of them and onto the stage, the boxes "are contemptibly thrust into the reare." Dekker meant the remark figuratively, of course, but it must have had its literal appropriateness as well if he was to avoid a mixed image. For a person sitting as a justice, in the throne of the stage, and under the state, "reare" could have meant only one thing, the back, at least as the bulk of the audience would have seen it. Leslie Hotson, finally, and others since have found evidence that important spectators were also at the rear of stages temporarily erected in churches and halls and at court.[18] These persons, it appears, were, like the people in the boxes at Blackfriars, at stage level.

Why should the boxes at Blackfriars have been at stage level rather than above? The height of the room, or that end of the room, may have had something to do with the arrangement.[19] Another reason depends less on conjecture. The Burbages could have had more box seats by putting the boxes down with the stage at its back than by putting them above the stage. Above the stage the problem was the difficult angle of vision created by the height and the proximity of the seats to the stage. Three pictures show spectators above the stage, but only eight spectators appear in the first, four in the next, and eight in the last, all of them in front. Even if the floor consisted of steps rising toward the back (as apparently it does not in any of the pictures but does in the Jones-Webb scheme), not many more persons could have seen much of the stage.

Whether putting the boxes of the Blackfriars playhouse along the sides of the stage or at the back, one must consider the space available for them, and here, too, the back seems the better choice.

To put boxes at one side of the stage is surely to put them on the other as well, for architectural and commercial reasons. The stage at Blackfriars was not small. Because the stage at St. Paul's *was* small, spectators preferred not to sit on it, supposing they would ''wrong the general eye...very much.''[20] Stage sitting was more closely associated with Blackfriars than any other playhouse, public or private. The room at Blackfriars was 46' wide by 66' long. If the stage was on one of the 46' sides, as no doubt it was, that much is available for boxes and persons standing, sitting, even reclining on both sides and the play itself in the middle. Wallace did not continue his boxes along the sides of the stage because he did not think there was room for them, persons in front of them, and the play. He allowed 10'6'' on each side of the room for boxes, thinking, probably, of the galleries of the Fortune, which were 12'6'' deep. Hence he also allowed 10'6 '' on each side of the stage for sitters and recliners. He supposed, therefore, that he could not put both boxes and sitters at the sides of the stage because they would take up 21' on each side and leave only 4' in the middle for the play. His allowances for boxes and spectators on the stage are, however, much too generous. Relatively comfortable boxes seating one row of pretentious people side by side can be 3' deep including the thickness of walls, and even a gaggle of sitters and recliners can be limited to 5'. Boxes and spectators on both sides of the stage, then, could occupy about 16' and leave something like 30' for the play. That might be enough.

One row of persons in boxes on each side is probably the maximum possible. Each row would have been as long as the stage was deep, 27'6 '' as at the Fortune, or, perhaps more likely, somewhat less, say 25' as Wallace guessed. Spectators side by side would have occupied from 50' or less to 55'. At the back, depth was not so great a problem. At least two rows of spectators could have sat in boxes there. If there were three stage doors in the back wall and each took up from 3' to 6' of the 46', spectators would have occupied from 56' to 74' side by side, more if there was a third row of spectators or only two doors. True, every foot of space used behind the stage was a foot of space lost in front of it. It was, however, a foot of space the Burbages could have afforded to lose when one recalls the prices exacted for seats in those boxes.

The amount of space available in the 66' length of the playhouse for boxes behind the stage, the stage itself, and pit in front of the stage involves the tiring house. If it was in the theatrical room, presumably behind the stage, one must allow some of the 66' for it and so diminish the amount available for boxes, stage, and pit. But was the tiring house in the theatrical room? The question, like many others in the history of the playhouses, takes one back to C. W. Wallace. That the room had in it a stage, boxes, pit, and galleries appears in places having nothing to do with him. Much else known about the room, however, especially its size, involves documents he found, and he dealt with these documents as he did with some others. He printed a few brief excerpts from them and a few assertions of his own about their contents, nothing more. He gave no citations. They were to accompany a fuller treatment in a great work that never appeared. Chambers grudgingly accepted this information. Then H. N. Hillebrand found and in 1926 published a document that repeated most of Wallace's excerpts. Irwin Smith eventually concluded that Hillebrand had found all Wallace's material. Hillebrand himself, however, must have known that he had not, though he did not say so. Wallace had found a lawsuit of 1608 involving the playhouse, another of 1612, yet another of 1640, and a contract of 1651 by which the Burbage family at last gave up the playhouse, nine years after it had ceased to be one. Hillebrand had found Wallace's lawsuit of 1608 and another of which Wallace did not know belonging to 1609. I have found Wallace's other documents and use them—with citations—below.[21]

All these documents are important, but two are more important than the others. They are Wallace's lawsuit of 1612 and Hillebrand's of 1609. Both describe the playhouse at some length, giving its size as 46' x 66', and both list repairs necessary to the place in 1602. Both resulted from the Burbages' leasing the playhouse to Henry Evans in

1600 and Evans's taking Edward Kirkham and others as partners in 1602. Both are between Kirkham and Evans, and both were argued in the King's Bench. Wallace gave the impression that his excerpts come from several documents, but they all come from the lawsuit of 1612. Though the two lawsuits have similar language, sometimes even spelling, Hillebrand's omits several things about the playhouse in Wallace's and confuses others. In these things, both recite statements in the lease of 1600 and contract of 1602, but Wallace's evidently has the more careful recital.

Before describing the playhouse at length and the repairs, the two lawsuits have an abbreviated description that is repeated over and over in the documentation. The playhouse is "all that greate hall or roome with the roomes over the same...the sayde greate hall or roome and other the p^rmisses," and the remark is translated into Latin several times. Though these two documents do not, much other documentation adds that the great hall was divided into seven rooms when James Burbage bought it. Smith tried to have a photogenic playhouse rising many feet to the hammer beam roof of a medieval hall. He strove, therefore, to explain away the most obvious meaning of rooms over the hall. In any event, the rooms over the hall are absent from the descriptions of the playhouse in Wallace's documents of 1640 and 1651. I translate the longer description of the playhouse in Wallace's lawsuit of 1612:

The Burbage-Evans lease was "of all that great hall or room with the rooms above the same as then [at the time of the lease] were erected, furnished, and built with a stage, galleries, and seats of a quantity specified in a schedule annexed thereto situated and being at the northern end of certain rooms then in the tenure and occupation of one John Robbinson or his assigns within the precinct of the Blackfriars, London, and being part and parcel of those houses and buildings in the same place which were then lately acquired and bought...by James Burbage...containing by estimation in length from the south to the northern part of the same sixty-six feet of assize be it more or less and in width from the west to the eastern part of the same forty-six feet of assize be it more or less together with all lights, easements, and commodities whatsoever pertaining to the same hall or rooms or other premises formerly let by the said indenture or any one of them."

Except for the formulaic statement at the end, all this is also in

Hillebrand's lawsuit, though a few of his words are different. Unlike Hillebrand's, however, Wallace's lawsuit goes on to say what was not included in Evans's lease: the vaults and rooms under the great hall or room, then occupied by Thomas Bruskett (''Briscitt'') or his assigns, with ''those rooms situated and being on the western side of the door of the stairs leading up into the said great hall'' (''illis locis anglice roomes scituatis & existentibus ex occidentali parte ostij graduum anglice of the stayres ducentium vsque anglice leadinge vpp in dictam magnam aulam''). The rooms were then (in 1600) occupied by Henry Duncalf. The repairs necessary to the premises in 1602 (''in decasu & minime reparatis existentibus'') were, as Wallace's lawsuit says, ''in the outside door leading to the said leased premises and in the walls on the right side of the same door, in the pavement along the eastern part of the said hall and in the pavement under the eastern end of a certain stage in the said hall and in the walls in the same place above the stairs and in the glass and in the wooden windows above as well as below on both sides of the said hall and in the walls on both sides and ends of the said hall and in the lead gutters and in the roofing [roof tiling?] of the said premises...and in the large purlin[s] on the southern side of the said hall and in the ceiling in the schoolhouse at the northern end of the said hall.''

Hillebrand's lawsuit somewhat confuses the remark about the pavement under the stage by having ''in'' rather than ''under.'' It omits the outside door and the wall beside it, the purlins, and the ceiling of the schoolhouse. Eventually it does get round to the school-house in another connection, but what it says about the place seems unlikely to be true. It says ''there was a certain chamber called the schoolhouse above part of the said great hall and a certain other chamber above the said chamber called the schoolhouse parcels of the said tenements'' (''fuit quedam camera vocata the schoolehouse supra partem predicte magne aule & quedam alia camera supra dictam cameram vocatam the schoolehouse parcelle tentorum predictorum''). A room over a room over a room seems odd.

In another lawsuit of 1612, printed in 1890, the plaintiff (Evans) and the defendant (Kirkham) agreed first that the playhouse com-prised the great hall with ''the roomes over same.'' They then agreed that ''there was a Certen Roome called the Scolehouse and a Certen chamber over the same...seuered from the said great Hall'' and included in the Burbage-Evans lease. Whether Evans or the Burbages or some predecessor severed the rooms does not appear, but Evans made one or both fit "to dyne and supp in" using his own furniture and implements. One implication is that, being mentioned separately, the rooms over the great hall were not the same places as the schoolhouse and room over. A second is that the schoolhouse and room over were severed from the great hall in the usual way—by a partition rising from the floor of the great hall. A third is that since the schoolhouse had a room over it and they had been part of the great hall, the great hall was at least two stories high. Kirkham said repeatedly that the schoolhouse and room over were valuable to him, and Evans eventually pointed out that those places had a value only when plays were performed. When, he said, the king stopped the boys from playing at Blackfriars in 1608, "the same Roomes were not worth almost any Rent." The schoolhouse and room over were, as Wallace's lawsuit of 1612 says, and Hillebrand's of 1609 does not, at the northern end of the great hall. They too, are absent from the documents of 1640 and 1651.

Nowhere in all the documentation about the Blackfriars playhouse is a tiring house mentioned or even hinted at. Where it was, even whether in the ordinary sense there was one, remain moot questions. Wallace's and Hillebrand's lawsuit of 1608, however, says that other rooms in addition to the great hall were used for plays: "when & soe often as anye enterludes playes or shows shalbe playde vsed showed or published in the greate hall and other the Roomes scituat in the Blackfriers london or any parte thereof." The remark is repeated in Latin, but later, when a specific occasion (June 16, 1604) is mentioned, the document reads simply that "a certain interlude was played in the said great hall" ("quoddam ludicrum anglice enterlude lusum fuit in predicta magna Aula"). Evidently plays were performed mainly in the great hall but other rooms could also be involved. The only other rooms mentioned are those on the south side of the great hall (occupied in 1600 by John Robbinson and later by John Bill), the rooms over the great hall, and the schoolhouse-cum-dining room with a room above, both severed from the great hall on the northern side. If the tiring house was in any of these places, it was not counted in the 66' length of the great hall.

The great hall was obviously a rectangle whose length lay north and south. The stairway leading up to it—described in Wallace's contract of 1651 as "the Stayres & Stayre case...leading vp into the late Playhouse out of the greate yard or Streete there now commonly called...the Playhouse yard"—seems in much evidence to have been at the northern end of the playhouse. The stage, therefore, would have been at the southern end. Smith calculated that in addition to the 66' of the playhouse, some 35' was available in the building at the southern end, behind the stage. He put the tiring house there, and for him 66' was the distance from the tiring house facade to the back wall of the auditorium. It is probably possible, however, that the tiring house was within the 66' but a relatively informal place so that nobody thought to mention it.

So the length of the room into which the boxes (if they were behind the stage), stage, and pit in front had to fit might well have been the full 66' or, allowing perhaps 11' for a tiring house, something like 55'. Either way, the size of the room would not have prevented the Burbages and their associates from carrying out a scheme in keeping with the drawings and the other specific evidence of the professional Shakespearean stage. In area the bare room was actually eleven square feet bigger than the yard at the Fortune before the stage was built in it. True, at the Fortune the galleries extended beyond the yard, making that house 80' square on the outside, or more than twice the size of Blackfriars in total floor area at the yard level. But the main concern must have been the size of the pit. Whether the Burbages would have built a gallery along the sides of the pit, as Wallace and others have done in reconstructions, would depend on whether the floor space would yield more revenue as gallery or pit. Because a gallery would accommodate fewer people and be expensive to build, the Burbages should have aimed at a big pit and thought of galleries as holding customers the pit could not. The idea was familiar in the 1590s and is not obsolete now. One runs the pit from wall to wall and hangs the galleries out over it rather than planting them beside it. In this way one can have the largest pit possible and still have extensive galleries.

This was apparently the arrangement at Paris Garden (1583)[22] and was clearly the arrangement in the yard of the Boar's Head Inn, Whitechapel, in both the primitive playhouse of 1598 and the better one of 1599. As the contractor, foreman, and one of the carpenters there all said, they "did buylde certeine roomes or galleryes in the yeard of the...Inne called the Bores head," and as one of the principals remarked of the primitive house, these "certeine galleryes or roomes" were "for people to stand in to see the playes." These galleries were on all four sides of the yard and, except for the gallery over the stage, were supported on posts "sett" in the yard. When another of the principals strove to achieve "the fitt placinge & makinge of the galleryes for the most advantage to hould & receave more store of people," the rebuilding of 1599 was begun. He remarked that "yf the case were myne...I would pull downe this older gallery to the ground, and buylde yt foure foote forwarder toward the stage into ye yarde...and qth he yf yt were buylt so farr forwarder then would there be roome for three or foure seats more in a gallery, and for many mo people, and yett nev*er* the lesse roome in the yarde." So he and the others had the new galleries pulled down and newer, larger ones erected.[23] It was this sort of thinking, I suggest, that would have prevailed at Blackfriars three years before. The theatrical room was high enough, if it was indeed at least two stories high.

In width, for example, the Burbages could have had as much of the pit between the sides of the stage and the walls as there was of the yard at the Fortune, 6' on each side, and galleries overhead of the same width (the northern and southern galleries at the Boar's Head were 6' deep from 1599). They would then have had a stage 34' across (that at the Fortune was 9' more and that at the Boar's Head 5'7'' more). As for depth, if the boxes, stage, and pit occupied the full 66', the stage and the pit in front of the stage could also have resembled the arrangement at the Fortune, where the stage and yard in front of it measured 27' 6'' each. The Burbages would then have had more room for boxes, 11', than even Wallace proposed. If boxes, stage, and pit occupied something like 55', the stage and pit could have measured about 24' each and the boxes about 7'. Either way, there would have been not only boxes capable of holding two or more rows of seats but plenty of room at the back of the stage for sitters, standers, and recliners. These dimensions are only postulates, of course; the stage and boxes, for example, could easily have been shallower and the pit deeper. But they demonstrate why the Burbages might have put their boxes at the back of the stage rather than at the sides. Laid out in this way, the room would have allowed, by the theatrical standards of the time, uncramped space for boxes, stage, audience on stage, pit, and galleries. The room would also have resembled the theatrical places the Burbages were used to in playhouses, at court, and elsewhere in 1596, when they took it in hand.

Such an arrangement, would provide seats for upward of fifty people in boxes, if three stage doors took up about 3' each, and there were two rows of seats in boxes. Thirty-two would have been in boxes across the stage and sixteen more in boxes continuing to the sides of the room. If three stage doors were twice as wide each, there would have been room for some thirty-six people in boxes. All would have been seated conspicuously, commodiously, and with good sight lines if people like Thurles did not interfere.[24]

Writers have striven mightily to establish what Shakespeare's contemporaries meant when they spoke of boxes, the twelve-penny room, the lords' room, the "orchestra"—the most expensive seats in their theatres. These places have been important because of the persistent struggle to prove the alcove and balcony stages. If these expensive seats were really where they seem to be in much of the best evidence, in a gallery above the back of the stage, then the theory of alcove and balcony stages falls into mortal difficulties at once. Spectators in such seats obviously could not have seen and very likely not heard what went on in the alcove, and occupied the space on which the balcony stage was supposed to exist. The main line of reasoning was begun by W. J. Lawrence and pushed to its logical end by J. C. Adams. Lawrence's part of the argument goes essentially as follows. 1) The allusions to the lords' room in the gallery above the stage seem to stop in 1607 or so. 2) Dekker in his *Gull's Hornbook* (1609) can be made to say in the sixth chapter that this lords' room had suffered a social eclipse, and he clearly said in the proem that lords were using an expensive place "next the stage." 3) Applying all these remarks to the same public theatres, one can assert that the gallery over the stage was the original lords' room and that by 1609 some sort of migration had occurred to a new one "next the stage," which Lawrence could only take to be the "orchestra" of the Swan drawing. Lawrence went only this far. He insisted that his migration was of the best patrons only, and that the gallery over the stage continued to be used by spectators of a much less illustrious sort until the closing of the theatres in 1642. His reason lay in those allusions to the lord's room over the stage. The literary ones do stop in 1607 or so, but the evidence in the pictures continues to show spectators there through Caroline times and even into the Restoration.[25]

J. C. Adams (pp. 70 ff.) and his followers chose to ignore or discount the pictures. They suggested that the social eclipse Lawrence had described in the gallery over the stage signified that the companies were banishing spectators from it altogether in order to use it for acting.[26]

In sometimes remarkably different ways, G. F. Reynolds, C. W. Hodges, Leslie Hotson, Richard Southern, Richard Hosley, and others have attacked Adams's conclusions with increasing force, so that now the alcove and balcony stages seem at last on the verge of extinction.[27] With Pory's account one can lend a little force to this attack. At Blackfriars, few if any of the persons in the best seats could have seen action in such places whether Pory's boxes were at side or back.

If Adams's part of the case has fared ill, Lawrence's has scarcely faltered. But now as a result of Pory's account, apparently one must reconsider it, not only after digesting Pory's evidence but after redigesting Dekker's. We no longer need to associate Dekker's place "next the stage" with the "orchestra" of the Swan and Hope and hence with the public theatres in general. We can acknowledge without creating a vacuum that the "orchestra" is not next the stage at all, though it is as close as, given his evidence, Lawrence could get. We now have a place very much "next the stage" about which Lawrence and everyone else has known nothing, in which lords really sat. This place belongs, as we have seen, not to one or more public theatres, but to the leading private one, Blackfriars. This piece of truth, in effect, separates Dekker's remarks and denies us the right to apply them together to Shakespearean theatres. In his remark about a place next the stage in *Satiromastix*, Dekker meant Blackfriars, and in his remark about the twelve-penny room next the stage in the proem, he probably meant Blackfriars. In his remark about gulls moving onto the stage from "boxes" vaguely in the "reare," however, he meant Shakespearean playhouses generally, since he specifically said he had both public and private theatres in mind. Lords, in other words, may have been moving onto the stage from the boxes, but they were *not* moving from one set of boxes in the "reare" to others next the stage.

One might add that the new clientele Dekker spoke of in the lords' room was not so depraved as Lawrence supposed. The new persons there were "waiting-women and Gentlemen-Ushers," the wearers of "much new Satten," all sweating together. Allowing at least a little overstatement for satiric effect, one will gather that the lords' boxes were not much worse off socially than they had been. And obviously by the 1630s those boxes in the great private house, at least, had fully regained anything they might have lost twenty-five years before.

In the end, it seems that the most expensive seats were in different places in different theatres. In all the public theatres for which suitable record survives, there were expensive seats in the gallery over the stage throughout the period.[28] In at least the Swan and Hope there were additional expensive seats in the portions of the lower gallery near the stage, the "orchestra." At Blackfriars the most expensive seats were literally next to the stage. To put it another way, we must stop freely associating all these expensive regions with each of the theatres.

Captain Essex was a younger, probably the second, son of Sir William Essex, a baronet of Beckett in Berkshire (while he still possessed it) who had ten years previously bade farewell to the final portions of a vast estate, nearly all of which he had lost through the good offices of Jacob Hardrett, a jeweller whose premises were adjacent to the theatre in Blackfriars.[29] The captain remained in Dutch service until there was a need for soldiers at home. Then, according to Clarendon again (VI, 95n), he persuaded the Queen of Bohemia to intercede for him with his Dutch masters for leave, swearing to her "that he would never serve against the King." He first appears thereafter serving in Ireland in 1640 as "Fourth Colonell" under no other than the former Thurles, now Earl of Ormond.[30] On May 2, 1642, he secured permission to return to his captaincy in the Low Countries, but when in July the Earl of Essex threw himself into the Parliamentary cause, the Dutch captain, English colonel was in England to do likewise. "He thought," wrote Clarendon, that "his gratitude obliged him to run the fortune of his patron, and out of pure kindness to the person of the earl, as many other gentlemen did, engaged himself against the King, without any malice or rebellion in his heart towards the Crown."[31] He very quickly became one of the principal commanders of foot in the Parliamentary army. He had command of a regiment of foot in the earl's army at the battle of Edgehill in October, where his history comes to an end. He "was esteemed," Clarendon declared, "the best and most expert officer of the army, and was killed by a musket shot in the beginning of the battle."[32]

That officer's companion in the playhouse, the countess, proved almost as much a trial for her husband as his first wife had, though apparently through much less fault of her own. The earl's new marital difficulties seem to have been on both sides. When she and the captain were set upon by Thurles, she had already acquired the reputation for indiscretion which (though far short of the scale of that founded on her predecessor's adventures) was soon to be her undoing. For his part, as a friend and apologist said, it was the earl's custom to show his new wife a "cloudy and discontented countenance." Within a very few months, he put her aside for what he fancied was improper conduct with Sir William Uvedale, the future army treasurer. She was then pregnant with a child who must have been conceived at about the time of the hearing in the Star Chamber. The earl declared that he would acknowledge the child only if it were born by Guy Fawkes Day. It was born *on* that day.[33] Essex accepted the child, a son, who died four years later.

Thurles became Earl of Ormond on his father's death less than three weeks after the playhouse episode. In these years of his youth, as his biographer says, he was "a great admirer of plays, and acquainted with all the good actors of the stage. He took such ·delight in the theatre, that it scarce ever wanted his presence." At the opening of the Irish parliament two years later, he conducted himself much as he had at the playhouse, but with a good deal more success. Wentworth, the Lord Deputy, "observing, that there were some refractory persons in the House of Commons...thought fit to issue out a Proclamation, that none of the Members of the Parliament...either Peers or Commoners, should enter the House with their swords." As Ormond himself related in subsequent years, "The Usher of the Black Rod was planted at the door of the House of Lords to take the swords of the Peers, and as the Earl of *Ormonde* was coming in, demanded his, but was refused. That Officer hereupon shewed the Proclamation, and repeating his demand in a rough manner, the Earl told him, that *if he had his sword, it should be in his guts*, and so marched on to his seat; and was the only Peer, who sat with a sword that day in the House.'' Wentworth ''considered seriously how he should behave himself towards'' such a person, supposing he must either crush him or befriend him. In the event, taking the advice of friends, he made Ormond a privy councillor.[34]

Pory was writing a professional news report, not a considered study of an important event or even, perhaps, an eye-witness account. There may be no more reason to trust some of Pory's details of the event than there is to trust those of professional news reports since. As no other account of the affair has appeared, one can merely look into what is known of the participants otherwise. Fortunately, all seems much of a piece. But even if one cannot accept all Pory's details of the event without qualification, one must accept his implications about the shape of the theatre. While Scudamore probably did not know much about the event, and Pory himself may have had it on hearsay, both men surely did know the theatre first hand, and each knew that the other knew. No sophisticated and well traveled nobleman like Scudamore, or professional snapper-up of unconsidered trifles like Pory, could in 1632 have failed to know Blackfriars well. Pory, therefore, was constrained to describe the event in such a way that, regardless of its accuracy in other respects, it fit the shape of the theatre in Blackfriars. For our purposes, one could ask no more.

APPENDIX

Wallace's transcriptions of his documents, including the citations, are in the Wallace Collection at the Huntington Library, San Marino, California, chiefly boxes 5 (no. 4), 7 (no. 11), and 8 (no. 3). The originals are, of course, at the P.R.O. in London.

His lawsuit of 1612 is K.B.27/1432/m.359. The Latin of the description of the playhouse reads: ''tocius illius magne Aule vel loci anglice Roome cum locis anglice roomes supra eandem sicut tunc fuerunt erecti ornati anglice furnished & edificati cum Theatro anglice a Stage porticibus anglice Galleryes & sedilibus de quantitate specificata in scedula ad inde annexata scituatis & existentibus ad borialem finem quorundam locorum anglice roomes tunc in tenura & occupacione cuiusdam Johannis Robbinson vel Assignatorum suorum intra precinctam de le Blackfryers london &

existen*tibus* pars & *parcella* illa*rum* domo*rum* & edificacionu*m* ibi*de*m que fuerunt tunc
nup*er* perquisit*e* & empt*e...per* Jacobum Burbidge...continen*tis per* estimac*i*onem in
longitudine ab austro ad borealem p*artem* eiusd*em* sexaginta & sex pedes Assise sit
plus siue minus & in latitudine ab occiden*te* ad orient*alem* p*artem* eiusdem quadraginta
& sex pedes Assi*se* sit plus siue minus Acetiam om*n*ia luminar*i*a easiament*a* &
comoditat*es* quecunq*ue* eisdem aule vel locis anglice roomes aut alijs pr*emissis* antea p*er*
d*i*ctam Indenturam dimiss*is* anglice letten vel alicui eo*rum*...pertinen*ti*a.''

The Latin of the part about repairs reads: ''in ext*eri*ori ostio ducen*te* ad p*r*edi*c*ta
dimissa pr*emissa* & in pariet*ibus* ex dextra p*arte* eiusd*em* ostii in paviament*o* p*er*
orient*alem* p*artem* in [*sic*] p*r*edi*c*te Aule & in paviament*o* subt*er* orient*alem* finem
cuiusdam Theatri anglice the Stage in Aula p*r*edi*c*ta & in pariet*ibus* ibi*de*m sup*er*
gradus anglice the Stayres & in vitro & in fenestris ligneis t*am* supra qu*am* infra ex
vtrisq*ue* part*ibus* predi*c*te Aule & in pariet*ibus* ex ambab*us* part*ibus* & finibus predi*c*te
Aule & i*n* gutturis plumbeis anglice gutturs of leade & in tegulac*i*one predict*orum*
premissor*um*...& in grosso Maheremio anglice the Purloynes ex australi p*arte* Aule
predi*c*te & in laqueario anglice the sealinge in schola anglice the schoolehouse ad
borealem finem Aule predi*c*te.''

In Wallace's lawsuit of 1640, the playhouse is described as ''All that great Hall a
[*sic*] roome p*ar*cell of ye p^rmisses as the same was then before devided into seaven
rooms and after converted into a playhouse as it is now erected furnished and built
wth. a stage and galleries for the shewing and acting of plaies and some other p*ar*cells
of the p^rmisses in the said Indenture p*ar*ticularly'' expressed (E.112/221/1215). The
indenture is that of 1620 (see below). In an order of the court, the playhouse is ''the
said greate Hall or roome p*ar*cell of the p^rmisses heretofore devided into seaven
rooms and afterwards converted into a Play house itt now [is] and some other
p*ar*cells of the p^rmisses'' (E.125/27/f.199-200).

In Wallace's contract of 1651, the playhouse and allied properties are: ''All that
greate Hall or Roome hertofore devided into seaven rooms & since converted into a
Playhouse & lately furnished wth. a Stage Galleries & Seats & for many yeares
together of late heretofore vsed for shewing & acting of Playes therein...together w^th.
the Stayres & Stayre case therevnto belonging & leading vp into the late Playhouse out
of the greate yard or Streete there now com*m*only called...the Playhouse yard And
alsoe all the rooms vnder the said late Playhouse & all other rooms Chambers
Galleries Sellers Sollers vaults curtilages yards & hereditam^ts. whatsoever scituate &
being w^thin the said Stone Wall And also all that other large messuage or ten*ement* w^th.
thapp*ur*ten*an*ces neere adioyning to the said late Playhouse on the south side thereof
late in the tenure or occupac*i*on of John Bill or his assignes & inclosed likewise wth. a
stone wall & abutting vpon the lane leading into the yard called the Printing house
yard towards the South And all Sh*o*ps rooms Cellers Sollers vaults yddraughts Court
yards curtilages backsides lights easem^ts wayes passages liberties pr*ivi*ledges ynnuities
profitts Com*m*odities advantages emolum^ts. hereditar*n*^ts. & app*ur*tenances whatsoever
to the said greate Hall messuages & p^rmisses and every or any of them severally &
respectiveiy belonging or in any wise app*er*taininge or accounted reputed or taken to
belong therevnto or to any of them or therewith or wth. any of them vsed occupied or
enioyed'' (C.54/3579/m.39-40).

See also K.B.27/1408/m.303, Wallace's and Hillebrand's lawsuit of 1608;
K.B.27/1414/ m.456, Hildebrand's lawsuit of 1609; C.2/Jas.I/K.5/25 and /E.4/9, two
lawsuits of 1612 found by James Greenstreet and published by F. G. Fleay, *A Chronicle
History of the London Stage* (London, 1890), pp. 208-51 (in the replication of /E.4/9 is

the remark I quote about the value of the schoolhouse and room above); and the discussions in Chambers, II, 475-514, Bentley, VI, 3-7, and Irwin Smith, *passim*, esp. pp. 166-69.

The documents of the lawsuit of 1640 explain what happened to the Burbage properties in Blackfriars after the death of Richard Burbage, the actor, in 1619. The story throws light on the descriptions of the playhouse above and probably connects the playhouse with English literature in a surprising way.

When James Burbage died in 1597, Cuthbert Burbage, as the oldest son and heir, could claim all his father's properties in Blackfriars. He regarded his brother, Richard, however, as effectively owning the playhouse, and it was Richard who leased it to Evans. Moreover, as the years went by the two of them bought more properties in Blackfriars. When Richard died, therefore, something had to be done about the Burbage estate in Blackfriars. In 1620, the properties were divided between Cuthbert and Richard's survivors: the widow, Winifred, who married next the actor Richard Robinson, and the children, William and Sarah. The survivors got the playhouse and allied properties and Cuthbert "the residue." The survivors, presumably, got the rents for the playhouse and other places (Evans had paid £40 a year) as well as what the places were worth to sell (in 1651 they were worth £700). The profits from the mounting of plays would have gone to the shareholders among the King's Men.

Because Winifred could lose control of her interest through marriage and her children were infants—William born in 1616 and Sarah posthumously in 1619—their part of Blackfriars had to be conveyed to them as a trusteeship. In a three-part contract dated July 4, 1620, Cuthbert and the survivors assigned the playhouse and allied properties to four men in trust for the survivors. In the order given, the first man was Edward Raymond, gentleman; then were Henry Hodge and Robert (also given as William) Hunt, alebrewers. The fourth was John Milton, gentleman, who may well have been the poet's father. The elder Milton was a scrivener by trade, and in every allusion to him in *The Life Records of John Milton* when he is given as anything it is as scrivener, not gentleman. Like many scriveners, however, he dealt also in finance, and he had become wealthy. The Burbages could have thought of him as a gentleman rather than a man who tended a scrivener's shop in Bread Street. People were often given as what they seemed to be rather than what they really were. Besides, he had to do with an Edward Raymond, gentleman, less than eighteen months after the contract of 1620. On February 9, 1622, he lent Raymond £50, which he had a great deal of trouble getting back. This Raynond was a lawyer who died in 1623.[35]

When Cuthbert Burbage died in 1636, his only surviving child inherited his part of Blackfriars. She was Elizabeth, married at the time to George Bingley, an official in the Exchequer. Eventually William Burbage was the only living survivor of Richard Burbage. It was he who in 1651 sold the playhouse and allied properties, which the contract says are all his possessions in Blackfriars.

The trustees must have been friends of the Burbages and admirers of the theatrical goings on at the Blackfriars playhouse. Trusteeships would have been no mystery to a scrivener. The elder Milton was also a notable musician, and in mixing business and art he had much in common with the Burbages. The poet was eleven years old when his father apparently became a trustee of the Blackfriars playhouse. Readers have wondered why the poet turned often to drama despite the antipathy for it that his religious views should have inspired. Perhaps, like music, an important part of his life at home was the work of Richard Burbage and the King's Men.

NOTES

* Originally published in *Studies in Philology*, LXIII, 2 (April 1966), 163-86.

1. See the Sharers Papers, L.C.5/133/pp.44-51; printed by J. O. Halliwell-Phillipps, *Outlines of the Life of Shakespeare* (London, 1882), I, 476-86, and much more accurately in the *Malone Society Collections* (Oxford, 1931), II, pt. 3, 362-73. In these papers the principal shareholders among the King's Men had very good reason to mention the main sums of money laid out on the two houses that company owned. They mentioned the original rebuilding at Blackfriars, the rebuilding of the Globe, regular sums laid out for ordinary repairs, etc., but nothing for serious alterations at Blackfriars after 1596.

2. C.115/M35/8391. These are "The Duchess of Norfolk's Papers," described by J. P. Feil in "Dramatic References from the Scudamore Papers," *Shakespeare Survey* 11 (1958), pp. 107-16, using an unofficial but more meaningful title for the collection. Like Prof. Feil, I am indebted to E. K. Timings, who also led me to these papers "in another connexion."

3. The only other Countess of Essex alive was the widow of the Elizabethan earl, who was very old and in her grave less than two weeks after Pory wrote (as Pory also reported). Moreover, she was then the wife of the Earl of Clanricarde, by whose name she might well have been known (G. E. C., *Complete Peerage*, [London, 1913]). The only other possibility was Captain Essex's stepmother (if he had one by then), who was also Lady Essex, but no countess. His mother was his father's first wife, Jane Harcourt, who had married in 1593 and died about 1618 (C.2/Chas.I/E.14/23; /Jas.I/E.1/42). Another wife survived his father in the winter of 1643-44 (*Commons Journal*, III, 213, 385).

4. Edward Hyde, first Earl of Clarendon, *History of the Rebellion*, ed. W. Dunn Macray (Oxford, 1888), VI, 7, 93. He had been in Dutch service at least since 1628, when the English apparently persuaded him to leave temporarily to command one of the foot companies of the English force sent under Sir Charles Morgan to assist the Danes against the Imperialists (*Acts of the Privy Council of England, 1629-30*, no. 356; S.P.16/184, no. 42; *C.S.P., Ven., 1628-29*, p. 214; *1629-32*, pp. 139, 257).

5. Thomas Carte, *An History of the Life of James Duke of Ormonde* (London, 1736), I, 9.

6. *C.S.P., Ven., 1628-29*, p. 216.

7. Something of the sort was one of J. C. Adams's many suggestions, but not proved by him nor repeated by others (*The Globe Playhouse* [New York, 1942], pp. 72-73). The arrangement could also have existed at other private theatres; Whitefriars, for one, had boxes (Chambers, II, 555).

8. Mark Eccles, "Martin Peerson and the Blackfriars," *Shakespeare Survey* 11 (1958), pp. 104-5.

9. *The Earl of Strafforde's Letters and Dispatches*, ed. William Knowler (London, 1739), I, 511.

10. V, ii, 303-5 (*Dramatic Works*, ed. Fredson Bowers [Cambridge, 1953], I, 382).

11. Lines 1605-10, the significance of which was pointed out by L. A. L. MacKichan, *TLS*, Oct. 6, 1961, p. 672.

12. See Glynne Wickham, *Early English Stages* (London, 1963), II, 253 and *passim*.

13. *The Children of the Chapel at Blackfriars 1597-1603* (Lincoln, Nebr., 1908), pp. v, 42-54; see also W. A. Armstrong, *The Elizabethan Private Theatre* (London, 1958), p. 1 and the frontispiece; and Irwin Smith, *Shakespeare's Blackfriars Playhouse* (New York, 1964).

14. One picture (in the title page of Nathaniel Richards' *Messalina*, [London, 1640]) has the usual gallery at back, but unlike the galleries in the other pictures, this one is apparently unoccupied and a curtain is drawn over it. One should not conclude, however, that the picture illustrates a different theatrical arrangement. This picture, unlike the others, shows a theatre not in use, for the stage is also unoccupied as is the yard.

15. *Skialetheia*, epi. 53; *Every Man Out*, II, iii, 189-93; *Jests to Make You Merry*, jest 45; see Chambers, II, 534-35 & n.

16. See my *The Boar's Head Playhouse* (Washington, D.C., 1986), chapters 12, 13.

17. John Eliot, *Poems* (London, 1658), p. 77 (S.T.C. E-524B). The poems were written in the 1630s and late 1620s if the occasions mentioned in many and the first remark in "To the Reader" are indications.

18. *Shakespeare's Wooden O* (London, 1959), chapter 6; also Wickham, *Early English Stages*, I, 357-59. Evidence recently announced leads to the same conclusion: Alan Nelson's and Robert Burkhart's essays presented at the meeting of the Shakespeare Association of America in Montreal, March 1986, "Hall Screens and Elizabethan Playhouses: New Evidence from Cambridge" and "Festive Performances in the Inner Temple and Middle Temple Halls."

19. Chambers, III, 153; see also Hosley, "Was There a Music-Room at Shakespeare's Globe?" *Shakespeare Survey* 13 (1960), p. 115.

20. Chambers, III, 133n.

21. See the appendix below, Wallace's *Children of the Chapel at Blackfriars*, pp. 39n.1, 40n.2, 41n.4, etc., and Hillebrand, *The Child Actors* (Urbana, Ill., 1926), pp. 179-85, 332-34.

22. Chambers, IV, 221-25.

23. C.24/278/71, Willys 2, Mago 1, Rodes 2; /290/3, Samwell 3. See my *The Boar's Head Playhouse*, chap. 3; app. 2. Like Blackfriars, incidentally, this theatre was used mainly in the winter.

24. See the space allowed for spectators at plays before the court in Oxford in 1605: John Orrell, "The Theatre at Christ Church, Oxford, in 1605," *Shakespeare Survey* 35 (1982), p. 135. Prof. Hosley believes the music room at Blackfriars was "above." It could have been in a special gallery over the stage boxes; it was in such a position over the side boxes of the Restoration theatres ("Was There a Music-Room at Shakespearee's Globe?" pp. 113-17).

25. *The Elizabethan Playhouse* (Stratford-on-Avon, 1912), pp. 7-8, 29-40.

26. This seems the logical drift of Adams's case as he had it from Lawrence and Chambers (II, 531, 537; III, 119-20, etc.). But Adams eventually stated the case as a perfect circle (pp. 78-79). On the suggestion also of Lawrence and

Chambers (III, 82, 90-95), he assumed the alcove and balcony stages and then argued that persons had to leave the place over the stage to see what was happening in the alcove and make room for actors in the balcony.

27. See, for example, Reynolds, *The Staging of Elizabethan Plays at the Red Bull Theatre* (New York, 1940), Ch. VII, esp. pp. 131-36, and *Essays on Shakespeare and Elizabethan Drama in Honor of Hardin Craig*, ed. Richard Hosley (Columbia, Mo., 1962), p. 366; C. W. Hodges, *The Globe Restored* (London, 1953), pp. 56-65; Richard Southern, "On Reconstructing a Practicable Elizabethan Public Playhouse," *Shakespeare Survey* 12 (1959), p. 34, and *Essays...in Honor of Hardin Craig*, p. 14; A. M. Nagler, *Shakespeare's Stage* (New Haven, 1958), pp. 26-32, 44-46, 47-51, etc. (but Nagler, who has followed Hodges closely for the public theatres, has installed an Adamsian alcove and upper stage at Blackfriars, pp. 96, 97-102).

28. Many writers now support this view: Richard Hosley, "Shakespeare's Use of a Gallery over the Stage," *Shakespeare Survey* 10 (1957), pp. 77, 83, 84, etc.; "The Gallery Over the Stage in the Public Playhouse of Shakespeare's Time," *SQ*, VIII (1957), pp. 23-25; Southern, "On Reconstructing...," see plate IV; Hotson, "Shakespeare's Arena," *Sewanee Review*, LXI (1953), 347 ff.; *First Night of "Twelfth Night"* (London, 1954), *passim*; *Shakespeare's Wooden O*, chap. 3 ff., esp. 8; and, apparently, Wickham, II, 320-22.

29. There are numerous echoes of his ruin: Fuller, *Worthies of England* (London, 1811), I, 109; an account of his lengthy imprisonment for debt in the Marshalsea in *C.S.P., Dom., 1639*, pp. 345-46; a comment in a lawsuit of 1648, C.2/Chas.I/E.14/23; and an extensive account of his ruin in his lawsuit against Hardrett in 1620, /Jas.I/E.3/51, where his heir, who was of age at the time, is William. See also *The Four Visitations of Berkshire*, ed. W. Harry Rylands (London: Harleian Soc., 1907-8), II, 125; Clarendon, VI, 95; and Chambers, II, 507.

30. H.M.C., *MSS. of the Marquis of Ormonde*, I, 122.

31. *Commons Journal*, II, 553; Clarendon, *History*, VI, 93.

32. He was commander of foot (as sergeant major general) in the Earl of Bedford's army before Sherborne in August, then joined his patron's army in the north, where he was for a time governor of Worcester after its seizure by the earl in September. He left a widow and a sister, Elizabeth. His father served as a captain in his regiment at Edgehill, was captured, and died in prison without heir in the winter of 1643-44 (*C.S.P., Dom., 1641-43*, pp. 366, 397; Clarendon, *History*, VI, 7, 93, 95n., 99; the lawsuit of 1648; *Commons Journal*, II, 910; III, 122, 213, 385).

33. Walter B. Devereux, *Lives and Letters of the Devereux, Earls of Essex* (London, 1853), II, 304-5; Frances Parthenope Verney, *Memoirs of the Verney Family During the Civil War* (London, 1892), I, 131-32. Essex had married his second countess March 11, 1631.

34. Carte, I, lxvii, 6, 64-65.

35. *The Life Records of John Milton*, ed. J. M. French (New Brunswick, N. J., 1949), I, 43, etc.; W. R. Parker, *Milton A Biography* (Oxford, 1968), pp. 17, 716-17.

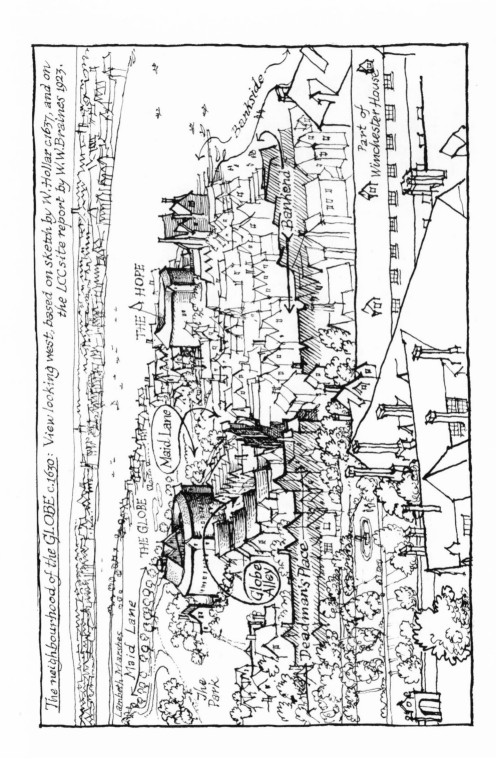

The neighbourhood of the GLOBE c.1630: View looking west, based on sketch by W.Hollar c.1657, and on the LCC site report by W.W.Braines 1923.

Banckside

Part of Winchester House

THE HOPE

Barm'end

Maid Lane

THE GLOBE

Maid Lane

Lambeth Marshes

Globe Alley

Deadman's Place

The Park

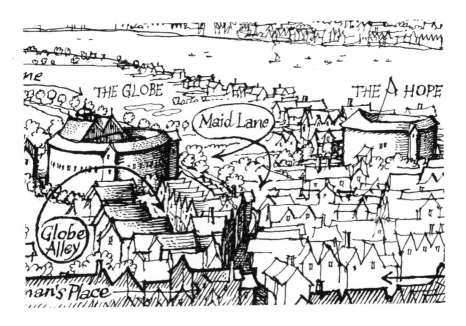

The Globe:
Documents and Ownership*

[Written for the Symposium for the Reconstruction of the Globe Playhouse, Detroit, 1979.]

My task has been to review the most likely classes of primary evidence to see whether I might in a few months find new information about the Globe as a building and to estimate whether, given more time or luck, anyone is likely to do so hereafter. That meant, in effect, holding W. W. Braines's book, *The Site of the Globe Playhouse Southwark* (London, 1924), the "second edition, revised and enlarged," against the documents he used to see what if anything he missed in those and similar documents. It also meant looking as he did at the maps and panoramic views of London to see whether the competitors of Hollar's Long Bird's-Eye View (1647) have much to tell us.

Braines strove mainly toward a limited and difficult conclusion. He was trying to prove that George Hubbard and C. W. Wallace,

among others, were wrong to put the Globe on the north side of Maid
Lane (or Park Street as it now is), and he had to defy a crucial and
palpably genuine document that places it there. He did deal with
much else about the Globe, including its features as a building, but
relatively in passing. He did not try seriously even to place the Globe
precisely on modern maps. He searched through the main classes of
primary documents   diligently, however, and he used accurately
those that concern the Globe. I have been able to find more information about the Globe in the same places, but nothing that contributes
much either to his case or to ours. I take his conclusion to be bril-
liantly proved. I suspect that we shall not find substantial new information about the building by seeking answers to likely questions in the
main kinds of documents. New information about the building probably exists somewhere in primary evidence, but in unexpected places
or in answers elsewhere to unusual questions. I am convinced, however, that an exacting study might well show more closely than Braines
attempted to do where precisely on modern maps the Globe was—
where, so to speak, one might dig for its potsherds.

I have not attempted that study, but even so, my journey through
primary evidence in Braines's rather intimidating shadow was not
without rewards. I can add something to his remarks about how early
cartographers and artists drew the Globe, and at much greater length
I can introduce its landlords. They are the people who collected the
payments of the rent, who, as I put it, owned the Globe, for its
builders, unlike those of its predecessor, the Theatre, had no clause in
their lease allowing them to remove the building. Neither Braines nor
anybody else has considered them in more than the vaguest way. Yet
they were interesting people who did interesting things, and if those
things often seem peripheral to our concerns here, they are not always
so, and, in any event, peripheries have their uses.

In the sixteenth and seventeenth centuries maps were of two
kinds. There were flat maps like ordinary modern maps, developed
toward the end of the period. There were picture maps, "map-
views," in which buildings and other features are not two-dimensional
outlines but three-dimensional pictures drawn from a vantage point in
the sky that deliberately varies from section to section of the map so
that the user sees many places clearly however illogical it might be for
him to see one from the vantage point of another. These maps are

very common throughout the period. Ida Darlington and James Howgego treat both kinds in their splendid bibliography, *Printed Maps of London* (London, 1978), the second edition, revised by Howgego alone. Hereafter I refer to this book as "D&H." Allied to maps are "panoramas," or "panoramic views," in which the maker's vantage point purports to be constant so that the result is meant to lie somewhere between cartography and fine art. Some of these have been used in studies of the Globe for a long time, like the Hondius, Visscher, Merian, and Hollar (1647) views. The maker of these means at least partly to produce an attractive picture. Irene Scouloudi deals with those made from 1600 to 1660 and their derivatives in her *Panoramic Views of London 1600-1660* (London, 1953).

I have not dealt extensively with these panoramic views because Braines (pp. 46-60) and I. A. Shapiro (*Shakespeare Survey I*) have dealt shrewdly with the early ones as they apply to the Globe, and others are now dealing with Hollar's view of 1647. Instead I have looked extensively at what others in pursuit of the Globe have usually ignored, the maps of London to the end of the seventeenth century. In doing so, I have found myself looking also at relatively unnoticed panoramic views, for almost from the beginning of the making of maps of London, publishers not infrequently included with their maps a "prospect" of the city which is simply a panoramic view. The idea, evidently, was to show in one part of a sheet of paper what the foot might travel and in another what the eye from a given vantage point might see. It occurred to me that where map and panoramic view appear together and have something to say about the Globe it might be worth comparing one kind of record with another. So in addition to looking for the Globe in maps, I looked for it also in those panoramic views that accompany maps.

Anyone who looks at early maps of London must be struck by their crudities. The Norden map of 1593 (D&H 5), for example, crudely shows the two entertainment places that stood south of the river when Norden drew it, the Beargarden and the Rose, labelled "The Beare howse" and "The Play howse." Worse was to follow, for the map was reissued without change in 1623 as "a guide for Cuntrey men," when, presumably, the rural user was to see the Beargarden as the Hope and the Rose as the Globe and not to miss the Swan nor notice that the Globe was on the wrong side of Maid Lane. It was reissued again in 1653 when all the playhouses south of the river were gone, and the printshop's only reaction was to add shading to the Beargarden and Rose to make them more realistic. Moreover, someone, apparently Norden, redrew the map to appear in John Speed's *The Theatre of the Empire of Great Britaine* of 1611 and 1614 (D&H 7), leaving the theatrical scheme of things south of the river exactly as in 1593, despite the appearance since of the Swan and Globe and the disappearance of the Rose, but mercifully omitting the labels for the two theatrical buildings.

Was this the spirit of the map trade throughout the period? To find out, I applied later maps to the question of when the Globe disappeared. According to a famous document often suspected to be a forgery, the Globe was pulled down in 1644. According to an obviously genuine contract of 1655, that Braines found quoted in two Chancery lawsuits and I in three more, the Globe had by then been replaced by "tenements...erected and built where the late playhouse called the Globe stood and upon the ground thereunto belonging." A remark in the records of the sewer commission for the area makes the same point in 1653. Local folklore in the eighteenth century, however, persistently had it that the Globe remained standing for a very long time after it had ceased housing plays in 1642, and at least one writer now accepts that it did.[1]

Chambers remarked that "The old maps...do not give much help in a pinch," but he did not look systematically enough at them. The first relevant map here is the Dankerts (D&H 9), which in its first edition, c.1633, shows not only the Globe and Hope more or less where they should be, but the Fortune and Curtain as well. In its second edition, c.1645, however, Southwark has been redrawn so as to remove the Globe and present a new picture of the Hope (the Fortune and Curtain remain unchanged), and this arrangement is repeated in the editions of c.1675 and c.1710. If one disregards for a moment the maps with which Hollar had to do and the 1653 edition of Norden's map (which is obviously useless here), of all the maps of London printed from the 1640s to the end of the century only two show the Globe. This muster includes the three maps issued between then and the Fire: two in the 1650's and one in 1661 (D&H 11-13). It also includes the first map of that part of London that may reasonably be described as accurate by modern standards, Morgan's of 1681-82

(D&H 33), and others like it that appeared later. It includes in all some forty-eight editions of twenty-four maps that deal with Bankside in a scale big enough to show playhouses.[2] Evidently the Globe really was pulled down in the 1640's or soon after. The Hope was pulled down in the same period and a new beargarden built south of it that continued to appear on maps until 1676 (D&H 29), from which time an open space usually appears instead, sometimes labelled Beargarden.

According to Darlington and Howgego, Hollar made nine maps of London, which were published from 1655 to c.1675. Four include Bankside and are to a scale big enough to show playhouses. The earliest of these four (1655) shows both Globe and Beargarden reasonably where they should be. The next (1666) shows neither. The next (1666) shows both, but the Globe unlabelled and on the wrong side of Maid Lane (this map was reissued in 1673 and twice thereafter). The last (1667) shows the Globe where it should be and not the Beargarden (reissued in 1668).[3] Can one argue that Hollar is right and so many others wrong? Even if he were consistent about the Globe, it might be a waste of ingenuity to try to do so. As it is, his inconsistency gives the game away and makes such argument impossible. One might better argue that on three occasions he drew the Globe not because he thought it still standing but because he liked drawing it. Perhaps it is significant that he was one of the very few map-makers of the time who took such an attitude toward their work as it applied to the Globe.

To 1700 or so, the Globe appears in seven printed maps: the Norden map of 1600, the Dankerts map, the three Hollar maps, and the Oliver? (D&H 32, c.1680) and Aa (D&H 51a, c.1700) maps. The Norden map perforce shows the first Globe, the others presumably the second. The Globe is on the south side of Maid Lane five times in these maps, on the north side twice (in the Aa map it is virtually on the river). It is polygonal in the Dankerts and Aa maps but round in the five others. It has a flag over it only in the Norden and Dankerts maps, and exterior staircases in none. It has a hut of a single gable in the Norden, Dankerts, and, probably, Aa maps. It has no hut in the so-called Oliver map, nor in the first two of Hollar's. In his third map, Hollar gave it a hut with the familiar double gable, but badly drawn so that the hut could be the tops of two houses standing in the yard and facing (as the true hut evidently did not) the southwest (D&H 21). The Norden map correctly shows the first Globe covered with thatch, and all the other maps equally correctly show the second covered with something apparently more solid. The Hope and its successor appear much more often, sixteen times in fifteen maps (twice in the Dankerts) that ran to twenty-six editions. They are polygonal eleven times and round only five. They have a flag only in the Dankerts and Porter (D&H 11) maps and external staircases not at all. They have a single-gable hut in the Dankerts and one other map (D&H 50), and a kind of cowl in the Porter and Aa maps that may be what Hollar shows in his view of 1647.[4]

Panoramas showing Bankside accompany the Norden map of 1600 and eight others dating from 1666 to the end of the century. All nine panoramas include the Globe, but only the Norden map does, and even here the map has a round Globe, the panorama a polygonal one. No map, that is, agrees with its panorama about the Globe. Moreover, all nine panoramas show what one might call the Beargarden-Hope, but only four of the accompanying maps do, and in each case the building is round in one and polygonal in the other. No map, that is, agrees with its panorama in the most obvious ways about either the Globe or Beargarden-Hope. The statistic is blatant: eighteen attempts at the same things, eighteen fundamental disagreements. One may look for significances.

Since eight of the panoramas were published when the Globe no longer stood, as all eight of the accompanying maps show, one significance seems clear. The maps and panoramas were the results of two different assumptions, the one pointing, however crudely sometimes, toward a record of the present and the other toward fancy, a pleasant picture, and the past. Shapiro argues that the same assumptions lie also behind the Norden map and panorama: the map is relatively accurate, much of the panorama "obviously purely conventional and 'artistic.'" Publishers and buyers, that is, expected the map and panorama to convey different kinds of intelligence about the same aspect of London. A glance at the Hondius, Visscher, and Merian views must suggest that what was true of the panoramas published with maps was equally true of many of those published on their own.

Five of the panoramas published with maps relate to Hollar's Long Bird's-Eye View. Four of these appeared within a year or so of the great fire of 1666 and are drawn from a vantage point in Southwark so as to show the buildings of Bankside standing starkly in the foreground while the city burns in the background. One of the four has the labels of the two playhouses reversed (D&H 16), as the Long Bird's-Eye View does, and another, much in Hollar's style, appears with one of his maps (D&H 14). The fifth and perhaps more interesting version of Hollar's View appears with his map of c.1675 (D&H 26). Here the city is shown as in the View, before the Fire, and here, too, the labels of the playhouses are reversed. In these five panoramas, the Globe is always round, the Beargarden-Hope polygonal once and round four times. The Globe has a double-gable hut four times, the sort of cowl once that the Beargarden-Hope has in the Long Bird's-Eye View. The Beargarden-Hope has that cowl twice and no superstructure three times. The Globe has a flag only once, but the Beargarden-Hope has one four times. The Globe has external staircases four times, the Beargarden-Hope three. The three remaining panoramas published with maps all date from the very end of the century or just after, and all have as their models not Hollar's Long Bird's-Eye View, which treats Bankside as it was in the early 1640's, but the Visscher and Merian views, which treat the place as of about 1600.[5]

What, then, may one say about Hollar's Long Bird's-Eye View, which has become so important in our calculations about the Globe? His Globe is conspicuously a more reasonable building than that in the Hondius, Visscher, and Merian views and their progeny. But it belongs to a convention the assumptions of which militate against accuracy, and Hollar was obviously no champion of accuracy as applied to playhouses in the maps that he also made. Did he defy convention and his own instincts as shown in his maps when he drew the view? Evidently not. Miss Scouloudi warns us against taking the view literally and points out several respects in which Hollar preferred to ignore fact: he does not show St. Katherine's by the Tower; he shows eight bays on the south side of the choir of St. Paul's but eleven in his elaborate plan of the building drawn on another occasion; he has the New Exchange incorrectly located (pp. 61-62). He left out the thirty-odd tenements that stood around the Globe. To suppose as we seem ready to do, that the Globe was polygonal rather than round as he has it, we must argue that he made it round not because he could not draw or take the time to draw a polygonal building, but because roundness, like the omission of the tenements, was right, in the mind's if not the real eye. The substitution of fancy for fact led him to a more attractive picture. The many differences between his partly inked-over pencil sketch and the finished engraving show that the process went on richly, and so even do the differences between the pencil lines and the ink ones over them. It is not unreasonable, therefore, to expect that Hollar made other adjustments to the fact of the building with the same motive. Nor is it unreasonable to conclude that where the evidence of the Fortune contract is at odds with that of Hollar's View, the View may not always be right.

And now let me proceed to proprietary matters.

A family named Brend (as they came to spell their name) owned the Globe through its whole history. The first of them who is important in that history is Thomas Brende, who acquired the site and passed it to subsequent generations but did not own it while the Globe stood on it. He was born in 1516 or 1517, became a citizen and scrivener of London, and in 1548 or so was living in the house of William Cawkett, scrivener, perhaps as his journeyman. Like other scriveners, Brende devoted himself at least partly to dealings in the money market of London and eventually in real estate. The Close Rolls are littered with the bonds and mortgages with which he secured the borrowings of his clients, and only one with which someone else secured one of his borrowings. These bonds and mortgages begin in 1547 and diminish sharply after 1558; most belong to 1548 and 1555-56. From 1554 to 1591, mainly from 1562 to 1566, the same rolls preserve numerous contracts by which he acquired a good deal of property in London, the Home Counties, and elsewhere. The first of these acquisitions, in October, 1554, was the site of the Globe in Southwark, which he bought for £240 from John Yong, a citizen and skinner of London who had inherited it from his wife, Christian, and she from her grandparents, Thomas and Christian Rede. Brende bought the place in his first wife's name as well as his own, so that perhaps the money was at least partly hers. From 1583, finally, to the last year of his life, these rolls also preserve contracts by which he gave up six pieces of property, one in a legal wrangle, one as a gift to a relative, four as sales.[6]

An antagonist of his said in 1578 that he "became" very "soone welthye" and that this sudden wealth was the result of "false or subtylle dealinge." A fellow lodger in Cawkett's house thirty years before, however, denied the assertion and offered a better reason for Brende's wealth: the "Rich mariages he hath had." We may well believe the man, for in addition to having known Brende more than thirty years, he had been called as a witness to sustain, not deny, the assertion, no doubt because Brende had once sued him for defamation.[7]

Brende's first wife was Margerie, who died June 2, 1564, having borne him ten children, four sons and six daughters. His second was Mercy, daughter of Humphrey Collet, a bowyer, it seems, of Southwark, and widow of Francis Bodley of Streatham. She brought a son into Brende's family, John Bodley, who becomes important in the history of the Globe, as does her brother, John Collet.[8] She set about bearing Brende eight further children, four sons and four daughters. Brende grew to be very old indeed. He outlived most of his children. His second wife died April 13, 1597, and he drew up a new will two months later, on June 15. He then had one son living, Nicholas, born between September 22, 1560, and September 21, 1561, hence the child of the first wife, and five daughters: Anne, Judith, Mary (who had married a man named Maylard and was a widow in 1601), Katherine (who had married George Sayers or Seares), and Mercy, born 1572-73 hence the child of the second wife (she was to marry Peter Frobisher, son of Sir Martin Frobisher the navigator).[9]

Among Brende's possessions were lands at West Molesey in Surrey (including the manor), the Star and other places in Bread Street, London, numerous properties grouped together in Southwark (including the site of the Globe), and a town house in St. Peter's Hill, London. He lived at his manor and in his town house.[10] He was sensitive about his progress from bourgeois to landed gentleman. From the 1540's to the 1570's he regularly described himself as citizen and scrivener of London, and he continued occasionally to describe himself so for the rest of his life. In one part (1578) of an extensive legal struggle, he is described as alive and "late Cytizen and scrivener of London," probably because he had by this time given up his shop. In another part, a deposition of his of 1582, the examiner wrote "gent" after his name; then, no doubt at Brende's insistence, crossed it out and wrote "esquyer" above the line; then at Brende's further insistence crossed that out, too, and wrote the unvarnished fact, "Exam[inan]t." He signed the deposition thus:

He gave himself as gentleman once, in 1583, but did not do so again. From 1580 he often preferred the splendid euphemism, citizen and writer of the court letter of London, suggesting not only that he had risen above plain scrivener but that he preferred to think of his scrivenership as having to do with palaeography rather than the lending of money.[11] He had one quite indirect brush with theatre, in 1581, and it cost him a great deal of money. He guaranteed a loan of £200 for that famous patron of a company of actors, the Lord Admiral. Brende had been led into the business by his neighbor in Surrey, Richard Drake, who was one of the Lord Admiral's chief followers and equerry to the Queen. When the Lord Admiral failed to repay the money, Brende had to do so. He had for his pains only a bond for £400 that Drake had given him as protection, which for some reason he did not pursue through the courts of law.[12] As his burial inscription in St. Peter's Church, West Molesey, reads, Thomas Brende "lived the age of fovrscore and one yeres And departed this worlde the xxj of September 1598."[13]

His son, Nicholas, married Margaret Strelley in 1595 or somewhat before, when Nicholas was thirty-four years old or so. It was a very unusual marriage and not merely because the groom was approaching middle age. He did not get his father's consent to the marriage or even tell him about it until some time after it had occurred. Neither did he give his wife a jointure, though she may well have brought him a portion (she could not have been a pauper, and eventually the Brends seem to have owed her something). They had their first child, Jane, in 1595 or 1596, another, Mercy (evidently they had taken his sister into their confidence), in 1597, and yet another, Frances, in 1598.[14] His father, who was eighty at the time, discovered

these arrangements by June 15, 1597, and was not amused. He took
"a very hard oppinion and conceit" of his daughter-in-law. He redrew
his will on that day and added a distressed note to explain: "I haue
stryken out my sonne to be one of my Execut[ors] in consideracion that
he did marry without my knowledge or consent." He named his
daughter, Anne (presumably the eldest) instead.[15]

Margaret Strelley had trusted Nicholas Brend to deal fairly with
her without carefully negotiated compulsion. It was a daring thing to
do, whether she was young and merely enthusiastic, or of responsible
years, perhaps even a widow, herself and her money at her own
disposal.[16] It was curious, to say the least, that a man of Nicholas
Brend's years should marry in such a way. Whether the lady was of
age in 1595 or so, she must have been many years younger than her
husband, for she lived to have at least twelve children, perhaps more,
and six years intervened between one group of children and another.
One can only guess at why Thomas Brende was hostile to her, and
why Nicholas anticipated his hostility. She was not lacking in social
pretensions. Indeed, hers were probably superior to those of the
Brends. She was cousin to Lady Jane Townsend and, more significantly, to that lady's brother, John Stanhope, a gentleman of the
privy chamber at court who shortly after the marriage was knighted
and made Treasurer of the Chamber (July, 1596). As such, he was
paymaster of, among others, the actors and musicians who performed
for the Queen. Eventually, Margaret Strelley's father may also have
been knighted, and her cousin became Vice Chamberlain and Lord
Stanhope (1605).[17] Perhaps her father-in-law was more impressed by
financial pretension, and hers was considerably less than he thought
those two marriages of his and a long life of lending and buying should
have yielded.

If Thomas Brende refused to make his son an executor, however,
he did not disinherit him. In his redrawn will he did not mention
either the properties in Southwark or some of his other principal
possessions, nor did he say that his son should not have them. When
Thomas Brende died, Nicholas was thirty-seven years old.[18] Nicholas
seems to have had no trouble taking possession of his father's
unmentioned properties. He had no ready cash, however, and he
must have been several hundred pounds in debt. Yet his first legal act
was to buy up the properties his father had left to his two sisters, Anne

and Judith.[19] He paid, or rather promised to pay, £1,150 for them on November 17, 1598, so keeping his father's estate more or less together, but also rendering his financial state difficult. Thanks to his wife's connections at court, perhaps, his next legal act was to lease a part of his property in Southwark to the Burbages and their associates. The arrangement was substantially agreed before Christmas 1598 (it was to take effect at that Christmas), but the contract was not signed until February 21 following, by which time the worthwhile pieces of the old Theatre in Shoreditch had probably been lying about the place for some six weeks, ready for assembly.

Once the players had taken up their lease there, the Brends' property in Southwark seems to have been worth at least £90 a year clear, of which the players paid £14.10s.0d. (16%). Their lease comprised two pieces of land separated by a lane, four gardens and various structures on one piece and three gardens and various structures on the other. Adjoining these pieces of land on both east and west were the other parts of the Brends' property, on which were numerous buildings during the whole history of the Globe. The whole property in 1601, two years after the Globe opened, comprised "small & ruinous howses" in thirty tenants' hands (two of whom represented the Globe), according to a man in whose interest it was to disparage them.[20] In that year the whole property was described twice in legal documents as "All those messuages tenements howses edifices buildings chambers roomes playhowse gardens orchards voidgrounds and other lands and heredytaments Whatsoever." The tenants of these places were given as four gentlemen (including Richard Burbage and Shakespeare), two tanners, two watermen, two beerbrewers, and a dyer, armorer, baker, porter, draper, tailor, saddler, and one person whose work was unidentified. Some of these people, like Hendrik Sturman (later Henry Stearman), the armorer, held more than one of the places. This description and these tenants were recited as current in 1608 and in 1622, suggesting, perhaps, that the neighborhood had not changed much in two decades. When the Globe was finally separated contractually from its neighbors in 1624, it was described as "All that the messuage or tenement and all that the Playhouse comonly called or knowne by the name of the Globe with their & either of their rights members & appurtenants set scituate lying & being in or neere Mayden lane...together with all & singuler edifices buildings cellers sollers chambers lights easem[ts] orchards gardeines Courts backsides walles inclosures waies pathes and all other profitts comodities & emolum[ts] whatsoeu*er* to the said messuage or ten*eme*nt & Playhouse called the Globe or either of them belonging.'' By that time, if not before, that is, the Globe was an extensive holding consisting of two main buildings and numerous subsidiary matters. Its occupiers, ''now or late,'' were John Hemings, Cuthbert and Richard Burbage, and Shakespeare.[21]

Nicholas' two unmarried sisters, Anne and Judith, both died in 1599, so that he became his father's executor after all, on May 8. Judith was living in John Collet's house when she drew her will on April 20.[22] What the two of them did with their brother's bonds does not appear, but his finances did not improve. He sold a small piece of property at West Molesey for £340 to Dame Dorothy Edmunds, one of the ladies of the Queen's privy chamber,[23] and he borrowed £105 from his widowed sister, Mary Maylard. Meanwhile his family continued to grow. His first son, Matthew, was born February 6, 1600,[24] and another son, John, little more than a year after, so that he now had five children. He owned a rich estate, but when he grew mortally ill early in the autumn of 1601 in his father's house in St. Peter's Hill, all he could contemplate were numerous debts either due already or shortly coming due, three daughters without portions, an heir who was less than two years old, and a second son who had just been born. He thought his debts amounted to £1,478, but they proved eventually to amount to £1,715. Not only had he no ready money with which to pay these debts, he needed £250 to see him through present difficulties. Moreover, his properties around the Globe and in Bread Street needed extensive repairs, so that his real indebtedness was something like £2,150, about half again as much as he thought.[25]

Evidently he saw no chance that his wife might be able to make sense of all this, anymore than he had. So in his last hours he summoned his step-brother, John Bodley of Streatham, now a cloth merchant, who quickly organized an elaborate scheme for rescue. Because Bodley could not finance his scheme himself, he summoned that other relative, John Collet, now a merchant tailor, and Sir Matthew Browne. Bodley would pay the debts and in return take a mortgage on the properties in Bread Street and Southwark, including, now, the Globe. Nicholas would provide other properties that Bodley would sell to raise portions for the daughters (£400 for Jane and £300 for each of the two others) and money to help maintain them while they were minors and to provide for Nicholas's wife and second son, John.[26] Bodley, finally, would see to it that Nicholas had £250 in cash at once. Bodley agreed to do these things, and Collet and Browne to finance him, because despite Nicholas's apparent difficulties, his estate was worth a good deal.

So on October 7, Bodley, Collet, and Browne agreed in writing to pay the debts and Collet to give Nicholas £250 in cash. In return, Nicholas mortgaged his properties in Bread Street and Southwark to Collet and Browne for the supposed amount of the debts, £1,478. On October 8 he signed a bond in which he promised to pay Collet and Browne £2500 if he did not perform the requirements of the mortgage. On October 10 he drew his will, providing among other things that Bodley and Browne should have various properties they would sell, including the house in St. Peter's Hill where all this was taking place. On the same day he signed a document making his mortgage of three days before look like an absolute sale, doubtless at Bodley's insistence, who had decided that he should control the properties until he had reimbursed himself for the debts out of the profits. He had probably grown nervous about the widow-to-be's ability to make the estate yield enough money over a reasonable time to cover the debts, and he knew the troubles he would have extracting the money from the estate through the courts should she fail. On October 11, Nicholas conferred with Bodley about the arrangements for the second son, which were manifestly inadequate.[27] And on October 12, 1601, at the age of forty or forty-one, the first owner of the Globe died.

Collet and Browne acted merely in trust for Bodley, and in any event, Browne died within two years and Collet formally sold his interest in the scheme to Bodley in 1608. Bodley collected the rents in Bread Street and Southwark from October 10, 1601, and otherwise managed the properties there.[28] From that day, therefore, it was he who effectively owned the Globe. The widow, meanwhile, lived with the children on the estate at West Molesey, which she would control until the heir came of age.

As the years went by, the family grew increasingly unhappy about these arrangements and eventually spent a great deal of time and money over them in the law courts. The family thought Bodley should have got more than he did for the properties sold to raise the portions—none the less so, perhaps, because the principal purchaser was a Peter Collet.[29] The family also came to believe that Bodley could have been more zealous in extracting money from the Bread Street and Southwark properties, and Bodley came to think of the mortgage on those properties as a sale, which according to the crucial document it was. But in the meantime, the King's Men had no trouble about their lease, and Margaret Brend took some interesting steps.

In 1602 or early 1603, she tried to collect the money due for her father-in-law's bond of £400 that secured a debt of the Lord Admiral's. Nicholas Brend had tried in vain to collect the money from Richard Drake, so his widow tried the Lord Admiral himself. She caught him one day as he was at the royal palace of Oatlands, near West Molesey, preparing to follow the Queen, who had just left for Hampton Court. He said he thought the debt had been paid, but he offered her £100 for the bond. Evidently she insisted on more and he refused to pay more, for in 1606, Richard Drake having died three years earlier, her next husband sued the son and heir, Francis Drake, at common law for the full value of the bond.[30]

If her previous marriage had been curious, her next, as Thomas Brende would have seen it, verged on the bizarre. In about 1605, she took as husband a man named Sir Sigismond Zinzan, who in several ways rivaled the King's Men in theatricality.[31] She brought him a portion of £1,000 "& vpwards," raised out of Brend properties and matched, one supposes, by a suitable jointure.[32] Sir Sigismond settled in as master of the lands at West Molesey and as foster father to the five Brend children, who were successively joined by seven Zinzan children: Henry, Sigismond, Robert, Charles, Margaret, Elizabeth, and Letticia. To this busy household, Dame Margaret Zinzan (as she now was) eventually brought two others, a brother, Henry Strelley, and a sister, Mary Strelley, who had been born in 1592 and hence was not much older than the oldest Brend children.[33]

The Zinzans were of Italian ancestry, or so some of Sir Sigismond's relatives and descendants thought (they occasionally called themselves Zinzano), as did Anthony Wood.[34] Sir Sigismond's father was Sir Robert Zinzan, who was born in 1547 or early 1548, joined the royal service in 1558, became (like Richard Drake) one of the Queen's equerries, was according to the King of Scotland a "discreet ...gentleman," battened on royal gifts (given "in Consideracione," as was said of one, "of his faithfull obedient longe & good service done vnto yor highnes"), acquired interests at Walton (near West Molesey) in 1589 and at the end of his life lived there, was knighted like hordes of others in the early days of James's reign, and died late in 1607.[35] From the 1540's until at least the 1640's, most of the male Zinzans of whom sufficient record survives were professional horsemen in the royal service. A Hannibal Zenzant, or Zenzano, was farrier to Henry VIII and Edward VI.[36] Sir Robert must have been a leading person in the royal stables. His brothers, Andrew and Alexander, were also royal equerries, as were both his sons alive in 1607, Henry and Sir Sigismond. A William was another in 1599, as, later, was Henry's son, Richard. His other son, Joseph, sought to conduct a riding school in the 1640's, and a "Signor Alex: *Zinzano*," who was "his Majesties *Cavalerizzo*," trained a horse for the diarist, John Evelyn, in 1643. Sir Sigismond's son Robert, may have been yet another royal equerry.[37]

All the Zinzans at least from Sir Robert and his brothers forward gave themselves also as Alexander, or even merely as Alexander. Because members of the family occasionally had to do with Scotland, one is tempted to think that the family acquired some valued connection in the middle of the sixteenth century with the Scottish house of Alexander out of which the Earls of Stirling were to come. And in the 1630s, if not eighty years earlier, the Zinzans did acquire such a connection, when Sir Sigismond's eldest son, Henry, married a woman whose sister was to be Countess of Stirling. That connection seems to be the only one, however, and a historian of the Scottish Alexanders convinced himself that the Zinzans used the name because an Alexander Zinzan of the mid-sixteenth century found his Christian name easier on English ears than his family one.[38]

Sir Sigismond had known the Brends since about 1598, when he would have been in his late twenties or early thirties, not yet knighted, and the second son of a man well placed at court and in the horse business. He was proceeding in both himself, as was his older brother, Henry, but along a rather different path than that their father had followed.[39] They were making themselves notable in the aristocratic sport of running at tilt. Their father had run at tilt, too, but not so persistently. He had run frequently from 1584 to 1591, only sporadically before and not at all after. Two of the tilts in which he had run, however, were famous, one of 1581 and that of 1590 in which Sir Henry Lee, the Queen's champion, resigned the "honour" and by way of explanation offered the Queen the celebrated poem beginning, "My golden locks time hath to silver turned."[40] When Sir Sigismond married Margaret Brend in about 1605, he and his brother had established themselves as a team of runners at tilt, and very likely he had been knighted. He was about as old as the lady's previous husband had been at her marriage to him ten or so years before. She was, of course, a widow who had five children to look after, but she was also lady of the manor of West Molesey.

Tilts were almost invariably run at the annual celebration of the monarch's accession, Accession Day—November 17 in Elizabeth's time, March 24 in James'—and they were sometimes run at other royal celebrations as well. The Accession Day tilts and most of the others took place in the tiltyard at Whitehall. They were lavish affairs that must have made the goings-on at the gorgeous Globe seem squalid by comparison. In the Accession Day tilt of 1621, Prince Charles alone spent £3,352.6s.6d. to participate, of which a John Shakespeare received £22.1s.0d. for providing bits to go with new saddles. The prince appeared with no fewer than thirty-six retainers, including six trumpeters, in his colors of white, green, and yellow, and perhaps as in the year before, with a tent of damasks of the same colors for his repose. When on Accession Day, 1613, the Earl of Rutland first ventured an appearance in these tilts, he paid William Shakespeare 44s. for composing an impresa and Richard Burbage, who was a painter as well as an actor, the same amount for "paynting and making it."[41]

In their time, nobody ran at tilt so often as the Zinzan brothers. Sir Sigismond first ran in the tilting for Accession Day in 1598 and his brother the next year. Except for one tilt each, they may well have run in every Accession Day tilt thereafter. Sir Sigismond did not run in 1602, nor Henry in 1600, but otherwise their names are on all the lists except those for 1606, which are informal and perhaps incomplete. They also ran in the tilts for special occasions and took part in other martial games. Henry took part in the challenge that followed the Accession Day tilting of 1602. The two of them ran with the Earl of Cumberland in a tilt at Grafton on June 27, 1603. The earl was mounting an entertainment for the new king and queen, who had just met there, she traveling south from Edinburgh to join in the coronation and he north from London to meet her. The earl may have defended the new royal house—he had succeeded Sir Henry Lee as royal champion—and the Zinzans challenged it. If so, the earl showed more zeal for that house than the game required, for as his daughter, Lady Anne Clifford, wrote, he hurt Henry Zinzan "very dangerously." Sir Sigismond performed in the elaborate challenge at barriers for Prince Henry on January 6, 1610, around which Ben Jonson wrote his masque, *Prince Henry's Barriers*. Both Zinzans ran in the tilt on June 6 following, that was part of the celebrations for the Prince's becoming Prince of Wales. Both ran, too, in the tilt on January 1, 1614, that accompanied Jonson's masque, *A Challenge at Tilt*, for the Earl of Somerset's marriage to Frances Howard. Neither, however, had joined in the game at barriers on January 6, 1606, in Jonson's masque, *Hymenaei*, for the lady's other marriage, to the Earl of Essex. Nor did they run at the ring on November 6, 1616, to celebrate Prince Charles's becoming Prince of Wales.[42]

The Zinzans' names appear together at the bottom of many of the surviving lists of these events, like John Chamberlain's list for the tilt of 1613. He gave the noblemen, then noted that there were six knights, named them omitting Sir Sigismond, and added "besides" the Zinzans. No doubt the Zinzans were socially inferior to other tilters, but also, being professional horsemen, they were probably the players and the others the gentlemen. Moreover, from 1610 onward, if not before, the Exchequer paid the Zinzans £100 a few days before Accession Day of every year in which an Accession Day tilt was run, also just before the tilt for the Somerset marriage.[43] They were to use the money "to furnish themselves wth necessaries against this Tiltinge," as their privy seal of 1613 reads, "for asmuch as that service is vsually a charge to them wch we of o^r Royal disposicion are pleased to defray," as that of 1622 adds. It was once specified that each of them should have £50. Nobody else received such payments for tilting. The money was paid to them as a "free gift" for which they did not have to account, or even go anywhere to collect, for the officers of the Exchequer were to take it to them.

If the Zinzans came to be something like professional runners at tilt, one may guess that they came also to be organizers and managers of tilts, as the lists of tilters in 1622 suggest. The Zinzans were not among the twenty-seven grandees summoned to join Prince Charles in the tilting, yet they were among the twelve who actually joined him, and they were paid as usual. If they did manage tilts, one of their duties would have been to see that no harm befell the great nobles who took part. From 1620 onwards, Sir Sigismond usually ran against novices, one of whom (in 1620) was the Marquess of Buckingham. Henry Zinzan in about 1625, his tilting days finished, sought royal relief because of "long service and extreme hurts he has received by Prince Henry and His Majesty" (Prince Charles, that is, who was now king), not to say the Earl of Cumberland, "which now grow grievous unto him." He must have acquired his extreme hurts in the strenuous training that took place before tilts, for he seems never to have run against either prince in the tilts themselves. In any event, he was probably believed, for he was given a patent to tax the transport of calf skins from Boston to Lynn.[44]

The Zinzans had to do, too, with less festive and dangerous ceremonials. In the great funeral procession for Prince Henry in 1612, each led a horse representing an important part of the crown the prince might have worn, Henry's horse the dukedom of Cornwall and Sir Sigismond's the kingdom of Scotland, "couered with blacke cloath, armed with Scuchions of that Kingdome, his Cheiffron and Plumes."[45] They signed themselves like this:

Their coat of arms was a blue shield on which a falcon in its natural color, wings expanded, stands on a golden rock and looks fiercely at a silver "estoile" in the upper left corner. The crest may have been a dove with wings expanded.[46]

Sir Sigismond was apparently a theatrical man of both kidney and choler. For example, he disapproved of a clergyman whom Francis Drake had appointed to a living near West Molesey. Drake, therefore, must withdraw the man and appoint one of Sir Sigismond's choosing. Drake refused, remarking that Sir Sigismond's man "was given to drink and notoriously unfit." Sir Sigismond then wrote "two scandalous and libellous letters, touching Drake in his place of justice of the peace" and "disturbed" Drake's man as he was about to conduct a service on a Sunday. Drake sought help from London, and Robert Cley arrived with a summons. Sir Sigismond, his brother-in-law, Henry Strelley, and probably others beat Cley "so that Cley was driven to run for his life into the Thames, where he continued for a quarter of an hour in the depth of winter." It may have been for this exploit that Sir Sigismond and thirteen others (not, however, Strelley) from West Molesey were fined in the Star Chamber in the autumn of 1609, he the huge sum of £500 and the others from £2 to £30.[47] He also managed to be outlawed for debt three times in 1612 and once more in 1619.[48] He contemptuously refused, that is, to appear in court to answer the charges against him.

This menage persisted at West Molesey, and John (Sir John after September, 1617)[49] Bodley persisted at the Globe until the heir, Matthew Brend, came of age on February 6, 1621, when many changes had to take place. First of all, Matthew sued Bodley in the Court of Wards for the return of the Brend properties in London and Southwark, including the site of the Globe. Bodley argued that the document of October 10, 1601, was an absolute sale, and Matthew argued that however worded the documents might be, his father's transactions as he lay dying amounted to a scheme of trusts, not sales. The case was heard on November 10, 1621, and again on February 8, 1622. Matthew won the case, but the court found that Bodley was still owed £540 for Nicholas Brend's debts and awarded him another £210 for his pains and travel. If, that is, Matthew should pay Bodley £750, Bodley would have to return both properties. Though Bodley lost the case, the court excused him from paying costs because it also found that "hee hath bin a Careful husband in the well orderinge of the *said* messuages landes & ten*ements.*"

Matthew promptly paid the money, and Bodley, joined by Collet, turned over the properties on February 21, 1622.[50] Matthew Brend now owned the Globe. As if to afix a royal seal on this coming of age, the King knighted Matthew at Hampton Court on April 6.[51]

Once Sir Matthew had established his ownership of the Brend properties, the Zinzans had to establish their place in the new scheme of things. Sir Sigismond and his wife concluded, rightly, that she was entitled by dower rights to a third of the income from Nicholas Brend's freehold lands from the time of his death and to a third of all his personal goods. None of the income had been paid before Sir Matthew's coming of age, and since that time he had been paying sums informally. A reckoning was obviously in order, and Sir Matthew urged the Zinzans to negotiate one with him. It was a time of family harmony. Sir Matthew had convinced himself that the Court of Wards had given Bodley more than his due, and the whole family agreed: the Zinzans. Sir Matthew's brother, John, and his sisters, Jane (unmarried), Mercy (married to Robert Meese), and Frances (unmarried). In the winter of 1622-23, they all sued Bodley, arguing generally that Bodley had greatly enriched himself out of the Brend properties and specifically that he had collected too little rent from the properties set aside for the girls' portions and then sold them for far less than they were worth. This muster of Brends was increased by others who testified for them, Sir Matthew's aunt, Mercy Frobisher (now a widow), his mother's sister, Mary Strelley, and his stepfather's servant, William Fellowes.[52]

In this congenial setting, Sir Sigismond negotiated with his stepson, and before the end of the summer of 1623 they arrived at an amicable understanding. Sir Matthew would pay the Zinzans £140 a year for his mother's interest in all the Brend properties. The Zinzans would vacate West Molesey the following spring, taking with them most of the goods and implements but sowing the fields first so that Sir Matthew could reap them. Sir Sigismond would file one or more writs of dower against Sir Matthew, who would not contest it or them nor have to pay costs. Apparently this was a device to determine how much the Zinzans should have for past years and for Dame Margaret Zinzan's interest in her late husband's personal goods. Sir Matthew guaranteed his part of the scheme by giving the Zinzans a bond of £3,000, and he agreed that the Zinzans could repossess West Molesey should he not pay whatever was due to them.

This harmony was ruined by love. Sometime during the summer of 1623, Sir Matthew conceived a passion for Frances Smith, the daughter of Sir William Smith of Theydon Mount in Essex. He wanted desperately to marry her, possibly bewitched by her wit or person or both, but openly by her considerable portion, with which he thought he might get his affairs into better order. He had had, no doubt, to borrow most of the £750 paid to Bodley and could have to borrow also whatever might be due Sir Sigismond. Smith was willing to give £2,000 with his daughter, but he and his two sons demanded a very convincing jointure in return, and this jointure would make parts of Sir Matthew's agreement with Sir Sigismond inappropriate and unenforceable.[53] They wanted the lady to have ownership for her life of two of the most important pieces of Sir Matthew's estate, the properties in Bread Street in London and West Molesey, and they would suffer neither to be encumbered by the dower rights of Sir Matthew's mother. Sir Matthew, that is, would have to give up these properties if he was to bring the marriage off, and, as he convinced himself, he would also have to give the Smiths an impression that he was wealthier than he really was.

During late August and the first three weeks of September, 1623, he negotiated with the Smiths, and in the midst of this time he turned to Sir Sigismond, whom he summoned to his lawyer's office in Gray's

Inn. In lieu of his mother's dower rights in the properties at West Molesey and in Bread Street, he offered the Zinzans ownership of the properties in Southwark, including the Globe, for her life. He proposed that the Zinzans lease these properties back to him for £100 a year, and, when the rents above that sum reached a total of £1,000, that he give the Zinzans two-thirds of this total and keep a third himself. In the meantime, they would strive to increase the rents. He suggested that the rest of their previous agreement remain unchanged: the Zinzans would leave West Molesey in the spring and Sir Sigismond would file the writ or writs of dower. He wanted to give the Smiths the impression that the goods at West Molesey were his, but Sir Sigismond could quietly take what he liked when he left. Sir Matthew also wanted to give the impression that he and Sir Sigismond would share the money yielded by the writs of dower, but Sir Sigismond would have it all.

Sir Matthew protested that the Zinzans would lose nothing by this new scheme, but Sir Sigismond saw his £140 a year shrinking to £100 and his wife's claim on the other major properties disappearing together with their right to repossess West Molesey should Sir Matthew not pay. So Sir Sigismond refused to agree and "went forth of the said Chamber downe the stayres." Sir Matthew "followed him into the Gallery," where he "much vrged and importuned." If Sir Sigismond did not agree, the marriage would not take place, and Sir Matthew "should bee vndone thereby and [he] did then wth teares and deepe oathes and imprecacions faythfully vowe and affirme" that Sir Sigismond would lose nothing by agreeing. Evidently, Sir Matthew promised that the Zinzans would get their £140 a year, though for the sake of impressing the Smiths the documents would mention only £100. Sir Sigismond was moved to agree, but only after extracting the promise of a further bond of £6,000 payable to his son, Henry, to guarantee payment of the first bond of £3,000 should Sir Matthew's performance fall short of the former agreement.

So Sir Matthew and his lawyer set about drawing up the documents that amounted to a marriage contract, and they suggested that for his part of the transaction Sir Sigismond seek legal counsel from Simon Wiseman, who was to prove a good deal cleverer than they thought he was. All was ready on September 22. The Zinzans joined Sir Matthew in conveying the properties at West Molesey and in

Bread St. to Frances Smith's trustees, and Sir Matthew conveyed those in Southwark to his mother for her life. Both conveyances were by foot of fine, a process requiring three law terms. The properties would formally change hands, that is, in Easter term, 1624. A contract was drawn providing for the Zinzans' leasing the properties in Southwark back to Sir Matthew and for the Zinzans' withdrawal from West Molesey.

Late in the winter of 1623-24, as the Zinzans prepared to leave West Molesey, Sir Matthew gained his Frances and her portion at an altar, but not before the Smiths had winkled one further concession out of him. They persuaded him that he should increase the lady's jointure by adding the Globe to it, in return for which they would add £100 (a fraction of its worth) to her portion. Evidently there was no time to draw up a document before the wedding, so the Smiths settled for the promise, and the lady's glad husband drew one up later, on March 12, 1624, separating the Globe and its appurtenances at last from the other properties in Southwark and conveying it to her for her life—after, of course, the death of Dame Margaret Zinzan.[54] If Sir Matthew's life at this critical moment could be complicated by the demands of in-laws, so could Sir Sigismond's and in a much more theatrical, and dire, way.

On Sunday evening, March 14, after Sir Sigismond had left for London, probably to see about the tilt to be performed in ten days (his and his brother's privy seal for their stipend that year is dated March 16), his teenage daughter, Margaret, covertly took a teenage husband in the house at West Molesey. The groom was William Shelley, son and heir of Sir John and Dame Jane Shelley of Michelmore in Sussex, a family of great pretension and extensive Catholic connections.[55] Lady Shelley called Sir Sigismond's daughter "cousin Megg," and the Zinzans had just kept Christmas with the Shelleys at a house of theirs in Kew. Young Shelley was nineteen years old, the bride younger. In two years he would be master, he thought, of £1,000 a year, at least sixteen times what Meg might have been mistress of, if Sir Sigismond could indeed have given her £650 as the locals thought. Both knew that the Shelleys energetically disapproved of the match and that Sir Sigismond would not have allowed it. But William had been a soldier in love's army for some time—he and a friend, for example, "had binne...in some Taverne...drinking of ye said M^{ris}

Margaretts health on there knees &...they did striue & contend together wch of them two did best loue her,'' and he had vowed to
friends that ''he would marry wth her, although he went A begging wth
her.''

So the parish priest, Israel Ridley, was summoned with his wife,
Alice, for a witness to the upstairs room called the chapel chamber,
and doubtless remembering her own daring and not unsuccessful
exploit with marriage thirty years before, Lady Zinzan sent up a
servant, John Barton, to give the bride away. Wisely, she did not go
herself. The ceremony over, the bride and groom called some friends
who happened to be in the house (including Henry Strelley) to the
same chapel chamber, where a small banquet was served in. Eventually bride and groom went to bed, also in the chapel chamber, and,
''in naked Bedd as man & wife,'' called their friends back to show that
they intended to consummate their marriage. The next morning the
groom, having sworn everyone to secrecy, took horse and rode away
and, as it turned out, lived with his bride no more, for William Shelley
proved no Nicholas Brend. Lady Zinzan presently found that the
marriage had been consummated ''to the full, for there were,'' she
said, ''such manifest toakens thereof in theire sheets that shee was
faine to hide the*m* fro*m* her seruants.''[56]

Perhaps Sir Sigismond found out about all this at once. Certainly
he knew in June or so, when he declared that he would tell the
Shelleys, and the groom pleaded with him for a chance to do so
himself. Marriage or no marriage, however, Sir Sigismond had to
devote himself to carrying out his agreement with Sir Matthew Brend.
The Zinzans left West Molesey two weeks after the marriage, at the
end of March, 1624, and moved temporarily into a house in Covent
Garden, near Drury Lane, where they stayed until the end of May,
when they moved into permanent quarters in Chiswick.[57] Sir Sigismond
filed one writ of dower against his stepson, who, according to the plan,
acquiesced in it.

Then Sir Sigismond went abroad, leaving his lawyer, Wiseman,
to look after the agreement with Sir Matthew Brend. He was taking
up a new career at a likely time. For as events were to prove, in 1624
he and his brother, Henry, had been paid to run at tilt on Accession
Day for the last time. A year later the King was to be mortally ill, so
that there could be no tilt, and thereafter the new King was to banish

tilting from Accession Day, apparently to reduce expenses at court. The brothers Zinzan had, therefore, come to the end of their careers as professional runners at tilt. Perhaps sensing that tilting was in decline, perhaps restless after removing from the manorial premises at West Molesey, perhaps in need of money, Sir Sigismond undertook to run at real enemies, as did two others from the house at West Molesey, his son, Sigismond, and Henry Strelley. The English government had agreed early in June to raise and maintain four regiments of English foot soldiers to help the Dutch. Sir Sigismond acquired the command of a company among them, as captain at £15 a month in the regiment of the Earl of Essex. The troops left for the Low Countries in July and August, Sir Sigismond among the first; he landed at Delft on July 13. His son went to the Palatinate as a lieutenant sometime during 1624, and Strelley joined during the winter of 1624-25 the ill-starred English army that Count Mansfeld tried to lead to Germany.[58]

At Midsummer Day and Michaelmas, Sir Matthew paid first and second quarterly installments of the rent for the properties in Southwark, but only £25 each time, as though the rent were £100 a year rather than £140. Wiseman protested and, it seems, more money was forthcoming. Wiseman, moreover, got £780 out of the writ of dower, which was much more than Sir Matthew had expected to pay, and to Brend's great annoyance he soon had a judgment issued in Sir Sigismond's name for that amount.

Sir Sigismond was back in England probably late in the autumn, when in addition to reporting these triumphs to him, Wiseman explained some other aspects of the case. Sir Sigismond had not yet executed the lease for the properties in Southwark nor had Sir Matthew executed the bond for £6,000. Furthermore, Sir Sigismond's contract with Sir Matthew, closely read, allowed but did not require the lease. Sir Sigismond, that is, owned those properties if he chose, as he decided he did. So with Wiseman's help, no doubt, he got the undersheriff of Surrey to put him into possession of them, including the Globe, and to instruct the tenants to pay no more rents to Sir Matthew. Enter, late in the autumn of 1624, Sir Sigismond Zinzan as owner of the Globe in the interest of his wife. And enter Sir Matthew Brend pleading in the courts to "secure his life from Sir Sigismond Zinzan...who resisteth ordinary justice."[59]

Presumably Sir Sigismond meant to keep the Southwark properties only until he could gain £780 from the rents and his stepson
guaranteed to pay £140 annually. Though the rents had probably
increased lately, they could hardly have amounted to more than £225
a year (which in his successful lawsuit against Bodley Sir Matthew had
insisted they were really worth), and they probably amounted to less
(Bodley had insisted on £90).[60] Hence Sir Sigismond might well have
had to hang onto the properties for ten or fifteen years to get £780 out
of them in addition to £140 a year. In December, perhaps on the
third, 1624, his stepson applied to the Court of Chancery for relief,
hoping mainly that the court might recalculate the debt to the Zinzans
and also require them to lease the Southwark properties to him. He
argued that the £750 he had paid Bodley should be taken into account
(since the money was for his father's debts and his mother and later
Sir Sigismond were his father's executors), as should all the rents the
Zinzans had collected through the years at West Molesey and various
items they, he said, had sold or taken away from the place.

Sir Sigismond answered on February 4, 1625. He had a good
case. He protested that his wife could not be expected to pay her
previous husband's debts because he had given her no jointure nor
enough money otherwise, and that she and he should not have to
account for the rents at West Molesey because the courts had given
her control of the properties there in her own right and not in trust for
her son. He added that the contract of September, 1623, allowed him
to lease the Southwark properties to Sir Matthew but did not require
him to do so. Sir Sigismond must have thought that a good case
deserved repetition, for ten days later he countersued in Chancery,
raising many of the same matters. This repetition should have been in
vain, however, for as Sir Matthew soon pointed out, his stepfather
had not removed the four judgments against him for which he had
been outlawed. Outlaws could defend themselves in the courts, but
they could not seek relief in them. Because of the strength of his
stepfather's case, perhaps, Sir Matthew did not take his lawsuit beyond bill and answer. Sir Sigismond, therefore, probably continued in
control of the Globe and other properties in Southwark, and eventually he and Sir Matthew probably negotiated toward a new bargain
providing for a cash settlement of somewhat less than £780 and a new
guarantee of £140 a year.

Sir Sigismond expected to return to his command in the Low Countries or some other during the spring of 1625, but in mid-February the Prince, Charles, ordered him to remain in England "for o^r service." That service kept him in England for eighteen and a half months, until the end of September, 1626. He was probably wanted for a tilt on Accession Day in March and when that was cancelled because of the King's illness and death, for the elaborate ceremonials that should have followed—the funeral on May 5, the coronation on February 2, 1626, the Queen's coronation (eventually given up), and a great procession through the City (planned for the summer of 1626 and also given up).

The royal order came at a good time. It gave Sir Sigismond a chance to negotiate personally with his stepson and, more urgently, personally to defend his daughter. For having learned of their son's marriage with Margaret Zinzan, the Shelleys did not propose to end the matter as Thomas Brende had done with Nicholas, by removing him as executor of their wills. They strove mightily to get the ecclesiastical authorities to annul the marriage, and Sir Sigismond responded with equal energy. In March, 1625, Archbishop Abbott recommended to one of the secretaries of state that the Shelleys and Zinzans take their quarrel to the Star Chamber because "what one affirms the other denies, and without swearing of witnesses, the truth cannot be found." There followed for thirty-two months a voluminous case in that court in which the Shelleys argued that the Zinzans had conspired against their son, and the Zinzans argued that young Shelley had loved the girl for some time and married her more than willingly. Many people from the house at West Molesey testified for Sir Sigismond and his daughter: his children Henry and Elizabeth, his stepson John Brend, his in-laws Henry and Mary Strelley, and various servants and visitors. The case was heard on November 23, 1627. The Star Chamber dismissed the charges of conspiracy against the Zinzans and refused to interfere with the marriage, but it came down very heavily on those who were present when the marriage took place. The priest was fined £50, his wife £3.6s.8d., and the servant who gave the bride away £10. Moreover, it awarded the Shelleys costs of £120 against the three of them. The servant managed to pay the fine, but the costs were beyond him, so the Shelleys sent him to jail and kept him there for several months. As for their son, he seems to have boasted to some of his friends that if his mother were dead all the world would not keep him from living with Margaret Zinzan, and to others that "if I cann putt of this gentlewoman," meaning Margaret Zinzan, he could now have a wife who had £1,000 a year in lands and £10,000 in ready money.[61]

While Sir Sigismond was thus engaged with the Shelleys in Star Chamber, his stepson, Sir Matthew Brend, was busy in Chancery, foolishly pursuing Sir John Bodley and occasionally protecting himself against his brother, John Brend, who had sued him and Bodley in December, 1624, for a larger share of Nicholas Brend's estate. Still convinced that the Court of Wards had been much too generous to Bodley, Sir Matthew pressed on with the family lawsuit of 1623 and launched at least one other. He was trying, in effect, to get Chancery to recalculate how much was due to Bodley for the return of the properties in Bread Street and Southwark, though he could not clearly say so in his argumentation because that matter had already been decided, the money paid, and property returned. He drove the case on in the names of all the plaintiffs long after at least two of them, Sir Sigismond and John Brend, would have had much interest in helping him, and he reached a hearing on June 26, 1626. He lost ignominiously. His case was so tortuously drawn that the court could not see how it legally affected him. The court threw it out and awarded Bodley £10 in costs, which Sir Matthew argued about until the end of January, 1627.[62] His brother had better luck. Though Sir Matthew for a time thought the case aimed at him and a connivance of Bodley's "for vexacion & for revenge & malice," it proved in the end to be aimed only at Bodley, and John Brend actually got on June 2, 1627, a recalculation of some of Bodley's dealings with Nicholas Brend's property.[63]

At the end of September, 1626, King Charles, as he now was, no longer needed Sir Sigismond's services in England. Presumably he returned to his post on the Continent (the regiments were now aiding the Danes), and presumably he was back in England during the winter following. He may well have arrived at an agreement then with his stepson about Lady Zinzan's dower rights, for Sir Matthew borrowed some £600 from a linen-draper early in December.[64] Sir Sigismond would then have executed the lease of the Globe and other properties in Southwark to Sir Matthew, so, in effect, returning them to him. Sir

Sigismond would have owned the Globe for about two years, living most of the time at Chiswick while attending on royal commands about festivities and ceremonials and negotiating his wife's dower rights with her son, but probably devoting most of his energies to his daughter's defense in the Star Chamber. His interest in the Globe ceased altogether about six months later when, sometime before June 20, 1627, his wife, Dame Margaret Zinzan, died.[65] The new owner then was Dame Frances Brend, Sir Matthew's wife, and she remained owner until the Globe was no more. That lady was, it seems, as effective at bargaining with Sir Matthew as her father and brothers had been, for in June, 1633, he increased her jointure yet again by giving her the properties it comprised, including the Globe, not merely for her lifetime but forever.[66]

From mid-1627, Sir Sigismond Zinzan fell increasingly into difficult times and eventually into what he saw as poverty and obscurity. He was cut off from Brend money and from tilting regularly in glittering surroundings. Somehow he had lost his pay as a royal equerry, though he still had the title. He had three daughters who needed portions and one who also needed an expensive legal defense. Presently he ceased campaigning in the Low Countries, perhaps finding it at £15 a month no pathway to riches. In 1628, probably, he pleaded with his old tilting companion, the King, to pay him for the eighteen and a half months in 1625 and 1626 when at the royal command he had stayed in England and earned no pay in the Low Countries. After an official inquiry in February, 1629, established that he had not earned £277.10s.0d., the King was pleased (as the privy seal reads) in July, 1630, to allow him at his humble suit £277.[67] The ink must have been scarcely dry on that document when Sir Sigismond pleaded again for money. This time the King granted him a pension of £100 a year to begin at Christmas, 1631, and to run not for life but during the royal pleasure. The pension, as this privy seal read, was "for the better accomodacion of the p'sent Accions" of Sir Sigismond and for "good and faithfull service heretofore done vnto o' late Deare and Royall father...and since vnto vs." This generosity, however, was not enough, either, and he soon began assigning portions of the payments to merchants to whom he owed money.[68]

He returned to the King, asking now that the pay and allowances for his equerryship be restored. He wrote a florid and humbling petition. Because of the loss of his pay and allowances, he began, "I was forced to such importunitie as had almost brought me to be insensible of All modestie and Ciuillitie, and had not yor sweete and Princelye nature pardoned manie great infirmities that want and dispayre brought vpon me, I might haue lost my selfe in a iust neglect deseruedly to haue ben cast vpon me in all my hopes presented in dayly peticions to yor Matie. But such was yor Princely goodnes and bounty towards me (when my great wants were truly diserned and knowne to yor Matie) as I am dayly releiued by a yearely guift of 100^{li}, or otherwise I had either rotted in Prison, or perrished with want." Alas, as he went on, that gift was being collected by others "to pay ould and Clamorous debts," so that he still felt "such wants as fewe can beare, with that patience I indure them." His pay and allowances would enable him "to appeare amongst Horsemen, whereas nowe I spend my time in a retyred way not able...scarce to walke abroad for debt much lesse to ride[,] a misery to great to accompany ould age that is otherwise pinched with greater wants then Horses. But," he concluded, "patience and dayly hopes of yor Ma^{ts} greater Compassion towards me sweeten my afflictions, and bringe me to peticion this grace and favo^r towards me presented with my prayers to the rewarder of all good Deedes to recompence yor Princely bounty towards me." Some twenty years later Sir Sigismond implied that the princely bounty was awakened yet again.[69]

Meanwhile, the Star Chamber had by no means ended the question of Margaret Zinzan's marriage. The Shelleys proceeded vigorously in the Ecclesiastical Court to get it annulled, arguing mainly that their son had been drunk at the time. Sir Sigismond presented much convincing evidence that he had not, including a remark by the priest that young Shelley did not "stammer, stumble, or lispe in speech more then he usuall[y] doth."[70] But eventually the Shelleys were successful, and Sir Sigismond appealed to the Judges Delegates. He was heard by six judges presided over by the Archbishop of Canterbury, William Laud. The Judges divided three to three and Laud resolved the question by siding with the Shelleys but allowing Sir Sigismond his full expenses as costs. When Sir Sigismond presented a claim for £2,000, however, Laud decided that £200 should suffice. So it was that William Shelley married again in 1636, the bride this time one of the French ladies of the Queen's privy chamber,

Christienne Marie de Luz de Vantelet, as she gave herself when she
was denizoned on February 23, perhaps to facilitate the marriage.
Whatever other financial inducements to marriage she may have had,
she had a royal pension of £150 a year, which hereafter she collected
as Dame Christiana Shelley, the groom having been knighted on
March 28, perhaps also to facilitate the marriage.[71] She bore the
Shelleys an heir, Charles, and less than four years after the marriage
both she and her husband had died, he before November 22, 1639,
and she in Paris describing herself as a Catholic in January, 1640.[72]

Far from rendering Margaret Zinzan's case ancient history, these
deaths caused new interest in it, even though she, too, had married (a
Robert Thomas of Kingston on Thames), for now the Shelley estates
were directly at stake. If Sir Sigismond could establish that his daughter was legally young Shelley's widow, he and she might come off very
well. So he took the matter to the House of Lords in March, 1641, but
apparently without success, the Lords having more urgent business
before them, like Strafford's attainder and the Army Plot.[73]

Though he must have been in his seventies, when the English
Revolution began in earnest in the summer of 1642, Sir Sigismond
Zinzan rushed to the colors—of his former chief, the Earl of Essex,
and the Parliament rather than of that king upon whose sweet and
princely nature he had called a few years before. He joined the cavalry
regiment of Arthur Goodwin, Hampden's friend, late in July as
sergeant major. He was also given the command of a troop as captain
a month later, on August 27, and remained with the regiment as both
until January 8 and as captain until March 24, 1643, presumably
taking part with the regiment (which was part of Essex's army) in
engagements at Daventry, Marlborough, Wantage, and Brill. This
campaigning gave him the chance to appear among horsemen again,
and it was considerably better paid than that in the Low Countries
had been. When he was both sergeant-major and captain, his net pay
was £8.8s.0d. a week. It would have been £3.10s.0d. more a week had
he supplied his own horse, as captains were supposed to do. Instead,
he paid the deduction and rode a government horse.

Both Sir Sigismond and his brother, Henry, grew to be very old
men living, as they thought, on the edge of starvation. Sir Sigismond
pleaded with Cromwell for relief in August, 1654. He wrote of "being
fill'd with many infirmities and weaknes of old age" and of being

"reduced to extremity of poverty and want, yea to such necessity that he is ashamed to expresse it, and without speedy supply must inevitably perish.'' He wrote that his pension was no longer paid. In his service under Essex, he said, he had used £4,000 of his own money to pay his troop, and the arrears of his salary came to £3,000. Whatever the truth of the rest of his plea, this last was the cry of a foolish fond old man fourscore and upwards. Cromwell's men had the records searched and found that Sir Sigismond had actually been overpaid for his soldiering by £306.11s.0d. Yet they, too, like the King before them, decided to relieve him. They gave him a pension of 20s. a week beginning May 10, 1655, little more than half his royal one, but they saw to it that it was paid.[74] Henry Zinzan made a similar plea. Because he "hath been allwayes faithfull to the Parlam^t and yor Highness,'' that is, Cromwell, "and is a very aged man, being 92 yeares of age, and reduced to a very great want and misery, being ready to perish,'' he asked for "such allowance as may preserve him from starving, during the short remaynder of his dayes (wch cannot be many).'' He, too, got 20s. a week, beginning February 22, 1656.[75]

Little more than a year after the Restoration, on July 16, 1661, the restored King restored Sir Sigismond's pension of £100 a year because of "his long service and Great Age.'' It was to recommence at Christmas, 1660—Sir Sigismond, that is, was to have a half year of it at once—and it was now for life rather than the royal pleasure. But it was too late. He died about then, probably over ninety years old, and it was his daughter, Letticia, his administratrix, who collected his £50.[76]

It is worth noting the both Puritans and Royalists were willing to help Sir Sigismond Zinzan, and that Royalists were the more generous, though they could easily have despised him as a traitor to their cause. Neither could have thought it remarkable that he had for a time owned the Globe or soldiered in the Low Countries and England. But perhaps neither could have thought it right that the more notable of the two best professional equestrian sportsmen of a vanished age in England should end his days in misery.

A person to be noted, finally, in the history of the Globe is George Archer, a porter who was born in 1562 or 1563. He was Sir Matthew Brend's rent gatherer in Southwark, had probably been Bodley's before that, and, since he was in the house in St. Peter's Hill when Nicholas Brend died there in 1601, may have been his as well. He lived in one of the Brend houses in Maid Lane from 1602, if not before, perhaps in the one "conteyning three severall roomes with a yard" that he occupied there on a lease from Sir Matthew in January, 1636.[77] He surely collected rents at the Globe, possibly for much of its history. The acquittances the Burbages and their associates received, therefore, probably bundles of them, bore this signature:

APPENDIX

The list below is to document my remarks in the text about tilting and other martial games, not to be a comprehensive statement about such things. I try, however, to give all the principal tilts and other martial games from 1598 to 1624 and most of the primary sources where the names of those who took part are preserved. I also give evidence for all the payments the Exchequer made to the Zinzans for tilting (expressed as call numbers of documents at the P.R.0.), but only one piece of evidence for each payment; there are several pieces for most of them. John Nichols printed the lists of those who joined in many martial games of Jacobean times in his *The Progresses...of King James the First* (London, 1828). His remarks are not without omissions and mistakes, but he used and cited most of the primary materials. When John Chamberlain happened to write a letter shortly after a tilt, he usually included an informal, sometimes abbreviated, list of participants and these lists, too, are in print; see *The Letters of John Chamberlain*, ed. N. E. McClure (Philadelphia, 1939).

1571-91 (Tilts in which Robert Zinzan appeared)—College of Arms, MS M.4, the unnumbered leaves at the beginning and f.3, 31, 33, 34, 36, 37, 38, 40; B.L., Cotton, Titus, C, X, f.16.

1598, November 17, 19—College of Arms, MS M.4, f.53, 54; B.L., Add. 12,514, f.154.

1599, November 19, 21—College of Arms, MS M.4, f.55; *Letters and Memorials of State*, ed. Arthur Collins (London, 1746), II, 142.

1600, November 17, 19—College of Arms, MS M.4, f.57, 58; B.L., Egerton 2804, f.128, 129.

1601, November 17?—H.M.C., *Salisbury*, XI, 540; B.L., Add. 10,110, f.68ᵛ.

1602, November 17, 20—B.L., Harl. 5826, f.361ᵛ, 128; Add. 10,110, f.67ᵛ, 68, 68ᵛ(2); Chamberlain, I, 172; *Diary of John Manningham*, ed. John Bruce (London: Camden Soc., 1867), pp. 86-87.

1603, June 27 (at Grafton)—*The Diary of the Lady Anne Clifford*, ed. V. Sackville-West (London, 1923), p. 10.

1604, March 24—No list, but see *C.S.P., Ven., 1603-07*, p. 141.

1605, March 24—B.L., Add. 38,139, f.192; H.M.C., *Salisbury*, XVII, 107; *Memorials and Affairs of State*, ed. Edmund Sawyer (London, 1725), II, 54.

1606, January 6—Ben Jonson, *Hymenaei*, in *The Complete Masques*, ed. Stephen Orgel (New Haven: Yale University Press, 1969), pp. 75-106, 476-77.

1606, March 24—Chamberlain, I, 217-18; *Memorials and Affairs of State*, II, 205.

1607, March 24—B.L., Cotton, Vesp., C, XIV, A-J, f.180.

1608, March 24—No list, but see *C.S.P., Ven., 1607-10*, p. 116.

1609, March 24—B.L., Stowe 171, f.6.

1610, January 6—B.L., Stowe 574, f.44-45ᵛ; Cotton, Vesp., C, XIV, L-W, f.285; Edmund Howes, *The Abridgement of the English Chronicle* (London, 1611), pp. 495-96; Chamberlain, II, 266-70; Jonson, *Prince Henry's Barriers* in *The Complete Masques*, pp. 142-58.

1610, March 27—B.L., Add. 14,417, f.4; E.403/2561/f.279ᵛ.

1610, June 10—H.M.C., *Downshire*, II, 317; *Memorials and Affairs of State*, III, 179.

1611, March 25—B.L., Add. 14,417, f.23; E.403/2561/f.297.

1612, March 24—B.L., Egerton 2804, f.207; Chamberlain, I, 342; S.O.3/5/March 1612. (The Egerton MS is a letter dated only March 26; "1613" is added in a later hand, but the news in the letter belongs to 1612, such as remarks about Lord Willoughby's military schemes [cf. Chamberlain, I, 342] and the illness of the lord treasurer [the Earl of Salisbury], who died in May, 1612, and was not replaced until July, 1614.)

1613, March 24—B.L., Harl. 1368, f.44; Chamberlain, I, 440; E.403/2601/f.103ᵛ.

1614, January 1—B.L., Harl. 5176, f.217; Chamberlain, I, 498; Jonson, *A Challenge at Tilt* in *The Complete Masques*, pp. 198-205; S.O.3/5/Dec. 1613 (first item).

1614, March 24?—B.L., Harl. 5176, f.218ᵛ; E.403/2602/f.16. (The Harleian MS gives the impresa each participant used, Sir Sigismond "Dum placeo pereo" and Henry Zinzan "My sufferan [i.e., sovereign] remedy.")

1615, March 24—B.L., Harl. 5176, f.220ᵛ; Harl. 1368, f.45; Chamberlain, I, 590; S.O.3/6/March 1615.

1616, March 25—B.L., Harl. 5176, f.221; Harl. 1368, p. 46; College of Arms, MS M.4, f.58ᵛ; Chamberlain, I, 617; E.403/2602/f.72ᵛ.

1616, November 6—Thomas Middleton, *Civitas Amor* (London, 1616), sigs. B4ᵛ-C.

1617, Accession Day—No tilt; see Chamberlain, II, 67.

1618, March 24—B.L., Harl. 5176, f.229; Chamberlain, II, 152; S.O.3/6/March 1618.

1619, Accession Day—No tilt; see Chamberlain, II, 225.

1620, March 24—College of Arms, MS 2.M.3, f.2^v; B.L., Add. 12,514, f.158, 158^v, 169^v; Chamberlain, II, 298; E.403/2602/f.170^v.

1621, March 24—College of Arms, MS 2.M.3, f.7; B.L., Add. 12,514, f.164, 165, 166, 167; Harl. 5176, f.242^v; Chamberlain, II, 359; S.O.3/7/March 1621.

1622, scheduled for March 24 but postponed to May 18 and perhaps abandoned— B.L., Add. 12,514, f.126, 125^v, 130, 163, 168; Chamberlain, II, 428, 430, 433; E.403/2562/f.55^v.

1623, Acccession Day—No tilt; see Chamberlain, II, 487.

1624, postponed and not yet run on April 2—B.L., Add. 12,514, f.128; *The Works of the Most Reverend Father in God, William Laud, D. D.*, ed. James Bliss (Oxford, 1853), III, 150; *C.S.P., Ven., 1623-25*, p. 268; E.403/2562/f.112. (The list is undated, but Buckingham is given as duke, a rank he acquired in May, 1623, and the man given as Lord Cromwell became Viscount Lecale in November, 1624.)

I have not included several relatively informal martial games for which the lists of participants are incomplete and contain only the names of a few great nobles, not the Zinzans. Three were performed for the amusement of the King of Denmark in August, 1606: running at the ring on the 4th and tilting on the next two days. Another is a challenge to a tilt to be run within forty days of June 1, 1606, also for the King of Denmark, which apparently began as and remained a purely literary thing. The last is a tilt on January 8, 1621, to show a new French ambassador "the pastime." See Henry Roberts, *Englands Farewell to Christian the fourth, famous King of Denmarke* (London, 1606), sigs. B4, B4^v; John Stow and Edmund Howes, *The Annales* (London, 1615), p. 886; William Drummond of Hawthornden, *The Works* (Edinburgh, 1711), pp. 231-34; *The Autobiography and Correspondence of Sir Simonds D'Ewes, Bart.*, ed. J. 0. Halliwell (London, 1845), p. 166.

NOTES

* Originally published in *The Third Globe*, ed. C. Walter Hodges, S. Schoenbaum, Leonard Leone (Detroit, 1981), pp. 29-57, 241-48.

1. See Braines, pp. 28-29; G.E. Bentley, *The Jacobean and Caroline stage* (Oxford, 1968), VI, 200; Chambers, II, 374-75, 428, 431, 433; Sidney Fisher, *The Theatre the Curtain & the Globe* (Montreal: McGill Univ. Library, 1964), pp. 6-8, and a paper presented to the theatre history seminar at the meeting of the Shakespeare Association of America held in Toronto, 1978, "Shakespeare's London and Graphical Archaeology," pp. 6-9 (Mr. Fisher finds that maps support his view, but he uses only a few of them). The documents are C.5/448/137, the bill (1675); C.6/245/25, answer of Francis Brend (1682.); C.7/616/26 (1703); C.9/320/16, the bill (1704); C.5/338/35 (1707). The dubious ms. is now at the Folger (Phillipps 11613).

2. D&H 9, 11-13, 16, 17, 24, 25, 29-31, 33, 35, 37-40, 42-45, 47, 50, 51b. Both exceptions are curious. One (D&H 32) is evidently a copy taken from an unfinished plate, and the other (D&H 51a) is one of six crude maps of English cities published c.1700 with many skillful engravings of English buildings (the

maps of Canterbury and Colchester show nunneries as apparently still functioning). See also *The Survey of London*, XXII, 70.

3. D&H 10, 14, 15, 21; 18-20, 26, 27 (the first four are those discussed in the text). No. 18 is to a scale too small for the engraver to show a playhouse clearly, but a tiny blob on the south side of Maid Lane may be another attempt to show the Globe. No. 35 is attributed to Hollar but is almost certainly not his work.

4. D&H 9-13, 15-17, 24, 25, 32, 37, 38, 50, 51a. No. 50 also shows a rectangular "Bare garde*n*" east of Maid Lane, near St. Saviour's.

5. D&H 14, 16 (2nd and 3rd edns.), 17 (2nd edn.), 24, 26 (1st edn.), 40, 43, 51b.

6. C.54/450/m.50; /462/m.36, 38, 43(2); /468/#25; /499/#29; /500; /504/#32 (the site of the Globe); /505/m.18-20, 13; /516/m.34; /518/m.9; /522/m.36-37, 37-38; /527/m.46; /550/m.21; /559/m.22; /597/#39; /624/#29, 30; /646/#67; /652/#12; /665/#33; /680/#58; /703/#55; /812/m.27; /859/m.22; /1080/m.15; /1112/m.34; /1123/m.28; /1151/m.21-22; /1217/m.1; /1273/m.31; /1274/m.6; /1337/m.30; /1347/m.8; /1382/m.9; /1613/m.25.

7. St.Ch.5/L.27/19, interrogatories (second last list) nos. 5, 10; Ilderton nos. 1, 2(where the allusion to Mr. Cawkett is), 3, 5, 7, 10.

8. A Humphrey Collet, bowyer of Southwark, died in Dec., 1558, having various unnamed married children and, presumably unmarried, Thomas (eldest son), Robert, and Nicholas. He owned property on both sides of the high street and, among other places, in Newington. Another Humphrey, also a bowyer of Southwark and son of Humphrey, bowyer, deceased, died childless in Jan., 1567, having brothers John, Thomas, Nicholas, and others (no Robert). See PROB.11/42A/f.122ᵛ-23ᵛ, /49/f.8ᵛ-9. The Collets who had to do with the Brends must have been related to these, and perhaps the first Humphrey was their father (in her will, Thomas Brende's daughter, Judith, wrote that John Collet had a sister, Mercy Pattenson, who could have been his wife's sister rather than his own). Bodley explained his relationship with the Brends and hinted at Collet's: WARD 9/94/f.632. In their wills Thomas Brende called Bodley son-in-law and Judith called him brother. Thomas Brende called Collet cousin. The matter is fully explained in a visitation taken in 1623: *Visitations of Surrey in 1530, 1572, and 1623*, ed. W. Bruce Bannerman (London: Harleian Soc., 1899), p. 147.

9. PROB.11/93/f.270ᵛ-71ᵛ. See also Nicholas's will, /98/f.325ᵛ-26ᵛ; Mercy Frobisher's deposition of Feb. 4, 1623 (where she gives her age as 50): C.24/496/#114; and a lawsuit of her husband's: C.2/Jas.I/C.17/44.

10. C.54/1273/m.31.

11. St.Ch.5/L.27/19, interrogatories (second last list) no. 1; /L.43/11, Brende no. 1; C.54/1151/m.21-22. In the first document, John Whythorne described him as "one Brende of Toowe Lane in London Scryven*or*" (no. 3-7). The signature reads, "*per* me Thom*a*m Brende." Four other signatures survive, all dated July 18, 1562 and all spelled "Brende": C.54/450/m.50; /462/m.36, 43(2).

12. At about the same time, in 1582 and 1583, a William Brende bought a lease from the Lord Admiral: C.54/1141/m.43; /1194/m.10. This Brende's financier in 1572 was Thomas Cure, who two decades later financed the Swan: /892/m.25.

13. Much information about Brende and his family comes from this inscription. The rest of it reads: "Here lyeth bvried the body of Thomas Brende of

Westmolsey Esqvire who had by his two wives eighteene children videlicit by Margerie his first wife foure son*n*es & six davghters who dyed the second of Ivne 1564. by Mercie his last wife he had fovre sonnes and fower davghters she left her life the xiij of April 1597 and lyeth here bvried he... left one son*n*e and five davghters at his death.'' V.C.H., *Surrey*, III, 455, mistakenly attributes his doings to a father and son. He did have a son and heir named Thomas in 1570 (C.66/1069/m.2), but by 1583 Nicholas was his son and heir (C.54/1151/m.21). He also had a brother named Thomas Brend, alive in 1599, whom he and his daughter, Judith, mentioned in their wills. That his doings belong to only one man is clear from a) the five signatures, 1562(4), 1578, which were written by the same person, those of 1562 cancelling loans made by Thomas Brende, citizen and scrivener of London, in 1547-48, and b) the history of two properties, the manor of Gloverswick and the advowson of Walkern. A Thomas Brende, citizen and scrivener of London, bought each in the 1560's, and the purchaser sold each in 1587, the first as citizen and scrivener of London who had a wife named Mercy, the second as citizen and writer of the court letter of London who had a wife, Mercy, and lived in a house in St. Peter's Hill. See C.54/624/#30; /646/#67; /1274/m.6; /1273/m.31.

14. They were certainly married by May 20, 1595, when Lady Jane Townsend (who obviously knew of the marriage) described George Sayers as a brotherinlaw to ''my cousin Margaret Brend'': H.M.C., *Salisbury*, V, 214. Moreover Nicholas Brend's sister, Mercy, said on Feb. 4, 1623, that she had known his wife for twenty-eight or twenty-nine years. She added that when Nicholas died his children were of the following ages: Jane five or six years, Mercy about four, Frances about three, and John a half or quarter year. See C.24/496/#114, nos. 1, 7.

15. The will is PROB.11/93/f.270^v-71^v; the remark was made by a neighbor, Francis Drake, in May, 1607: C.24/333/pt.2/#36, interrogatory no. 5.

16. Who Margaret's parents were is a puzzle. Her senior Brend grandson said in 1662 that she was the daughter of Sir William Plummer, and a person of the name was knighted as of Surrey in 1616: *Visitation of Surrey, 1662-68*, ed. Sir George J. Armytage (London: Harleian Soc., 1910), p. 14; W. A. Shaw, *Knights of England* (London, 1906), II, 159. Her senior Zinzan grandson, however, said in 1665 that she was the daughter of Sir Philip Strelley of Strelley in Notts., and a person of that name was knighted as of Leicester in 1603: *The Four Visitations of Berkshire*, I, 320; Shaw, II, 103. A Henry Strelley is described by others as her brother and Sir Sigismond's brother in-law, and by himself as uncle to her children; and a Mary Strelley described herself as aunt to those children: S.P.16/256/#1/f.13, 19, 22; H.M.C., *11th Report*, pt. 7, p. 159. Yet it must have been this Mary Strelley who in testifying for Margaret and her second husband in Jan., 1623, gave herself as daughter of Humphrey Strelley of Strelley in Notts.: C.24/496/#114. Lord Stanhope and his sister, Lady Jane Townsend, were nephew and niece to an Anna Strelley: *Visitations of...Nottingham...1569 and 1614*, ed. George W. Marshall (London: Harleian Soc., 1871), pp. 7-8, 19-22.

17. H.M.C., *Salisbury*, V, 214; Chambers, I, 63-65. An antagonist of hers asserted at the end of her life that her brother, Henry Strelley, had been more a servant to her next husband than an equal, an assertion that husband vigorously denied: S.P.16/256/#1/f.22-23.

18. So Thomas Brende's inquisition post mortem reads, and it agrees with the funeral inscription that he died on Sept. 21, 1598: C.142/257/#68. His will is PROB.11/93/f.270ᵛ-71ᵛ.

19. C.54/1612/m.22(2).

20. Sir John Bodley made the remark in 1621-22: WARD 9/94/f.631ᵛ-32. The description of the property before the Globe was built is from the lease, recited in K.B.27/1454/m.692 (see Braines, p. 17, and Chambers, II, 416-17). Thomas Brende's inquisition post mortem reads that there were forty tenants in the property.

21. C.54/1682/m.11 and /1722/m.7 (both of 1601); /1947/#5 (of 1608); #2471/#15 (of 1622); /2594/#15 (of 1624). For Hendrik Sturman, see also /3063/#18.

22. PROB.11/93/f.270ᵛ-71ᵛ, 298ᵛ-99.

23. C.54/1674/m.26.

24. 0ne of the two copies of Nicholas Brend's inquisition post mortem reads that Matthew was one year, eight months, and six days old when Nicholas died on Oct. 12, 1601, and Matthew himself said so in June 1621, adding that he had come of age the previous February: C.142/271/#151; E.112/126/179, Matthew's reply. The other copy reads that he was one year old and the words following are perished: WARD 7/26/134. The decree in the Court of Wards, however, reads that he was only eight months and six days old—thereby perhaps qualifying the matter more obviously for that court in the winter of 1621-22, since with that birthdate Matthew would have been a minor until Feb. 1622: WARD 9/94/f.632.

25. How Bodley (whose accounting this is) arrived at £2,150 is unclear. After Nicholas's death, he discovered additional debts of £237, and the repairs cost him nearly £300. Hence Nicholas's indebtedness should have been some £2,265. The heir, Matthew, eventually argued that his father's debts totalled only £1,865. See Nicholas's deathbed mortgages and allied documents: C.54/1722/m.7 (Oct. 7, containing a list of the debts Nicholas could remember, for £1,478), /1705/m.26 (Oct. 8), /1682/m.11 (Oct. 10); and a summary of Matthew's lawsuit against Bodley of 1621-22: WARD 9/94/f.631ᵛ-33. For the place of Nicholas's death, see C.24/496/#114, Archer no. 2, and for its date, the lawsuit and inquisition post mortem (C.142/271/#151). His will is PROB.11/98/f.325ᵛ-26ᵛ, proved by his widow on Nov. 6, 1601.

26. Whatever was realized above the amount necessary for portions and maintenance was to be divided between the widow and John. This was the only provision made for him. Bodley was able to give his own second daughter, Jane (aged 7 in 1623) £3,000 when she married Robert Brocas in 1638: C.8/77/80 and *Visitations of Surrey in...1623*, p. 147.

27. So John Brend eventually said, informed, perhaps (as Matthew Brend thought), by Bodley: C.2/Chas.I/B.153/39, bill and answer.

28. C.54/1947/#5 and some of Bodley's and Collet's remarks in the lawsuit of 1621-22: WARD 9/94/f.632ᵛ.

29. C.54/1721/m.21-22(3)

30. To stop these proceedings, Drake launched a lawsuit in Chancery of which I have found only three orders together with some interrogatories and two depositions for Drake: C.33/109/f.535 and /113/f.153, 183; C.24/333/pt.2/#36.

The Zinzans filed a demurrer in reply to Drake's bill. In May, 1606, Drake got the court to stop the case at common law until they should answer directly, and when they did that in Nov., 1607, he got it stopped until Chancery should hear the case. His interrogatories belong to May, 1607, and his depositions to Jan. and May, 1608. That there seem to be no more orders suggests either that the Zinzans abandoned the matter or that they settled it privately with Drake. Drake argued that the Lord Admiral had repaid the loan by giving Brende timber from the manor of Esher.

31. They were certainly married by May 21, 1606, when as her husband Zinzan acquired an interest in the estates of her father-in-law and previous husband: PROB.11/93/f.271^v. Zinzan said on Feb. 14, 1625, that he had made a payment on behalf of his stepson, Matthew Brend, twenty years before, C.2/Chas.I/Z.1/17, the bill.

32. So Matthew Brend said on Jan. 12, 1625, in response to a lawsuit of his brother's that had nothing to do with Zinzan: C.2/Chas.1/B.153/39, the answer. Three weeks later, Zinzan said in another lawsuit that because his wife had no jointure with which she might support her children after Nicholas's death, the Court of Wards gave her control in her own right, rather than in trust for the heir, of the Brend properties (presumably those not committed to Bodley) during the heir's minority: /B.126/62, the answer. That she could then raise £1,000 from Brend lands to bestow on Zinzan suggests that she brought the family a portion when she married Nicholas and so was entitled eventually to a jointure or new portion from them. That Matthew Brend did not tax Zinzan with the portion money suggests that his mother received a reasonable jointure for it.

33. Once, at least, Sir Sigismond took an active interest in collecting his stepdaughters' portions from Bodley, when in Lent, 1621, he discussed the matter with Bodley: C.24/496/#114, Fellowes, no. 2. His grandson, Henry, certified the list of children in March, 1665, together with the names of most of their wives or husbands: *The Four Visitations of Berkshire*, I, 320. For the two Strelleys, see S.P.16/256/#1/f.13, 22-23, and Mary's deposition (which accompanies that of Fellowes) in which on Jan. 31, 1623, she said she was 30 years old. Sir Sigismond's more remote descendants seem to have thought he had an additional son: Charles Coates, *The History and Antiquities of Reading* (London, 1802) pp. 445-46. His uncle, Andrew Zinzan of Reading, mentioned several of the sons in his will (March 14, 1622): PROB.11/148/f.196-96^v.

34. Sir Sigismond's grandchildren called themselves Zinzano throughout one part of an extensive lawsuit but Zinzan before and after, and his uncle, Andrew, was buried as Zinzano in 1625 but had drawn his will as Zinzan: C.7/328/113; /392/23; C.8/341/208; /465/40; Coates, p. 229; and PROB.11/148/f.196-96^v. See also Anthony Wood, *Athenae Oxoniensis* (London, 1721), I, 625.

35. He gave himself as fifty years old on Jan. 24, 1598, and wrote on July 3, 1593, of his 35 "painful years of service" to the Queen. Giving himself as of Walton, he declared his will orally on Sept. 21, 1607; his widow, Margaret, proved it on Jan. 27, 1608, and his son, Henry, succeeded to one of his offices on Dec. 21, 1607. See Req.2/183/62 (where there are three of his signatures); H.M.C., *Salisbury*, XIII, 268, 282 (and E.403/2559/f.225); Shaw, II, 116; PROB.11/111/f.5^v; S.O.3/3/Dec.1607. His royal gifts are recorded among the

patent rolls and state papers (see esp. *C.S.P.*, *Dom.*, *1591-94*, pp. 359, 483, and *1595-97*, p. 304), occasionally in lawsuits (see esp. St.Ch.5/Z.1/1, the bill, from which the quotation comes).

36. Zenzant owned a farm at Parkbury, near St. Albans, in 1547; Sir Robert and probably his brothers, Alexander and Andrew, were of St. Albans respectively in 1588 and after, 1586, and 1607, though Andrew was of Reading when he died in 1625: Req.2/8/143 and /19/40; V.C.H., *Herts.*, III, 92, 94; *Marriages Licences Issued by the Bishop of London* (London: Harleian Soc., 1887), I, 148, 172; *C.S.P.*, *Dom.*, *1603-10*, pp. 145, 157; C.54/1906/m.21.

37. A list of the horsemen who served the late King James includes Sir Sigismond, Henry, Andrew, and Robert Zinzan (a yeoman): H.M.C., *6th Report*, pp. 324-26. It omits Alexander (whose place was filled by John Prichard in Jan. 1626) and Richard (who had the reversion of Andrew's place). See *C.S.P.*, *Dom.*, *1598-1601*, p. 216; *1611-18*, p. 28; *1623-25*, p. 295; *1625-26*, p. 558; *1635*, pp. 134, 492; C.54/2949/#21 and /3169/#26 (for Henry's two sons and wife, Elizabeth); and H.M.C., *5th Report*, pp. 57-58, 116 (for Joseph, who in 1643 wanted to site his school in the stable and yard of Winchester House, not far from the deserted Globe). An Alexander Zinzan was the King's servant in 1553: *Calendar of Patent Rolls*, *1569-72*, nos. 1108, 3328. For Evelyn (who was first cousin to Bodley's wife), see E.S. deBeer's edn. of the *Diary* (Oxford, 1955), I, 10&n., 54.

38. Charles Rogers, *Memorials of the Earl of Stirling and of the House of Alexander* (Edinburgh, 1877), II, 172-78, where, however, some details are wrong. Henry Alexander married Mary Vanlore in December, 1637, and became third earl in 1640; Henry Zinzan alias Alexander married Jacoba Vanlore before 1635 (his eldest son was twenty-eight years old in March 1665): *C.S.P.*, *Dom.*, *1635*, p. 566 and *1637-38*, p. 496; *The Four Visitations of Berkshire*, I, 320. Sir Sigismond's youngest son, Charles, eventually settled in Leith: C.10/159/187.

39. On Feb. 4, 1623, Mercy Brend Frobisher said that she had known Sir Sigismond for twenty-five or twenty-six years: C.24/496/#114, no. 1. His brother, Henry, is regularly mentioned first in both their father's and uncle's wills and in 1638 described himself as heir: PROB.11/111/f.5^v; /148/f.196-96^v; C.54/3169/#26. Henry was born in 1563 or 1564, for on Feb. 22, 1656, he said he was ninety-two years old: *C.S.P.*, *Dom.*, *1655-56*, p. 197. Sigismond's knighting is not recorded, but it took place between 1601, when he is mentioned as unknighted, and March 24, 1605, from which time he is invariably mentioned as a knight: H.M.C., *Salisbury*, XI, 540; XVII, 107.

40. A description of the tilt of 1581 (May 15-16) was printed in Robert Walgrave's *The Tryumphe Shewed before the Quene and the Ffrenche Embassadors* and that of 1590 in George Peele's *Polyhymnia*. See Chambers, III, 402; IV, 63-64.

41. E.101/435/15; *The Letters of John Chamberlain*, II, 298; H.M.C., *Rutland*, IV, 494, 508.

42. See Appendix.

43. Before 1610 the Zinzans could have received payments out of one of the branches of the royal household, whose payments are not so well recorded as those of the Exchequer. Rogers (II, 175) cited "the Warrant Book of the Exchequer," II, 141, as recording that the Zinzans were paid £100 for the Accession Day tilt of 1608, but I cannot identify the book nor find any other

indication that they received such a payment out of the Exchequer in 1608. Nichols (II, 287n.; III, 78n.) reported that the Zinzans received additional payments of £1,000 in 1614 and 1615, appparently out of the Exchequer, but I cannot verify these payments in the records of the Exchequer, either.

44. H.M.C., Cowper, I, 195, 199. Sir Thomas Somerset (1612), Lord North (1612), Lord Hay (1618), the Earl of Montgomery (1620), and the Earl of Oxford (1624) were seriously hurt practicing for tilts.

45. *The Funerals of the High and Mighty Prince Henry* (London, 1613), sigs. B2, B3.

46. At least fifteen signatures of Henry Zinzan survive because several of the issue books survive of the teller who paid his annuities: E.36/134/pp.53ᵛ (*sic*), 172 (where this one occurs); E.405/548-51. Sir Sigismond's signature is from his petition to the House of Lords (see below). Four others purport to be his, but none is genuine. Three are in the hands of the clerks who wrote the documents to which they belong and not Sir Sigismond's: E.406/47/f.41, 47ᵛ, 154. One is in the same hand as two others at the end of a petition; each of the three has been traced over by another hand holding another pen, possibly those of the purported signer who when he came to sign the document found that a scrivener had already signed for him: S.P.18/73/#34. The coat of arms as reported in 1665 by Sir Sigismond's son, Henry, is shown in black and white, but with colors indicated, in *Four Visitations of Berkshire*, I, 320, and is described, the color of the estoile mistaken, in Sir Bernard Burke, *The General Armoury* (London, 1884), p. 1153 (see also "Alexander" on p. 10). For the crest, see *Fairbairn's Book of Crests of the Families of Great Britain and Ireland* (London, 1905), I, 611; II, pl. 94, no. 2.

47. The quotation is from an undated note among the Lord Keeper Egerton's papers about a case in the Star Chamber: H.M.C., *11th Report*, pt. VII, 159. For the fines, see E.159/440/Easter 9 Jas.I/m.256. In 1633 Strelley was a Brend tenant on seventy acres in Walton: C.54/2985/#6.

48. So Matthew Brend asserted in 1625, offering chapter and verse: C.2/Chas.I/Z.1/17, the answer.

49. Shaw, II, 165.

50. WARD 9/94/f.631ᵛ-33; C.54/2471/#15. Another result of Matthew's coming of age was that Sir Sigismond's brother, Henry, living as their father had done in Walton, sued Sir Matthew in the summer of 1621 about a house and some sixty-four acres near Walton Common. Henry argued that the properties belonged to him but that the Brends had appropriated them about three years before. Had he sued a few months earlier, of course, the defendant would have been Sir Sigismond. See E.112/126/179.

51. Shaw, II, 178.

52. The lawsuit survives as a replication dated merely Easter (C.2/Chas.I/Z.1/6), interrogatories and depositions (taken between Jan. 24 and Feb. 4, 1623) for the Brends (C.24/496/#114), and various decrees and orders (see below).

53. When Sir Matthew and Sir Sigismond came to sue one another about Dame Margaret's dower rights and their ramifications (C.2/Chas.I/B.126/62 and /Z.1/17) it was not in Sir Matthew's interest to admit that the first arrangement existed, nor was that arrangement of first importance to Sir Sigismond. So what one knows about it derives from allusions, sometimes confused, in Sir

Sigismond's parts of the lawsuits. He and Sir Matthew both described the new arrangement and the trouble it caused. See Sir Matthew's bill of Dec.3? 1624 (the day begins "tr" and is then illegible); Sir Sigismond's answer of Feb. 4, 1625, and his bill of Feb. 14, 1625; Sir Matthew's undated answer. Sir Matthew also alluded to the matter in his answer of Jan. 12, 1625, to his brother's lawsuit about something else: C.2/Chas.I/B.153/39.

54. C.54/2594/#15. I quote the description of the property above. The rent for the land on which the Globe stood was still £14.10s.0d. a year (it would eventually be £40). At twelve years purchase that land alone should have been worth £174.

55. Sir John Shelley was one of the original baronets in 1611. Two of his uncles were implicated in Catholic plots, one of whom was attainted though not hanged. Two of his great uncles were knights of St. John (one the last grand prior in England). See G.E.C., *The Complete Baronetage* (Exeter, 1900), I, and *D.N.B.* ("Sir Wm. Shelley" and "Sir Richard Shelley"), and the pedigree in the visitations of Sussex: *1530...1633-4*, ed. W. Bruce Bannerman (London: Harleian Soc., 1905), pp. 36-37, and *1662*, ed. A. W. Hughes Clarke (London: Harleian Soc., 1937), p. 99.

56. S.P.16/256/#1, a brochure of forty-four leaves in which the Zinzans' case was summarized in the early 1630's from what must have been massive documentation in the Star Chamber. The whole brochure is relevant, but see esp. f.1-4, 6-9, 14, 17, 19-20, 33, 36-38, 44. Because her parents were married in 1605 or a little after, the bride cannot have been more than eighteen years old and may have been a good deal less. One witness said that Sir Sigismond could have given between £600 and £700 with his daughter and another said a thousand marks (£666).

57. S.P.16/256/#1, f.15-16.

58. For Sir Sigismond, see S.P.14/168/#27, 28; S.P.84/118/f.172, 174, 176; /119/f.152ᵛ. For Sigismond the son, see *C.S.P., Ireland, 1647-60 and Addenda, 1625-60*, pp. 47-48, where in Feb., 1625, he is said to have served as a lieutenant in the Palatinate. For Henry Strelley (who served under the Earl of Lincoln), see S.P.16/256/#1, f.23. One of Sir Sigismond's men was apparently Shackerley Marmion, author of *Holland's Leaguer*, who found advancement under him slow and soon returned to England: Anthony Wood, I, 625.

59. See Sir John Coke's notes of Sir Matthew's and Sir Sigismond's lawsuits: H.M.C., *Cowper*, I, 185.

60. Brend's figure is my extrapolation drawn from an exchange between him and Bodley in their lawsuit of 1621-22. Bodley said that the properties in Southwark were worth £90 a year and those in Bread Street and Southwark together £160. Brend argued that the two groups of properties were worth £400. Though Brend won the case, the Court seems to have sided with Bodley in such matters, as Brend thought. See WARD 9/94/f.631ᵛ-32. In two contracts of Oct., 1601, Brend's dying father agreed with Bodley that the Southwark properties were worth £90 a year: C.54/1682/m.11 and /1722/m.7.

61. *C.S.P., Dom., 1623-25*, p. 490; S.P.16/256/#1, f.19, 20, 30, 42; E.159/466/Hil. 3 Chas.I/32/62-64. See also House of Lords, Papers 27 Feb.-10 March, 1641, f.113.

62. The decrees and orders for Sir Matthew's case are (in the A books)

C.33/147/f.932^v; /149/f.537, 936-36^v; /151/f.485^v, 528. Bodley said on Feb. 8, 1625, that Sir Matthew had made him defend three lawsuits in Chancery about the matter, one of which was probably John Brend's. The Court ordered that if Lady Zinzan had consented to the lawsuit Sir Sigismond should pay part of the costs. Sir Matthew asserted that she had, and he suggested that all five plaintiffs should pay £2 each (John Brend had dissociated himself from the case).

63. The case survives as a bill and answer: C.2/Chas.I/B.153/39; and decrees and orders (in the A books): C.33/147/f.183^v, 508, 552, 665, 949; /149/f.391, 476, 537, 818; /151/f.31, 337, 1097, 1320; /153/f.52^v. It became a question of how the interest should be calculated on money Bodley got for the properties sold to raise portions. Should his disbursements and expenses come first from the principal (so reducing the interest) or first from the interest (so that the principal continued to produce interest)? The Court decided the latter on June 10, 1625, but two years later ordered a judge and master of the Court to review the question while negotiating a final settlement with John Brend and Bodley. The gross sum at stake was £230.2s.0d. Eventually Bodley seems to have had to pay £30 each to Brend and his mother's estate, which is to say Sir Sigismond, whom the Court excluded from collecting his part, presumably because he was still an outlaw.

64. C.54/2690/#84, a performance bond for £1,200, dated Dec. 11, 1626. Usually such bonds were for twice the amount borrowed. The lender was Hilary Mempris, to whom Sir Matthew's brother, John, had been apprenticed.

65. She was mentioned on Jan. 29, 1627, as alive: C.33/151/f.528. She left no will, and the administration of her goods was granted to her husband on June 20, 1627: PROB.6/12/f.151^v.

66. C.54/2985/#6 (June 20).

67. S.P.16/135/#39; E.403/2565/f.152. It is not known whether he served with military enterprises abroad after Sept., 1626. The four regiments were to be withdrawn in Nov., 1626. He was one of the commanders proposed in Feb., 1625, for service in Ireland (*C.S.P., Ireland, 1647-60, and Addenda, 1625-60*, p. 47), where evidently he did not go. He does not appear in Henry Hexham's books about the siege of Bois-le-duc in 1629, the campaigns of 1632, or the siege of Breda in 1637, though many Englishmen do: *A Historicall Relation of the Famous Siege of the Busse* (Delft, 1630), *A Journal of the taking in of Venlo*, etc. (The Hague, 1633), and *A True and Brief Relation of the Famous Siege of Breda* (Delft, 1637).

68. E.403/2567/f.7^v-8 (dated Dec. 14, 1632). Two of his assignments are recorded: E.406/47/f.41, 154 (July 18, 1633, and Feb. 9, 1636).

69. S.P.15/43/f.295 (undated). In 1654 Sir Sigismond claimed that he had received from Charles I not only his pension of £100 a year but a salary as equerry of almost as much (S.P.18/74/f.82). He certainly received his pension then (see, for example, E.403/1753/14 June 1639 and 10 Jan. 1640), but his salary then and earlier, unlike his brother's, must have been paid out of the royal household rather than the Exchequer directly. Henry had a patent in 1603 for £100 a year as equerry and another in 1607 for £10 a year as keeper of armor in the Tower (C.66/1624/m.3; /1737/m.4), and his payments are regularly recorded.

70. S.P.16/256/#1, f.30-38, 42-44.

71. *C.S.P.*, *Dom.*, *1635-36*, p. 250; *1636-37*, p. 105: E.405/548/f.102, etc.; House of Lords, Papers 27 Feb.-10 March, 1641, f.113; Shaw, II, 204. The marriage took place between Feb. 23 and Aug. 28, 1636. The lady was apparently the daughter of the Queen's nurse.

72. PROB.6/17/f.79 (Sir Wm. Shelley's admon. act, Nov. 22, 1639); PROB.11/182/f.44ᵛ-45 (Lady Shelley's will, dated at Paris Jan. 2/12, 1640, and proved at London on Jan. 28 by her executor in England, Sir James Vantelet, her father, not one of the Shelleys); E.405/550/Easter/f.9 (her father collected the last payment of her pension).

73. House of Lords, Papers 27 Feb.-10 March, 1641, f.113.

74. S.P.18/74/f.82 and attachment; E.403/2523/p.63 (July 19, 1655); *C.S.P.*, *Dom.*, *1659-60*, pp. 228, 587, 590; *Commons Journal*, IV, 179. Four Strelleys also joined Essex's army, including a Henry as lieutenant in John Gunter's troop of horse: *The List of the Army Raised under the Command of his Excellency, Robert Earle of Essex* (London, 1642).

75. S.P.18/124/#91; E.403/2608/p.40 (March 31, 1656).

76. E.403/2569/f.107ᵛ; /1761/f.39. A Mrs. Zinzan of Reading had a picture of him in 1809: Charles Coates, *A Supplement to the History and Antiquities of Reading* (Reading, 1809), sig. F4.

77. See his testimony for the Brends on Feb. 1, 1623 (where his signature appears): C.24/496/#114. He gave his age as sixty and his address as Maid Lane. He said he had known Sir Sigismond twenty and a half years, Dame Margaret twenty, and Bodley well for ten but by sight much longer. He also said he had delivered to the Zinzans, and got acquittances for, the quarterly sums Bodley contributed to the maintenance of the Brend children while Matthew was still a minor. Curiously, this remark and others of his pointedly did not make the case against Bodley that the Brends wanted him to make. Sir Sigismond said on Feb. 14, 1625, that Archer was Sir Matthew's rent gatherer and had delivered the two payments (at Midsummer and Michaelmas, 1624) meant as rent for the properties in Southwark: C.2/Chas.I/Z.1/17, the bill (see above). For Archer's house see Braines, p. 72n., and a contract by which Sir Matthew sold it and six others on Jan. 13, 1636: C.54/3063/#19.

The Late Lancashire
Witches / Act 2 · Sc. 1.

The Globe Bewitched
and *El Hombre Fiel**

We have no reviews of the thousands of productions that passed over the stages of Shakespearean playhouses. Nor have we many accounts otherwise of what happened in those playhouses on specific occasions, and of those that we do have none is very long or thorough. This silence about how plays were played and received is one of the most important ways in which our understanding of drama in Elizabethan, Jacobean, and Caroline times is sadly inferior to our understanding of drama in later times.

I have found an account of what happened at the Globe one afternoon in August, 1634. It is nearly four hundred words long and is virtually a little review. Nothing quite like it has appeared before. The play being performed was Thomas Heywood's and Richard Brome's *The Late Lancashire Witches*, as it is called in its printed version, and the man who saw and wrote about the production was Nathaniel Tomkyns.

His remarks provide a good deal of new information about a much-discussed play. They allow us, among other things, to hold a detailed, first-hand account of one of the King's Men's productions against a script licensed for printing less than eleven weeks after the production, and to see more clearly into its curious link with a famous event. Apart from writing this account, Tomkyns had other noteworthy brushes with drama and literature and one momentous brush with English history. He deserves to be remembered.

His account is among the Phelips papers now at the Somerset Record Office in Taunton. It is the last third of a letter that Tomkyns wrote from London on August 16, 1634, to "S^r," evidently Sir Robert Phelips, who was then at Montacute House in Somerset. The account has not appeared in literary history before because when surveying the Phelips papers for their *First Report* of 1870 and *Third Report* of 1872 the editors of the Historical Manuscripts Commission skipped over this letter along with many others.

Sir Robert's father, Sir Edward, had been master of the rolls and speaker of the House of Commons, and he had built Montacute House. Sir Robert had been head of the family at Montacute House since 1614. In the parliaments of the 1620s, he had been one of the leaders of the popular party and, in company with Sir Edward Coke, Sir Edwin Sandys, and Sir John Eliot, had outraged the King and his ministers repeatedly. He was also a magnate of his shire, and in 1634 he had been so for two decades. As one gathers from Tomkyns' letter, Phelips had recently written Tomkyns asking for information. Some men of Stoke-sub-Hamdon had been fined in the Somerset Assizes and had asked Phelips to help them get the fines reduced. Although Phelips had apparently agreed to help them, he did not really want the fines reduced. So he asked Tomkyns to tell him why he could not help the men. Stoke-sub-Hamdon is an easy walk from the west gate of Phelips' park, but its nearness was not its residents' reason for seeking Phelips' help. The Crown owned the manor of Stoke-sub-Hamdon, and Phelips was steward. Phelips turned to Tomkyns because he was an old friend who often corresponded with him and was also clerk to the council in London that managed the manor and many other pieces of royal property.[1]

Tomkyns gave Phelips several impressive reasons why the fines of "those ill neighbors of your's" could not be altered, adding, "I hold yor desire easie to be effected." His business finished, Tómkyns turned to current events that he thought might interest Phelips. He wrote shrewdly and rather lengthily about the Attorney General, William Noy, who had died recently (August 9). He concluded these remarks by alluding to a celebrated former attorney general, "yor grandfather Sr Edw: Coke," who lay languishing at Stoke Poges "expecting daylie the good hower" (he died September 3).[2] Then Tomkyns finished his letter by turning to events at the Globe, "some meriment," as he wrote, "after this sad accident [the death of Noy] wch in the course of this world are commonly mixed togither (most dayes in ye yeare producing weddings and funerals):

"Here hath bin lately a newe comedie at the globe called *The Witches of Lancasheir*, acted by reason of ye great concourse of people 3 dayes togither: the 3^d day I went with a friend to see it, and found a greater apparance of fine folke gent^{men} and gent^{weomen} then I thought had bin in town in the vacation: The subiect was of the slights and passages done or supposed to be done by these witches sent from thence hither and other witches and their familiars; Of ther nightly meetings in severall places: their banqueting with all sorts of meat and drinke conveyed vnto them by their familiars vpon the pulling of a cord: the walking of pailes of milke by themselues and (as they say of children) a highlone:[3] the transforming of men and weomen into the shapes of seuerall creatures and especially of horses by putting an inchaunted bridle into ther mouths: their posting to and from places farre distant in an incredible short time: the cutting off a witch = gent$^{woman's}$ hand in the forme of a catt, by a soldier turned miller, known to her husband by a ring thereon, (the onely tragicall part of the storie:) the representing of wrong and putatiue fathers in the shape of meane persons to gent^{men} by way of derision: the tying of a knott at a mariage (after the French manner) to cassate masculine abilitie, and ye conveying away of ye good cheere and bringing in a mock feast of bones and stones in steed thereof and ye filling of pies with liuing birds and yong catts &c: And though there be not in it (to my vnderstanding) any poeticall Genius, or art, or language, or iudgement to state o^r tenet of witches (wch I expected,) or application to vertue but full of ribaldrie and of things improbable and impossible; yet in respect of the newnesse of ye subiect (the witches being still visible and in prison here) and in regard it consisteth from the beginning to the ende of odd passages and fopperies to provoke laughter, and is mixed with diuers songs and dances, it passeth for a merrie and ex^cellent new play. *per acta est fabula. Vale.*"

Perhaps in deciding to write about this particular event, Tomkyns remembered that it was the House of Commons of which Phelips' father had been speaker that had passed the act presently in force "against Conjuration Witchcrafte and dealinge with evill and wicked Spirits" (1 Jas. I, Cap. 12). In any event, Tomkyns signed the letter, "Yo^r^s: most devoted to loue honor and serue y^ou [—] Na: Tomkyns," then added the date, August 16, 1634, and "My humble service to my most noble ladie is never to be forgotten." He meant, evidently, Sir Robert Phelips' wife, Bridget.[4]

The play Tomkyns saw has been much written about. We have known that it has a great deal to do with actual witches from Lancashire who were the object of serious attention by the government in the summer of 1634. We also know that the play was in gestation on July 20, 1634, as, apparently, another on a similar subject was. The players at the Globe, the King's Men, petitioned the Lord Chamberlain on that day complaining that other players were "intermingleing some passages of witches in old playes to ye p^riudice of" the King's Men's "designed Comedy of the Lancashire witches." They wanted the Lord Chamberlain to prohibit the playing of another such play "till theirs bee allowed & Acted." Their play was licensed to be printed on October 28, 1634, and issued before the end of the year as "A well received Comedy, lately Acted at the *Globe* on the *Banke-side*, by the Kings Majesties Actors."[5]

Tomkyns' remarks add greatly to this store of information. For a start, he tells us that the play was acted as *The Witches of Lancashire* rather than as *The Late Lancashire Witches* of the printed version. We could have guessed, because Tomkyns' title is the running title of the book and that by which the book was licensed. Besides, in the summer of 1634 the title used for the book was inappropriate (the witches were current, not "late"). In August, evidently, Tomkyns' title was enough to tell playgoers in London that the play had to do with actual witches. Three or four months later it was necessary to add the word "late" to show that the play dealt with a real event of the previous summer rather than with fancy or with Lancashire witchcraft of other years (such as a famous outbreak there in 1612). Should we now refer to the production, and even the text, by the title that Tomkyns used? and to the printed book by the one that we have been using for all aspects of the play but that properly belongs only to the book?

Hitherto, we have had to date the first performance of the play as between July 20 and October 28, 1634. We can now see that the play was first performed at least three days, and at most not many more, before Tomkyns wrote about it. Tomkyns wrote on Saturday, August 16. The play probably opened, therefore, early in the week of August 10, and no later than August 13—between, that is, August 11 or so and August 13. A reasonable guess might be that it opened on Monday or Tuesday, August 11 or 12. On the day Tomkyns wrote, the Lord Chamberlain licensed another play about witches, *Doctor Lambe and the Witches*, for performance at the playhouse in Salisbury Court. Bentley guessed that this was the play that had worried the King's Men a month before. If it was, the King's Men, as Bentley also guessed, had "had their way as usual," for the Lord Chamberlain licensed it only after the play at the Globe had finished its run.

We can also see at a glance, and rather unexpectedly, that the King's Men's play was a huge success, the more so because it found its audience during the long vacation between the end of Trinity Term and Michaelmas, when many residents of London were away on holiday. Obviously, the Globe could have great successes as late as 1634, when its custom is supposed to have been in decline. Moreover, this particular success was not among the rude multitude, as we might have expected, but among "fine folke," who were especially scarce in London at the time and in any case are supposed to have preferred the King's Men's other house, Blackfriars. Success at the Globe was not impeded, either, by the great troubles the King's Men were having just then about the lease on its site, which was to expire sixteen months later.[6]

The many things Tomkyns wrote of seeing and hearing at the Globe are nearly all, one way or another, in the printed text. If it is so in these respects, that text may well be a good indication generally of what happened in the original production. Yet, the text is not perfectly explicit, and Tomkyns' remarks supply some of its lacunae.

A bridegroom in the play, for example, cannot consummate his marriage because (as he eventually discovers) he has fastened a magical "point" to his codpiece (sigs. F4-F4^v, H3). Tomkyns tells us that the point was a "knott" tied at the marriage "after the French manner," hence perhaps a piece of French lace. At the equally abortive marriage feast in the play, seven characters enter with dishes of food that is "transform'd" by "*A Spirit* (*over the doore*)." One dish becomes "horne," according to the text, and another contains "live Birds" that escape when the pie is opened, "look where they flye." The text does not say what the audience is to see in the other dishes, but it does say that food off stage has become snakes, bats, frogs, and the like (sig. E4ᵛ). At the Globe, Tomkyns says, some of the dishes comprised "a mock feast of bones and stones," and others were pies actually filled "with liuing birds" and also with "yong catts &c"—at least one pie for the birds, presumably, another for the cats, etc. Since Tomkyns says nothing of them, the snakes, bats, and frogs probably remained off stage. Those "catts &c" are, so far as Tomkyns' remarks show, the only business the players used that they did not find in the script as printed.

At their more successful feast in the play, the witches say that "we must pull for" food, and "Pull, and pull hard / For all that hath lately bin prepar'd" and "Pul for the Poultry, Foule, & Fish," and "Pull for the posset, pull." The reader, however, finds nothing to tell him either what is being pulled or how the food gets on stage as a result of pulling. Moreover, at the end of the feast a witch tells "those that are our waiters nere, / Take hence this Wedding cheere," but the reader has no hint about who the waiters are (sigs. Gᵛ-G2ᵛ). Tomkyns explains: at the Globe the witches banquetted "with all sorts of meat and drinke conveyed vnto them by their familiars vpon the pulling of a cord"—who also, no doubt, took the food off stage. In the play, finally, the witches attack a sleeping miller with a clearly inadequate stage direction. It reads, "*The Witches retire: the Spirits* [familiars] *come about him with a dreadfull noise: he starts,*" and the miller several times describes his assailants as cats (sigs. I3, I4ᵛ-Kᵛ, K2ᵛ-K3). Because one of the witches loses a hand here, the miller must lash out after he wakes, and at least one witch must be close to him. Because Tomkyns says the injured witch was "in the forme of a catt," the miller must mean his cats literally, and the witches, if not the familiars, are to be dressed as cats.

More importantly, perhaps, Tomkyns' remarks add to our knowledge of what the play has to do with the actual Lancashire witches and the government's treatment of them.[7]

A young boy, Edmund Robinson, accused people of witchcraft in the autumn of 1633. Others soon laid further accusations against these people and accused yet more. The accusers and accused all came, it seems, from the region of the Pendle Forest in Lancashire. The authorities took depositions from young Robinson and his father (another Edmund) on February 10 and from at least one of the accused persons, who admitted being a witch, on March 2, 1634. Twenty-one people were then tried before a jury at the Lancashire assizes on March 24 for killing or injuring people by witchcraft, and all but one of them were found guilty. As the law stood, the circuit judges who presided over the trial had to sentence the twenty people to death, but the judges were not satisfied with the trial and refused to pronounce sentence. Leaving the convicted people in prison at Lancaster, they took the matter back to London and laid it before the King.

He directed the Privy Council on May 16 to summon "some of the principall, and most notorious offenders" to London "to attend his...farther pleasure." That body promptly ordered writs of habeas corpus drawn up requiring the Sheriff of Lancashire to release some of the people and send them to London. The writs, however, needed a specific name in each, and the Privy Council evidently did not know who the principal offenders were. The judges reminded the King and Council on May 23 that the convicted people were still unsentenced. By the end of the month, the Privy Council had the names of seven suitable people and also some information about the Robinsons. It took three steps on May 31: it supplied the names for the writs and ordered them into execution; it sent one of the messengers of the King's chamber to bring young Robinson to London (in the event, he brought the elder one, too); and it directed the Bishop of Chester, John Bridgeman, in whose diocese Lancaster was, "to examine" the seven people "perticularly" before they started south so that the King could have a preliminary opinion, "as cleare informacion as may be, of the qualitie and nature of their seuerall offences."

The Privy Council soon decided not to have seven writs of habeas corpus sent but one of mandamus containing seven names, dated June 2—a saving of parchment, no doubt, and also a more seasonable procedure, for the writ of mandamus was addressed not to the sheriff of the county but to the chancellor of the Duchy of Lancaster, who was Lord Newburgh, an active member of the Privy Council. The bishop's instructions reached him on June 13, when he happened to be in Lancaster on his triennial visitation, and he carried them out that day. He found three of the seven people dead and one apparently dying. So he took depositions from the other three, one of whom was the person who had admitted being a witch. She still admitted, but the other two strenuously denied having to do with witchcraft. The bishop sent these depositions to London with a covering letter dated June 15 in which he suggested that none of the three was guilty of anything and, moreover, that the elder Robinson might have profited from his son's accusations by taking money to exclude people. By the time an under sheriff set out with the prisoners, the person whom the bishop had thought dying had recovered enough to go along, too, so that four people, all women, arrived in London and were lodged at the Ship Tavern in Greenwich. The Robinsons had arrived there by June 28, when the elder one was put into the Gate House prison. The boy, it seems, was lodged at Richmond and watched over by the King's coachman. There was a royal palace at Greenwich and another at Richmond.

On June 29, the Privy Council ordered two royal surgeons to have midwives examine the women physically. No fewer than ten midwives, gratuitously joined by eight royal physicians and surgeons led by the celebrated Harvey, conducted examinations. They reported on July 2 that they also could find little amiss. The Privy Council then had depositions taken from the Robinsons separately, the boy on July 10 and his father two days later. The boy broke down, admitting readily and in detail that his accusations were "a meere fiction of his owne," and his father protested that he had never fully believed the boy and had accused no one of witchcraft himself. The Council had father and son interrogated again on July 16 and got the same results. Curiously, here the matter stopped. The four women and at least the elder Robinson remained in confinement in or near London, and the King's Men and their two writers prepared the play for performance, assuming that the Lord Chamberlain would guarantee them first use of the material, as, it seems, he did. The women were still confined nearby when the play opened at the Globe and when Tomkyns wrote his letter on August 16.

The play is a piece of what one writer has called "dramatic journalism."[8] Heywood and Brome exploited the actual Lancashire witches literally from one end of the play to the other. The four women confined in or near London and the elder Robinson all figure in it by name, and though not by name, young Robinson is there, too. So are many details of the story otherwise, and because a full report of what was said at the trial does not exist nor do many depositions that might have been taken before the trial (twenty from the accused alone), even more of the story could be in the play than now appears. Ten depositions survive, the three taken by the authorities before the trial, the three taken by Bishop Bridgeman seven weeks after the trial, and the four taken by the Privy Council later still. Some ten pages of the play closely retail the story as it appears in two of these, Margaret Johnson's second deposition, taken by the bishop, and young Robinson's first deposition, taken by the authorities before the trial. A brief exchange in the play derives inaccurately from Margaret Johnson's first deposition, taken by the authorities before the trial.[9] Another matter in the play derives either from the charges against Mary Spencer at the trial or, perhaps more likely, from her refutation of them in her deposition, taken by the bishop.[10]

Much of the material in Margaret Johnson's second deposition appears in one conversation at the end of the play. She was the person who admitted being a witch. In the deposition she said "That shee hath beene a Witch about 6. yeares last past....And, about that time...there appeared to her a Man in blacke Attire trussed wth blacke points....In this manner hee ofttimes resorted to her, till at last shee yeilded to him....And shee asked his name, and hee called himselfe *Mamilion*: and shee saith that most commonly at his coming to her, hee hath the vse of her Body; and shee had some lust and pleasure therby." In the play, Peg Johnson and the witch hunter, Doughty, speak to one another like this:

Dought. And that *Mamilion* which thou call'st upon
   Is thy familiar Divell is't not?...
Peg. Yes Sir.
Dough. ...how long hast had's acquaintance, ha?
Peg. A matter of six yeares Sir....
Dought. And then he lay with thee, did he not sometimes?
Peg. ...twice a Weeke he never fail'd me.

Dough. ...was he a good Bedfellow?...
Peg. He pleas'd me well Sir, like a proper man.
Dought. There was sweet coupling....and did he weare good clothes?
Peg. Gentleman like, but blacke blacke points and all.

(sigs. L3-L3ᵛ)

Heywood and Brome ignored a similar passage in her first deposition, where she had put the beginning of her witchcraft at "betwixt seauen and eight yeares since," given her devil "a suite of blacke tyed about wᵗʰ silke points," and omitted to say that she had found her sexual experiences with him pleasurable.

The play retails material in young Robinson's first deposition even more closely than that in Margaret Johnson's second. In both deposition and play, for example, the boy finds two greyhounds and tries to make them chase a hare. When they do not, in the deposition he "tied them to a little bush at the next hedge, and with a switch that he had in his hand he beat them. And in stead of the black Grayhound one Dickensons Wife stood up, a Neighbour whom this Informer knoweth. And instead of the brown one a little Boy, whom this Informer knoweth not." In the play he says to the greyhounds, "nay then...you shall to the next bush, there will I tie you, and use you like a couple of curs as you are, &...lash you whilest my switch will hold....Now blesse me heaven, one of the Greyhounds turn'd into a woman, the other into a boy! The lad I never saw before, but her I know well; it is my gammer *Dickison*" (sigs. E-Eᵛ).¹¹

Indeed, what Heywood and Brome meant is occasionally clearer in the deposition than in the printed version of the play. The pulling of a cord to produce food is an example. Young Robinson said he saw six witches "kneeling, and pulling...six several ropes, which were fastened or tied to the top of the Barn. Presently after which pulling, there came into this Informers sight flesh smoaking, butter in lumps, and milk as it were flying from the said ropes." Another example follows immediately. Young Robinson said that during this pulling the witches "made such ugly faces as scared" him, "so that he was glad to run out and steal homewards: who immediately finding they wanted one that was in their company, some of them ran after him near to a place in a High-way called *Boggard-hole*, where he...met two Horsemen. At the sight whereof the said persons left following of him." In the play, young Robinson says, "Now whilest they are in their jollitie, and do not mind me, ile steale away, and shift for my selfe, though I lose my life for't," and he exits. One witch says "But stay, wheres the *Boy*, looke out, if he escape us, we are all betrayed," and another adds merely, "No following further, yonder horsemen come, / In vaine is our pursuit" (sig. G2ᵛ). Evidently Heywood and Brome wanted here what the deposition prescribes but the printed text of the play barely hints at, a chase round the stage.

Heywood and Brome knew that many of the accused persons stoutly denied being witches and that the denials were sufficiently credible first to cause the assize judges to postpone sentencing and then to cause the King and Privy Council to investigate. They noted in their prologue that the four convicted women had been brought "to Town" and in their epilogue that they might find "great Mercy"—be pardoned by the King. Yet they managed to keep any hint of the denials out of the play, or of the case for the accused otherwise. The play represents the case for the prosecution alone. The elder Robinson in the play "is as liberall a gentleman, as any is in our countrie," and his son is "a made man" (sigs. D4, I4ᵛ). In the last passages of the play, all the rational people who have had doubts about the existence or seriousness of witchcraft are convinced that they have been wrong. The witches have been rounded up and arrested. Three characters, including the one representing young Robinson, lay young Robinson's accusations against the witches, who are then driven off to prison like "untoward Cattell" to await the next assizes. The current act against witchcraft distinguished sharply between witchcraft that caused injury or death and witchcraft that did not, and it prescribed the death penalty only for the former. The doings of Heywood's and Brome's witches were neither especially injurious nor mortal, but the reader is assured that at least the chief of them will die "about a day after" the trial (sigs. L2, L3ᵛ).[12]

That much of the play is the case for the prosecution written and performed while the defendants were unsentenced, in effect still before the courts, is not just our view as we assess ancient documents. It was also Heywood's and Brome's view, as they explained in their prologue and epilogue. In their prologue, they note that their "Scene" is grounded on real events well known in London:

The Project unto many here well knowne;
Those Witches the fat Iaylor brought to Towne,

though the events are "so thin, persons so low" that they

Can neither yeeld much matter, nor great show.

In their epilogue, Heywood and Brome explain the legal implications of what they were about. Those actual "Witches must expect their due / By lawfull Iustice," they write; "what their crime / May bring upon 'em ripenes yet of time / Has not reveal'd." The play represents "as much / As they have done, before Lawes hand did touch / Vpon their guilt"—before, that is, law's hand touched *finally* upon the charges against them, and before, as far as the play goes, a word was heard from the defense. Having sent the stage witches off to the assizes in the last lines of the play, Heywood and Brome could hardly say in their next utterance that the actual witches had already been to the assizes. Heywood and Brome dared "not hold it fit"

That we for Iustices and Iudges sit.
And personate their grave wisedomes on the Stage
Whom we are bound to honour; No, the Age
Allowes it not. Therefore unto the Lawes
We can but bring the Witches and their cause,
And there we leave 'em....
What of their storie, further shall ensue,
We must referre to time....

Heywood and Brome were also well aware that the actual witches might go free. They allowed in their epilogue that "great Mercy may / After just condemnation [the conviction at the Lancashire assizes, presumably] give them day / Of longer life." Besides, at the end of the play they sent off their most attractive witch crying to her erstwhile boyfriend, "Well Rogue I may live to ride in a Coach before I come to the Gallowes yet."

Writers have assumed that Heywood and Brome got their information about the actual Lancashire witches through either gossip or interviews with the people confined in or near London (Barber, p. 79). We are even told that the appearance in the play of information about the witches proves that the information was circulating widely before the play was written (Notestein, p. 159). Tomkyns' letter and much else, however, prompt us to doubt these assumptions.

Information about the Lancashire witches did not sweep through the country like wildfire. Though according to Mary Spencer the trial on March 24 was attended by a vast throng, the Privy Council itself did not know the names of the chief offenders until the end of May and even then did not know that three of them were dead. Moreover, none of the three surviving remarks casually written about the witches before the play was acted so much as hints at the story as it appears in the play. The first (dated May 16) reports that nineteen people had been found guilty and that "it is suspected y^t they had a hand in raysing ye greate storme, wherein his Mayjestie was in so greate danger at Sea in Scotland," a matter that appears nowhere else. The second (dated June 3) simply mentions "the discovery of our Lancashire witches." The third (dated June 28) reports that "Four witches are sent out of Lancashire to the King to be re-examined."[13] These remarks point to the kind of information that certainly was widely known, that a trial had taken place at which some twenty people had been found guilty, that the judges had refused to pass sentence, that the King and Council had summoned four convicted people to London—the well known "Project," evidently, on which Heywood and Brome said they grounded their scene but, except for the allusions in the prologue and epilogue, actually avoided altogether. It must be likely that the spreading of other aspects of the story was the result and not the cause of the play, and Tomkyns encourages us to think so. The play was such a success, he wrote, partly "in respect of the newnesse of ye subiect."

Moreover, the information in young Robinson's first deposition appears so similarly in the play and at such length that Heywood and Brome could not have got it by gossip or perhaps even by an interview with young Robinson. In any case, he and the four women may have been lodged outside London to prevent such interviews,[14] and he was apparently in no mood to maintain his accusations once he had arrived in London and been separated from his father on June 28. He voluntarily confessed all, he said, at Richmond to the King's coachman before confessing formally to the Privy Council's examiner on July 10. Neither could Heywood and Brome have got the information in Margaret Johnson's second deposition by an interview with her, for, as the bishop found, that distraught woman could not keep her story together. The details of her second deposition differ in many ways from those of her first, and evidently details constantly wavered as the bishop interrogated her. He told the Privy Council that she often said "That shee was a Witch but more often faulting in the particulars and circumstances of her Actions, as one having a stronge Imagination of the former, but of too weake a memory to retaine or relate the other."

Heywood and Brome, then, seem to have had accurate copies of young Robinson's first deposition and Margaret Johnson's second. They knew a little about Margaret Johnson's first deposition, too, but if they had a copy of it they preferred not to treat it closely. They probably had at least part of Mary Spencer's deposition. Where did they get these things?

The prosecution must have used young Robinson's and Margaret Johnson's first depositions at the trial, and sooner or later the depositions themselves circulated widely. They survive together in three old manuscripts and separately in one more each; and young Robinson's was printed in 1677 from yet another manuscript.[15] We could suggest that Heywood and Brome acquired copies much as they acquired books, if we could show that the information in them was current before the play was written. But we cannot and so must suspect that the playwrights acquired them in a less open way, and even that copies circulated because of, hence after, the play. As for Margaret Johnson's second deposition and Mary Spencer's deposition, they were taken at Lancaster on June 13 and dispatched to London on or after the 15th. They could hardly have arrived there sooner than seven weeks or so before the play was acted at the Globe. They were intended, moreover, for the eyes of the King and his privy councillors alone, who would not have made copies of them promptly available for wide circulation.[16] The only surviving copies are the originals still lying among the papers of the secretaries who served the King and Council. Heywood and Brome, then, must have acquired a copy of Margaret Johnson's second deposition in some covert way and also, probably, information from Mary Spencer's deposition.

There is, too, that petition of July 20 in which the King's Men demanded that the Lord Chamberlain prevent another company from exploiting witchcraft in a play before they had dealt with the Lancashire witches. As we have seen, he probably did as the King's Men wanted, for he did not license another company to do a witch play until immediately after the King's Men had finished the run of their play. Could the King's Men really claim a right to the first use of material that was widely available, and would the Lord Chamberlain agree that they had such a right and enforce it? If so, we must rewrite a good deal of our theatre history. It seems more likely that the Lord Chamberlain saw to it that the King's Men had the first use of these witches as part of some extraordinary arrangement.

What can Tomkyns tell us? We could hardly have a more likely person to whom we might turn. He was a senior civil servant in the Queen's establishment, and he made it his business both to know about such things and to report them to Phelips.

Tomkyns knew that much of the play was about the people convicted of witchcraft in Lancashire, especially those "sent from thence hither," as he put it, and "in prison here." He thought the subject new as he saw it on stage. He went to the play expecting it to include a judgment about the state or the "tenet of witches," about, that is, national politics or a matter equally contentious, the current doctrine about witchcraft. So he knew, it would seem, that there was a quarrel in Whitehall about witchcraft in which playwrights and players might well meddle. Having seen the play, however, he concluded that it did not take sides in such a quarrel. The play was meant, he thought, merely "to provoke laughter, and is mixed with diuers songs and dances," so that it "passeth for a merrie and ex^{c}ellent new play."

This conclusion about a play that obviously does have a point of view, not only about witchcraft in general but about the guilt of actual persons accused of it, must lead us to two further conclusions. First, Tomkyns could not have known how close the matters in the play are to the actual evidence against the convicted people. Hence that evidence was probably not widely known in London, even in the upper reaches of the government, and Heywood and Brome are the less likely to have got their knowledge of the evidence openly. Second, the point of view about witchcraft could not have been persuasively in evidence on the stage of the Globe. Tomkyns should have recognised a bias in favour of the validity and seriousness of witchcraft, for his remarks about the injuries "done or supposed to be done by these witches" and their "still" being confined suggest that he was not a confident believer. So whatever the instigation of the play and however grim some of its statements could be made to seem on stage, the King's Men played it as its writers saw to it they could—for the fun and not the message.

How was it, then, that Heywood and Brome came to write their play and to include in it some remarkable material? The thing could have proceeded like this. A quarrel developed in the Privy Council when in mid-May, 1634, the King laid the case of Lancashire witches before it. On one side were councillors who shared the doubts of the assize judges about witchcraft in general or about the guilt of these persons accused of it. They saw their doubts reinforced by the reports of Bishop Bridgeman (June 13) and the physicians and midwives (July 2) and finally by the collapse of the accusations (July 10 and 16). On the other side were councillors who convinced themselves either that these persons were indeed guilty of a serious offence or that it was a bad idea to annoy a great many people in the north who obviously had no doubts. So when these councillors saw their position decaying, they decided to buttress it by making a public display of the case against the witches. They made a bargain with the King's Men sometime in late June or early July. In return for the promise of a suitable play, the councillors guaranteed the King's Men the first use of spectacular material and provided much of it. They gave the King's Men copies of young Robinson's and Margaret Johnson's first depositions and of Margaret Johnson's second one, and a snippet of Mary Spencer's deposition. Young Robinson and Margaret Johnson must have been the best parts of the case against the convicted people. The councillors did not give the players the other deposition of June 13, Frances Dicconson's, which was a stout denial; nor the part of Mary Spencer's that was another stout denial; nor the later depositions of the Robinsons, in which the accusations collapsed.

The King's Men then engaged Heywood and Brome to write the play, allowing about six weeks for writing and staging. The playwrights set about demonstrating the case against the witches, and when they came to deal with Margaret Johnson, they preferred her second to her first deposition because the second was more recent and more privileged. They kept in mind, however, that they were writing a play that had to make its way on the public stage and not a polemical tract. They omitted the charges of serious injury and death, and they infiltrated the witches with a great deal of good fun and high spirits. They specified music, dance, and song some sixteen times, mostly in the third and fourth acts—not in the last—and probably intended them several times more. The bewitched marriage feast is "such a medley of mirth, madnesse, and drunkennesse shuffled together," as one character says, that "My sides eene ake with laughter" (sig. F2ᵛ). The chief witch says of another bewitched occasion, "'Tis all for mirth, we mean no hurt," and soon even the chief witch hunter sums up the witches' doings as "such Villanies...such mischievous tricks, though none mortall" (sigs. Iᵛ, I4). Eventually Heywood and Brome felt it necessary to add prologue and epilogue in which they could make their responsibilities about the witches clear: they had brought the witches to trial, in effect, but what happened to them thereafter was somebody else's business. It is a facile apologia, no doubt, but more conscience than was strictly necessary. On such terms, the players and playwrights soon had a huge success on their hands in an unlikely season. Perhaps such a quarrel in high places and such a success in lower ones caused the King to hesitate about either authorising a pardon or directing the judges to proceed to sentence, so that despite the failure of the accusations against them, the famous Lancashire witches of 1634 simply rotted in prison.[17]

The way the Lancashire witches were treated at the Globe in 1634 proved durable. Thomas Shadwell pinched the general structure and method of Heywood's and Brome's play and even many of its details for his *The Lancashire-Witches* of 1682. He used three of the women confined at Greenwich by name, along with Margaret Johnson's familiar, Mamilion, and Heywood's and Brome's witch hunter, Doughty. He said that his witches came from "near *Pendle-Hills*," as those of 1634 did, and he made them perform several of the tricks that Heywood and Brome had got from young Robinson's accusations. At the end, Shadwell's witches, like Heywood's and Brome's, are rounded up and sent off to jail at Lancaster. Shadwell took great pains to tell his reader where he had found the material in the play, and in his preface he wrote that his witchcraft was "from some antient or Modern Witchmonger. Which you will find in the notes." But curiously, while those prodigious notes mention a great deal of bewitched scholarship, they do not mention Heywood and Brome or their play. Thanks also, finally, to Heywood and Brome and the King's Men, we are assured a hundred years later still that Lancashire witches "chiefly divert themselves in merriment, and are therefore...more sociable than the rest."[18]

If the play did grow out of a quarrel in the Privy Council, who were the quarrellers? The Council was dominated by the Archbishop of Canterbury, William Laud, who would have agreed with the judges in doubting the business. The Church of England, especially under his leadership, regarded belief in witchcraft as superstitious and irrational, hence un-Christian. Moreover, he would have suspected that the affair in Lancashire was a symptom of puritanism, which he had been hounding Bridgeman to be more energetic in stamping out. Nineteen other members attended one or more of the twenty-three meetings of the Privy Council from May 16 to July 16, when meetings ceased until September 15. Of these, the Lord Chamberlain, the Earl of Pembroke, must be Laud's most likely opponent. He was an "intolerable choleric and offensive man" and the only visible puritan on the Council. He had opposed and almost defeated Laud in the election of 1630 for the chancellorship of Oxford. Above all, as Lord Chamberlain he controlled the theatrical industry, especially the companies sponsored, like the King's Men, by the royal family. He alone was able to guarantee the King's Men the first use of the Lancashire witches on stage by licensing another witch play only after theirs had finished its run. He might have connived with the crypto-Catholics, who often opposed Laud: the Earl of Portland, Lord Cottington, and the secretary, Windebank (who, Laud wrote on May 14, had just become an opponent); or the soldiers who had served often on the Continent, the Earl of Lindsey and Lord Wimbledon; perhaps also the old Scot, the Earl of Kellie.[19]

Nathaniel Tomkyns may have been the person of the name at Magdalen College, Oxford, from 1596 to 1610. If so, he was born in 1584 or 1585, and probably had to do there with two future notables, the musician, Thomas Tomkins, whose brother he may have been, and the poet, John Davies of Hereford, for whose book, *Microcosmos* (1603, sig. B4), a Nathaniel Tomkins wrote Latin verses.[20] He became a quiet politician and a friend of an unquiet one, Sir Robert

Phelips. Tomkyns sat in the Parliament of 1614 for Carlisle and then in all those of the 1620's for Christchurch in Hampshire. Phelips sat in all those parliaments, too, save that of 1625-26, when the royal party managed to exclude him. In 1615 and 1617, Phelips joined the English mission in Spain scouting a Spanish match for Prince Charles. Perhaps Tomkyns did, too, as a secretary. Tomkyns married Cicelie Waller, the sister of the poet Edmund Waller, and so connected himself with a family of pretensions in Buckinghamshire as great as those of the Phelipses in Somerset.[21] In January, 1624, Tomkyns was elected to sit in Parliament for both Christchurch and Ilchester in Somerset, a place then virtually in Phelips' gift. He chose to sit for Christchurch, and Waller succeeded him at Ilchester.[22]

Tomkyns also took up a career in Whitehall and, according to Clarendon, acquired a "very good fame for honesty and ability." He belonged to the household of Prince Charles from 1620 and by the winter of 1623-24 was clerk of his council. He may have joined the negotiations in Paris for that other match, the French one, 1624-25 (for from 1626 to 1629 he was serving the Earl of Holland, who had led them, and he remarked eventually that he had known the Earl "both in the Courte of England and in other *partes* beyond Sea"). He continued a member of Charles' household and in 1630 became also clerk and registrar of the Queen's council, a position he held for the rest of his life.[23] This council existed chiefly to manage the many properties that had been made part of the Queen's jointure.[24]

Phelips and Tomkyns adopted Spanish nicknames for one another. Phelips was "El hombre de bien" and Tomkyns "El hombre fiel." The use of the phrases suggests that the two men were close friends, but the phrases themselves suggest the significant gulf between them: one was the head of a great provincial family, the other a loyal official. It was a gulf, however, that at least Phelips found useful. For Tomkyns became a shrewd and knowledgeable figure in the labyrinths of central government, hence a reliable source of information and advice for a man like Phelips, who had ideas about the governing of the country but alienated those in authority and preferred to spend much of his time in Somerset. When in 1622 Phelips was imprisoned in the tower for noisily opposing among other things the Spanish match, he seems to have confided, or thought of confiding, in Tomkyns. He wrote a long letter in his own hand explaining his situation and asking for advice. He addressed the letter only to "S^r," but he signed it "Your Hom de bien" and wrote on the back, "Guarde v[sted] a esta carta a causa que no tengo copia" and "El hombre." Since the letter is among the Phelips papers, evidently he did not send it, or kept a copy after all.[25]

Phelips and Tomkyns must have corresponded often. Seven of Tomkyns' letters to Phelips survive among the Phelips papers, and they allude repeatedly to other letters Tomkyns wrote to and received from Phelips. Their call numbers and dates are as follows:

DD/PH 219/#33—March 30, 1625[26]
,,   ,,   #35—November 27, 1626
,,   ,,   #42—January 13, 1633
,,   ,,   #43—July 29, 1634
,,   ,,   #44—August 2, 1634
,,   ,,   #45—August 4, 1634
,,   212/#12—August 16, 1634

the last being the letter in which Tomkyns discussed Heywood's and Brome's play. All were evidently written from London. All are addressed only to "S^r." All except the last are signed only "El hombre fiel," but all are in the same handwriting, which is clearly that of our Tomkyns. "S^r" is identified in one as Sir Robert Phelips (#35) and in two as "El hombre de bien" (#42, 43) an "antient and noble freind."[27] The letters amount mostly to personal newsletters, full of informed comments about the workings of government. In one (#42) Tomkyns remarked that he was older than Phelips, who was born in about 1586.[28] In March, 1625, Tomkyns warned Phelips that further trouble like that of 1622 was on the way, as indeed it was, and urged Phelips to blunt it by writing the Duke of Buckingham. In November, 1626, Tomkyns wrote lengthily in reply to a request for advice about how Phelips might react to animosity from the court. On August 4, 1634, Tomkyns wrote ironically about the recent "noble Acts" in Dublin of Lord (once Sir Thomas) Wentworth, Phelips' former colleague on the opposition benches of the House of Commons, or as Tomkyns put it, "your *quondam* parlamentarie friend now his Maties active minister in Ireland."

Tomkyns wrote about theatrical matters in two letters other than that in which he dealt with the play of 1634. In his letter of January,

1633, he noticed the recent performance and a projected one of Walter Montagu's diffuse pastoral, *The Shepherd's Paradise*. His remarks have become a commonplace of stage history because they were printed in the *Third Report*. One can add now only the identity of the writer and recipient, and suggest that the writer might have known what he was writing about because the performance took place at Denmark House, where the council of which he was clerk held its meetings and where he probably had an office. In his letter of July, 1634, Tomkyns wrote from London that "The Queen is preparing to entertain ye King with a Galanteria (as they call it) at Holdenbye wch being within her ioynture, she holds as her own howse." This remark was also printed in the *Third Report* but with the name of the place mistranscribed as "Hulembey." Stage historians have not used the information, perhaps because they could not locate Hulembey. The King, Queen, and much of the court were on progress, and the King spent three nights at Holdenby in Northamptonshire while the Queen stayed nearby.[29] On one of those three nights, presumably, the Queen organized and the Prince's Men (who were paid £100 to accompany the progress) mounted a "galanteria" there, the Queen amusing herself by protesting that she was entertaining a royal guest in a house of hers. Again, of course, Tomkyns was in a position to know, at least about the house, because his council managed the Queen's jointure.

Evidently Tomkyns was writing Phelips weekly during the summer of 1634, and four of his letters among the Phelips MSS. are all but one of those written from July 29 to August 16. Tomkyns must have assumed that Phelips was interested in the Attorney General, Noy, because he wrote of his illness on July 29 and August 2, and he began the section about him in the letter of August 16 by writing, "I certified you in my last of m^r Attorney's death." Hence he probably wrote a missing letter on the day of Noy's death, August 9, or a day or two later, and in it reported that bad news. In the letter of August 2, Tomkyns wrote that "my Lo:" had just reduced a fine by £1,000, a remark that probably prompted Phelips to ask for the information that Tomkyns supplied at the beginning of the letter of August 16.[30] Tomkyns reported on August 2 that he had "little worthie ye writting this being (as you well describe it) a dull and dead time here, when both the K: and Q: are absent and in progresse, Westminster-hall shutt vp, the exchange but rarely frequented, and the streets thinne, in regard most people of qualitie are gone to take ye fresh ayre of ye countrie.'' Hence his astonishment on August 16 at the vast numbers of such people who had just been appearing at the Globe to see *The Witches of Lancashire.*

Phelips died in 1638. Five years later, Tomkyns fell a victim partly to his brother-in-law, Edmund Waller, partly to the times, mostly, perhaps, to his being indeed an ''hombre fiel.'' In the spring of 1643, when the King and his Parliament were at war with one another and the King had his headquarters at Oxford, Waller was in London as a member of Parliament and Tomkyns was there, too, presumably looking after shreds of the Queen's business. The royal party persuaded Waller to assist in a scheme to overthrow the parliamentary cause. Waller would arm people in London loyal to the King, and on an appointed day they would beat down the parliamentary troops there so that royal troops could march in from Oxford. Waller enlisted Tomkyns as his second. Tomkyns' job was to find people sufficiently loyal. The leaders of Parliament, however, soon fathomed the business. They had Waller, Tomkyns, and others arrested on May 31. As Clarendon wrote, Waller, ''was so confounded with fear and apprehension that he confessed whatsoever he had said, heard, thought, or seen,'' and did ''ill very well.'' So Tomkyns and four others (not Waller, because he was a member of Parliament) were tried for treason at Guildhall on June 30. Tomkyns and three others were sentenced to death on July 3 and 4. Tomkyns was hanged on July 5 ''in the sight and presence of many thousands of Citizens'' on a gibbet erected outside his house at the Holborn end of Fetter Lane.[31]

Tomkyns was allowed to make the customary speech from the ladder. He said that he was neither an atheist nor a Papist, but he admitted having dealt with Catholics in England. As Catholics were civil to him abroad, he said, so he was civil to them here. ''Touching the businesse for which *I* suffer,'' he went on, ''I do acknowledge that affection to a Brother-in-Law, and affection and gratitude to the King...drew me into this foolish businesse.'' He repented his part in it, ''because it might have occasioned very ill consequences.'' He thanked God for taking him ''away from the dayes of sin,...from the evils of the time to come, which God avert,...from the infirmities of age now approaching upon me.'' Lt. Col. Washborn then asked him to reveal any other plots he might know of. Tomkyns replied, ''*Pray trouble me not, I have done my duty,''* and with that the hangman turned him off.[32] As for Waller, he eventually escaped with a large fine, partly because of another, more effective relative of his, Oliver Cromwell.

NOTES

* Originally published in *Medieval and Renaissance Drama in England*, I (1984), 211-30.

1. Phelips was made steward in 1616, and Tomkyns addressed him and other stewards in 1637 as "Clerke vnto vs his Ma:[ts] said Commissioners" (Somerset Record Office, DD/PH 223/#5, 6; V.C.H., *Somerset*, III, 239). There are accounts of both Sir Edward and Sir Robert in *D.N.B.*

2. Neither Sir Robert Phelips nor his wife was one of Coke's grand-children in the usual sense, and both were too old to be. The elder Phelips and Sir Robert must have known Coke well, however, and they came to be related to him, though distantly. Coke was born in 1552, the elder Phelips in about 1560; both became successful lawyers in London, Coke of the Inner and Phelips of the Middle Temple. The elder Phelips was Coke's assistant in the prosecution of Raleigh, and Sir Robert almost invariably was an ally of Coke's in the parliaments of the 1620s. The elder Phelips' oldest brother married a grand-daughter of the Berkeleys of Stoke in Gloucestershire, and eventually Coke's daughter, Elizabeth, married Sir Maurice Berkeley of that family. Perhaps Tomkyns' remark was a joke deriving from Coke's being senior to the elder Phelips in the law and vastly senior to Sir Robert in politics. See the elaborate pedigree of the Phelips family, DD/PH 250/pt.1/pp. 120-21; *The Visitation of the County of Gloucester in 1623*, eds. Sir John Maclean, W. C. Heane (London: Harleian Soc., 1885), pp. 8-9; *D.N.B.*, "Family of Berkeley."

3. *N.E.D.*: "Quite alone, without support."

4. DD/PH 212/#12. The letter is the original document sent to Phelips. It is bound in a volume with some fifty-five other documents dating from about 1589 to 1709.

5. Bentley, III, 73-76. See also Wallace Notestein, *A History of Witchcraft in England* (Washington, D.C., 1911), pp. 146-63; Otelia Cromwell, *Thomas Heywood* (New Haven, 1928), pp. 177-84; Arthur M. Clark, *Thomas Heywood* (Oxford, 1931), pp. 120-27, 240-43; C. L'Estrange Ewen, *Witchcraft and Demonianism* (London, 1933), pp. 244-51; F.S. Boas, *Thomas Heywood* (London, 1950), pp. 154-55, 157; etc. The best account of the play is in L. H. Barber's dissertation (Michigan, 1962), an edition of the play, reproduced as *An Edition of The Late Lancashire Witches* (New York, 1979).

6. See below, pp. 156 ff. Barber thought the play a conspicuous example of what the rough audience at the Globe demanded, unlike the refined one at Blackfriars (pp. 85-87, 98, 101).

7. For the early depositions, see below. For other aspects of the affair, see B.L., Add. 36,674, f. 197 (a list of charges against the convicted people); P.C.2/43/pp. 652, 656, 657-58 and /44/pp. 56, 73 (the actions of the Privy Council); K.B.29/283/m.76 (the writ of mandamus and Lord Newburgh's reply giving an account of the trial as it applied to the seven people, including its date as Monday in the fifth week of Lent); S.P.16/269/#85, and /270/#50, and /271/#9, 56, 57 (the Bishop's interrogations and letter, the physical examinations, the later interrogations of the Robinsons, the imprisonment of the elder Robinson—all calendared in *C.S.P.*, *Dom.*, *1634-35*, pp. 77-79, 98, 129-30, 141, 144, 152-53); H.M.C., *Cowper*, II, 53(2) (the trouble about the names of the offenders and a remark by their judges); and John Webster, *The Displaying of Supposed Witchcraft* (London, 1677), pp. 276-78, 346 (a reminiscence by an eye witness to part of the affair).

8. Clark, p. 242.

9. She said nothing about meetings of witches in her second deposition but several things in her first: she did not attend a meeting "vpon all sn^{ts}-day" last but did attend one the next Sunday; "Good friday is one constant day for a yearely gen^{r}all meeteinge of witches"; and "on Good friday last they had a meeteinge neare Pendle wat^{r} syde" (she did not say whether she attended). In the play, a witch says that Meg Johnson did not attend a meeting "last *Goodfriday* Feast," and another adds that she did attend an earlier one on "*All-Saints* night" (sig. I).

10. In the play Mal Spencer has a milk pail that, she says, "shall come to me," and the stage direction adds, "*The Payle goes.*" We hear later, "they say shee made a payle follow her t'other day up two payre of stayres" (sigs. E2^{v}, F4). One of the charges against her was "causeing a Pale or Collocke to come to her full of water 14 yards vp a hill from a Well." In her deposition she denied being able "to call a Collocke or Peal, wch came running to her of its owne accord vpon her call," and she explained how the charge came about: "when shee was a yong Girle and went to the Well for water, shee vsed somtimes to tumble or trundle the Collock or Peal downe the hill, and shee would run along after it to overtake it, and did overye it sometimes; and then might call it to come to her."

11. Young Robinson's story of his first deposition appears in the play at sigs. D4-D4^{v}, E-E2^{v}, G^{v}-G2^{v}, I3^{v}-I4^{v}. Perhaps significantly, where Webster has "switch" in young Robinson's deposition here, all other versions have "rod" (see below).

12. The act also provided the death penalty for those convicted a second time of non-injurious witchcraft; but neither the chief witch in the play nor any of the others had been convicted before.

13. S.P.16/268/#12 (calendared in *C.S.P.*, *Dom.*, *1634-35*, p. 26); Sir William Brereton, Bt., *Travels in Holland*, etc., ed. Edward Hawkins (London, 1844), p. 33 (Chetham Soc., vol. 1); H.M.C., *Gawdy*, p. 147. The matter of the storm may derive from a remark in Margaret Johnson's first deposition: she said that witches' familiars "can cause foule weather and stormes, and soe did at theire [the witches'] meeteings."

14. Eventually the women may have been put in the Fleet prison and become a public attraction, for we hear in 1677 of "great sums gotten at the Fleet to shew

them" (Webster, p. 346).

15. Copies of Margaret Johnson's and young Robinson's first depositions occur together in Dodsworth 61 (ff. 45-47^v) and Rawlinson D 399 (ff. 211-12^v) at the Bodleian, and Harleian 6854 (ff. 22-29^v) at the B.L. Another copy of each, not written by the same person nor on the same kind of paper, occurs in Additional 36,674 (ff. 193, 196), the so-called Londesborough MS., also at the B.L. The Dodsworth, Harleian, and Additional versions have been published wholly or partly several times, first in Thomas D. Whitaker, *An History of the Original Parish of Whalley* (Blackburn, 1801), pp. 184-88; Edward Baines, *History of the County Palatine and Duchy of Lancashire* (London, 1836), I, 604-8; Thomas Wright, *Narratives of Sorcery and Magic* (London, 1851), II, 109-11, 114-17 (where the version of Margaret Johnson's deposition is from the Additional MS., but the parts of young Robinson's are from Dodsworth).
Of these versions of Margaret Johnson's first deposition, Dodsworth and Rawlinson derive from the original via one route and Harleian and Additional via another. Dodsworth is clearly superior to Rawlinson, and Harleian to Additional. Where the versions differ, Dodsworth very often has the most likely reading. Additional is very rough, omitting or simplifying many passages and confusing others. Rawlinson is also rough (its relative, Dodsworth, agrees less often with it than with Harleian) and it may have been influenced by the play: it is the only version that spells "Mamilion" as the lady's second deposition and the play do, and in the passage I quote above it has "six and seaven" against "seauen & eight" in Dodsworth and "seaven or eight" in Harleian and Additional. Dodsworth and Rawlinson omit the date of the deposition; Harleian gives March 2, Additional March 9.
All the ms. versions of young Robinson's deposition are quite inferior to the version printed as a last-minute addition to Webster's book of 1677 (sigs. Yy2-Yy3), which is regularly more logical and consistent and more like a deposition. I use this version and the version of Margaret Johnson's deposition in Dodsworth.

16. Privy councillors took an oath of secrecy: "You...shall keepe secret all matters comitted and revealed vnto you or shall bee treated of secretlie in Councell..." (P.C.2/44/p. 5).

17. The women in London were sent back to Lancashire in December, 1634, still "condemned," and nine of the convicted people were still in prison there in 1637, including three who had been in London: H.M.C., *Tenth Report*, IV, 433: *The Farington Papers*, ed. Susan M. Ffarington (Manchester, 1856), p. 27 (Chetham Soc., vol. 39). The King is often said to have pardoned them all, and at least once a specific date is given, June 30, 1634, but a source of the information is not given: see, for example, Whitaker, p. 187; Baines, I, 607-8; Clark, pp. 124-25. Though many pardons are noted among the records of the signet bills, privy seals, and patents of the time, I can find none for these people: see esp. S.O.3/10, 11; IND.6748; C.82/2112 ff. S. R. Gardiner suggested that they were kept in prison partly to protect them from their neighbors: *History of England...1603-1642* (London, 1883-84), VII, 325-26.

18. *The Famous History of the Lancashire Witches* (London, 1780?), p. 22.

19. For Laud, see, for example, H. R. Trevor Roper, *Archbishop Laud* (London, 1962), pp. x, 114-15, 173-74, 211-14, 223, etc.; *The European Witch-Craze of the*

16th and 17th Centuries (Harmondsworth, Middx., 1969), chap. 4: Keith Thomas, *Religion and the Decline of Magic* (London, 1971), chap. 15; and Laud, *Works*, VI, 372-73. For the meetings of the Privy Council, see P.C.2/43, 44. See also Chambers, I, 39n.

20. The man at Magdalen matriculated on March 3, 1598, when he was thirteen years old, and took the M.A. in 1605 (*Alumni Oxoniensis*, "Nathaniel" and "Thomas Tomkins"; *D.N.B.*, "Thomas Tomkins"). Our man has been confused with the musician's son, another Nathaniel, who became a prebendary at Worcester Cathedral, also took an interest in drama (in 1635 he had turned "Diuerse vestments and other ornaments of" the Cathedral "into Players Capps and Coates and Imployed" them "to y^t vse": S.P.16/298/#43 and *C.S.P., Dom., 1635*, p. 395), and died in 1681. In versions of our man's letters printed in *C.S.P., Dom., 1640-41*, pp. 130-31, 539-40, 547, 555-56, 559-60, and *1641-43*, pp. 193, 259-60, he is often said to be the prebendary, but by the editor not the writer.

21. H.M.C., *First Report*, pp. 59-60; S.P.94/22/f.241. In his will of December 21, 1615, the poet's father mentioned unmarried daughters but not by name; in her will of November 8, 1652, the poet's mother mentioned a daughter, Cicelie Tompkins, as still alive (PROB.11/129/ff.143-44; /229/f.262-62^v). The Debates compiled for the parliaments of the 1620s mention a person named Tomkins as speaking only four times, and only once when Nathaniel was the sole member of the name: in 1621 he urged outspoken puritans to act with charity, wisdom, and moderation. See *Commons Debates, 1621*, ed. Wallace Notestein, et al. (New Haven, 1935), V, 501n.; *Commons Journal*, I, 524; and Robert E. Ruigh, *The Parliament of 1624* (Cambridge, Mass. 1971) p. 223.

22. V.C.H., *Somerset*, III, 195; *Members of Parliament* (London, 1878), I, 453, 459, 463, 465, 471, 477; III, xxxvii. At Christchurch Tomkyns may have been the nominee of Lord Arundell, who had the choosing of one of the members (V.C.H., *Hampshire*, V, 87).

23. The handwriting of the person who wrote about Heywood's and Brome's play is the same as that of the clerk of the Queen's council. Many of the clerk's letters survive among the state papers and one among the Phelips papers. At least part of each of these, including in every case the signature, is in the hand of the writer about the play (see, for example, S.P.16/469/#11; /479/#27, 34, 62, 74; /486/#34; /488/#72; /535/#6; and DD/PH 223/#6). In one of these letters the writer mentions "my Bro: Waller" (/479/#27), and in two he mentions staying at Beaconsfield, where Waller's chief residence was (/469/#11; /488/#72). In 1642 this man noted that he had been "Clearke of the Counsell" to Prince Charles and described his work for the Earl of Holland (C.2/Chas.I/T.20/4). Just before he died, he said he was Waller's brother-in-law and had served Charles as prince and king and eaten his bread "it will be 23 yeers in August next [1643]," adding that he had been a servant (meaning, perhaps, clerk) to him for twenty. The House of Commons then, like Clarendon later, described him as both Waller's brother-in-law and clerk of the Queen's council. See below and John Rushworth, *Historical Collections* (London, 1692), pt. 3, II, 322; Conrad Russell, *Parliaments and English Politics 1621-1629* (Oxford, 1979), p. 149; *C.S.P., Dom., 1641-43*, pp. 111, 118-19.

24. The Queen's councillors were sometimes called the commissioners for her

revenue (Rushworth, pt. 3, II, 322). The person to whom they were responsible, hence Tomkyns' superior, was her chancellor, Lord Savage to 1635, then Sir John Finch to 1640, then Sir John Lambe.

25. DD/PH 224/#88, 89.

26. The paper is torn where the day was written, so that only "Mar: 1625" survives clearly written; but an "o" seems faintly to survive before the month, and one piece of news reported in the letter belongs to March 28, 1625 (Sir Humphrey May's becoming a member of the Privy Council: *C.S.P.*, *Dom.*, *Addenda, 1625-49*, p. 1). The letter enclosed a document that "should haue come by Mr Gresley" to Phelips but inadvertently had not—Walsingham Gresley, perhaps, the Earl of Bristol's steward. The earl, who lived some ten miles east of Montacute at Sherborne Castle, had been head of the mission in Spain to which Phelips and perhaps Tomkyns had for a time belonged, and at least in 1622-23 Gresley had been a messenger journeying between Madrid and London (*C.S.P.*, *Dom.*, *1619-23*, pp. 424, 540, 544, 550, etc.). In 1625, the earl was as much out of royal favor as Phelips was. All the letters signed "El hombre fiel" are noticed in the *Third Report*, pp. 282-83, some of them extensively.

27. All these remarks refer to the addressee only indirectly as Sir Robert Phelips or "El hombre de bien." In the first Tomkyns wrote, "I will tell you plainly what I would do were I Sr Rob: Phelips" and then told the addressee plainly. In the second he wrote that "our friend (el hombre de bien) was pleased to require my opinion" and then gave the opinion. In the third he wrote that "the arrowe of Bristol came out of the quiuer of their neighbo^r and our antient and noble friend El hombre de bien," meaning that the mayor and aldermen of Bristol were opposing royal schemes as Phelips had done. After this essay was printed in 1984, Mr. D. M. M. Shorrocks, the county archivist of Somerset, kindly referred me to an essay of which I had not known. In it H. F. Brown identifies "El hombre fiel" as I do but offers different and not fully developed reasons. See "El Hombre Fiel" in *Notes and Queries for Somerset and Dorset*, XXX (March, 1977), 238-41, especially 238.

28. At the death of Sir Edward Phelips (September 30, 1614), according to his Inquisition Post Mortem, the heir, Sir Robert, was twenty-eight years old. Yet Sir Robert is given as thirty-one years old "or thereabouts" in a deposition of May 3, 1616. On January 31, 1588, the future Sir Robert was, according to his grandfather, a "lyttle boy." See DD/PH 238-39/#6/f.62; 122/#5/f.1; 224/#3/f.4^v.

29. Bentley, IV, 917-21; I, 310-11.

30. Tomkyns had a hand in the remitting of a small fine in November, 1634 (S.P.16/535/#6 and *C.S.P.*, *Dom.*, *Addenda, 1625-49*, p. 484). In the same month, a fine imposed in the Somerset assizes on John and James Chaffy and Nicholas Pettibone for assault and battery was remitted via a pardon procured by Sir Sidney Mountague at the suit of Morris Aubert, the Queen's surgeon (S.O.3/11). By "my Lo:" Tomkyns probably meant his superior, Lord Savage.

31. The affair is usually known as Waller's plot. A full account of it is in *Cobbett's Complete Collection of State Trials* (London, 1809), IV, cols. 625-52. See also Clarendon, *History*, VII, 54-73; *The Poems of Edmund Waller*, ed. G. Thorn

Drury (London, 1905), pp. xxxix-lvii; etc.

32. *The Whole Confession and Speech of Mr. Nathaniel Tompkins...Made upon the Ladder at the time of his Execution...5 July 1643* (London, 1643), which was printed by authority of the "Committee of the House of Commons...concerning printing," granted on the day the speech was made. A *Satyrick Elegie* about the execution was published at Oxford in 1643; it attacked the parliamentary cause and defended "brave Tomkins" who "stood undaunted" before his judges.

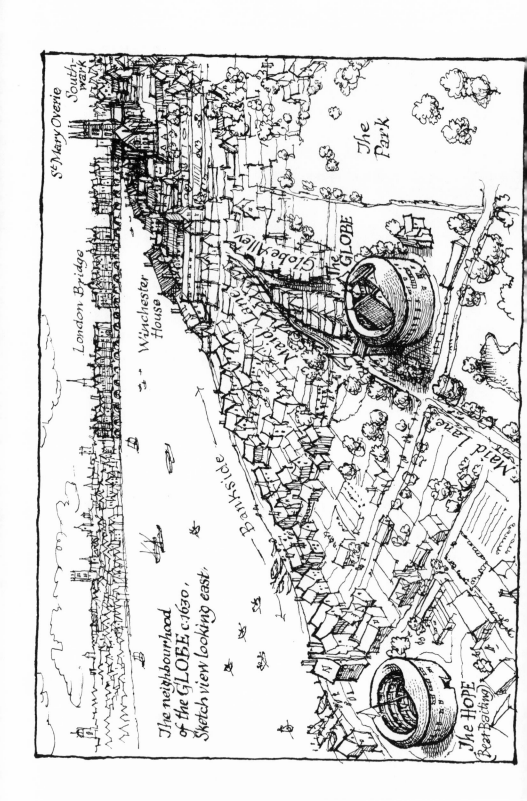

St Mary Overie

South-wark

London Bridge

Winchester House

The Park

GlobeAlley

The GLOBE

Maid Lane

Maid Lane

Bankside

The neighbourhood
of the GLOBE c.1630,
Sketch view looking east.

The HOPE
(Bear-baiting)

A New Lawsuit
about the Globe[1]

In an article published in *The Times* on April 30 and May 1, 1914, C. W. Wallace reported having found at the Public Record Office many new documents about the Globe Playhouse. He was willing to share with his readers, however, only a few tantalizing echoes from the documents and not the magic numbers that would allow those readers to find the documents easily and see for themselves. He promised to publish the documents properly later, but he did not keep the promise. W. W. Braines then identified and used apparently all these documents in his book, *The Site of the Globe Playhouse Southwark*. Some years ago, I noticed that Braines had not found one or one group of Wallace's documents. I eventually concluded that it or they must belong to the lawsuit in the Court of Requests about the Globe alluded to in the so-called sharers papers of 1635 (in print since 1882) and never identified.

151

Wallace, I deduced, had found a bill of complaint filed by the Globe people and perhaps some allied documents attached to it. The document or documents would lie among a vast pile of such things in the Court of Requests, 326 bundles for the reign of Charles I and 50-odd bundles and boxes of, literally, bits and pieces for all the reigns from Henry VIII to 1642. The pile must contain well over 40,000 documents, none of them indexed, calendared, or arranged chronologically. I decided that my remaining years were too few and my remaining eyesight too dim for me to start through them. So I tried looking in the books of decrees, orders, notes, and whatnot having to do with the progress and conclusions of lawsuits in the Court of Requests. These books are also (with a few exceptions) unindexed, but they were kept chronologically, and only fifty record the doings in the thousands of lawsuits passing through the court during what I took to be the period of Wallace's lawsuit. Besides, Wallace's tantalizing hints suggested that he had not found anything about the progress and conclusion of his case. I was lucky. I found entries about the case detailing much of its progress and explaining a first conclusion and then a second and final conclusion. I discussed these things and transcribed them in an article in *Shakespeare Quarterly*, Autumn, 1981, pp. 339-51. They provide a good deal of new information about the Globe.

I continued to worry, however, about Wallace's document or documents and once or twice was on the point of plunging into that pile. Then a year or so after the article had appeared, I remembered that Wallace's papers had fetched up in the Huntington Library in San Marino, California. He had left them to his wife, Hulda, and she had left them to her sister, Miss Victoria Berggren, who in 1962 had passed them to the Huntington. Could Wallace's notes about this lawsuit be among those papers? If they could, surely they would give a call number at the P.R.O. If they could not, perhaps some scrap of paper would contain doodlings of Wallace's among which would be some numbers I could try at the P.R.O. In April, 1983, I went to the Huntington to see.

In the Huntington's list of Wallace's papers, I found first an accurate notation about the lawsuit. Then in the papers themselves I found what must be Wallace's complete file about the lawsuit, P.R.O. numbers and all. Wallace had apparently meant to make a monograph or small book of the lawsuit, much like his book about the documents of the Theatre in Shoreditch, *The First London Theatre* (Lincoln, Nebr.: University of Nebraska, 1913), containing, that is, a discussion and then the documents themselves transcribed *in extenso*. As I had deduced, he had found the bill of complaint, which has many attachments. He had also pursued the case up to its first conclusion. He had not only transcribed everything he had found, but he had had somebody prepare a fair copy of his transcriptions. He had then gone over the fair copy, adding new headings to documents, a few explanations, and some queries. On his own transcription of the document reporting the first conclusion (no. 26), he had noted, "End—final decree" and "Proof read against original, 27 Jan, [19]10. C.W.W." He drew up three pages of numbered notes (1-83), about the contents of various documents for, it seems, the discussion that would precede the transcriptions, but the work stopped there, evidently in the early months of 1910.[2]

I propose to publish the work that Wallace did not. I shall discuss the events that led up to the lawsuit and trace its whole progress up to not the first conclusion, which Wallace thought final, but the second one, which really was final. I shall then discuss how some of the information in the new documents adds to our knowledge of the Globe. I shall use the matters I reported in my article in *Shakespeare Quarterly* (with the kind permission of the editor), corrected where necessary in the light of the documents I did not have when I wrote the article. I shall, finally, append my own transcriptions of the documents belonging to the lawsuit, and I shall include the magic numbers.

These documents provide yet more information about the history of the Globe and the theatrical enterprise in it, and they also provide information about other things. They tell us at last, for example, what it cost to build and rebuild the Globe. They tell us much we did not know about the lease by which the people at the Globe held the land on which their playhouse stood. If the documents do not reveal the size and shape of the building, they do suggest what it was made of and how much these materials were worth. They hint at the arrangements for rebuilding the Globe. They even give us a glimpse of that rival playhouse, the Swan, as it was four years later than our latest glimpse heretofore.

When James Burbage's sons and their associates—the Lord Chamberlain's Men as they then were, the King's Men as they became—could not renew the lease on the property in Shoreditch where their old playhouse, the Theatre, stood, they leased a site in Maid Lane in Southwark. They then had the Theatre pulled down during the last days of December, 1598, and its "timber" (the main members) and "wood" (facings, doors, wainscoting, and the like) taken to the new site.[3] There, by about June, 1599, these pieces of the Theatre and, no doubt, much else became the Globe. This building was burned to the ground in June, 1613, but was rebuilt and open again for business within about a year. It remained in business until the general closing of the Theatres in 1642.

Before Wallace appeared in the Public Record Office, we knew very little about the lease on the site in Maid Lane—only that the King's Men did indeed hold the property by lease and that in 1635 they had trouble getting the then owner of the property, Sir Matthew Brend, to renew the lease. This information derived from the sharers papers, about which more presently. Then Wallace found not only accurate allusions to the terms of the lease in one lawsuit but a long paraphrase of it in another. He formally announced these discoveries in 1909 and 1910, giving citations. The original lease was granted by Nicholas Brend, Sir Matthew's father. It took effect at Christmas, 1598, though it was not signed until February 21 following. It was to run for thirty-one years, until Christmas, 1629, and the rent was £14.10s.0d. a year.

These new details invited new questions. What effect did the fire and rebuilding of 1613-14 have on the lease? Could the King's Men afford to rebuild their playhouse with only fifteen years of their lease remaining? How was the lease renewed until 1635, and how was the trouble of that year resolved so that the King's Men could continue in the Globe until 1642? Did the rent increase as the lease was renewed, and if so by how much? As we can now see, Wallace knew the answers to all these questions when he was publishing information about the original lease in 1910. For the lawsuit he finished transcribing in January, 1910, and mentioned briefly but did not identify in 1914 concerns mainly these very matters.

The sharers papers consist of three kinds of documents: (1) petitions addressed to the Lord Chamberlain in the late spring or early

summer of 1635 in which three players among the King's Men
(Robert Benfield, Eliard Swanston, and Thomas Pollard) argued that
they should be allowed to acquire shares in both playhouses used by
the company, the Globe and Blackfriars; (2) the replies written during
the month or so following by those who owned most of the shares (the
Burbages and an old player, John Shanks); and (3) the Lord
Chamberlain's decisions, dated July 12 and August 1, 1635.

The players, Shanks, and the Lord Chamberlain all alluded to
our lawsuit. The players said that they had "suffered lately the sayd
Housekeepers [i.e., the then shareholders] in the name of his Ma^{ts}
servants, to sue & obtaine a decree in the Court of Requests against S^r
Mathew Brand, for confirmation vnto them of a lease paroll for about
9 or i0 yeeres yet to come, which they could other wise haue prevented, vntill themselues had beene made" shareholders. They listed
the current shareholders in both playhouses and opposite those in the
Globe noted, "of a lease of 9 yeeres from o^r Lady day last [March 25]
1635—not yet confirmed by Sr Mathew Brand to bee taken to feofees."
Shanks wrote that he had bought one of his shares "about allmost 2
yeeres since" and the other two "about 11 months since." When he
bought these three shares, "there was a chargeable suit then depending in the Court of Requests betweene Sr Mathew Brend Kn^t & the
lessees [i.e., the then shareholders] of the Globe & their assignes for
the adding of nine yeeres to their lease in consideration that they and
their p^{r}decessors had formerly beene at the Charge of 1400^{li} in building of the sayd House vpon the burning downe of the former, wherein,
if they should miscarry[,] for as yet they haue not the assurance
perfected by Sr Mathew Brend," he would have laid "out his money
to such a loss, as the pet^{rs} will neuer bee partners wth him therein."
The Lord Chamberlain, finally, noted on July 12, 1635, that "five
yeeres" remained in the lease of the Globe, and he added that a lease
of the Globe "is to bee made vpon the decree in ye Court of Requests."[4]

Hence the lawsuit was in the Court of Requests. The plaintiffs
were the King's Men, either the whole company or just its shareholders, and the defendant was Sir Matthew Brend, who owned the Globe
property. The King's Men were seeking an extension of their lease on
the property for five, nine, or ten years. The current lease expired in
1635. The lawsuit was in progress in 1633 or 1634. The King's Men

argued that they should have an extension because they had spent
£1,400 rebuilding the Globe after the fire of 1613. By the summer of
1635 the King's Men had won a preliminary victory but still did not
have an extension.

In his article of April 30 (pp. 9-10) and May 1 (p. 4) in *The Times*,
Wallace turned to this lawsuit mainly on May 1. He did not even tell
us in what court the lawsuit was argued, but he did assure us that it
contains some intriguing things. On October 26, 1613, after the Globe
had burned down, the King's Men got John (later Sir John) Bodley to
extend the original lease for six years, until Christmas, 1635. Bodley
controlled the Globe property from 1601 to 1622. Wallace went on:
"It was soon found necessary to reckon with the young heir, Mathew
Brend. So on February 14, 1614, Cuthbert Burbage, Richard Burbage,
John Heminges, and Henry Condell, on behalf of themselves and
their partners, went out to West Moulsey and got the signatures of
young Mathew, his mother as his guardian, and his uncle as witness,
to a renewal of the original Brend lease with an extension to December
25, 1644. The long and lively sequel to this step cannot here be
touched upon." In 1633, as Wallace added, Sir Matthew Brend "was
giving the Globe company trouble. But in his attempt to abrogate the
lease signed during his minority in 1614, and to lease the Globe now
to others over the heads of the old company at an enormous rent, he
was defeated at the end of a long litigation, of which I am publishing
the complete records."

Chambers took Wallace's word for all this, and with it partly in
mind he guessed at, among other things, how much the King's Men
paid as rent during the various stages of their lease on the Globe
property. Bentley, however, chose to ignore this aspect of Wallace's
article.[5]

As customary, both sides in the lawsuit reviewed past events in
their opening documents, the King's Men in their bill of complaint
(no. 1), Sir Matthew Brend in his answer (no. 2). The King's Men
said that Nicholas Brend had granted his original lease in return "for
divers greate and valuable Consideracions." But Sir Matthew Brend
protested that his father had received only what the lease specified—
that is, the annual rent of £14.10s. 0d. The King's Men said that
they, or, rather, their predecessors, had then laid out at least £1,000

"in the erecting newe building and setting vp there in and vpon the said demised [i.e., leased] premisses of a howse structure or building vsed for a Playhowse and Commonly called the Globe." Brend did not believe that the Globe people had spent £1,000 "or neere any such summe." As to the fire of 1613, the King's Men reported that the Globe "was by Casualty of fire vtterly ruinated burnt downe and Consumed" so that they lost their £1,000 "at the leaste." Brend was reluctant to admit that there had been a fire, but "in Case any Casuallity happened therevnto," it was caused by the King's Men's "negligence or ill keepeinge."

Both sides then discussed the rebuilding. The King's Men reckoned that they needed a lease of thirty-one years at £14.10s. 0d. a year "to inhable and incourage them to newe erect build and sett vp the said Playhowse," just as their predecessors had needed a similar lease to build the place originally. Since they had sixteen years remaining in the old lease, they needed an extension of fifteen years at no increase in rent. Cuthbert and Richard Burbage, John Hemings, and Richard Condell went on behalf of themselves and the other shareholders (including Shakespeare) to John Bodley, who held the mortgage on and controlled the property. He took "notice of the greate losse and charge susteined and to be susteined by them...in reedifying" the Globe, and on October 26, 1613, he renewed the lease for six years at no charge and no increase in rent. He refused, it seems, to countenance a longer extension. So in February, 1614, the Burbages, Hemings, Condell, and John Atkins, a scrivener who was Hemings' son-in-law, repaired to Brend, the heir apparent. They were looking for a further nine years but would ask for all fifteen, so that if Bodley's control of the property proved imperfect they would also have the heir's word for the first six.

He had just reached his fourteenth birthday and lived with his mother, stepfather, an aunt, an uncle, and numerous siblings in the family mansion at West Molesey in Surrey, across the Thames from Hampton Court Palace. The Globe people found the boy, his mother, and uncle at home. Despite his youth, Brend seemed to the King's Men "well able to iudge not onely of the greate losse which had befallen" them, "but also of the greate charge and expence" they "were to be putt vnto in and about the newe erecting and building of the" Globe. He was also, they thought, well aware "of the benefitt

and advauncement that should come to his lands and ground thereby.''
The boy, his mother, and uncle, therefore, were ready to give the
King's Men their further nine years at neither charge nor increase in
rent. Because he was under age, however, no contract he signed could
be binding on him. So the King's Men offered him an unusual
document to sign. It gave its purpose as to encourage the King's Men
to rebuild the Globe, and it declared that they meant to spend £1,000
doing so. It provided that when Brend was twenty-one years old he
would confirm an extension to their lease of fifteen years from Christmas, 1629, and they would pay him £10 to do so. The boy signed the
document on February 15, and his mother and uncle "attested and
witnessed'' it, as did the scrivener, Atkins.[6] Partly on the dubious
strength of this contrivance, the King's Men set about rebuilding the
Globe. Presently, "at theire owne proper Costs and chardges,'' they
"erected builte and sett vp there vpon the said demised premises in
the same place where the former howse stood a very proper newe and
faire howse or Playhowse Called the Globe.'' They spent, they said,
£1,500 "at the leaste being the greatest parte of'' their "substance
and estates.'' But Brend came to believe "that the nowe playhouse
called the Globe'' did not cost more than £500.

The two sides could agree, however, on what had happened since
the rebuilding of the Globe. In 1621 Brend came of age and in 1622
took control of his properties (confirming Bodley's extension of the
Globe lease in the process) and was knighted. The King's Men offered
him £10 "in all gentle and Courteous manner,'' but he refused to take
the money "or to doe any other thinge that may giue or Confirme any
longer tyme or Terme of yeares'' to the King's Men. By then he
thought the property worth a good deal more than £14.10s. 0d a year
and so wanted to repossess it as soon as he could. As the King's Men
put it, he took "advantage of his...minority'' in 1614 not to carry out
the terms of the document he signed in that year; as he put it, he "was
greately abused therein...and...is not Compellable in equity to make
the same good.''

This state of affairs persisted until the end of 1631, by which time
the original lease had run out and Bodley's extension had only four
years to run. Brend had convinced himself that he could never get
enough out of the place to make up for the money he and his father
had lost because of the low rent. He did not propose to pull the Globe

down when he would acquire it at Christmas, 1635, but he thought that "if fitt dwellinge houses had beene erected vpon" his property instead, "it had bene farre better for" him. He thought he should be able "to dispose of the same play house and premisses as pleaseth him and to whom he will and att such better yearely rentes as he can gett." According to the King's Men, he had been threatening to dispossess them "of the said house and grounds" in 1635 "and to thrust" them "out of the possession thereof and to sell it to others." Now he was threatening to sell his interest in the place to others at once, and those others, the King's Men feared, would not have the contractual obligations to them that Brend had. Despite its seventeen years of existence and the success of the King's Men's other house, Blackfriars, the Globe was still "for theire exercise and practise of theire quality very fitt and Comodious."

Late in 1631, the King's Men decided not to adopt the commonplace legal strategy for cases like theirs. That would have been simply to carry on at the Globe and when Bodley's extension ran out at Christmas, 1635, to try to keep possession according to the extension Brend had signed as a minor. Brend, or a successor, or a new tenant would try to take possession a few days later. Fights could occur. Soon Brend or somebody else would sue the King's Men for trespass in one of the main courts of common law, King's Bench or Common Pleas. There the whole issue would be the validity of that unenforceable extension. When defeat seemed close, the King's Men would take their case to one of the main courts of equity, Chancery or Requests, to ask that the case at common law be stopped and the matter be decided at equity. They would argue that while the extension might not be valid at common law, it should be valid at equity because of extenuating circumstances. The King's Men's predecessors had successfully followed this strategy at the turn of the century against their landlord in Shoreditch, Giles Allen, when they simply took down the Theatre and moved much of it to Southwark.[7] While that matter was perhaps no better in King's Bench than the present one, however, the extenuations they urged later in Requests were impressive. The present extenuation was that they had rebuilt the Globe in 1614, and so vastly improved the value of Brend's property, on the understanding that they could keep the property until 1644. Brend's reply was obvious and telling: they had rebuilt the Globe knowing that their lease was legally good only until Christmas, 1635, and if they had suffered losses, or not gained so much as they would have liked, they could hardly hold Brend accountable.

The King's Men hired two Northamptonshire men for their legal counsel, Richard Lane and Samuel Maunsell. Lane was an obvious choice. He had been a barrister for twenty years. He was a most prominent member of the Middle Temple and a busy figure in the Court of Requests, with which his family had been associated for at least sixty years and where people named Lane now held two of the principal jobs. He was also well connected at Whitehall and one of Clarendon's friends. He would become a leading royalist lawyer and judge, soon attorney general to the Prince of Wales, one day defender of Strafford before the House of Lords, and ultimately Lord Keeper. Moreover, the Globe people had reason to remember Lane's father, another Richard. He was the deputy registrar of Requests whom Giles Allen had accused thirty years before of illicitly helping them to defeat him.[8]

Maunsell, however, was not an obvious choice. He had been a barrister longer than Lane, for about twenty-four years, but his practice at the bar of the Court of Requests was fitful, and his personal affairs were chaotic, partly as a result of his inept management of his own legal occasions. He had impoverished himself by 1613 and "for manie yeares together lived retyred and was not in all probabilitie able to paye" his debts. For at least ten months in 1614-15 he was at liberty only because the officers of the Fleet Prison could not find him, his creditor being a lawyer or legal official named Richard Lane, but not the King's Men's counsel or his father. Maunsell married an heiress, Nightingale Fortho, but by the time he acquired her estate, her brother had wasted much of it. Maunsell then had numerous judgments issued against him for his own and his brother-in-law's debts. One creditor who tried to seize Maunsell's lands in 1625, and was still trying in 1629, found that they had been seized by others with prior claims. During the Easter term of 1629, another succeeded in having him imprisoned in the Wood Street Counter. He admitted to carelessness in one transaction and complained that his lawyer had been at fault in the lawsuit that followed. He was nonsuit in another of his lawsuits—dismissed because he had no case. In addition, he had ten small children by 1628, whom he said he could not maintain. Like

Lane, he belonged to the Middle Temple, but from 1627 he was not paying his bills there and in 1631 finally gave up his chamber. He died probably in the latter half of 1634, long before the King's Men's lawsuit came to an end.

For his part, Brend hired John White, who had been a barrister for about fourteen years. He, too, belonged to the Middle Temple, and, like Lane, he was a prominent member. Unlike Lane, however, he did little business in the Court of Requests, and he was becoming a leading puritan lawyer. As a member of the Long Parliament for, appropriately, Southwark, where the Globe was, White was to direct the plundering of royalist clergy in the early 1640's. Clarendon described him as "a grave lawyer, but notoriously disaffected to the Church."[9] Perhaps Brend thought a man like White could get his heart into discomfiting a theatrical enterprise.

In addition, each side was perforce supervised by one of the three attorneys of the court, who was supposed to see that his side did not outrage the court in some way. The man who supervised the King's Men was another Richard Lane, probably the one who tried to have Maunsell imprisoned in 1614-15. The man who supervised Brend was Peter Langley. Both had been attorneys in the court for a long time.[10]

Advised, no doubt, by their counsel, Maunsell and Richard Lane, the King's Men decided to keep Brend out of King's Bench or Common Pleas by taking the offensive against him well before their current extension ran out. The King's Men would have to do this by raising their extenuating circumstances in a court of equity, and they chose the court of their former triumph, Requests, where justice was a quicker, more deliberate process than in Chancery. Besides, Chancery had been known to throw out cases about players and playhouses because, as the Lord Keeper Egerton himself had said in 1602, they were "noe meete matter for this Court."[11] The strategy was that in Requests Maunsell and Lane would not try seriously to test the validity of the extension Brend had signed as a minor, but they would try to maneuver him into a court-supervised negotiation leading to an increased rent the King's Men could afford.

The King's Men assumed that Brend was interested in rents and not in equipping another company with a playhouse, or in running one himself, or even in pulling the Globe down and putting up houses instead. They were ready to concede that they should pay more rent for the Globe property. They assumed, too, that one way or another they would keep the Globe. For in 1633 or so, according to his remarks in the sharers papers, Shanks paid £156 for one of William Hemings' shares in the Globe and one in Blackfriars, and early in the autumn of 1634, before the court had ruled in the case, he paid £350 for Hemings' other two shares in the Globe and another in Blackfriars. While balancing the obvious equations,

$$x + y = 156$$
$$2x + y = 350,$$

to guess at the value of shares in the Globe at the time does not lead to a sensible result, it does suggest that those shares were far from worthless, even though the lease was about to expire. (Shanks went on to suggest that a share in Blackfriars might have been worth £60.) Another of the King's Men's assumptions was that the reasonable period for a valid extension was not twenty-one years or more but only the nine remaining of the dubious extension. Were they predicting that the Globe would be at the end of its useful life by Christmas, 1644, because either the structure or its custom would be in serious decline?

Maunsell drafted the bill of complaint that summoned Brend to defend himself, and Lane took charge of the case in the court room. The Court of Requests received the bill on January 28, 1632—in Hilary Term—and Brend in the person of John White hastened to file his answer, on February 6. The players who protested in the sharers papers of 1635 were wrong to think that the lawsuit was in the name of the King's Men in general, the whole enterprise at the Globe, and that they, therefore, could have exercised some control in it. The lease had originally been granted to the shareholders (or sharers) only, when that group consisted (except for Cuthbert Burbage) of leading players. The lease, therefore, still belonged to the shareholders, though thanks mainly to the scattering of shares on the deaths of the original holders the shareholders no longer had much to do with the playing of plays. It was partly this development that brought about the protest of 1635. So it was only the shareholders who filed the lawsuit, and it was to them that Brend replied. They are given as Cuthbert Burbage, Richard Robinson, and William Hemings, the three principal shareholders at the time, and two others whose names soon dropped from the documents of the case, John Lowin and Joseph Taylor. Cuthbert Burbage held three and a half of the sixteen shares then in the Globe, and he was the only surviving person in whose name the original lease had been made. Richard Robinson was an actor who had married Richard Burbage's widow and controlled the three and a half shares she had inherited. William Hemings, who was not an actor, held three shares he had inherited from his father, John, who had not only been an actor but, in effect, the company's treasurer. William Hemings sold all three of his shares to the ancient actor, Shanks, while the lawsuit progressed. Lowin and Taylor were actors who temporarily controlled a share or shares and, more important, had succeeded John Hemings as treasurer.[12]

Technically, Sir Matthew Brend did not own the Globe property. He had given it to his mother in 1624 as part of her dower, and when she died in 1627 to his wife, Dame Frances, as part of her jointure. Moreover, Dame Frances had given it to her two brothers to hold in trust for her, and on June 30, 1633, would give it instead to John Kingsnorth of London, gentleman.[13] The King's Men sued Brend himself because he had signed the extension of 1614 that they wanted confirmed. Moreover, it was he who actually managed the property, and in all the legal maneuvers that were to ensue neither he nor anybody else mentioned Dame Frances or any of her trustees.

Maunsell drew the bill of complaint to give the impression that Brend owed the King's Men a great deal and hence should carry out the extension signed in 1614 as a simple matter of equity. The King's Men, he suggested, had somehow given Nicholas Brend something of great value for the original lease.[14] They had spent great sums improving the Brend property by building the Globe on it, and then rebuilding it, "theire whole stocks and estates," indeed, by rebuilding it, which without Brend's word, promise, and agreement "they would not haue done." Maunsell admitted that the King's Men had no case at common law. It was usual in equity courts to argue that the question belonged there rather than in a place like King's Bench. "But nevertheles," he went on, "in equity...Brend ought to be bound" to carry out the extension he signed in 1614. And while Brend was not of age when he signed this document, "he was then of the age of Twenty or eighteene yeeres at the leaste." Maunsell implied that the document was already partly in force, hence that the rest should be, too. He did this by describing the document of 1614 first and then, many words later, the Bodley extension, which, he wrote, was "in parte of performance and towards the accomplishment" of the document of 1614. Naturally, he omitted to give the date of the Bodley extension. Maunsell concluded his argument by pointing out that the King's Men were required by their patent to perform before the King and that the Globe was a very suitable place in which to practice against these occasions. Moreover, that patent authorised them "to exercise theire said quality of acting and playing of Interludes Comedies and Tragedies in the same howse Called the Globe."

White seemed to destroy this argument in Brend's answer and in so doing rehearsed parts of the original lease about which we have not known. He denied that the King's Men and their predecessors had spent great sums, and he announced both Brend's true age in February, 1614, and the date of Bodley's extension. But he thought these things largely irrelevant. The original lease, he declared, gave the Globe people the right to pull down buildings on the site, provided they built as good or better instead. It required them to keep all the buildings on the site, whether there originally or built later, in good repair and to leave them so at the end of the lease. Once the Burbages and their associates had built the Globe, that is, they had to keep it in good repair and deliver it so to the Brends at Christmas, 1629. It was because of these provisions that Nicholas Brend had asked for so little rent in the first place. Sir Matthew Brend conceived now, therefore, that the King's Men were bound "att theire owne Charges to haue repayred whatsoeuer the said fire destroyed and leaue the same buildinges in good repaire...att the end of the said old Lease." Neither Brend nor Bodley had to extend the lease at the time of the fire or since. Bodley's extension, indeed, gave the King's Men "much more profitt and advantage" than Brend "was bound either by Lawe or equity to giue vnto them." The fire at the Globe, in short, was the King's Men's problem and not Brend's.

The King's Men decided to respond to this logic before going on to the next stage of lawsuits in such places as Requests, the examining of witnesses. They were in no hurry, however, and when they did respond in a replication of May 10 (no. 3), they simply swore that Brend's answer "is very vncerteine vntrue and insufficient" and their bill "iust true certeine and sufficient," as they were "ready to averre and prove." For his part, Brend must have thought his answer to the King's Men's bill needed no gilding, nor this response of the King's Men any comment. So he put in no rejoinder.

Early in the autumn, the King's Men pressed on. They framed questions (no. 4) to be put to witnesses, who were supposed to confirm the main parts of the bill of complaint and refute part of Brend's answer but not his central contention. First the King's Men challenged Brend's assertion that the rent for the Globe property had been low from the beginning and that the property would have been worth more had the Globe not been built on it. "Is not the same rent" of £14.10s. 0d. they asked, "much more then the said parcells of ground and garden plotts would haue yeilded yeerely in rent before the erecting of the said Playhowse therevpon?" Then the King's Men wanted to show that the Globe had indeed cost £1,000 "or very neere so much" at its first building. They wanted to confirm what they had said in their bill about the document Brend signed as a minor, "the better to incourage them to newe build the said Playhowse." They wanted especially to confirm that the Globe had cost a great deal to rebuild after the fire of 1613. They wanted, finally, to confirm that since Brend had come of age they had been "always ready and willing" to pay him £10 to carry out the terms of that document he had signed as a minor. They had five witnesses. One was John Atkins, the scrivener and brother-in-law of William Hemings, who had been performing legal tasks for the King's Men for many years. He was supposed to know about the inner workings of the Globe enterprise and to answer all the questions. The other four were literate workmen, two carpenters, a bricklayer, and a plasterer, who were supposed to say how much the Globe had cost to rebuild after the fire.

They all testified at Westminster Hall on September 18 (no. 5). Atkins could not say much about either the original lease or the original Globe. He had heard about and seen the original lease and did not believe that the Globe property could be worth £14.10s. 0d. a year without the Globe on it. He believed that the original Globe "might Cost the best parte of" £1,000 to build and hence that the King's Men had lost that much when it burned. But having been present when it was signed, indeed signed it himself as a witness, he did know about the document of 1614. The King's Men wanted the extension to their lease, he said, "the better to incourage them to reedify and newe build the said play howse"; and eventually Brend agreed to sign the document "if" the King's Men "would reedifie & newe build the said Playhowse." Atkins did not know how old Brend was at the time, but he conceived "that he was then of an age & Capacitie sufficient to be sensible both of the greate Losse...susteined by the burning downe of the said Playhowse as also of the greate benefitt that would accrewe vnto him...by the reedifieing & building thereof." The reedified Globe was "a very faire building or structure nowe vsed for a playhowse," which Atkins had heard "and doth verely beleeve did Cost" £1,400 or £1,500. Atkins also knew that the King's Men had asked Brend to carry out the terms of the document of 1614, who "hath denyed...or at the Least...deferred & delayed the performaunce thereof."

The four workmen were Richard Hudson and Thomas Spurling, carpenters, John Wathen, a bricklayer, and Richard Fisher, a plasterer.

Hudson had a very long history in the affairs of the Burbages and the King's Men. He was born in 1560 or 1561, and in his twenties he worked for Bryan Ellam, a carpenter whose daughter he married. When James Burbage hired Ellam to work on the buildings in Shoreditch that included the Theatre, Hudson was one of the workmen. That was in about 1580, Hudson said, and so it was that he had known James' son, Cuthbert Burbage, "of a Child." He was one of the workmen in July, 1586, whom James Burbage had evaluate the work done on the buildings in Shoreditch. He testified for the Burbages in February, 1592, in the lawsuit John Brayne's widow aimed at them in Chancery over the ownership of the Theatre. He testified for them again in May, 1600, in their lawsuit against Giles Allen in Requests over their right to pull down the Theatre and take much of it away—so that it could become the Globe. He was one of those at whom Allen aimed a counter lawsuit in 1601, claiming, among other things, that Hudson had perjured himself in his testimony for the Burbages (Hudson replied that he did not have to respond to such an assertion). Both times, he had testified only about work he and others had done on the buildings in Shoreditch other than the playhouse, because the Burbages' arguments had required him to do so. But he must have worked on the playhouse, too, and it is at least conceivable that he was one of the dozen unnamed workmen who did most of the work of pulling it down

in the Christmas season of 1598-99. The King's Men asked him to
help in the rebuilding of the Globe in 1614, but he had other work to
do at the time. He did join in the work on the house that was then
built adjoining the rebuilt Globe.[15] Now, in 1632, he returned to
Requests to testify a third time for a theatrical enterprise he had
known for over fifty years.

He thought the original Globe, which he said he had known from
the beginning, had cost about £700 to build. Evidently Cuthbert
Burbage had recently asked him to put a value on the timber and
carpentry in the rebuilt Globe, remembering, perhaps, James Burbage's
strategem forty-six years before. Hudson said they could not be worth
less than £1,100, but he must have been unsure, because a fortnight
before the examination he had asked another carpenter, Spurling, for
an opinion. Spurling, who said he was twenty-nine years old and
knew only Burbage among the litigants (and him "but of late"),
arrived at the same conclusion as Hudson about the timber and
carpentry. Wathen was a fifty-three year old who had known Burbage
about five years and none of the others. Burbage had asked him about
ten days before to look at the brickwork and tiling in the Globe.
Wathen reported that in materials and workmanship the brickwork
and tiling could not be worth less than about £240. Fisher was sixty
years old and had known shareholders among the King's Men for
about twenty years. A fortnight before the examination, Burbage had
asked him, too, to "considerately view" the Globe. He reported that
the plastering, work and materials, was easily worth £300.

The King's Men then waited almost two months for Brend to
have his witnesses examined, and when he did not, they forced his
hand. In the equity courts of the time, each side of a lawsuit had its
witnesses examined without telling the other what either the questions
or the answers were. The two sides eventually agreed that they were
ready for "publication." When the court granted it, all examining
ceased and the two sides made public what they had been asking and
getting from their witnesses. The case was then ready for negotiation
or a hearing. The King's Men asked the court on November 13 for
publication, and the court gave Brend two weeks, until November 27,
to finish his examinations (no. 6).

Brend hastened to get questions and witnesses ready. He had
three questions put to three witnesses (no. 7). He wanted to confirm

that Bodley had extended the lease on the Globe property for six years, to prove when he himself was born—hence how old he was in February, 1614, and to establish how much the King's Men made yearly "of and by reason of the said play-house." His first witness was George Archer, aged seventy or more, who was Brend's rent gatherer in Southwark, had been Bodley's, and may well even have been Nicholas Brend's. Archer was supposed to answer all the questions. The other two witnesses were John Cheswell, a haberdasher forty-three years old, and John Page, a twenty-nine year old servant of Brend's. These two had looked up the record of Brend's baptism.

The three men were examined at Westminster Hall on November 22 (no. 8). Archer reported that Bodley had indeed extended the lease six years from Christmas, 1629. Archer had not seen the record of Brend's baptizing, but he did know (not quite correctly) that when Nicholas Brend died in November, 1601, Matthew "was in his Cradle and not above xij monethes olde." He must have disappointed Brend when he said that the King's Men had made about £6 a year on the Globe property since the beginning of their lease—meaning, probably, the rents they collected on parts of the property separate from the Globe. Cheswell and Page reported that according to the register for burials and baptisms for the parish of St. Mary Aldermanbury, London, Brend was baptized in the parish church on March 6, 1600, and that, as they did not report, was exactly one month after he was born.[16] On February 15, 1614, he was fourteen years and nine days old.

The King's Men pushed both Brend and the court toward publication. On November 23, they had Atkins' apprentice, John Bell,[17] serve on Brend the court order of November 13 giving him two weeks to finish examining witnesses. Though Brend had actually finished with his witnesses by then, he did not offer to proceed to publication. So the King's Men had Bell report to the court on December 3 that he had served the order, presumably so that the court could compel Brend to agree to publication (no. 9). But the court did not grant publication, and the case simply disappeared from the court's records for over a year. Perhaps Brend and the King's Men fell to negotiating about a new extension to the lease, or perhaps the King's Men had other things to do and because Bodley's extension still had three years to run preferred to stay out of the Court of Requests for a time.

Both sides, it seems, took their lawsuit back to Requests early in 1634. The two lawyers, Lane for the King's Men and White for Brend, drew up and signed a statement (dated February 5, 1634) of the facts in the quarrel (no. 10). Though the court had not granted publication, the examinations of both sides were mutually available. For the statement gives Brend's age in February, 1614, as Cheswell and Page had done, as reckoned from the date of his baptism, and the cost of the original Globe as Hudson's figure, £700. The rest of the statement derives not from the King's Men's bill and Brend's answer but from Nicholas Brend's original lease, the document Brend signed in 1614 as a minor, and Bodley's extension, all of which the lawyers no doubt had before them. It rehearses again parts of the original lease, including the King's Men's right to pull down buildings provided they built as good or better instead and their obligation to keep buildings in good repair. It adds a detail: when the King's Men or their predecessor pulled down a building, they had one year to put up another. The statement summarizes, apparently neatly, the document of 1614. It declares that the King's Men spent £1,400 rebuilding the Globe—the lawyers had accepted the lower of Atkins' two figures—and that they wanted an extension of nine years from the end of Bodley's extension, from, that is, Christmas, 1635, to Christmas, 1644.

This statement is odd. Lawyers were not prone to put their names to objective statements of their clients' quarrels. Wallace, indeed, noted, ''This is different from any other document ever met in this court.'' Lane and White agreed about what the facts of the case so far were. They may also have agreed that these facts led to subtle questions which court-appointed commissioners could best answer. (The King's Men, at any rate, wanted such commissioners to consider the case.) Most of the facts as Lane and White agreed to them probably amounted to a new formulation of the King's Men's extenuating circumstances. The original lease required the King's Men to rebuild the Globe after the fire, but only to its original value, which Lane and White put at £700. Encouraged by Brend, his mother, and uncle in the document of 1614 to spend more than that, £1,000, in return for a fifteen-year extension of their lease, the King's Men had actually spent £1,400. They had, therefore, increased the value of Brend's property by £700 more than he had a legal right to demand.

Another fact was that the document of 1614 was clearly invalid, as the King's Men admitted. The questions to be answered were: could the facts-cum-extenuations cause the invalid document to acquire force, and if so, how much, given that the King's Men had already received some reward in the form of Bodley's extension of their lease?

Whatever the reason for Lane's and White's statement, the case reached open court the next day, February 6 (nos. 11, 12), when Lane moved that the court hear both sides on Monday next (February 10). The court agreed to do so and noted that the case was delivered into court that day by the King's Men under the hands of both Lane and White, "of Counsaill severally wth the said parties." Neither Brend nor White seems to have been present to hear Lane, however, for the court ordered that the defendant was to have notice forthwith of the hearing.

On February 10, the two lawyers paraded their clients' cases in court, and Lane seems to have had by far the better of it. The clerk who kept notes summarized the exchange in a single sentence that expressed the heart of Lane's, not White's, case: "Recompence & advantage may make a voyd contract good" (no. 13). Moreover, and much worse for Brend, the court ordered that commissioners look into the dispute whose commission (that is, mandate) was, at least as the clerk expressed it, wholly on Lane's terms. The commissioners were to study the state of the property as Nicholas Brend had leased it and see whether the King's Men had improved it, or, as the clerk noted, whether "the thing [is] so much betterd that it is now in case to render more in proffitt then before." There were to be four commissioners, two chosen by each side.

Needless to say, Brend was not enthusiastic about pursuing such an inquiry, so he dithered. He did not name his commissioners, nor did he challenge the court's order that created their commission. After three months, the King's Men harried him. They got the court on May 12 to renew the order for the commission and to add, or spell out, several details (no. 14). The commissioners were to be able to act if any three of them could agree, and they were to report on the octave of Trinity Term—a month hence. The commissioners were also "to mediate an end if they can," and if they could not, the court promised to grant publication at last and set a day for a decisive hearing in the next term (Michaelmas).

Still Brend dithered. Two and a half weeks later, on May 30, the King's Men had Atkins take him a copy of the order of May 12 under seal of the court. Atkins "desired" Brend to join in the execution of the commission by naming his commissioners, and Brend replied "that he would advise thereof & wthin 2. or 3. dayes give his Answeare whether he would or not." Brend went to Atkins' house a few days later "& told him that he would not ioyne...in the execucion of the said Commission." Atkins reported these events in an affidavit of June 6, which Lane presented in court the same day (nos. 15, 16). The court responded as Lane and his clients could have wished. It renewed the order for the commission yet again and added yet another detail: if Brend did not name his commissioners, the King's Men's commissioners could proceed on their own.

This stroke impelled Brend instantly into action. White (presumably) appeared in court the next day, June 7, demanding that the commissioners be instructed to study matters other than whether the King's Men had improved the value of the Globe property (no. 17). A specific question Brend wanted the commissioners to study was both a fit riposte to the King's Men's argument and an indication of how Brend was reckoning what the rent for his property should be: would the playhouse yield more income if it were converted into small holdings? The answer was probably much more, as the owner of the Boar's Head had realized about that playhouse some fifteen years before. The court refused to allow a general broadening of the commissioners' mandate, but it did allow the commissioners to seek an answer to Brend's question.

Brend now named his commissioners, and the King's Men had the commission formally issued. Atkins swore out the document, which was dated July 1 and issued in the King's name (no. 18). In it, the court began by repeating its previous instructions to the commissioners. That body was to find what the state of the property was when the Globe people acquired it and what "advantage may redound" to Brend as a result of the money they spent building on it. It was to ask Brend's question, how much more would the property have been worth if the King's Men had built tenements on it rather than the Globe. But the heart of Brend's case figures only once, and that in an obscure remark reflecting the King's Men's point of view—about their "Costs vpon it [the property] in his nonage," meaning, no doubt, the money they spent rebuilding the Globe after he had signed the document of 1614 as a minor. As before, the commissioners were "to end and determine the same matter...if ye can."

The court, however, added two new instructions about how the commissioners might end the matter. They were to examine further witnesses proposed by both sides, endeavoring "by all meanes to search and try out the veritie of the premisses." Moreover, "in case that by the obstinacie of any of the said parties or otherwise ye cannot," they were to tell the court on October 6 and turn over the examinations they had taken. The commissioners were George Bingley, Thomas Mainwaringe, Richard Daniell, and Henry Withers; and ominously for Brend should he do more dithering, the court said, as before, that its instructions were not only for all the commissioners but for "any three or two of them." Bingley was an officer of the Exchequer who had adjudicated matters before; he was also the second husband of Cuthbert Burbage's daughter, Elizabeth. Mainwaringe seems to have been a lawyer of the Inner Temple and Daniell a money broker of St. John Street, London. Henry Withers may have been a relative of Brend's by marriage.[18] If the list of names follows the protocol of such things, the first two men were the King's Men's nominees and the second two Brend's.

So the King's Men and Brend once more set about finding witnesses and framing questions. Eventually the King's Men had seven witnesses to answer six questions, and Brend had three witnesses to answer four questions. Three of the commissioners (Daniell was absent) put all the questions to all the witnesses "at the Howse Comonly Called or knowne by the name...of the Swan on the Banckside," appropriately enough, the old playhouse, on October 1.

Though the Swan is shown in existence as late as January, 1638, in drawings, this is the latest reference to it by name and use yet found. Heretofore we have known only that it was used occasionally by prize-fighters in the 1620s and that, according to Nicholas Goodman in 1632, it "was now fallen to decay, and like a dying *Swanne*, hanging downe her head, seemed to sing her own dierge."[19] Either Goodman was wrong, or at least part of the Swan had been put back into repair by 1634. The commissioners of the Court of Requests would not take official evidence in a hovel.

If we may judge from the questions the two sides now framed for their witnesses, the commissioners had moved the quarrel toward something that might more readily be settled by mediation. The invalid document of 1614 had vanished, and so had the King's Men's extenuations. The issue now seemed to be not whether the King's Men would stay at the Globe after Christmas, 1635, but how much they would pay for doing so. The King's Men meant their questions to show that the rent should not be great because Brend would be much enriched when he finally acquired the Globe. Brend meant his questions to show that the rent had always been too low and that when he should acquire the Globe he would not have a thing worth all those years of low rent. The arguments, however, were tricky for both sides. The King's Men had to establish that the Globe was worth a great deal on one hand but not a greatly increased rent on the other. Brend had to argue that the Globe was not worth much on one hand yet a large increase in rent on the other.

The King's Men summoned their scrivener Atkins again, Brend's rentgatherer Archer, three carpenters (Hudson again and Hugh Standish and Henry Segood, who said they were forty-two and sixty years old respectively), and two watermen (Thomas Blackman and Thomas Godman, aged sixty and fifty-five) to testify for them. They wanted to establish that the Globe property was practically worthless when they acquired it, and that Nicholas Brend had leased it to them so that they could build a playhouse on it. They wanted to show, too, that it had cost a great deal to rebuild the Globe, and now they included the cost of the house adjoining. That must have been the taphouse mentioned in the sharers papers, built and occupied by John Hemings, perhaps as a private venture. Why did the King's Men concern themselves with it now and not in 1632? William Hemings must have acquired his father's interest in it when his father died in 1630, and he could have sold that interest to the King's Men in 1633 or 1634 much as he sold his father's shares to Shanks then.[20] The King's Men, finally, believed that Brend had once said he thought the Globe worth £200 a year, so they also asked about that (no. 19).

They probably got less out of their witnesses than they wanted (no. 21). Three men described the property as worth very little at the time of the original lease—all three said there were no houses on it and two said it was subject to flooding, "overflowne by the Spring tides" because there was "no wall or fence to keepe the same out," though the ground did lie "betwene two ditches." But a fourth, Archer, was a more impressive witness. He said that the property consisted of "garden grounds and had two Tenements thereon of two roomes in each," and he added quite properly that Nicholas Brend estimated its value at £14.10s.0d. a year. Atkins believed that Nicholas Brend made the lease so that the King's Men's predecessors could build a playhouse on the property, but Archer *knew* he did. Three men were nearly agreed about what the house adjoining the Globe had cost to build, £200, including Hudson, who had helped to build it, but they and two others were curiously at odds about what it had cost to rebuild the Globe. Their estimates ranged from £1,400 "at the Least" to only £800. Three of them also gave, as we shall see, equally curious estimates of what the Globe and its adjunct might have been worth a year. As to what Brend had said about the value of the Globe, Atkins reported that he had heard Brend tell the two lawyers, Lane and White, that it was worth £200 a year, but Atkins did not say whether Brend had meant the place as a playhouse or as the matter much closer to his heart, a collection of small dwellings.

Hudson, incidentally, made an interesting remark about the effect of the Globe on its neighbors. Had it diminished the quality of the area? He believed "that the building of the Playhowse hath byn an advauncem^t to the yeerely value of all the howses therevnto neere adioyninge."[21]

Brend's three witnesses were men whom his opponents also summoned, Standish, Segood, and Archer. In effect, he wanted them to say three things: that the Globe property was valuable at the time of the original lease, that the property would be worth more to him when he should acquire it if it had houses on it rather than a playhouse, and that the materials of which the Globe was built were worth little as scrap (no. 20). His result must have been even less satisfying to him than the King's Men's was to them (no. 22). Only Archer said anything about the value of the property at the time of the original lease, a tight-lipped remark that it was worth £14.10s.0d. a year, "and further [he] saieth not." Only Archer, too, said anything about what the property might be worth if it had houses on it—double if not treble at Christmas, 1635, he said, judging by what neighboring houses yielded, and he meant £29 if not £43.10s.0d. Standish and Segood, being both carpenters, had shrewd ideas about the scrap value of the materials in the Globe. The first thought only £200, and the second thought even less, £160.

The commissioners did not bring about an agreement between the King's Men and Brend, nor do they seem to have pronounced either side obstinate. They passed the examinations on to the court, and then, though their commission was renewed (no. 27), they disappeared from the quarrel.[22] Brend, it seems, decided to bide his time, but the King's Men decided to press the case to a decisive hearing in open court, as well they might, their lease having only a little more than a year to run. On November 3, their lawyer demanded such a hearing (nos. 23, 24). The court ordered the case to be heard two weeks later whether Brend agreed or not: he was to have only "convenient notice" and not a chance to disagree. On November 17, the court set the case over until the next day (no. 25), and on November 18, the principal shareholders among the King's Men, Brend, and their lawyers all attending, the Court of Requests addressed itself decisively to the Globe (no. 26). The Lord Privy Seal, who was the chief judge of the court, was on the bench. He was the Earl of Manchester.[23]

The King's Men decided to accept the figure the two lawyers had arrived at in February for the cost of the Globe, £1,400, and the one the witnesses had recently agreed on for the cost of the house adjoining, £200. They also decided, as did Brend, that they would not be bound by the truncated form of the case the commissioners had pursued. They said in court that they had been induced to spend £1,600 "by the hopes" that the fourteen-year old Brend, his mother, and uncle had given them of an extension of their lease to 1644. Brend replied that Bodley's extension to 1635 was "a sufficient recompence for their charge in building & reedyfying the Play house." Moreover, "The streight of the Case" was how the contract signed by "the Infant shall binde him / Where the person is disabled there no Court can make him able." At that sticky point, someone proposed a compromise. Brend agreed to it, and the court enshrined it in a decree. The King's Men would have their extension of nine years from Christmas, 1635, but they would pay a great deal more rent, almost three times as much, £40 a year. They would also give security (that is, bonds) "for keeping the house[s] in repayre & Leaving them sufficiently in repayre at the end of the [new] terme." On these conditions Brend was to make a new lease and the King's Men were to accept it. Other than the new term, the new rent, and the new security, this lease was no doubt to be exactly like the original one granted by Brend's father, and Brend was to demand no fine for it, not even the £10 mentioned in the document of 1614.

The King's Men were evidently pleased with this settlement, but Sir Matthew Brend soon decided that it was inadequate. He declined to draw up a new lease according to the court's decree, and he began haggling with the King's Men for more rent, or a shorter term, or both. On January 17, 1635, the King's Men got the court to issue an injunction against Brend, requiring him to "performe" the decree, but the injunction seems to have had little effect on him (no. 28). He was behaving as he had done a decade earlier in his dealings with Bodley. A court had decreed a settlement between Bodley and Brend, and the two of them had actually carried out all its terms. Brend, however, decided that he should have done better in the settlement and spent four years arguing vainly with Bodley in Chancery.

Brend may have offered the King's Men a five-year extension during the summer of 1635, or so one may guess from the Lord Chamberlain's remarks about the lease in the sharers papers. If Brend did, they eventually refused it. For they were in a quite secure position, though their lease was on the point of expiring. The current shareholders, indeed, argued strenuously that shares were worth a good deal when on July 12 the Lord Chamberlain ordered that the three protesting players should have shares allotted to them. The shareholders argued that these players should pay the real value of the shares they were to acquire, and the Lord Chamberlain appointed a committee on August 1 to decide how much shares then were worth.

When the lease expired at Christmas, 1635, the King's Men offered Brend the new rent in return for a new lease drawn according to the court's decree. He refused to draw such a lease without more money. So they regarded themselves as still renting under the terms of the old lease and tried to pay him the old rent. Brend, of course, refused this, too, for to accept it was to suggest that he had extended the old lease, rent and all. Brend had now worked himself into a thoroughly self-defeating position reminiscent of his quarrels with Bodley. He received no rent, yet because of the decree in the Court of Requests he could ask no court to evict the King's Men. Instead of speedily drawing up a new lease that the King's Men would have to accept, he once more took up dithering. He did nothing for nearly two years, and with every successive quarter made his position worse. For the King's Men asserted that every quarter without a new lease was a quarter under the old lease at the old rent.

In mid-autumn, 1637, Brend finally gave up. He offered to draw up the requisite new lease, beginning, as the court had decreed, at Christmas, 1635. The King's Men refused to accept it. They would accept only a lease beginning at Christmas, 1637. They would not, that is, pay the new rent for the two years (including the current quarter) during which they had had no lease. So on November 9, 1637, Brend sent his lawyer back to the Court of Requests (nos. 29, 30), protesting that Brend was ready to draw up a lease in keeping with the court's decree and that the King's Men had refused to accept it. They had, moreover, paid no rent at all for two years, nor had they given him security to guarantee that they would keep the Globe in repair.

At last Brend had a legal triumph. Ignoring all the available legal hesitations, the court ordered that the King's Men "shall att their perill accept of the said lease in wryting...and pay" Brend "all his rent in arrere, and shall give the Security intended by the said decree by or before Monday next w^{th}out further delay." Monday next was November 13.

The King's Men were no ditherers. They let November 13 go by, but they were vigorously back in court a week or so later. Someone delivered an affidavit to the court on November 20, certifying, perhaps, that an agent of Brend's had served the order of November 9 on the King's Men and that they still refused to accept the new lease (no. 31). Another affadavit appeared in court the next day, November 21, in which the King's Men's agent certified, perhaps, that Brend had refused for many months to accept the new rent in return for a new lease (no. 32). The affidavits are now lost, and only dated entries in an index survive.

The court, therefore, turned again to the Globe, on November 28, 1637, the last day of the current term, Manchester now joined on the bench by Sir Edward Powell (no. 33). One Herbert, possibly Edward Herbert, seems to have argued Brend's case this time instead of White. If he was Edward Herbert, he was Brend's attempt to fight fire with fire. Edward Herbert was, like Lane, an eminent royalist lawyer, the Queen's attorney general (Lane had been the Prince of Wales' attorney general since September, 1634), who seven years later would lay before the House of Commons the King's disastrous case against the five members. Clarendon remarked that "the knack of his talk" was to seem "the most like reason without being it," and "His greatest faculty...in which he was a master" was "to make difficult matters more intricate and perplexed; and very easy things to seem more hard than they were."[24] If Edward Herbert was indeed Brend's man, the Court of Requests was no more impressed by him than Clarendon, for Brend came off badly. The court ordered the King's Men to pay the new rent for only one of the two years and, presumably, to pay the old rent for the other year. The new lease that Brend was to draw up and the King's Men were to accept was to accord with the decree of 1634, except that, in effect, it was to begin at Christmas, 1636, and continue for eight rather than nine years. As to the security the King's Men were to give to keep the Globe in repair, the court ordered a Mr. Lane to decide whether they should give Brend one bond or two. He could have been Richard, their counsel; or Richard, their attorney (perhaps the best guess); or yet another Lane at the Court of Requests, William, the deputy registrar, who may have been their counsel's brother.

There the matter seems to end. Presumably both Brend and the King's Men carried out the requirements of this order, and presumably the King's Men could contemplate the untroubled possession of their playhouse until Christmas, 1644.

One part of the history of the Globe about which there has been no question for a long time is the original lease of the Globe property granted by Nicholas Brend in the winter of 1598-99. In 1909 and 1910, Wallace published a lawsuit of 1616 containing a paraphrase of it, and then another of 1619 containing accurate allusions to matters in the paraphrase. Chambers made both paraphrase and allusions current coin by publishing much of the first in his *Elizabethan Stage* of 1923, II, 416-17, and all of both in his *William Shakespeare* (Oxford, 1930), II, 52-62. Nobody has wondered whether the paraphrase represents the whole of the lease, and Chambers took the paraphrase to be a quotation. With one exception (the tenants' right to use an alley), that paraphrase mentions only the basic provisions found in the first half or two-thirds of many leases of the time: the date, the parties, the description of the property, the term, and the rent. The present documents show that the lease was more complex than that. Like Wallace's lawsuit of 1619, they allude accurately to matters in the paraphrase, and, as the lawsuit of 1616 implies, they show that the paraphrase is just that and not a quotation. Above all, they reveal matters in the lease that are not in the paraphrase.

The paraphrase says that Nicholas Brend's lease was in the form of an indenture among three parties, but it does not say who the three parties were, probably because one can deduce who they were from what follows. The lease would have set out who they were. In the King's Men's bill of complaint (no. 1), their lawyer, Maunsell, ran through parts of the lease, having, no doubt, a copy of it before him. He wrote that the first party was Nicholas Brend, the second comprised Cuthbert and Richard Burbage, and the third comprised Shakespeare, Augustine Phillips, Thomas Pope, John Hemings, and William Kempe. Then in Brend's answer (no. 2), his lawyer, White, explained two provisions in the lease that do not appear in the paraphrase or any other document we have had. The King's Men did not deny the provisions, and eventually the lawyers for both sides agreed that they were part of the lease. The first provision allowed the King's Men, as the lawyers put it in their agreement (no. 10), ''to take and pull downe alter or Change any howses shedds pales fences or other buildings which then were [in the winter of 1598-99] or after should be in or vpon the premisses Soe as there be as good or better reedified and built on the premisses within a yeere then next ensewing.''[25] The second provision is found in many leases of the time. According to the lawyers' agreement again, it required the King's Men ''to maintaine and support...with all necessary reparacions'' the buildings and fences on the property, whether there in the winter of 1598-99 or erected later, and at the end of the lease to yield them up ''soe repaired made mayntayned and amended.''

The lease could easily have had several other provisions not mentioned in the paraphrase, and one is hinted at in the present documents: the lease could have said that the Burbages and their colleagues meant to build a playhouse on the property. In their interrogatories of 1634 (no. 19), the King's Men asked whether the "intent" of the lease was "to build a Playhowse" on the property. Their scrivener, Atkins, who knew the lease well, agreed (no. 21) that "the intent (as this deponent beleeveth)" was "to build a Playhowse thereon," then added, "But for the more Certentie therein he referreth himself to the said lease." Brend's rentgatherer, Archer, said flatly that the intent was "to build a Playhowse," but he did not mention the lease. In Wallace's lawsuit of 1616, the first sentence after the paraphrase reads, translated from the original Latin, "upon some part of the property a certain playhouse suitable for showing and acting comedies and tragedies came into existence [existebat]." The sentence cannot be part of the paraphrase because the Globe was built after the drawing up of the lease.[26]

Glancing at Wallace's remarks in *The Times* in 1914 and at the sharers papers, Chambers guessed that Bodley raised the rent to £20 when in 1613 he extended the lease by six years, from Christmas, 1629, to Christmas, 1635. Chambers did not say, but he must have meant that the increased rent would be paid from Christmas, 1629. Chambers also guessed that the Court of Requests raised the rent to £55 from Christmas, 1635. The present documents, however, make it quite clear that both guesses are wrong. The rent remained £14.10s.0d. from the beginning at Christmas, 1598, until the end of Bodley's extension at Christmas, 1635. The court decreed that the rent from then until Christmas, 1644, should be £40, not £55, but thanks to Brend's dithering, the King's Men paid £14.10s.0d. a year longer, until Christmas, 1636, and presumably £40 from then on (nos. 26, 33).

Chambers made his guesses partly because in the article in *The Times* Wallace remarked, without a citation, that Bodley demanded and got £20 from the King's Men in 1609 for him to recognize the original lease. Where Wallace found this information, I cannot discover. It is not in the present documents, and no lease then or now could require the lessee to pay a fee every time the ownership of the property changed hands or, as in this case, the lessor mortgaged the property. Wallace also remarked, without citation, that the King's Men paid Bodley a fee of £2 in 1615 for permission to build the house adjoining the Globe. That payment is not mentioned in the present documents, either, and, from what we now know of the terms of the original lease, it, too, was quite unnecessary. The King's Men had the right to build what they liked on the property. The present documents seem to show that the King's Men and their predecessors paid only their rent for the property—no fine to Nicholas Brend in 1598-99, none to Bodley in 1613, none to Matthew Brend in 1614, and none to the same Matthew Brend in 1637.

The present documents also explode one other venerable notion about the history of the Globe. As we have seen, the protesting players of 1635 thought the last extension of the lease was for nine years from Lady Day, 1635, rather than, as we might have expected, from Christmas, 1635. Moreover, a much-quoted document now at the Folger has Brend pulling down the Globe on April 15, 1644, exactly three weeks after Lady Day. The two pieces of evidence tally nicely. So Chambers, T. W. Baldwin, and others have concluded that the lease expired on Lady Day, 1644, and that Brend promptly took possession of the playhouse and had it pulled down. They have skipped over an awkward question. How could a lease that should have ended at Christmas, 1635, have actually ended nine months earlier?[27] One of these pieces of evidence, however, has recently lost some of its credibility: the document at the Folger is suspected of being a forgery. Now the other piece, the players' remarks in the sharers papers, must also lose credibility.

When the players wrote their petition in 1635, the final extension did not exist and would not exist for another two and a half years. We can hardly rely on them, therefore, to be accurate about its terms. Besides, in their brief remarks about the lease and the lawsuit, they made several mistakes. They were wrong to think 1) that the lawsuit was in the name of the King's Men in general, 2) that the final extension would be taken to "feofees" (by then Lady Brend had only one feofee, or trustee), 3) that the decree of 1634 required a "confirmation" of the document Brend had signed as a minor (the decree ignored that document and required at least two important things not in it: a great increase in rent and security that the King's Men would keep the Globe in repair), 4) that the document of 1614 was a "lease paroll," a verbal extension of the lease (it was a written and signed contract that promised an extension to be made later). This last mistake probably points to why the players made mistakes: they got their information by hearsay. The document of 1614 could not remotely be called a "lease paroll" by anybody who knew at first hand about either the document or the lawsuit. But it was, in legal jargon, something that sounds like that—a deed poll, an agreement made by one party rather than an agreement made by two or more parties (see no. 10).

Not yet being shareholders, the three players evidently knew only approximately what the management at the Globe was doing. Shanks' remarks in the sharers papers are not at odds with the present documents, and he was a shareholder. It is quite clear in these documents that the original lease expired at Christmas, 1629, Bodley's extension at Christmas, 1635, and the court-ordered extension at Christmas, 1644. If by any chance Brend did pull the Globe down on April 15, 1644, he had got possession by then not because the lease had expired but because the King's Men had ceased paying their augmented rent.

We have had no idea what it cost to build the Globe in 1599 and only Shanks' remark in the sharers papers about what it cost to rebuild the Globe after the fire. He said that the King's Men "had formerly beene at the Charge of 1400^{li} in building of the sayd House vpon the burning downe of the former." Both Chambers and Bentley accepted this figure, Chambers adding that it represented the cost of both the rebuilt Globe and the house adjoining, Bentley keeping his peace about the matter.[28] The present documents explain where Shanks' figure came from and show that Chambers, at least, was wrong. They also provide many new figures, perhaps too many.

There are, first of all, figures at last for the original building of the Globe in 1599. In their bill of complaint (no. 1), the King's Men said it had cost £1,000 "at the leaste," and when it had burned down they had lost the same amount, "at the leaste." Brend then said in his answer (no. 2) that they had not spent that much "or neere any such summe." The remark is no doubt predictable, but the King's Men themselves retreated from the amount in their bill. In their first interrogatories (no. 4), they gave the amount as £1,000 "or very neere so much," and in the answers to the interrogatories (no. 5), they retreated even more. Their scrivener, Atkins, said he believed that the original Globe "might Cost the best parte of" £1,000, and their carpenter, Hudson, "verely believeth [it] Cost them" £700 "or thereabouts," though Hudson added that when it burned down they lost £1,000 as he "verely believeth." Lane and White, the lawyers for the two sides, then agreed to accept Hudson's first figure in their statement of fact (no. 10). The Burbages and their associates, as Lane and White wrote, "therevpon spent about Seaven Hundred pounds in building a Playhowse Called the Globe." Presumably that included the value of the timber and wood of the old Theatre in Shoreditch which had been carried across the Thames and built into the Globe. The official figure for the cost of building the Globe in 1599, therefore, is £700, about what the Theatre itself had cost in 1576, rather more than the Fortune in 1601 (£520).

As for the cost of rebuilding the Globe in 1614, the King's Men began in their bill by saying they had spent £1,500 "at the leaste," not counting, it seems, money spent on the house adjoining. They then retreated from this amount even before they had finished with the bill, for they added that the rebuilding had enriched Brend's inheritance by £1,500 and they did not add "at the leaste." In his answer, Brend thought they had spent only £500, "if...so muche." Their man Atkins said on September 18, 1632 (no. 5), that he "doth verely beleeve [it] did Cost them" £1,400 or £1,500, not counting the adjoining house, and he thought himself an authority because he had drafted contracts with the builders who rebuilt the place. On the same occasion, the King's Men got two carpenters, a bricklayer, and a plasterer to say that the materials and labor in the Globe were worth £1,640. In the statement of fact, however, the two lawyers agreed to accept the lower of Atkins' two figures: the King's Men "new built the said Playhowse and expended about One Thowsand and foure hundred pounds therevpon," and that figure must not have included the adjoining house, either. The King's Men (hence Shanks) accepted this figure, for they used it in the hearing of November 18, 1634 (no. 26). Two of the King's Men's witnesses said on October 1, 1634 (no. 21), that the house adjoining the Globe had cost £200: Atkins and the carpenter Hudson, who had worked on it. The figure is probably reasonable, for even Brend's rentgatherer, Archer, thought this house had cost between £200 and £300. The King's Men accepted £200 and also used this figure in the hearing of November 18, 1634. The official figure for the rebuilding of the Globe, therefore, is £1,400 and for the building of the house next to it £200, or £1,600 altogether.

The documents, however, mention further figures. Those witnesses of the King's Men said some peculiar things on October 1, 1634. They were asked to give the cost of rebuilding the Globe and of building the house adjoining and also the annual value of both buildings. They responded as follows:

	Globe	House	Globe p.a.	House p.a.
Atkins	£1,300 or £1,400	£200	£40	£13.6s.8d.
Blackman		£30	£10	
Standish	£1,000			
Hudson	£1,400 at least	£200	———£66.13s.4d———	
Segood	£800			
Archer	£1,000	£200 or £300	£40 or £50	£8 or £9

Why should Atkins, an intimate in the business of the King's Men, admit that the rebuilt Globe might have cost only £1,300? Why should Standish, a carpenter, give only £1,000 and Segood, another carpenter, even less, £800? Moreover, all the figures for the annual value of the places seem odd. If twelve years' purchase, or a little more than 8% a year, is a fair guide to the value of property at the time, Atkins was saying that the Globe was worth only £480 and the house about £160. Hudson was saying that the two together were worth about £800. Even Archer thought the two places could be worth more a year than Atkins did. Could the commissioners who examined these people have inspired more caution than was necessary? Or could the Globe people have tried not to make the place seem too valuable, especially yearly, for fear that Brend could then demand more rent? In any event, these figures for yearly value are obviously artificial, as further figures arrived at by a public body only five months later and shown below also suggest. The Globe ought to have been worth about £116 a year and the house next to it about £16.

The costs of building and then rebuilding the Globe suggest, if nothing else, that the rebuilt playhouse was a splendid place. The King's Men must have been right to describe it in their bill of complaint as "a very proper newe and faire howse or Playhowse Called the Globe." John Chamberlain heard soon after it opened that it was the fairest playhouse that ever was in England. The second Globe occupied the same geographical space as the first, indeed could have sat on some of the same pilings, yet it cost twice as much to build. It actually cost as much to build as the Boar's Head, Fortune, and Hope combined. The second Globe had a lot more money spent on it than was strictly necessary in a playhouse of the time, and since that money did not increase its size on the ground, it must have gone into some remarkable appointments and structural features.

This idea that the first and second Globes occupied the same geographical space is one of those truisms in the history of the theatre that one neither doubts nor looks into. The truism takes one to a striking conclusion, for the ground plan of the first Globe was, it seems, the one with which James Burbage had begun the age of the great public playhouses at the Theatre in 1576. He and his successors, therefore, seem to have used the same ground plan from one end of the age to the other. The truism, however, is based on a single piece of evidence the reporting of which is a thorough muddle. William Rendle published an inaccurate and incomplete report of the evidence in 1877, and Chambers (II, 426), then Bentley (VI, 186) reprinted Rendle's remarks more or less faithfully except for further omissions. Moreover, Rendle, followed by Chambers and Bentley, misdated the evidence as 1634 and, confusing a remark of Rendle's, Chambers offered a second date, 1637, also wrong.[29] Even so, the truism is not untrue, as a remark in the present documents makes clear.

For many years the government had been trying in vain to stop the growth of London. It was worried about inhabitants multiplying "to such an excessiue number, that they could neither be gouerned nor fedd" and about the spread of infection and the danger of fire. Ferocious proclamations appeared laying out three principles, that no new houses be built except on old foundations, no new or existing houses be divided or otherwise occupied by more than the original number of dwellers, and new houses be solidly built of stone or brick. These proclamations were supposed to be enforced by Commissioners for Buildings who reported directly to the Privy Council. The government systematically watered its own wine, however, by allowing new buildings on new foundations if the builders paid a fee and acquired a license. So builders put up a vast number of illegal buildings, often in great haste during vacations, even at night, when the commissioners were not looking, and if caught offered to pay the fee. The commissioners sometimes sprang into vigorous activity, bundling offenders off to the Star Chamber for punishment and driving the sheriffs to pull down buildings whose owners would not. One such spell of activity began in November, 1633, and intensified in January, 1634. The commissioners, many of them privy councillors, were to demand from each parish a survey of new buildings put up since 1605 and to meet twice weekly to decide which had been built legally, which had not but should be suffered to stand on payment of a "rent" to the King, and which should be demolished. As spring came on this enthusiasm waned a good deal, especially as it applied to twice-weekly meetings. It waxed a little, however, toward the end of January, 1635, and it was then that the commissioners got round to the large parish on the south side of the river, in which the Globe was.[30]

By now the leading commissioner was the Earl Marshal, who was the Earl of Arundel. He and his colleagues ordered the churchwardens and constables of the parish of St. Saviour to report on buildings erected since March 1, 1605. The parish officials were to say by February 5, 1635, whether such buildings stood on new or old foundations; when, where, and at whose expense they had been erected; who occupied them now; who owned the ground on which they were; and how much a year they would fetch if rented out. The parish officials got together a rough draft of their report, dated merely February 1635. It was organized into the three main sections of the parish: boroughside, the liberty of the Clink, and Paris Garden. Under the liberty of the Clink appears the following remark about the Globe, much crossed out and interlineated: "The globe playhouse nere Maidlane [wth the dwelling house thereto adioyninge built—CO] built by the company of players wth timber about 20 yeares past vpon [w—CO] an old foundac*i*on worth [14 to 20—CO] p*er* Ann*um* & one [tent—CO] house thereto adioyning built aboute the same tyme wth timber in the possession of Wm Millet gent*leman* worth p*er* Ann*um* [4^{li} p*er*—CO] 4^{li}." In the margin is "playhouse & house Sr Mathew Brands inheritance."

The report itself was organized like the draft and dated February 27, 1635. Each section was signed by the officials responsible for that part of the parish. The churchwarden for the Clink liberty was John Hancock, whose signature is curiously reminiscent of that of a later and better known man of the name. The constable was none other than George Archer, Sir Matthew Brend's rentgatherer. Of the Globe property Hancock and Archer reported: "The Globe Playhouse nere Maidlane built by the Company of Players wth timber aboute 20 yeares past vppon an old foundac*i*on worth 20^{li} p*er* Ann*um* being the Inheritance of Sr Mathewe Brand K^t." In the margin they wrote

"10^{li}." The next entry reads, "One house thereto adioyninge built aboute the same tyme wth tymber in the possession of William Millet gent*leman* also of the Inheritance of Sr Mathew Brand K^t worth 4^{li} p*er* Ann*um*," and in the margin is "3^{li}." I do not know what the sums in the margin signify.[31]

Among the parish officials who drew up the report, Archer, at least, knew the Globe very well. There is no need, however, to believe that the foundation under the Globe was literally old, or any other foundation the report describes as old. The commissioners, hence the parish officials, were interested not in whether foundations were old or new, but in whether buildings stood where none had stood before. Besides, foundations did not last forever in marshy places like Maid Lane, where they could be wooden piles, nor in drier places where the floor plates of timber buildings sometimes lay directly on the ground. Yet over two-thirds—seventy—of the entries in the report have buildings on old foundations; only fourteen have buildings on new foundations, and eighteen either say nothing of foundations (like the entry about the house adjoining the Globe) or say the officials did not know. Two entries have buildings on partly old, partly new foundations, but dozens could probably have had buildings on such foundations had the officials meant "old" and "new" literally. Rather, both commissioners and officials probably described a foundation as old that followed an old line, whether the foundation was old in other respects or not. The writer of the most recent proclamation (July 16, 1630) inferred as much while explaining that new buildings on old foundations could not be divided into more dwellings than the former building was. No "person or persons," he wrote, "who shall erect a new house vpon, or within the precincts of an old foundation, shall diuide the same...."

The new building on an old foundation, that is, lay on or within the lines of its predecessor. The new building on a new foundation lay where no building had been before. Unless the second Globe was somewhat smaller on the ground than the first, it was the same size and shape, and it need not have lain on the singed piles of the first. In the present documents, a remark the King's Men made three years before the report of the parish officials comes to the same thing. The second Globe, they said in their bill of complaint (no. 1), was "erected builte and sett vp...in the same place where the former howse stood."

It is curious, incidentally, that the yearly values the parish officials, including Archer, put on the Globe and house adjoining were even less than the King's Men's witnesses and Archer had put on those buildings just a few months earlier.

Two passages in the present documents concern what the second Globe was made of. One comprises the remarks of the four workmen in 1632 about the value of the materials and labor involved in its building, the second the remarks of two workmen in 1634 about the scrap value of some of those materials. Both passages hint at what kind of structure the second Globe was.

The four workmen were testifying for the King's Men, and they answered this question (no. 4): "what somme or value doe you knowe beleive or haue heard" the King's Men "haue laid out and bine at in the erecting and newe building of the same Playhowse?" The two carpenters, Hudson and Spurling, agreed almost word for word, Hudson saying that "the timber and Carpenters worke...Could not be Lesse worth then ii00^{li}. or thereabouts," and Spurling that they "Could not Cost lesse then Eleaven hundred pounds." The brick-layer, Wathen, said "the brickworke & tylinge" of the Globe, "the materialls and workemanshipp...Could not be lesse worth then two hundred and forty pounds or thereabouts." And Fisher, the plasterer, said the "plaistering worke and the materialls in and aboute the" Globe "were very well worth 300^{li}" (no. 5). These figures add up to £1,640, which is £240 more than the figure on which the King's Men themselves eventually settled as the cost of rebuilding the Globe. The figures are, therefore, too high, but only 15% if they included every-thing, as they must have done. Timber and carpentry, for example, could well have included ironwork (for nails among other things) and wood other than timber; brickwork and tiling could have included leadwork in gutters and flashings. In any event, these figures suggest that the building was a great wooden palace. Its timber and carpentry were worth a good deal more than the whole cost of the orginal Globe and as much as the whole cost of the Fortune and Hope combined. Yet that timber and carpentry were worth only two-thirds of the value of the building. The other third was in brickwork, tiling, and plaster-ing, which are a measure of the sophistication and comfort of a wooden building. In the second Globe, those things alone were worth nearly what it had cost to build the Boar's Head and Fortune and more than it had cost to build the Hope.

Yet on October 1, 1634, two of Brend's witnesses could say that the scrap value of the timber and lead was only £200 or £160. Brend had them asked (no. 20), "what doe yo^u conceiue the Materialls of the said play house may be truly worthe to be sold in case the same should be pulled downe?" He believed that he could make more money if his property had houses on it rather than the Globe, and he was trying now to show that the building was not worth much to him. Both witnesses were illiterate carpenters, one a middle-aged, the other an old man. Both implied that the only materials of real value as scrap were the timbers, the main members. Both implied, too, that these timbers were worth much less as scrap than one might think (seeing them, presumably, in the playhouse) and tried to explain why. The first, Hugh Standish, said that "the materialls of the play house being puld downe to bee sold, may bee worth Twoe hundred poundes," because "the said materialls beinge puld downe wilbee shorte it beinge the most parte ffurr Tymber, and the lead thereof very thynne." The second, Henry Segood, said the "play house to bee puld downe wilbee worth Eightscore poundes," because "the same beinge builded with old Pollard, to bee puld downe will not bee soe vsefull as younger tymber is" (no. 22).

Brend's question is fair enough as a piece of logic, and what Standish said in reply evidently satisfied the examiners. His logic, however, is confusing. If *all* the materials of the second Globe were sold as scrap, they could not be short because *most* of them were a certain kind of timber. All the materials were not timber. Even if, being a carpenter, he meant by materials just the timber, his words give one pause. *All* the timber could not be short because *most* of it was "ffurr Tymber." Nor did he help by switching from plural to singular, from "materialls" to "it" to "Tymber." None the less, he thought he was saying something meaningful about the timber and lead in the second Globe, and it is easy to guess at what that is. Offered for sale as scrap, the greater part of the timber would be too short for ordinary building purposes because it was "ffurr Tymber"; and the lead was much thinner than prime lead should be. Our problem is not Standish's tortured syntax but what he meant by "ffurr Tymber."

In his mind, the shortness of most of the timbers of the Globe had to do not with the size or shape of the building but with their kind, "ffurr Tymber." He might have meant that they were cut from fir trees. Fir timber was available in England in the time of the Globe, and carpenters could use it as a cheap substitute for oak. The contract for the Hope (drawn up only a few months before the second Globe was built) both forbids and allows it to be used so: "the principalls and fore fronte of the saide Plaie house are to be made of good and sufficient oken tymber, and no furr tymber to be putt or vsed in the lower most, or middell stories, except the vpright postes on the backparte of the said stories (all the byndinge joysts to be of oken tymber)." But Standish would not have made his point if he had the timber of fir trees in mind. They provide very long pieces of wood, which were generally used for such things as masts, poles, rails, and scaffolding. The greater part of the timbers of the second Globe were probably not cut from fir trees, any more than those of the Hope were.

He must have meant that the timbers were "furred." The term usually applied to timbers that were warped or otherwise not straight and had boards nailed to them to provide a straight edge. Warped timbers had to be furred where they held up a floor, for example, if the floor was to be straight. In plain view, timbers might be furred, that is boxed, to make them appear straight and formidable. The term could also apply to timbers that were short and had "extra pieces of timber" nailed to them "to extend their length." The pieces of wood used for furring could be substantial, like the four-by-fours used to fur the floors and walls of Carpenter's Hall in the 1570's and 1580's. This sense of the word "fur" is not reported in *NED* until 1678, but it had been commonly used since at least the 1450's. The surveyor of the King's Works reported paying for the following tasks performed virtually as Standish was speaking:

> furring the Joysts Lifting shooting playning and laying downe the bourds of the Princes w[th]drawing Chamber presence and the passage to the Lady Maryes Bedchamber...and the like furring lifting shooting the Bourds of the privie chamber,

and

> taking vp the old bourds of the flore of the passage over the bowling Alley leading to the Cockpitt and furring out the Joysts

there and planing lifting and shooting of Dealebourds and new bourding the same,

and

ripping vpp the old rotten planks at the Kings privy stayres, putting in of new Joysts and laying and furring of others Lifting & nayling downe of dealebourds vppon the flatt formes of those stayres,

and

furring the floore of the Kings Presence Chamb[r].[32]

Standish meant that most of the timbers of the second Globe had had to be furred—to provide straight edges and perhaps extra length. Such timbers might well be too short to be prime materials for use in other buildings, either because they were so warped that they would have to be cut up to yield reasonably straight pieces, or because they were short to begin with.

Such timbers might well be old ones, and Segood probably meant his remark to complement Standish's. The important word for Segood was "old." The timbers of the second Globe were old, so old as to be defective in some way, warped, for example. He meant, too, that they were cut from pollarded trees, and he implied that that also had something to do with their lack of value.

Pollarded trees produced much of the building material used in the time of the Globe. Oaks were often pollarded and so were many other kinds of trees. The pollarded tree was cut off some seven to eighteen feet from the ground, and shoots were allowed to grow at the top, where grazing cattle could not disturb them. These shoots were eventually harvested as poles and the like, not timber because the shoots could not become thick enough for timber. Pollarded trees live a very long time and produce many crops of shoots, but eventually the trunks wear out and have to be cut down. When they are, they can presumably produce timber, but it is likely to be knotty, partly rotted, and short. The general point appears in an exchange of 1624 and 1625 between Sir Matthew Brend and his stepfather, Sir Sigismond Zinzan. Brend accused Zinzan of taking down and selling valuable trees on the Brend estate at West Molesey during the nineteen-odd years Zinzan had been master there—"diuers Tymber trees," as Brend put it, "Coppices and woods." Zinzan replied that he had taken down no "tymber trees coppices or woods" but only "some fewe pollards," which he had used to repair estate buildings and had used, sold, or exchanged to make palings for estate fences.[33] Segood's "old Pollard" must refer to such timber and his word, "old," not only to the timber but perhaps to the pollarded trees as well. Hence according to him the timbers of the second Globe had been inferior from the start and were now more so by being old.

Whatever else Standish and Segood may have meant, therefore, they implied that the King's Men had used second-rate timbers in the rebuilt Globe, as we know they had done in the original one. Because lead does not grow thin in twenty years, Standish also implied that the King's Men had used very thin, hence second-rate, lead, too, in the rebuilt Globe. Philip Henslowe and his son-in-law, Edward Alleyn, had doubts about the timber in the first Globe. They hired the builder of the first Globe to build their new playhouse, the Fortune, two years after he had built the Globe. They specified that the frame of the Fortune was to be made of "good, stronge and substancyall newe tymber," and added that "all the saide fframe" was to be "in every poynte for Scantlinges lardger and bigger in assize then the Scantlinges of the timber of the saide newe erected howse called the Globe." Evidently the King's Men believed that money could be saved in timber and lead. What then of the great value two other carpenters placed on the timbers of the second Globe and the things that went with them, not as scrap but parts of the playhouse? The two pairs of carpenters might both have been right. For if less of the value than we might expect was in such basic things as the main members and lead, more could have been in relatively cosmetic (and less scrap worthy) refinements of wood and carpentry.

We catch a tantalizing glimpse in the present documents of how the shareholders organized the building of their very proper, new, and fair playhouse in 1614. Their scrivener, John Atkins, said on October 1, 1634 (no. 21), that he knew how much it cost to rebuild the Globe because—or as he put it, "is the rather induced so to beleeve for that"—he played a part in organizing the work. He had "marryed the daughter of the said John Hemings," a player, shareholder, and, in effect, treasurer of the company. Hemings "was a principall agent ymployed in and about the oversight of the building of the said Playhowse," and he used Atkins "in and about the making of Certen Covenants betwene the Carpinters and the" shareholders. Two years before, Atkins had defended another remark about the cost of the project by saying that he "did make certen Covenants & agreaments betweene the" shareholders "and a Carpenter & others concerning the building thereof" (no. 5). The erecting of the second Globe was, it seems, largely the responsibility of the man who kept the company's books, and one of his important assistants was a scrivener, his son-in-law, who apparently drew up the builder's contract. It was Hemings, too, who (according to Archer on October 1, 1634) built the house adjoining the playhouse and (according to Atkins and Hudson on the same occasion) occupied it (no. 21).

The present documents, finally, prompt us to think about the calculations James Burbage, his sons, and their associates must have made as they went about building three playhouses. In 1576, James Burbage proposed to spend about £500 building the Theatre and in the end spent £700. He calculated that he needed a piece of property for his playhouse on which he could have a thirty-one year lease at £14 a year rent, and he was willing to pay a fine of £20 for such a lease. He needed to make at least enough money a year, clear of expenses, to pay his rent, earn 8% on his capital, and retire his investment—about £95. He seems to have made about twice that a year.[34] When in 1597 and 1598 his sons and their associates found that they could not have the last ten years of their lease, they decided simply to repeat his scheme. They found a piece of property on which they made certain that they had thirty-one years. They paid 10s. more a year in rent for it but no fine, so that their rent was practically identical to James Burbage's. They then dismantled the old playhouse and took much of it with them to the new site, where they erected a new playhouse also costing £700.

They must have done even better than James Burbage had. For when the Globe burned down in 1613, the Burbages and associates proposed to spend not £700 but £1,000 rebuilding it and in the end actually spent £1,400. They were not proceeding recklessly, however, because to lay out such sums they insisted on having a new 31-year lease at the old rent. The amount they had to clear annually with such a lease was only about £172. James Burbage had probably done better at the Theatre between 1576 and 1597, and no doubt they had done still better at the Globe between 1599 and 1613. Nor were they reckless to proceed even when they found that they could reliably have only twenty-two years. With that term they needed to clear some £191 a year, just about what James Burbage had done. So it was that they were willing first to get involved in the document of 1614, which they must have known was merely a theatrical gesture, and second to pay a great deal more rent for the last nine years. They needed to clear about £197 a year when paying £40 a year in rent.

If the King's Men knew what they were doing after the fire at the Globe, did Bodley and the Brend family? Both Bodley and the family wanted to encourage the King's Men to rebuild the playhouse, since they were willing to renew the lease with no fine and no increase in rent. Both thought, therefore, that the property would be more valuable with a rebuilt Globe on it than anything else they could see being put on it. So both had to ask themselves what the shortest term might be that would cause the King's Men to think they could build a reasonable playhouse and make a fair amount of money in it. In giving them twenty-two years (the remainder of the current term plus six years), Bodley calculated nicely indeed. The King's Men spent three and a half months thinking that term over, then went to the Brend family for what they knew would be a dubious gesture at best, then rebuilt the Globe. The Brend family, however, was at first glance over-anxious and naive in being ready to give them all thirty-one years at the old rent. The Court of Requests eventually decided that from 1635 the property with the Globe on it was worth 276% more in rent than in 1614 the Brend family had thought. If Sir Matthew Brend had accepted the court's decision promptly and Parliament had not closed the playhouses in 1642, he would have made £229.10s.0d. (not counting interest) more than he and his relatives thought possible in 1614. He probably made £104 more as it was. Or did the family agree in 1614 to give the King's Men thirty-one years at the old rent knowing as well as they that the heir could do as he pleased when he came of age?

TRANSCRIPTIONS OF THE
DOCUMENTS

I have organized and numbered these documents chronologically, and I show this organization in a table that precedes the transcriptions. I begin the transcription of each document with a remark in which I give my number for the document, its date, its current call number at the P.R.O. (many of the call numbers used by Wallace were changed after his time), and its category. Then I quote whatever belongs to the main text of the document but is written elsewhere, like the date of an entry in a book (which often appears some pages before the entry), notations on the back of a document written mainly on one side of a single sheet (like a bill or answer), and marginalia. I describe these peripheral matters in brackets and use three abbreviations: D for the date, B for on the back, and M for marginalia. Where there are several notations on the back of a document or in the margin, I separate them with a plus sign. I leave a space between peripheral matters and the main text of a document.

I have transcribed each document completely except for some crossings out that seem immaterial or are illegible. The writers of some of these documents fairly often confused plaintiffs and defendants. Sometimes the writer himself or a colleague saw the confusion and corrected it; where not, I correct it in brackets. The notations in the margins of the procedural books of the Court of Requests are much abbreviated, and an entry that should have a given notation beside it may well not have it. A sum of money beside an entry must represent a fee to be paid by whichever side instigated the procedure reported in the entry. The phrase I have written as "*per* co[nsiliarium] test*atum*," but perhaps should have written as "…test*atur*," means attested by counsel; the procedure reported in the entry was pursued by the litigant's counsel rather than the litigant himself. I have expanded the abbreviations, "La:" and "Lang:," which mean Richard Lane and Peter Langley, the attorneys of the court who supervised respectively the King's Men and Brend.

Table of Documents

1. January 28, 1632. The bill of complaint.
2. February 6, 1632. The answer.
3. May 10, 1632. The replication.
4. Before September 18, 1632. Interrogatories for the King's Men.
5. September 18, 1632. Depositions for the King's Men.
6. November 13, 1632. An entry in the order book.
7. Before November 22, 1632. Interrogatories for Brend.
8. November 22, 1632. Depositions for Brend.
9. December 3, 1632. An entry in the affidavit book.
10. February 5, 1634. Statement of fact for both sides.
11. February 6, 1634. An entry in the note book.
12. February 6, 1634. An entry in the order book.
13. February 10, 1634. An entry in the note book.
14. May 12, 1634. An entry in the note book.
15. June 6, 1634. An entry in the affidavit book.
16. June 6, 1634. An entry in the note book.
17. June 7, 1634. An entry in the note book.
18. July 1, 1634. The commission.
19. Before October 1, 1634. Interrogatories for the King's Men.
20. Before October 1, 1634. Interrogatories for Brend.
21. October 1, 1634. Depositions for the King's Men.
22. October 1, 1634. Depositions for Brend.
23. November 3, 1634. An entry in the note book.
24. November 3, 1634. An entry in the order book.
25. November 17, 1634. An entry in the note book.
26. November 18, 1634. An entry in the note book.

27. Michaelmas, 1634? Notice of the renewal of the commission.
28. January 17, 1635. An entry in the process book.
29. November 9, 1637. An entry in the note book.
30. November 9, 1637. An entry in the order book.
31. November 20, 1637. An entry in the indexes to a missing affidavit book.
32. November 21, 1637. An entry in the indexes to a missing affidavit book.
33. November 28, 1637. An entry in the note book.

1. January 28, 1632. Req.2/706/[bottom]. The bill of complaint.

[B] xxviij° die Januarij Anno. R[eg]ni R[eg]is Caroli septimo + per warrantum + Burbage, Robinson, Heminges, Lowen et Taylor Complts

To the Kinges most excellent Matie.
In all humble manner Complayning shewe vnto your most excellent Matie. your true faithfull and obedient subiects Cuthbert Burbadge of London gentleman Richard Robinson yor Ma^{ts}. servaunte and Winifride his wife late wife and Executrix of Richard Burbadge deceased William Hemings sonne and Executor of John Hemings your Ma^{ts}. late servaunte deceased and John Lowen and Joseph Taylor your Ma^{ts}. servaunts assignees of the said William Hemings Executor of the said John Hemings That Nicholas Brend late of West Moulsey in the County of Surrey Esquire deceased was in his life time about Thirty and two yeeres since seised in his demeasne as of ffee of and in all that parcell of ground then lately inclosed and made into fowre seuerall gardens which were then late in the tenures or occupacions of Thomas Burte Isbrand Morris Dyers and Lactantius Roper Salter Citizens of London and of and in all that parcell of ground then also lately inclosed and made into three severall gardens two of them being then or lately in the severall tenures or occupacions of one John Roberts Carpenter and the other of them then late in the tenure or occupacion of Thomas Ditcher Citizen and Merchauntaylor of London being all of them scituate in the parrish of S^t. Saviour in Southwarke in the County of Surrey by his Indenture of lease tripartite bearing date the One and twentith day of January in the One and ffortith yeere of the raigne of our late soueraigne Lady Queene Elizabeth made betweene him the said Nicholas Brend on the firste parte the said Cuthbert Burbadge

and Richard Burbadge of the second parte And William Shakespeare Augustine Phillips Thomas Pope the said John Hemings and William Kempe of London gentlemen on the third parte for divers greate and valuable Consideracions him therevnto especially moveing in the said recited Indenture specified did demise graunte and to ferme lett vnto the said Cuthbert Burbadge Richard Burbadge William Shakespeare Augustine Phillipps Thomas Pope John Hemings and William Kempe All those before recited parcells of ground or garden plotts with thappurtenances in the said recited Indenture specified for the terme of one and thirty yeeres from the ffeaste of the Birth of our lord God then last past before the date of the said Indenture of lease for severall yeerely rents amounting in the whole to the somme of ffowrteene pounds and tenn shillings As by the said Indenture of lease wherevnto relacion being had more at large appeareth And your said subiects and servaunts further informe and shewe vnto your most excellent Matie. that the said Cuthbert Burbadge and other the said Leassees did then enter into and vpon the aforesaid recited demised premisses by force and virtue of theire said lease and demise and became of them lawfully and quietly possessed and did at theire owne proper Costs and chardges expend disburse and lay out in the erecting newe building and setting vp there in and vpon the said demised premisses of a howse structure or building vsed for Playhowse and Commonly called the Globe the somme of One Thowsand pounds of lawfull English money at the leaste And that about eighteene or nineteene yeeres sithence the said howse or playhowse called the Globe so by them erected and builte in and vpon the said demised premisses was by Casualty of fire vtterly ruinated burnt downe and Consumed to the damage and losse of the Leassees theire partners and assignes of whatsoever had bine by them formerly expended disbursed or laid out in or about the erecting building or setting vp of the same (it being to the value of One thowsand pounds at the leaste) And your said subiects and servaunts further also shewe vnto your most excellent Matie. That in or about the moneth of ffebruary 1613 and in the Eleaventh yeere of the raigne of our late soueraigne lord Kinge James of pious memory (it being some shorte time after the greate Casualty of fire) The said Cuthbert Burbadge Richard Burbadge and John Hemings being surviving Leassees and others theire partners interested in the said lease by assignement from other the Leassees became suitors and peticioners vnto Sr Mathewe

Brend then Esquire and nowe Knight who was then interessed in the
imediate revercion of the said demised premisses as sonne and heire
vnto the said Nicholas Brend his late father deceased and was then to
haue the same after thexpiracion of the said lease so made by the said
Nicholas Brend as aforesaid in Consideracion and respect of theire
said greate losses by Casualty of fire as aforesaid and the better to
inhable and incourage them to reedify erect and new build the same
againe to graunte vnto them a further and longer time therein And
your said subiects and servaunts further also shewe vnto your most
excellent Majestie that the said Sr Mathew Brend (albeit he the said S^r
Mathewe Brend was not then of the full and perfect age of one and
twenty yeeres yett he was then of the age of Twenty or eighteene
yeeres at the leaste and well able to iudge not onely of the greate losse
which had befallen the said Leassees by the said greate Casualty of fire
but also of the greate charge and expence which the said Leassees and
theire partne[r]s were to be putt vnto in and about the newe erecting
and building of the said howse and of the benefitt and advauncement
that should come to his lands and ground thereby) did then most
worthily and willingly with the assent of his mother his vncle and other
freinds and allies at the peticion and request of the then surviving
Leassees theire partners and assignes in consideracion of the said
greate losse and the better to inhable and incourage them to newe
erect build and sett vp the said Playhowse not onely graunte and yeild
to make a further and longer terme of yeeres of and in the said
demised premisses vnto them the said then surviving Leassees and
theire partners for the space of ffifteene yeeres to Comence and
beginne imediatly after thend and expiracion of theire said old lease
made by the said Nicholas Brend his late father But also by his writing
vnder his hand and seale bearinge date in or about the moneth of
ffebruary 1613 in further expression of his the said Sr Mathewe Brend
his willingnes to make the said newe Lease in Consideracion of the
greate losse charge and expence susteined by the said Casualty of fire
and to be susteined by newe building as is aforesaid and for theire
better incouragement towards the reedifying thereof and for the
somme of Tenne pounds of lawfull money of England to be paid vnto
him the said Sr Mathewe Brend when he should accomplish his full
age of one and twenty yeeres did Covenante and graunte to and with
the said Cuthbert Burbadge Richard Burbadge John Hemings and

Henry Condell who was then an assignee of parte of the said howse theire executors and assignes and to and with every of them that hee the said Sr Mathew Brend at such time as he should accomplish and Come to his full age of one and twenty yeeres should and would make graunte and confirme vnto them the said Cuthbert Burbadge Richard Burbadge John Hemings and Henry Condell theire executors and assignes the full terme of ffifteene yeeres more in the said garden plotts grounds and premisses to Comence and beginne imediatly from and after thend and expiracion of theire said former lease made and graunted by his said late father Nicholas Brend deceased as aforesaid for and vnder the like and the same yeerely rent of ffourteene pounds and tenne shillings and such other Covenants and Condicions as are or were conteined and specified in the said former lease made by his said late father As by the said writing subscribed sealed and delivered by the said Sr Mathewe Brend and attested and witnessed by dame Margarett Zinzan naturall mother of the said Sr Mathewe Brend and by Henry Strelly Vncle of the said Sr Mathewe who were both present at thensealing thereof and gave theire Consent therevnto wherevnto referrence being had more at large also appeareth And your said subiects and servaunts further shewe vnto your most excellent Matie. that your said subiects and servaunts and those whose estates they have in the said Playhowse and grounds relying vpon the word prom- ise and agreament of the said Sr Mathewe Brend and of his Covenante in writing vnder his hand and seale as aforesaid did and haue sithence at theire owne proper Costs and chardges erected builte and sett vp there vpon the said demised premisses in the same place where the former howse stood a very proper newe and faire howse or Playhowse Called the Globe to theire further charge of ffifteene hundred pounds of lawfull English money at the leaste being the greatest parte of your said subiects and servaunts substance and estates And sithence the said Sr Mathewe Brend hath accomplished his age of one and Twenty yeeres your said subiects and servaunts and those whose estates they haue, in all gentle and Courteous manner haue tendred the said Tenne pounds vnto the said Sr Mathewe Brend and haue requested him to accept thereof and according to his said promise graunte and Covenante in writing to make graunte and Confirme vnto them a newe lease or estate of the said howse and ground for the said terme of ffifteene yeeres to Comence after the expiracion of theire said ould lease vnder the like yeerely rent of ffourteene pounds and tenne shillings and other the Covenants and agreaments conteined in the same ould lease But may it please your most excellent Matie he the said Sr Mathewe Brend takeing advantage of his said then minority when he did make seale and deliver the said writing hath and doth refuse to accept of the said somme of Tenne pounds and to graunte and Confirme vnto your said subiects and servaunts such further terme of yeeres as he promised agreed and Covenanted to doe And your said subiects and servaunts further also shewe vnto your most excellent Matie That the interest and estate of and in the said howse and grounds (amongest other things) Comeing by some lawfull wayes or meanes vnto the hands and possession of Sr John Bodley then Esquire and nowe Knight The said Sr John Bodley takeing notice of the greate losse and charge susteined and to be susteined by them the said Cuthbert Burbadge Richard Burbadge John Hemings and Henry Condell by the burning of the former howse and in reedifying the same anewe did therevpon graunte and demise the same premisses vnto the said Cuthbert Burbadge Richard Burbadge John Hemings and Henry Condell for the terme of Sixe yeeres to Comence and beginne at thend and expiracion of the said Lease made by the said Nicholas Brend as aforesaid at the said yeerely rent of ffourteene pounds and tenne shillings and vnder such other Covenants as were Conteined in theire said old lease according to the said Covenante and agreament of the said Sr Mathewe Brend and in parte of performance and towards the accomplishment thereof And the same lease so made by the said Sr John Bodley of the same premisses for the said terme of Sixe yeeres as aforesaid was and hath bine amongest other leases sithence accordingly ratefied Confirmed and decreed vnto them in his Ma^ts Courte of Wards and liveryes But nevertheles May it please your most excellent Matie the said Sr Mathewe Brend (the said lease made by the said Sr John Bodley drawing on and comeing neere to an end and being to end about foure yeeres hence) The said Sr Mathewe Brend doth not onely refuse to make the said newe Lease for the remainder of the said terme of ffifteene yeeres according to his said Covenante but doth threaten when the said lease made by the said Sr John Bodley is ended to dispossesse your said subiects and servaunts of the said house and grounds and to thrust your said subiects and servaunts out of the possession thereof and to sell it to others and offereth also nowe to sell the same presently from your said subiects and servaunts (who haue the present estate and terme therein) vnto others who are not nor cannott be bound by lawe by or vnto the performance of the Covenants graunts or agreaments of the said Sr Mathewe Brend) which is Contrary to all equity and wilbe to your said subiects and servaunts vtter vndoing haueing disbursed and laid out theire whole stocks and estates in and vpon the reedifying and newe building thereof and your said subiects and servaunts are become remediles at lawe therein for that the said promise Covenante and agreament of the said Sr Mathewe Brend was by him had and made in his minority and the same neither doth or can binde or conclude him at the Common lawe being had made and done in his minority as aforesaid But nevertheles in equity the said Sr Mathew Brend ought to be bound therevnto for that the inheritance of the said Sr Mathewe Brend is advaunced & bettered thereby to the somme of ffifteene hundred pounds which hath bine so done and improved by the whole Costs and chardges that hath bine expended and laid out by your said subiects and servaunts and those whose estates they haue in the newe building and reedifying thereof and your said subiects and servaunts were therevnto drawne to expend and disburse the said moneys (which otherwise they would not haue done) but by and vpon the promise Covenante and agreament of the said Sr Mathewe Brend as aforesaid The premisses therefore tenderly Considered and for that your said subiects and servaunts are otherwise remediles but onely by peticion vnto your most excellent Matie. And for that also the said howse is for theire exercise and practise of theire quality very fitt and Comodious the better to inhable your Ma^{ts}. said servaunts to doe theire service to your Highnes And that your most excellent Matie. by your Highnes Letters Patents vnder the greate Seale of England for the purposes aforesaid hath also licenced and authorized your said servaunts to exercise theire said quality of acting and playing of Enterludes Comedies and Tragedies in the same howse Called the Globe As by your Ma^{ts}. said Letters Patents wherevnto relacion being had truly appeareth May it therefore please your most excellent Matie. to graunte vnto your said subiects and servaunts your Ma^{ts} most gratious writt of Privy Seale to be directed to the said Sr Mathewe Brend thereby Comaunding him at a Certen day and vnder a Certen paine therein to be lymitted personally to be and appeare before yor

most excellent Matie. and your highnes Councell in your Ma^{ts} hono^{ble}.
Courte of Requests then and there to answer the premisses vpon his
Corporall oath and to stand to and abide such further order and
direction therein as to your Matie. shall best seeme to stand with
equity and good Conscience And as &cetera/

S. Maunsell

2. February 6, 1632. Req.2/706/[bottom]. The Answer.[35]

/vj° die ffebruarij Anno R[egni] R[eg]is Caroli septimo./
The Answeare of Sr Mathew Brend Knighte to the Bill of Complaynte
of Cutbert Burbage Robert Robinson and Winifrid his wife William
Henings John Lowen and Joseph Taylor Comp^{lts}./

The said defend^{te} saueinge to himselfe nowe and att all tymes hereafter all advantages and benefitt of Excepcion to the incertaynty insufficiency and other imperfeccions of the said Bill of Complaynte for
Answeare therevnto saith that he beleeueth it to be true that his late
ffather in the said bill of Comp^{lt} mencioned did make such a Lease of
the parcells of ground gardens and Lands in the Bill mencioned vnto
the said Cutbert Burbage Richard Burbage William Shackspeere Augustin
Phillipps Thomas Pope John Hemminges and William Kempe and
vnder such yearely rentes as in the said Bill is sett forthe, But this
defend^t neither knoweth nor beleeueth That the same was made vpon
any other Consideracions then are in the said Lease expressed, And
this defend^t further saith That by the said Indenture of Lease the said
Lessees had powre to pull downe all such houses and buildinges as
then were vpon the premisses so as they would build as good or better
instead thereof, And the said Lessees for them theire Executors and
assignes did thereby Covenante att theire owne proper Costs and
Charges to mayntaine and Supporte the said Buildinges and fences of
the p^rmisses in and with all needefull and necessary reparacion and
amendementes from tyme to tyme when and as often as need should
require duringe the Terme in the said Lease mencioned and the same
so repaired and made mayntayned and amended together with all
such edifices and buildings whatsoeuer as should be builte and sett vpp
by them the said Lessees or theire assignes in and vpon the premisses
or others as good and Conveniente for the place at the end expiracion

or other determinacion of the said Lease to leaue and yeeld vpp vnto this defend[ts] said late ffather his heires and assignes as in and by the said Lease to which this defend[t] for certainty therein referreth himselfe doth and may appeare, And afterwards S[r] John Bodley in in [*sic*] the bill named pretendinge Title to the said parcells of land and *pre*misses and the Play house nowe called the Globe therevpon errected by his Indenture beareinge date the Six and Twentith day of October in the yeare of our Lord God One Thousand six hundred and thirteene and in the Eleauenth yeare of the raigne of Kinge James of pious memory did make a further Lease thereof vnto the said Cutbert Burgage and others therein named for Sixe yeares from the end and expiracion of the said former Lease made vnto them by this defend[ts] said late father vnder the like yearely rentes as in the said old Lease was reserued vnder Coven*a*ntes to the same and like effecte as are Contayned in the said old Lease whereby it may appeare as this defend[t] Conceyueth very cleerely to this hono[ble]: Co[rt] that the said Lessees in the said firste and old Lease menc*i*oned and theire Executo[rs] and assignes were bound in Case any such fire happend as in the Bill is pretended and dammage thereby to the said Lessees theire executo[rs] or assignes [That by theire agreamentes and Coven*a*ntes in theire said Lease they were bounde—CO] to haue borne the same and att theire owne Charges to haue repayred whatsoeuer the said fire destroyed and leaue the same buildinges in good repaire to this defend[ts] said late father his heires and assignes att the end of the said old Lease, and therefore this defend[t] Conceyueth there was noe Just cause or motiue or Consideracion for him to enter into any such Coven*a*nte for the makeinge of any newe lease [att—CO] to commence from the end of the said old Lease as in the said Bill of Complaynte is pretended, And this defend[t] further saithe That he doth not knowe nor beleeue that there was One Thousand pounds disbursed for the errecting of the Play house aforesaid or neere any such summe, neither doth this defend[t] knowe that the same was by fire burnte downe as in the bill is *pre*tended neither is the same materiall vnto this defend[t] as he Conceyueth vnder fauoure of this honorable Courte for that the said originall Lessees theire executors and assignes were by Coven*a*nte as aforesaid bounde to errect buildinges vpon the said parcells of grounde and premisses and for that Consideracion the same were lett vnto them att such small yearely rentes by this defend[ts] said late father as aforesaid,

and in Case any Casuallity happened therevnto they were to mayntaine
repaire rebuild and amend the same buildinges and in the end of
theire said old Lease to leaue and yeeld vpp the same in good repaire
vnto this defend', and therefore theire negligence or ill keepeinge of
theire fire ought not as this defend' Conceyueth in Lawe or equity to
moue this defend' to Make them any longer lease of it or graunte them
any longer terme in the said playhouse called the Globe then they had
by vertue of the said first Lease, And as to the Covenante in the Bill
suggested to be entred into by this defend'ᵉ in the Eleauenth yeare of
the raigne of Kinge James of blessed memory this defend' saith that in
Case any such Covenante was entred into by this defend' the same was
as this def' conceueth & hopeth to proue when this defend'ᵉ was either
within the age of ffoureteene yeares or when this defend' had but
newly attayned therevnto and this defend' was greately abused therein
[and drawne therevnto wᵗʰout any consideracion att all for it this
defend' cann discerne—CO] as he also conceiueth and therefore as he
is not by Lawe bounde to performe the same, So he conceyueth vnder
the fauoure of this most honorable Courte he is not Compellable in
equity to make the same good or performe the same Covenant in any
parte especially seinge by the Compˡᵗˢ owne shewinge it appeares That
without any Consideracion att all they haue obtayned a further terme
of Sixe yeares from the said Sʳ John Bodley then they had by the said
old lease which this def'ᵉ agreeth to Confirme, And in regard that
thereby the Compˡᵗˢ are to enioy the same play house and premisses for
so many yeares more att so small [a—CO] yearely rentes wᵗʰ out any
valuable benefitt or advantage att all to this defend' whereby this
defend'ᵉ hath sustayned so much losse in the improuemente he mighte
raise the yearely value and rentes of the said play house and premisses
vnto this defend' is not willinge [nor will—CO] to agree to make any
further Estate therein vnto the said Complaynants then they haue by
the said Lease of the said Sʳ John Bodley made vnto them as aforesaid,
Without that that this defend' was att the tyme when the Compˡᵗˢ
pretend the said Covenante to be entred into by him of the age of
Twenty or Eighteene yeares or of any other age to this def'ˢ knowledge
then is aboue herein sett forthe, or that this defend' was then able to
Judge either of the losses or charges and expences in the Bill
mencioned And whether this defend'ˢ mother Vncle or any other of his
friends did assente to this defend'ˢ enteringe into such Covenante as in

the bill is pretended or not this defend[t] [knoweth—CO] remembreth
not neither doth he conceyue the same to be materiall vnto this defend[t]
or to binde him att all, And this defend[t] further saith that he doth not
beleeue that the nowe playhouse called the Globe euer Coste ffifteene
hundred pounds the buildinge or any more then ffiue hundred poundes
as the def[t] conceiueth if it did so muche and that whatsoeuer it Cost
this defend[t] beleeueth that they were bound by the said Couenantes to
errecte the same, And that by the said newe addicion of Six yeares
vnto the said old Lease which they haue and inioy by this defend[tes]
agreem[t] and Confirmacion they haue had and receyued much more
profitt an advantage then this defend[t] was bound either by Lawe or
equity to giue vnto them for the same, And therefore hopeth vnder the
fauoure of this Honorable Courte it shall and may be lawfull for him
after the end of the said newe lease of Six yeares to dispose of the
same play house and premisses as pleaseth him and to whom he will
and att such better yearely rentes as he can gett for the same
notwithstandinge the said Couenante abusiuely and surreptisiously
obtayned from him when he had not discretion to knowe what he did
or wherefore he did it, And this defend[t] doth not knowe nor beleeue
that the said play house and groundes ever came to S[r] John Bodley by
any lawfull meanes or waies as in the bill is pretended But this defend[t]
Confesseth that the said Lease by him made of the said play = house is
Confirmed by the assente of this defend[t] and by the decree of his Ma[ts]
Courte of Wards and Liveries and this defend[t] is willinge the Comp[lts]
shall enioy the benefitt of that Lease so made vnto them by the said S[r]
John performinge the Condicions and Couenants thereof, but this
defend[t] because he intendeth to dispose of the same after the
expiracion of theire said newe lease for Six yeares att his owne
pleasure and as he shall thinke most meete to be for his best profitt and
Commodity this defend[t] doth refuse to accept the Tenn poundes in the
bill mencioned or to doe any other thinge that may giue or Confirme
any longer tyme or Terme of yeares vnto the Comp[lts] therein then the
said Terme of yeares graunted vnto them by the said S[r] John Bodley,
And this defend[t] doth not beleeue that his inheritance is advanced or
bettered by any buildinges nowe [vnto—CO] vpon the premisses but
verily thinketh that if fitt dwellinge houses had beene erected [vnto—
CO] vpon it in value Answeareable to the longe terme of yeares the
Comp[lts] and theire predecesso[rs] haue enioyed it and are to enioy it att

such meane yearely rentes as aforesaid it had bene farre better for this
defend^{tes} inheritance then nowe it is or can bee, And that whatsoeuer
benefitt this defend^{t} shalbe able to make of the buildinges nowe vpon
it, after the end of the said Terme of Six yeares the same will neuer
Countervaile the losse his ffather and he hath sustayned and he is yett
to sustaine by the letting of the same parcells of grounde gardens and
groundes originally lett [vpon—CO] vnto the said first Leasees att
such small yearely rentes, Without that that any other matter or
thinge Clause sentence Article or allegacion in the said Bill of Complaint Contayned materiall or effectuall to be by this defend^{t} Answeared
vnto and not herein before well and sufficiently Answeared Confessed
and avoided trauersed or denied is to the knowledge of this defend^{t}
true All which matters and thinges this defend^{t} is ready and willinge to
averr mayntaine and proue as this most honorable Courte [of Chancery—CO] shall award, And humbly praieth to be dismissed out of
the same with his Costs and and [sic] Charges in this behalfe most
wrongfully vniustly had and sustayned./
                                   John White

3. May 10, 1632. Req.2/706/[bottom]. The replication.

x° die Maij A°. Regni R[eg]is Caroli octauo
The Replication of Cuthbert Burbage Richard Robinson and Winifride
his Wife William Hemings John Lowen and Joseph Taylor Comp^{lts} to
the Answer of Sr Mathewe Brend Knight Def^{t}.

The said Comp^{lts} doe and will averre maintaine and prove theire said
Bill of Complainte and all and every the matters and thinges therein
Conteined to be iust true certeine and sufficent in the lawe to be
answered vnto and that the Def^{ts} Answer for so much as is not therein
Confessed is very vncerteine vntrue and insufficient in the lawe to be
replyed vnto for divers and sundry faults and imperfections therein
evidently appearing The benefitt and advantage of exception to the
incertenty and insufficiency whereof being vnto theis Comp^{lts}. nowe
and at all times hereafter saved and reserved for further replicacion
therevnto they say in all things as in theire said bill of Complainte they
haue said Without that that any other matter or thinge in the said
Def^{ts} Answer conteined materiall or effectuall for them theis Comp^{lts}.

to reply vnto herein not sufficiently replyed vnto Confessed and
avoyded traversed or denyed is true in such sorte manner and forme
as in and by the said def^{ts} Answer the same are surmised All which
matters theis Comp^{lts} are ready to averre and prove as this most
honourable Courte shall award And humbly pray as in theire said Bill
of Complainte they haue prayed

4. Before September 18, 1632. Req.2/706/[bottom]. Interrogatories
for the King's Men.

[B] Burbadge et alius versus Brend termino Michaelis viij Caroli 1632

Interogatoryes to be ministred vnto Witnesses to be produced and
examined on the parte and behalfe of Cuthbert Burbadge Richard
Robinson and others Comp^{lts}. against Sr Mathewe Brend Knight def^t

1 Inprimis whether doe you knowe the parties p^{lts}. and defend^t.
and whether did you also knowe Nicholas Brend deceased late
father of the def^t Sr Mathewe Brend and doe you knowe Sr John
Bodley late Esquire and nowe Knight if yea then howe longe
haue you knowne them or any of them.

2 Item whether doe you knowe that the said Nicholas Brend did
heretofore by Indenture of lease demise graunte and to ferme lett
vnto the Comp^{lt} Cuthbert Burbadge Richard Burbadge and
others whose estate and interest afterwards came vnto the rest of
the nowe Comp^{lts} Certen parcells of ground gardens and garden
plotts scituate in the parish of St Saviour in Southwarke in the
County of Surrey wherevpon a Certen Playhowse Called the
Globe is sithence therevpon erected and builte for the terme of
Thirty and one yeeres for seuerall yearely rents amounting in the
whole to the somme of ffourteene pounds and tenne shillings And
whether is not the same rent of ffourteene pounds and tenne
shillings much more then the said parcells of ground and garden
plotts would haue yeilded yeerely in rent before the erecting of
the said Playhowse therevpon Declare what you knowe or haue
heard concerning the same.

3 Item whether doe you knowe that the said Comp^{lt} Cuthbert
Burbadge and other the said Leassees after they had the same
Lease from the said Nicholas Brend did at their owne proper

Costs and chardges erect build and sett vp a Playhowse vpon the said demised parcells of ground Called the Globe and whether as you knowe beleive or haue heard did the said Comp^lt Cuthbert Burbadge and the said other Leasses expend and lay out in the erecting and newe building of the same Playhowse the somme of One Thowsand pounds in money or very neere so much And whether was the same Playhowse so by them erected and builte as aforesaid afterwards about eighteene or nyneteene yeeres sithence by Casualty of fire vtterly burnt downe and Consumed if yea then what damage and losse and to what somme or value doe you knowe or beleive the said Leassees theire partners and assignes did susteine thereby Declare your knowledg and what you beleive concerning the same -/

4 Item whether doe you knowe or haue heard that the def^t Sr Mathewe Brend within some shorte time after the greate Casualty of fire and burning downe of the said Playhowse did vpon the request and desire of the then surviving Leassees theire partners and assignes in Consideracion of theire said greate losse and the better to incourage them to newe build the said Playhowse willingly Condiscend and agree to graunte vnto the said nowe Comp^lt Cuthbert Burbadge and other his partners the then surviving Leassees a further terme of ffifteene yeeres to beginne at thend and expiracion of the said Thirty and one yeeres graunted vnto them by his said father Nicholas Brend and that vnder the same yeerely rent of ffourteene pounds and tenne shillings and the like Covenants as in the said former lease were conteined and mencioned And whether to your knowledge did the said Sr Mathewe Brend in expression of such his willingnes by his writing vnder his hand and seale Covenante with the said nowe Comp^lt Cuthbert Burbadge and other of the then surviving Leassees theire executors and assignes That he the said Sr Mathewe Brend at such time as he should accomplish and come vnto his full age of one and twenty yeeres for the Consideracions aforesaid and for the somme of Tenne pounds to be paid vnto him as in and by the said writing is mencioned should and would make graunte and Confirme vnto them the said nowe Comp^lt Cuthbert Burbadge and other his partners the then surviving Leassees theire executors and assignes the full terme of ffifteene yeeres

more in the said garden plotts grounds and premisses to Comence and beginne imediatly from and after thend and expiracion of theire said former lease made by his said late father Nicholas Brend for and vnder the like yeerely rent of ffourteene pounds and tenne shillings and other Covenants as were Conteined in the said former lease if yea then of what age or howe many yeeres old doe you knowe or beleive the said def[t] was at the time of his makeing of the said Covenante and agreament and whether was he then of sufficient Capacity and iudgment to conceive and iudge of the said Comp[lts] losse by the burning of the said howse as you beleive And whether was the same Covenante and agreament made by the said def[t] S[r] Mathewe Brend and the said Complainant and his partners with the assent and good likeing of his the said def[ts] mother Vncle and other his freinds and Allyes or of some of them Declare the truth Concerning the same -/

5 Item doe you knowe or beleive that the writing nowe shewed vnto you at the time of this your examinacion and which beareth date the ffifteenth day of ffebruary 1613 and in the eleaventh yeere of the raigne of our late soueraigne lord Kinge James &c was made by and from the said def[t] S[r] Mathewe Brend to the said Comp[lt] Cuthbert Burbadge Richard Burbadge John Hemings and Henry Condell the then surviving Leassees And whether did the said def[t] S[r] Mathewe Brend seale and deliver the same writing as his act and dede vnto them the said Cuthbert Burbadge Richard Burbadge John Hemings and Henry Condell or to theire vse And doe you knowe or beleive that the name (Mathewe Brend) subscribed at the bottome of the said writing is of the handwriting of the said def[t] and that the said seale fixed to the said writing was marked with the seale of the said def[t] And whether doe you knowe who were the severall Witnesses that were present at thensealing and delivery thereof and haue subscribed theire names vnto the said writing And whether doe you knowe the same names so subscribed to be the handwriting of the same Witnesses Declare what you knowe or beleive Concerning the same and the reasons why you so knowe or beleive

6 Item whether doe you knowe that the Comp[lts] and those whose estate they haue in the said Play howse and grounds being incouraged by the said promise and agreament of the def[t] and by

his said Covenant in writing haue sithence at theire owne proper
Costs and chardges erected and builte a very faire newe howse or
Playhowse Called the Globe vpon the said demised premisses if
yea then what and howe much in moneys Chardges and expences
and to what somme or value doe you knowe beleive or haue
heard the Comp^lts. and those whose estate they haue in the said
Playhowse and grounds haue laid out and bine at in the erecting
and newe building of the same Playhowse and howe much and to
what value doe you knowe or beleive the inheritance of the said
def^t Sr Mathewe Brend of and in the said garden plotts and
premisses is advaunced and bettered thereby Declare your knowledg
and what you haue heard & beleive Concerning the same

7 Item whether doe you knowe or haue heard that the Comp^lts.
and those whose estate they haue or some of them sithence the
def^t hath accomplished his age of one and Twenty yeeres did
make request vnto him in performance of his Covenante to
Confirme vnto them a further estate and terme of ffifteene yeeres
of and in the premisses to beginne after thend and expiracion of
the said Lease made by the said Nicholas Brend his late father
vnder the like yeerely rents and Covenants as in the former lease
and to accept and take the said somme of Tenne pounds to be
paid vnto him the said def^t vpon the doing thereof And whether
were the Comp^lts to your knowledge alwayes ready and willing
vpon his performance therein to pay him the said somme of
Tenne pounds Declare your knowledge and the truth Concerning the same -//

5. September 18, 1632. Req.2/706/[bottom]. Depositions for the King's
Men.[36]

[M] Ex parte querentium

Depositiones capt[ae] apud Westmonasterium 18°. die mensis Septembris,
Anno Regni [domini—CO] Regis Caroli Angliae &c octauo 1632 ex
parte Cuthberti Burbage et aliorum querentium v^rsus [Mathew—CO]
Matheum Brend militem Def^t/

[To—CO]

John Atkins of the parish of St Botholph wthout Aldersgate London Scrivener aged ffiftie yeeres or thereabouts sworne & examyned saith as followeth (vizt)

1 To the first Interogatory this dep^t saith that he knoweth the parties p^{lts} & def^t and hath knowne them & euerye of them for divers yeeres past

2 To the second Interogatory this deponent saith that he hath [&— CO] heard & doth veryly beleeve that the said Nicholas Brend in the said Interogatory named fath^r to the said def^t [Sr Mathew Brend—CO] did heretofore by Indenture of Lease demise graunte and to ferme Lett vnto the said Complainant Cuthbert Burbadge & vnto Richard Burbadge John Hemings & oth^{rs} deceased whose estates are sithence Come to the said nowe Complainants Certen parcells of [gardens—CO] ground [and—CO] or garden[s—CO] plotts in the said Interogatory menc$i$oned for such terme of [yeer—CO] xxxj yeeres and for such yeerely rent of xiiij^{li} x^s as in the same Interogatory is also expressed [ffir—CO]. And that he this dep^t hath seene such Lease of the same wch is menc$i$oned to be vnder the hand & seale of the same Nicholas Brend father of the said def^t [Sr Mathew Brend—CO]/ But this dep^t saith that he doth not beleeve that the said parcells of ground and garden plotts [Co—CO] at the time when they were so letten by the said Nicholas Brend Could be of any such yeerely worth or value as xiiij^{li} x^s or neere so much But that the buildings vpon the same since erected by the Leasees [hath—CO] raised & made them of such value and worth in yeerely rent

3 To the [second—CO] third Interogatory this dep^t. sayth that (as he verely beleeveth) the said nowe Comp^{lts} & others the said leasees (whose estates the said nowe Comp^{lts} haue) did at theire owne proper Costs & chardges build and sett vp a playhouse vpon the said parcells of ground which playhouse was called the Globe & [w^{ch}—CO] (as this def^t [i.e., deponent] doth beleeve) the same might Cost the best parte of one thowsand Pounds And wch said playhowse afterwards about xviij or xix yeeres since was by Casualtie of fier vtterly burnt downe & ruinated to the damage & Losse of the Complainants & others the then Leasees (whose estates & interests therein the nowe Complainants haue)

to the some & value of one thowsand Pounds of Lawfull money of England

4.5 To the ffourth and ffiveth Interogatoryes this Dep^t. saith he knoweth that [the said def*endant* Sr Mathewe Brend—CO] within some shorte tyme after the [the greate Casualty of fire and—CO] burning downe of the said Playhowse Called ye Globe so formerly erected & sett vp by them vpon the said p*ar*cells of ground as aforesaid the said Comp^{lt} Cuthbert Burbadge together with John Hemings deceased & oth^{rs} wth them did repaire and goe to the said Def*endan*t Sr Mathewe Brend who (as this [deft—CO] dep^t taketh it) was then liveinge and residing with the Lady Zinzan his mother at Moulsey [(as this def*endan*t taketh it)—CO] in the County of Surr*ey* and then & there in the behalfe of themselues and others theire p*ar*tners the then Leassees who had suffered a greate losse by the said fire did request and desire the said [Sr Mathewe Brend—CO] def^t in Consideraci*on* thereof and the better to incourage them to reedify and newe build the said playhowse so burnt downe as aforesaid to graunte vnto them a further and a longer terme of yeeres to be added vnto theire terme then in beinge vnder the same yeerely rent of ffourteene pounds & tenne shillings and such other Coven*an*ts and Condici*ons* as were conteined in theire former lease then in beinge And this dep^t. saith that the said def*endan*t [Sr Mathewe Brend—CO] and his said mother the Lady Zinzan and one Mr Henry Strelly [his—CO] vncle to the said def^t did then Condiscend & agree to & wth the said Comp*lainan*t Cuthbert Burbadge & John Hemings that they the said Cuthbert Burbadge John Hemings & theire p*ar*tners should haue a further terme of ffifteene yeeres to be [add—CO] graunted vnto them by him [the—CO] this said [Sr Mathewe Brend—CO] def^t when he should accomplish and Come vnto his age of xxj yeeres to beginne and take effect at thend & expiraci*on* of theire said lease then in being vnder the like yeerely rent of xiiij^{li} x^s and such other like Coven*an*ts & Condici*ons* as in theire said former lease were conteined [if the said—CO] for theire better incouragement if they the said Comp^{lt} Cuthbert Burbadge & the said John Hemings and theire p*ar*tners would reedifie & newe build the said Playhowse. And this dep^t further saith that accordingly the said def*endan*t [S^r

Mathewe Brend—CO] by the name of Mathewe Brend gentleman sonne & heire of the said Nicholas Brend deceased by a
writing vnder his hand and seale bearing date the ffifteenth day
of ffebruary 1613 and in the Eleaventh yeere of the raigne of our
late soueraigne lord Kinge James [nowe shewed vnto this dep^t at
the time of his examinacion—CO] by & with the Consent &
agreament of his said mother & Vncle did Coven[a]nte promise
& graunte to & with the said nowe Comp^{lt} Cuthbert Burbadge &
wth Richard Burbadge John Hemings & Henry Condell (sithence
deceased) theire exec^{rs} & assigns & to & with euery of them that
he the said [Sr Mathewe Brend for the some of ten—CO] def^t
assone as he should come vnto his full age of xxj yeere for the
somme of x^{li} should & would graunte & Confirme vnto them the
said Complainant Cuthbert Burbadge & to Richard Burbadge
John Hemings & Henry Condell theire exec^{rs} & assigns the full
terme of ffifteene yeeres in the said playhowse & grounds to
Comence & beginne imediatly after thend & expiracion of the
[said—CO] Lease made and graunted vnto them by the said
[Brend—CO] Nicholas Brend his father deceased then in being
& that for & vnder the like yeerely rent of xiiij^{li} x^s & such other
Covenants & condicions as were Conteined & [specied—CO]
specified in the said former lease made by the said Nicholas
Brend [his late father—CO] as aforesaid And this dep^t also saith
that the writing now shewed vnto this [deft—CO] dep^t at the
time of his examinacion & subscribed by thexamyner of this
Courte and bearing the date aforesaid is the same writing and
that [he this dep^t did see—CO] the same writing was subscribed
& sealed [& deliuered—CO] by the said [Sr Mathewe Brend—
CO] defend^t. & deliuered as his acte & dede in the presence of his
said mother & vncle and that his said mother & vncle were
witnesses vnto his subscribing sealing and delivery of the same
and did subscribe theire names as witnesses vnto the said writing
All which this deponent knoweth to be true for that this depo^t.
was then present at the doing thereof and did also subscribe his
name vnto the said writing as a witnes therevnto But this dep^t
saith that he doth not certenly knowe of what age the said
defendant then was at the time [of—CO] when he did so seale &

deliver the said writing but Conceiveth that he was [of age—CO]
then of an age & Capacitie sufficient to be sensible both of the
greate Losse of the complainant Cuthbert Burbadge & his partners susteined by the [said Casualtie of fier—CO] burning downe
of the said Playhowse as also of the greate benefitt that would
accrewe vnto him the said def' having the inheritaunce thereof by
the reedifieng & building thereof

6 To the sixth Interogatory this depn'. saith that after the time of
thensealinge and delivery of the said writing by the said defendant
for the graunting of such further terme of ffifteene yeeres as
aforesaid the said Comp'lt [an—CO] Cuthbert Burbadge John
Hemings Richard Burbadge and other theire partners at theire
owne proper Costs & chardges did [er—CO] reedifie erect build
& sett vp a very faire building [and—CO] or structure nowe vsed
for a playhowse and Called by the name of the Globe which (as
this [defendant—CO] dep'. hath heard) and doth verely beleeve
did Cost them fourteene or fifteene hundred pounds And this
dep'. saith that he is the rather so induced to beleeve for that he
this dep'. [at—CO] did make certen Covenants & agreaments
betweene the said then Leasees and [the—CO] a Carpenter[s or
workemen—CO] & others concerning the building thereof. And
this dep' also sayth that he doth verely beleeve that the said
Comp'lt Cuthbert Burbadge John Hemings & the rest of theire
partners were so incouraged to rebuild the same vpon such
graunte of a further terme of yeeres to be added vnto theire lease
[then—CO] & terme then in being as is aforesaid and that the
newe building thereof is a greate advauncem' to the inheritaunce
of the def' in the same —

7 To the seaventh Interogatory this dep' saith that he knoweth that
the Complainants sithence the accomplishm' of the def'ts age of xxj
yeeres haue requested the def' S'r Mathew Brend in performaunce
of his Covenante Conteyned in the said writing bearing date the
said xv'th day of ffebruary as aforesaid to graunte vnto them such
further terme vnder the Like yeerely rent of xiiij'li x'ts [&—CO] as
by the same writing it was & is Covenanted and agreed w'ch the
said def' hath denyed [or delay—CO] to doe or at the Least wise
hath deferred & delayed the performaunce thereof albeit he hath

byn oftentimes by the said Complainant Cuthbert Burbadge &
oth[rs] therevnto required.

per me Johannem Atkins

Richard Hudson of the parishe of S[t] Albanes Woodstreete London
Carpenter aged 6i yeares or thereabouts sworne &cetera/

    i To the first Interrogatory this dep[t]. saith he hath knowne the
plaintiffs specified in the title of this interrogatory 20 yeares and
vpwards, the defend[t]. nor any other of the parties in the Interrogatory mencioned this depon[t]. neither doth [not—CO] nor did
knowe./

  3. To the third Interrogatory this dep[t]. saith that about Eight and
twenty yeares since (as this dep[t] now remembreth) the plaintiff
Cuthbert Burbage and the other Lessees of the lease in question
did at their proper Costs and charges erecte build and set vpp a
playhouse vpon the parcell of ground Called the globe in the
interrogatory mencioned, w[ch] this dep[t] verely believeth Cost them
700[li] or thereabouts, W[ch] said erected playhouse was afterwards
aboute i8 or i9 yeares since by casualty of fyre vtterly burnt
downe to the Losse and damage of i000[li] to the said Lessees as
this dep[t] verely believeth. And more or otherwise &cetera /

  6. To the 6th interrogatory this dep[t] saith that the p[lts]. and those
whose estate they haue in the said playhouse and grounds haue
erected and builte a very faire New playhouse vpon the premisses
at their proper Costs and charges, the timber and Carpenters
worke whereof Could not be Lesse worth then ii00[li]. or thereabouts, And this Depon[t]. saith that the Inheritance [and—CO]
of the defend[t]. in the premisses is thereby bettered and advaunced
but how much this dep[t] knoweth not. Nor Can more or otherwise hereto depose./

To the rest he Cannot depose at all. /

Richard Hudson

Thomas Spurlinge of the parishe of Alhollowes in the wall london
Carpenter aged 29 yeares or thereabouts sworne &cetera /

    i To the first Interrogatory this dep[t] saith he hath knowne the
Complainant Burbage but of late, the other parties in the interrogatory mencioned he did neuer knowe./

6. To the 6th interrogatory this dep^t saith that aboute a fortnight
since this dep^t at the request of Richard Hudson Carpenter
viewed the playhouse in question, and this deponent verely
believeth the timber and Carpenters worke of the *said* buildinge
Could not Cost lesse then Eleaven hundred pounds. And more
or other wise &*cetera* /

Thomas Spurling

John Wathen of the p*arishe* of S^t. Giles wthout Criplegate London
Bricklayer aged 53 yeares or thereabouts sworne &*cetera* /
    i To the first int*errogatory* this dep^t. saith he hath knowne the
    Comp^{lt}. Burbadge 5 yeares or thereabouts, but did neu*er* knowe
    any other of the p*arties* in the Interrogat*ory* menci*on*ed
  6. To the 6th int*errogatory* this dep^t saith that at the request of the p^{lt}.
    Burbadge aboute i0 dayes since this dep^t. viewed the brickworke
    & tylinge of the [house in—CO] playhouse in question, the
    materialls and workemanshipp whereof Could not be lesse worth
    then two hundred and forty pounds or thereabouts as this dep^t.
    verely believeth And more or otherwise hereto &*cetera* /

John Wathen /

Richard ffisher of the p*arishe* of S^t. Dunstanes in the East London
Playsterer aged 60 yeares and vpwards sworne &*cetera* /
    i To the i int*errogatory* this Depon^t. saith he hath knowne the p^{lts}.
    20 yeares or thereabouts, but knoweth none other of the p*arties*
    in the int*errogatory* Spec*ifi*ed./
  6. To the 6th int*errogatory* this dep^t. saith that about a fortnighte
    since at the request of the p^{lt}. M^r. Burbadge this dep^t. did
    considerately view 0 [*sic*] all the Playstering worke in and aboute
    the playhouse in question and this dep^t. saith he is confidente
    that the same plaistering worke and the mat*eri*alls in and aboute
    the same [could not—CO] were very well worth 300^{li}. And more
    or otherwise to any p*articler* pr*oposition* in this int*errogatory* this
    dep^t. cannot depose./

Richard R ffisher

6. November 13, 1632. Req.1/61/13 Nov. An entry in the order book.

[D is four pages earlier] Decimo tertio Novem*bris*
[M] La[ne]

In the cause at the suite of Cuthbert Burbage [plaintif against—CO]
Wm Hemings and Joseph Taylor Complaynaunts against Sr Mathew
Brend *knight* def^t It is Ordered that the same matter shalbe published
vpon the last Tuesday of this present Terme if the said defendaunt
having convenient notice of this Order shall not then or in the meane
time shew good matter in this Court to the contrary.

7. Before November 22, 1632. Req.2/706/[bottom]. Interrogatories for
Brend.

[B] Brend mil*es* ag*ainst* Burbadge ter*mino* Micha*el*is viij.° Carol*j* 1632

Interogatories to be administred to wittnesses to be produced for and
in the behalfe of Sr Mathewe Brend Knight defendant to the bill of
Complainte of Cutbert Burbage Richard Robinson and Winifrid his
wife Wm Hemmings John Loen and Joseph Tayler Compl*ainan*tes:/

   1 Imprimis did not Sr John Bodlett Knight by Indenture bearing
      date the Six and Twentith day of Octob^r. Anno domin*i* 1613
      make a lease of the playhouse called the Globe vnto the said
      Burbage and others for Six yeares and is not this Indenture nowe
      shewed forth vnto yo^u the said Indenture of lease was not the
      Counterparte of the said Indenture of lease sealed and deliu*e*red
      by the said Sr John Bodlett declare yor knowledge heerein:
   2 Item when was the said Sr Mathewe Brend baptised and at what
      parish Church; is there an entrie made in the booke, kept in the
      said parish, of baptisings and burialls of the baptising of the said
      Sr Mathewe and of the time thereof; and when doth the said
      entrie thereof menc*i*on the said baptising to haue beene declare
      yor knowledge thereof:
   3. Item what proffitt and advantage haue the Compl*ainan*ts yearlie
      had and made of and by reason of the said play-house declare yor
      knowledge and what you Conceaue herein and the reasons thereof

8. November 22, 1632. Req.2/706/[bottom]. Depositions for Brend.

[M] Ex p*arte* def^{tis}:./

Deposic*iones* capt*ae* apud Westm*onasterium* xxij° die 9br*is* A°. 8°. R*egni* R*egis* Carolj 1632 Ex p*arte* Mathei Brend Milit*is* def^{tis}. ad*vers*us Cuthbert*um* Burbage et al*ios* quer*entes*./

George Archer of the p*arish* of S^t. Saviours in Southwarke in the County of Surr*ey* yeom*an* aged [60 yeares and—CO] 70 yeares and vpwards sworne &*cetera*

1. To the firste Int*errogatory* this Dp^t. saith that S^r. John Bodly K^t. by the name of [S^r.—CO] John Bodly esq^r. did by his Indenture dated the six and twentith day of October 1613. make a Lease of the Playhouse called the globe after thexpirac*ion* of xxxj yeares in the Int*errogatory* menc*ion*ed vnto the Comp^{lt}. Burbadge and others for 6. yeares and this Dp^t. saith that the Indenture in p*archem*^t. nowe shewed to this Dp^t. at the tyme of this his ex*amination* subscribed by the Ex*aminer*s of this Courte is the Counterp*arte* of the same Lease and more hee sayeth not./
2. To the 2 Int*errogatory* this Dp^t. saith hee doth not knowe where or when the s*aid* Def^t. S^r. Mathewe Brend was baptised, but this Dep^t. saith that at the decease of the s*aid* Def^{ts}. father wch. was in or about November A°. 43° R*egi*ne Eliz: the s*aid* Def^t. was in his Cradle and not above xij monethes olde and more hereto hee saith not./
3. To the 3 Int*errogatory* this Dp^t. sayeth that the s*aid* Comp^{lts}. eu*er* since the sealing of the s*aid* Lease haue made of c*erten* ground to them granted by the s*aid* Lease the som*me* of [v—CO] vj^{li}. or thereabouts yearely, besides the benefitt and advantage of the s*aid* Playhouse. And more or otherwise hereto hee cannot say./
   George: Archer

John Chiswell of the p*arish* of S^t. buttolphes wthout Aldersgate London Haberdasher aged xliij. yeares or thereabouts sworne and p*ro*duced &*cetera*/

2. To the 2 Int*errogatory* this Dp^t. saith that hee hath of late veiwed the Register booke for Baptismes and Burialls for the p*arish* [Ch—CO] of Alderman Bury London and this Dp^t. saith that it thereby appeareth that the [Comp^{lt}—CO] Def^t S^r. Mathewe

Brend was Baptized in the said parish Church the sixt day of March 1599; And more or otherwise to this or any other of the Interrogatories this Dp^t. cannot depose./

John Cheswell

John Page of Islington in the County of Middlesex Servt. to the [Co— CO] Def^t. aged xxix. yeares or thereabouts sworne and produced to bee examined &cetera/

    2. To the 2 Interrogatory this Dp^t. saith hee of late veiwed the Register booke for Burialls and Baptismes for the parish of Aldermanbury London, and this Dp^t. saith that thereby it appeareth that the Def^t S^r. Mathewe Brend was Baptized in the said parish Church the sixt day of March 1599. And more or otherwise to [any—CO] this, or any other of the Interrogatories this Dp^t. cannot depose./

John Page

9. December 3, 1632. Req.1/135/3 Dec.; another copy: /136/[f.1^v]. An entry in the affidavit book.[37]

3^{tio} die Decemb: 1632

In the cause at the suite of Cuthbert Burbadge William Hemmings and Joseph Taylor Comp^{lts} ag^t Sr Mathew Brend k^t def^t John Bell of Barwicken london scriven^r maketh othe that vpon the 23th day of November last he served the said def^t [Sr Mathew—CO] with the copy of an Order vnder teste of this Court made betweene the said parties dated the xiijth day of November last aforesaid and delivered it vnto him./

John Bell.

10. February 5, 1634. Req.2/789/[top]. Statement of fact for both sides.

[B] 1633 + The Case betweene Cutbert Burbadge &cetera p^{lts} & oth^r Sr Mathew Brend Def^{ts}

february 5to. 1633

        The Case betweene Cutbert Burbadge & others p^{lts}. and S^{ir} Mathew Brend deft^t./.

Nicholas Brend being seised in ffee of a parcell of ground in length Twoe Hundred and Twenty foote of assize, and of one other parcell in length 156 foote of assize and in breadth 100 foote with buildings therevpon [made—CO] erected did by his Ind*enture* 21° ffebruarij 41 Eliz*abeth* lease the same to Cutbert Burbadge and others for One and Thirty yeeres from Christmas before vnder severall yeerely rents amounting in the whole to ffoureteene pounds and Tenn shillings In which Ind*enture* the said Nicholas Brend doth Coven*a*nte that it shallbe lawfull for the Leassees their execuⁿtoᵗs and assignes to take and pull downe alter or Change any howses shedds pales fences or other buildings which then were or after should be in or vpon the premisses Soe as there be as good or better reedified and built on the premisses within a yeere then next ensewing, And the Leassees Coven*a*nte for them their execuⁿtoᵗs and assignes at their Costs and Charges to maintaine and support as good and better buildings and fences as then were vpon the pᵗmisses in and with all necessary reparac*i*ons dureing the said terme and the same soe repaired made mayntayned and amended Togeather with all such edifices and buildings whatsoever as should be built and sett vp in or vpon the pᵗmisses or others as good and Convenient for the place to leave at thend of the said Lease and yeild vp vnto the said Nicholas his heires and assignes./.

The Leassees therevpon spent about Seaven Hundred pounds in building a Playhowse Called the Globe vpon the pᵗmisses, and the same beïng burnt downe by Casualtie of fier that happened therein dureing the said terme Sᵗ Mathew Brend the defᵗ by his dede poll dated 15°. ffebruarij 1613 reciteing the said Lease made by his father and the burneing downe of the said Playhowse by Casuality of fier and the Leassees intenc*i*on to lay out One Thowsand pounds more vpon the reedifieing of the said Playhowse in Considerac*i*on of their said losse and expence and for their encouragement to reedify the same, and for Tenn Pounds to be paid him at his full age of xxj yeeres (if he shall then make them the Lease hereinafter menc*i*oned,) Covenants that when he shall attaine his said full age to make them a further lease of ffifteene yeeres to beginne after thexpirac*i*on of the said Lease of One and Thirty yeeres vnder the like rent and Coven*a*nts as were in the said lease of One and Thirty yeeres At thensealing of which dede the Mother and vncle of the said Sᵗ. Mathew were present and were privy and acquainted with the said S^r. Mathew his Covenante and agreament in and by the same dede Poll made and did subscribe their names as witnesses to expresse their Consents therevnto, and at the time of thensealing of the said dede Poll the said S^r. Mathew was within one moneth of the age of ffowreteene yeeres and was in ward to the King./.

And S^r. John Bodley takeing notice of the said losse by fire and Charge of new building and p^{r}tending to have some estate in the premisses by his Indenture dated xxvj^o Octobris 1613 for good Consideracions him moveing made therevpon vnto the said Leassees a lease of the premisses for Six yeeres to beginne from thend of the said Lease for xxxj yeeres vnder the like rent and Covenants as are in the said lease for One and Thirty yeeres wherevpon [and vpon hope of performaunce of Sr Mathew Brends Covenante—CO] they new built the said Playhowse and expended about One Thowsand and foure hundred pounds therevpon and haue ever sithence quietly enioyed the same./.

This Lease of S^r. John Bodleyes was vpon suite in the Courte of Wards betweene S^r. Mathew Brend and S^r. John Bodley Confirmed and the Leassees and their assignes sue to haue a further Lease made by the def^t S^r. Mathew vnto them for Nyne yeeres from thend of S^r. John Bodleys lease which the def^t S^r. Mathew Brend doth refuse to make../.

> Richard Lane
> John White

11. February 6, 1634. Req.1/156/f.91^v. An entry in the note book.

[D is one page earlier] Thursday the sixt of february

Burbage et alii v^s Brend mil$item$ to be heard vpon the Case Monday next.

12. February 6, 1634. Req.1/63/6 Feb. An entry in the order book.

[M] La[ne] + Burbage Brend

Jovis Sexto die Februarij

In the Cause at the suite of Cuthbert Burbage Richard Robinson William Hemings & others p^lts ag^t Sr Mathew Brend Knt def^t[:] vpon the mocion of Mr Richard Lane of Counsaill wth the said Comp^lts It is ordered that the Councells on both sides shall attend this Court vpon Monday next to be heard vpon the Case this day delivered into this Co^rt by the said Comp^lts vnder [their Councells hande—CO] the hands of [of Richard Lane & John White esq^rs of Councell—CO] Richard Lane & John White esq^rs of Counsaill severally wth the said parties And therevpon such further direction shalbe given in the cause as shalbe meet And the said def^t is forthw^th to have notice of this present Order.

13. February 10, 1634. Req.1/156/f.97^v. An entry in the note book.[38]

[D is one page earlier] Monday the xth of february
[M] 18^d + La[ne]

Burbage et al^ii v^s Brend mil^item   Recompence & advantage may make a voyd contract good / A Commission to examin the [bo—CO] state of the things demised at the time of the p^lts entry & [how—CO] what advantage may redound to the def^t by the charge they have been at in building vpon the premisses & whether there be a melioracion of it now by their charge & the thing [made—CO] so much betterd that it is now in case to render more in proffitt then before[:] Vpon hearing Councells on both sides super Casum in praesencia pertinentium.

14. May 12, 1634. Req.1/156/f.147^v. An entry in the note book.[39]

[D is on the same page] Monday the xij^th of May

Burbage et al^ii v^s Brend Mil[item] et al^ios   The Commission to be renewed[,] anie three of the Com^rs[,] & made returnabile octavo trinitatis next & the Com^rs to mediate an end if they can & the name of the Com^r mistaken to be amended & therevp[on] publication [granted] & a day to be appoynted for hearing next terme.

15. June 6, 1634. Req.1/137/6 June. An entry in the affidavit book.

[D is two pages earlier] 6to. die Junij a^o. x^o. 1634
[M] Burbage Brand

John Atkins gent*leman* maketh oath, That according to an Order of this Court of the 12th. of May last in the Cause at the suite of Cuthbert Burbadge & others p^{lts}. ag^t. Sr Mathew Brend K^t. def^t. the Com*mis*sion in the said Cause awarded was renued & continued vnto the Com^{rs} therein already named or to any three of them and made returnable Octav*o* Trinit*atis* next coming And that he this dep^t. about the 30th. of May last did thereof give notice vnto the said def^t. Sr Mathew Brend K^t. by shewing vnto him the said Order & Com*mis*sion vnder seale of this Court, and desired him the said def^t. to ioyne by his Com^{rs} wth the p^{lts}. & their Com^{rs} in the execuc*i*on of the same Com*m*ission And this dep^t. also maketh oath, That the said def^t. answeared this depon^t. that he would advise thereof & wthin 2. or 3. dayes give his Answeare whether he would or not. And this dep$^{t·}$ further maketh oath, That the s*a*id def^t. did sithence come to this dep^{ts}. house & told him that he would not ioyne wth the p^{lts}. in the execuc*i*on of the said Com*m*ission./

16. June 6, 1634. Req.1/156/f.171. An entry in the note book.

[D is five pages earlier] friday the Sixt of June

Burbadge v^s Brend mil*item*　　The Com*m*ission to be [proceed—CO] renewed to 3 or 2 [if—CO] but the [def^t do not forthwth give in his names to ioyne therein—CO] p^{lts} may execute the same by their owne Com^{rs} if the def^t sup*er* notic*iam* refuse to bring his Com^{rs}[.] M^r Ri: Lane cu*m* def^t [i.e., plaintiff].

17. June 7, 1634. Req.1/156/f.171^v. An entry in the note book.

[D is on the same page] Satterday the vijth of June
[M] 2^s + Lang[ley]

Burbadge et al*ii* v^s Brend mil*item*　　The Com*m*ission not to be inlarged & no further exa*m*inac*i*on but vpon the poynts already directed & whether the house be made Worse as to the def[t] in regard it was not converted into Tenements[,] And the Commission to be renewed to 4 3 or 2. as formerly[:] in presence of Counsaill.

18. July 1, 1634. Req.2/706/[bottom]. The commission.[40]

[B] Complanctores Burbidge et alii contra Brend Militem r[eturnabile] vj° die Octobris 1634 super sacramentum Joh[ann]is Atkins generosi iuratum + Execucio Comissionis infra mencionata patet in Quibusdam scriptis huic annex[is]/. + To the Kings most Excellent Ma[tie] & his highnes Counsell in his Courte at Whitehall. [Lower right corner] 13[s]-4 [i.e., one mark]

By the King

Trustie and welbeloved we greete you well And send vnto you here inclosed the true Coppies or transcripts of two seuerall orders of late made by vs and our Counsell in o[r] Court of Whitehall in the cause there depending in variance betweene Cuthbert Burbage and others Comp[lts]: and S[r] Mathew Brend Knight defendant the one bearing date the tenth day of ffebruary last and the other the seaventh day of June last past Wherevpon we trusting in your approoued wisdomes learnings and indifferences for the due administracion of Justice in this behalfe will and desire you that by authoritie hereof calling afore you in our name the said parties togeather wth such witnesses and proofes as by any of them shalbe nominated vnto you, ye then doe according to the effect purport and true meaning of the said seuerall orders in every behalfe duely and substantially examine them the said witnesses by theire oathes in due forme of lawe sworne aswell for proofe of the state of the things demised at the tyme of the p[lts]: entry therevpon (in the said order menconed) As alsoe what advantage may redound to the defendant by the chardge the p[lts]: have bine at in building vpon the premisses And whether there be a Melioracion thereof by the p[lts]: chardge whereby the premisses are like to render more in proffitt to the defendant by theire Costs vpon it in his nonage then it would otherwise have done or not And to what value the said Melioracion amounteth vnto by the Play howse built therevpon And if the said Comp[lts]: had built and erected Tenements vpon the premisses then how much and to what value the premisses would have bine bettered thereby Endeavo^ring your selues by all meanes to search and try out the veritie of the premisses by your said examinac*i*ons And therevpon finally to end and determine the same matter betweene the said p*a*rties if ye can And in case that by the obstinacie of any of the said p*a*rties or otherwise ye cannot conveniently soe doe ye then doe duely Certifie vs and our said Councell of our said Court of Whitehall at Westm*inster* in the Vtas of St Michaell Tharchangell next com*m*ing Of the very true deposic*i*ons of the said witnesses like as ye shall fynde by your said examinac*i*ons To thintent that vpon view thereof wee and our said Counsell may make and settle such finall order in the cause as to Justice shall app*er*teyne Not failing hereof as ye tender our pleasure and thadvancement of Justice Given vnder our Privie Seale at our Pallace of Westm*inster* the first day of July in the tenth yeare of our reigne./

> W: Lane dep   Ja: Mylles

> To our trustie and welbeloved George Bingley Thomas Manwareing Richard Daniell Esq^{rs}: and Henry Withers gen-*tleman* or to any three or two of them.

returnabile octavo Michae*l*is *proximi*

19. Before October 1, 1634. Req.2/706/[bottom]. Interrogatories for the King's Men.

Interrogatories to be ministred to the Witnesses to be produced for and in the behalfe of Cutbert Burbadge Richard Robinson William Hemings and others Comp^{lts}. against S^r. Mathew Brend Knight def^t./.

1. Inprimis doe you knowe the parties p^{lt}. and def^t. or any of them and how long haue you knowne them or any of them, and whether did you knowe Nicholas Brend Esquire deceased late father of the def^t S^r. Mathew Brend Knight./.

2. Item doe you know the howse or building now Called or knowne by the name of the Globe scituate on the Banckside in the parrish of S^t. Saviour in Southwarke in the County of Surrey now vsed

for a Playhowse and whether Doe you knowe one other howse or building adioyning to the said Playhowse late in the occupac*i*on of John Hemings deceased late father of William Hemings one of the Comp^{lts}. and whether did you know the ground and soyle whereon the said Playhowse and the said other howse or building therevnto adioyning doe now stand before the said Playhowse and the said other howse or either of them were built vpon the same/.

3. Item doe you know or haue you heard about what time the said ground and soile was demised and leased by the said Nicholas Brend deceased to the p^{lt}. Cutbert Burbadge and to others his partners or any of them yf yea then for what time and for what yeerely Rent or other Considerac*i*on was the same soe lett and to what intent whether to build a Playhowse thereon haue you seene the Lease thereof or the Counterp*arte* of the same declare your knowledge therein and how you knowe the same./

4. Item doe you knowe or haue you heard that the ground and soile whereon the said Playhowse and the said other howse therevnto adioyning now stand at the time when the same was leased by the said Nicholas Brend to the said Burbadge and others was a meere void peece of ground or Laystall without any building at all then standing therevpon And that the same ground and soyle was then of little or noe worth or yeerely value declare yor. knowledge therein and what you knowe Concerning the same./.

5. Item doe you know or haue you heard That the said p*laintiffs* or those vnder whome they Clayme did bestowe great Costs and charges in building of the said Playhowse and the other howse adioyning to the same what Costs and Charges and to what value doe you know haue you heard or doe you beleeue that the said p*laintiffs* or those vnder whome they clayme did bestowe and lay out in and about the building of the said Playhowse and the said other howse. And whether by theire said Costs and Charges will there Come a great advancement in yeerely rent and proffitt to the def^t. for the said howse when the same shall Come into his hands and be out of lease for what rent or proffitt doe you Conceiue or beleeue the said Playhowse and the said other howse adioyning may be lett yeerely or may be worth to be lett when the same shalbe out of Lease and how much will the inheritance

of the def[t]. then be bettered yeerely by the p[lts]. said Costs and at what yeerely rate or value doe you know haue you heard or doe you beleeue the def[t]. hath estimated and valued the same Playhowse declare what you know beleeue or haue heard and the truth Concerning the same./.

6. Item whether doe you know or haue you heard that the said def[t]. S[r]. Mathew Brend Knight vpon some Conference by him here-tofore had with you or some others either touching the sale of the inheritance of the said Playhowse or the leaseing thereof for yeeres did value the same Playhowse Called the Globe at the yeerely Rent or value of Twoe or one hundred pounds or of some other good yeerely Rent or value declare yo[r]. knowledge therein what yeerely value you knowe or haue heard he did rate and value the same Playhowse at./.

20. Before October 1, 1634. Req.2/706/[bottom]. Interrogatories for Brend.

Interrogatories to be administred to Witnesses to be produced for and on the behalfe of S[r] Mathew Brend Knighte defend[t] ag[t] Cutbert Burbage and other Comp[lts]./

1 Inprimis doe yo[u] knowe the playhouse called the Gloabe and the other Tenementes and groundes there in the possession of the Comp[lts] there assignes or vndertenantes the inheritance whereof is in the defend[t] did yo[u] knowe the same groundes before Nicholas Brend the defend[ts] late father did lease the same to the Comp[lts] or summe of them, In what estate were the same att the tyme of the makeinge of the said Lease and of the p[lts] entry therevpon what buildinges and howe many houses were there then errected and standinge vpon the same and to what vse and employm[t] were the rest of the premisses then put and what yearely rent was the same then worthe to be lett/

2 Item had not the premisses bene then worthe ffourteene pounds Tenn shillings a yeare to be lett to any man to build Tenem[ts] and houses vpon the same for the habitacion and dwellinge of men so as the Lessee that should haue vndertaken such buildinges att his owne Charge might haue had a terme of seauen and Thirty yeares in the same att the said yearely rente in Lieu and

satisfaccion of his said buildinges And howe much more yearely rente doe yo^u conceiue the same might haue yeelded to the defend^t and his Ancestors in Case the same had bene so imployed after the said Seauen and thirty yeares were ended and determined/

3 Item what doe yo^u conceiue the Materialls of the said play house may be truly worthe to be sold in case the same should be pulled downe declare the vttermost value thereof and the reasons of your opinion Conceringe the same./

4 Item doe yo^u conceiue that the buildinges of the said play house as they nowe are, in case they should be lefte to the defend^t are a sufficient recompence to him for the p^{lts} quiet enioyinge and holdinge the said leased premisses seauen and Thirty yeares att no greater yearely rent then ffourteene poundes Tenn shillinges whereby he hath bene during all that tyme hindred of the better improuem^t of his inheritance in the premisses by better and more vsefull and profitable buildinges, and yf yo^u shall conceiue the said buildinges to be a full recompence to the defend^t for all those many yeares past att so small a yearely rente and more, then sette downe to what value more./

21. October 1, 1634. Req.2/706/[bottom]. Depositions for the King's Men.

[M] on the parte of the plaintiffs

Deposicions of witnesses taken before vs George Bingley Thomas Maynwaring Esquiers and Henry Withers gentleman this p^{r}sent ffirst daie of October 1634 and in the Tenth yeere of the raigne of our Soueraigne Lord king Charles at the Howse Comonly Called or knowne by the name or signe of the Swan on the Banckside in the Countie of Surrey by virtue of a Commission out of the Courte of his Matie and his highnes Counsell of Whitehall to vs directed in a Cause there depending betwene Cutbert Burbage Richard Robinson William Heminges and others Complainants, and Sr Mathew Brend Knight def^t as followeth (vizt)

John Atkins of the parish of St Botholphe without Aldersgate London

Scrivener aged ffiftie yeeres or thereabouts [sworne—CO] to the ffirst
and second Interogatoryes sworne & examyned

1 2 saith That he knoweth the plaintiffs and def' and the Howse
Called the Globe and the other Howse adioyning to the Globe
late in the occupacion of John Hemings deceased in the
Interogatorye Menconed and hath knowne them for divers yeeres
past And further to theis two [Interogato—CO] deposeth not/

3 To the third Interogatory saith That by the sight of an old Lease
made by Nicholas Brend father to the def', to the plaintiffs or to
others vnder whome they clayme that Certein ground vpon
which the said Playhowse and the oth' howses standeth was lett
for one & thirtie yeeres in the One and ffortith yeere of Queene
Elizabeth at the yeerely rent of ffourtene Pounds and ten shillings to the intent (as this deponent beleeveth) to build a Playhowse
thereon, But for the more Certentie therein he referreth himself
to the said lease/

5 6 To the ffiveth and Sixth Interogatory saith This dep' hath heard
and doth beleeve that the Playhowse at the last building thereof
did Cost the plaintiffs and those vnder whome they Clayme the
some of Thirteene or fourteene hundred Pounds and that the
other Tenement adioyninge therevnto late in the tenure of the
said John Hemings did Cost in building the some of Two hundred pounds And this dep' is the rather induced so to beleeve for
that this dep' marryed the daughter of the said John Hemings
who was a principall agent ymployed in and about the oversight
of the building of the said Playhowse and bore parte of the charge
and this dep' was by him vsed in and about the making of Certen
Covenants betwene the Carpinters and the plaintiffs And this
dep' further saith and beleeveth that there wilbe a good
advauncem' to the def' when it Comes into his hands by the
plaintiffs Costs in building the same ffor this depon' thincketh
that the howse Called the Globe if it be ymployed as a Playhowse
may be worth ffortie pounds a yeere and the oth' howse Twentie
Marks a yeere/ And this dep' further saith That he hath heard
the def' S' Mathewe Brend vpon some Conference had by him
touching the p'misses in question in the p'sence of m' White and
M' Lane Counsell seuerally wth the plaintiffs and def' did value

the Playhowse to be worth two hundred Pounds a yeere And further saith not/.

per me Johannem Atkins /

Thomas Blackman of the parish of St Savio^r in Southwarke in the Countie of Surrey Waterman aged Threescore yeeres or thereabouts sworne & examyned

1.2 To the first and second Interogatoryes saith He knoweth the plaintiffs in this suite but not the def^t And also saith that he knoweth the howse or building Called the Globe and also the other howse therevnto adioyning Late in the occupacion of the said John Hemings deceased in the Interogatoryes mencioned and hath knowne the said building Called the Globe ever since the same was builte and did knowe the ground whereon the same building Called the Globe and the said other howse nowe standeth Longe before there was any building vpon the same/

3 To the third Interogatory he Cannott depose

4 To the fourth Interogatory this dep^t saith that the ground or soyle whereon the said Playhowse and the said other Howse standeth at the time when the same was lett by the def^{ts} ffather Nicholas Brend to the plaintiffs or those vnder whome they Clayme was a void peece of grounde of litle or no value not worth aboue ffortie shillings a yeere overflowne by the Spring tides There being no wall or fence to keepe the same out but the same ground lay betwene two ditches/

5 To the ffiveth Interogatory this dep^t saith he doth not knowe to what value the plaintiffs did bestowe in and about the building of the said Playhowse and the other Howse But he saith they build them newe vpon the said ground there being before no building vpon the same But this dep^t saith That he beleeveth that the said building Called the Globe Playhowse is worth to be lett by the yeere Thirtie pounds and the other howse Tenne pounds by the yeere

Thomas Blackman /

Hugh Standish of the parish of St Gyles without Creplegate London Carpinter aged ffortie two yeeres or thereabouts formerly sworne & examyned for the def^t and nowe sworne and examyned for the plaintiffs

To the ffiveth Interogatory this dep^t saith That he beleeveth that the Playhowse besides the other Howse did Cost in building the somme of One Thowsand Pounds in lawfull money of England And further he Cannott depose/

> The marke HS of Hugh Standish.

Richard Hudson of the parish of Saint Alban in Woodstreate [in—CO] London Carpinter aged Threescore and Thirteene yeeres or thereabouts sworne and examyned

1.2 To the first and second Interogatoryes this dep^t saith He knoweth the plaintiffs and def^t and also knoweth the Howse or Playhowse Called the Globe and the other howse therevnto adioyning and did knowe the ground and soyle whereon the said Playhowse and the other Howse nowe standeth before there was any building vpon the same

4 To the fourth Interogatory this dep^t saith That the ground and soile whereon the said Playhowse nowe standeth was before it was built into a Playhowse a void peece of ground of litle or no value and a meere laystall

5 To the ffiveth Interogatory this dep^t saith That he verilie beleeveth that the howse nowe vsed for a playhowse did Cost at the least ffourteene hundred Pounds in building at the last building thereof and that the said other Howse late in the occupacion of the said John Hemings adioyning to the Playhowse Cost the building two Hundred Pounds which he this dep^t is the rather induced to beleeve for that this dep^t was ymployed by John Hemings deceased as a Carpinter in the building thereof and was to haue byne ymployed in the building the Playhowse also But that he was at the tyme of the building thereof ymployed in other worke elswhere And this dep^t also saith that he beleeveth that there will Come a greate advauncem^t in yeerely benefitt to the def^t by the plaintiffs Costs in building of the Playhowse and the said other Howse therevnto adioyning when the same shall Come into his hands to be lett and that the building of the Playhowse hath byn an advauncem^t to the yeerely value of all the howses therevnto neere adioyninge And this dep^t also saith that he verily beleeveth that the Playhowse and the said other howse therevnto adioyning

are both worth to be lett by the yeere the some of one hundred marks of Lawfull money of England

Richard Hudson /.

Henry Segood of the parish of St Gyles in the ffeilds in the Countie of Midd*lesex* Carpinter aged Threescore yeeres or thereabouts formerly sworne and examyned for the def^t and nowe sworne and examyned for the pl*aintiffs*

> 5 To the ffiveth Interogatory he saith That he beleeveth that the Playhowse in the Interogatory menc*i*oned besides the other Howse did Cost in building the some of Eight Hundred Pounds in Lawfull English money/

The marke of HS Henry Segood.

George Archer of the parish of St Savio^r in Southwarke in the Countie of Surrey

> 1. 2 yoman Rentgatherer for the def^t Sr Mathewe Brend aged Threescore and ffourteene yeeres or thereabouts form*er*ly sworne and examyned for the def^t and nowe sworne & examyned for the pl*aintiffs* To the ffirst and second Interogatoryes he saith That he knoweth the pl*aintiff* Burbage and the def^t Sr Mathewe Brend Knight and doth also knowe the Playhowse and the other Howse in the Interogatory menc*i*oned and did knowe the ground whereon the same Howses doe nowe stand before the same Howses were built therevpon/
>
> 3 To the third Interogatory this dep^t saith That he knoweth that Nicholas Brend deceased in the Interogatory menc*i*oned about the one and ffortith or Two and ffortith yeere of Queene Elizabeth did lease the said ground to the pl*aintiffs* or to oth^{rs} vnder whome they clayme for a Certen terme at the yeerelie rent of ffourteene pounds [and—CO] ten shillings (as he Conceiveth) to build a Playhowse on But for the Certentie of the terme the same was Lett for he referreth himself therein to the lease/.
>
> 4 To the fourth Interogatory this dep^t saith that the ground whereon the Playhowse & the said other Howse nowe stand at the time of the letting thereof by the said Nicholas Brend were ymployed in garden grounds and had two Tene*me*nts thereon of two roomes in

each Ten*eme*nte and were estimated by the said Nicholas Brend as this dep' supposeth at fourteene pounds tenne shillings a yeere letting and taking/

5 To the ffiveth Interogatory this dep' saith That he beleeveth that the Playhowse in the Interogatory menc*i*oned Cost the p*laintiffs* One thowsand pounds in lawfull English money the building and that the other howse built by the said John Hemings and adioyning to the playhowse did Cost in building betwene two and three hundred pounds in Lawfull English money And he further saith That he beleeveth that the Playhowse if it shalbe ymployed as a Playhowse is worth to be lett by the yeere ffortie or ffiftie pounds and the said other Howse is worth to be lett by the yeere Eight [or Nyne—CO] pounds or Nyne pounds

George Archer /

Thomas Godman of the p*ar*ish of S' Savio' in Southwarke in the Countie of Surrey Waterman aged ffive and ffiftie yeeres or there-abouts sworne and examyned

1. 2 to the ffirst and second Interogatoryes he saith that he knoweth the p*laintiffs* in this suite but not the def' and doth also knowe the Playhowse and the other Howse in the Interogatory menc*i*oned and did knowe the ground or soile whereon the same are built before there was any building therevpon/

4 To the ffourth Interogatory This dep' saith That he knoweth that the ground & soile whereon the Playhowse and the other howse doe nowe stand before the said playhouse and the other howse were built [therevpon—CO] thereon was a meere void peece of ground of Litle or no value and no Howse or building therevpon and subiect to be overflowed by the Thames for want of ffences or any bancks to keepe out the water/

Thomas Godman /.

Geo: Bingley
Tho: Mainwaringe
Henry Withers

22. October 1, 1634. Req.2/706/[bottom]. Depositions for Brend.

Deposicions of Witnesses taken before vs George Bingley Thomas Maynwarynge Esq^{rs} and Henry Withers gentleman this presente first day of October 1634: And in the Tenth yeare of the reigne of o^r Souereigne Lord Kinge Charles of England &ceterj att the house Commonly Called or knowne by the name or signe of the Swann, on the Banckside in the Countye of Surrey, by virtue of a Comission out of the Co^{r}te of his Ma^{ts}, and his highnes Councell of Whitehall to vs directed in a Cause there dependinge betwene Cutbert Burbage Richard Robinson William Hemings and others Comp^{lts} and Sr Mathewe Brand Kn^t def^t as followeth (vizt)

Hugh Standish of the parish of St Giles Criplegate London Carpenter, aged Twoe and ffortye yeares or thereabouts, sworne and examined

1 to the first Interrogatory saieth, That hee knoweth the def^t but not the p^{lts}, and alsoe saieth that hee knoweth the Globe and further saieth not/

3 To the Third Interrogatory Saieth, That hee doth Conceiue that the materialls of the play house being puld downe to bee sold, may bee worth Twoe hundred poundes, his reason is that the said materialls beinge puld downe wilbee shorte it beinge the most parte ffurr Tymber, and the lead thereof very thynne, and further saieth not /

the marke of the said
Hugh HS Standish

Henrye Seagood of the parish of St Giles in the feildes in the Countye of Middlesex Carpenter, aged Threescore yeares or thereabouts sworne and examined

1 to the first Interrogatorye saieth that hee knoweth the def^t Sr Mathewe Brand and the play house, and further this dep^t saieth not /

3 To the Third Interrogatorye saieth That hee doth Conceiue the said play house to bee puld downe wilbee worth Eightscore poundes of lawfull money of England, his reason is the same beinge builded with old Pollard, to bee puld downe will not bee soe vsefull as younger tymber is and further this dep^t saieth not/

the marke of the said
Henery HS Seagood

George Archer of the parish of St Savio^r in the Countye of Surr*ey* yeoman, aged Threescore and ffoureteene yeares or thereabouts

1 sworne and examined to the first Interrogatory, this dep^t saieth that hee knoweth the def^t and the p^{lt} Mr Burbage and the house Called the Globe, and did knowe the ground before the play house was therevpon errected, and did knowe it to bee certeyne gardens vallued att ffoureteene poundes Tenn shillinges p*er* ann*um*, and further saieth not/

2 To the second Interrogatory saieth, that the said gardens to bee letten att that tyme for Seaven and Thirtye yeares to build thereon was worth ffoureteene poundes a yeare, and the Lessee to haue a good bargayne, as hee supposeth, and hee beleiveth, that if the said ground whereon the said play house standeth, had had Tenem^{ts} thereon insted ereccted, had amounted double the rent if not treble att thend of the said Seaven and Thirtye yeares, by reason of the neighbour houses by nowe yeildes the same and further saieth not/

3 To the Third Cannott depose/

4 To the ffourth Interrogatory saieth he Conceiueth it had bene better for the def^t if a Play house had not bene thereon builded but Tenem^{ts} by the advantage of the rent nowe att this tyme paid and further saieth not/

p*er* me George Archer

Geo: Bingley
Tho: Mainwaringe
Henry Withers

23. November 3, 1634. Req.1/157/f.37. An entry in the note book.

[D is one page earlier] Lune. Tertio die Novembr*is*
[M] La[ne] + p*er* co[nsiliarium] test*atum*

Cutbert Burbage et al*ii* p^{lts} Sr Mathew Brand K*nigh*t def^t to be heard 17° Novem*bris* sup*er* notic*iam*.

24. November 3, 1634. Req.1/64/3 Nov. An entry in the order book.

[D is three pages earlier] Lune Tertio die Novembris
[M] La[ne] + Burbage Brend

In the Cause at the suite of Cuthbert Burbage & others p^{lts} ag^t S^r
Mathew Brend Knt def^t It is ordered that the same matter shalbe
heard in this Co^{rt} vpon the xvij^{th} day of this present moneth the said
def^t having convenient notice of this Order /

25. November 17, 1634. Req.1/157/f.64. An entry in the note book.

[D is three pages earlier] Monday the xvij^{th} of November

Burbage v^s Brand militem sett ouer till to morrow the first cause.

26. November 18, 1634. Req.1/157/f.65^v. An entry in the note book.

[D is one page earlier] Tuesday the xviij^{th} of Novem[ber]

Burbage et alii v^s Sr Mathew Brend Knight def^t 14^l. 10^s. per Annum the
rent now reserved & the same rent answered before Question for the 9
yeres addicion to the terme of 6 yeres[.] The first six yeres allowed
them by Sr Math: vrged as a sufficient recompence for their charge in
building & reedyfying the Play house[.] 1400^l bestowed in reedyfieing
the Play house, & 200^l vpon the house / The Charge of the p^{lts} induced
by the hopes given them for inioying the further terme by the def^{ts}
Coven^t in his infancy[.] The def^{ts} Mother & his Vncle witnesses to the
Coven^t / The streight of the Case how the Coven^t of the Infant shall
binde him / Where the person is [ab—CO] disabled there no Court
can make him able, for an end of the cause It is Ordered by consent of
the [p^t—CO] def^t That the p^{lts} shall inioy their Terme of nine yeres
after the expiracion of the six yeres in those things comprised in their
Lease [vnder—CO] vpon the increase of their rent to [of—CO] xl^l per
Annum during the contynuance of the said nine yeres[.] Vpon full
hearing in presence of Counsaill & parties[.] And they to putt in
sufficient [security] for keeping the house[s] in repayre & Leaving them
sufficiently in repayre at the end of the terme And the p^t [i.e.,
defendant] to make a Lease accordingly to the said Comp^{lts}.

27. Michaelmas, 1634? Req.2/617/[bottom]. Notice of the renewal of the commission.[41]

renued 10 Com*mission* to Bingley Burbadge Brend 6-6

28. January 17, 1635. Req.1/185/f.14ᵛ. An entry in the process book.

[D is one page earlier] xvij°. die Januarij
[M] La[ne]

An Iniunc*i*on to [i.e., against] Sʳ. Mathew Brend Kᵗ. to performe a decree at the suit of Cuthbert Burbage and others.

29. November 9, 1637. Req.1/160/f.101ᵛ. An entry in the note book.

[D is five pages earlier] Jovis ix° die Novem*bris*
[M] Lang[ley] + p*er* co[nsiliarium] test*atum*

Burbage et al*ii* vˢ Brand mil*item* The defᵗ is ready to make the lease so he may have his rent[.] The [defᵗ—CO] pᵗ to accept thereof & pay the rent in arere by Monday next—in p*rese*nce of Co[unsel].

30. November 9, 1637. Req.1/76/p.232. An entry in the order book.

[D is one page earlier] Jovis Nono die Novem[bris]
[M] Lang[ley] + Burbidge Brennd

Whereas in the cause att the suite of Cuthbert Burbidge Richard Robinson Wᵐ Hemings & others Compˡˢ agᵗ Sʳ Mathew Brennd Kt defᵗ By the decree in this Cause made dated the xviijᵗʰ day of November Anno xj [i.e., x] R[eg]is nunc It was ordered that the pˡᵗ should enjoy the messuage or play house in question for the Terme of nyne yeares after the expiration of their form*er* Terme of six yeares in their old lease The s*ai*d Compˡ increasing their old Rent of xiiijˡⁱ xˢ to the som*m*e of xlˡ from the com*m*encemᵗ of their s*ai*d new Terme of nyne yeares during the contynuan*c*e And by the s*ai*d decree the s*ai*d defᵗ was required to make vnto the pˡˢ a lease in Wryting of the same pʳmissˢ conteyned in the s*ai*d old lease wᵗʰ the like Covenants for the said Terme of nyne yeares vnder the said Rent of xl^{li} per Annum accordingly And by the said decree the p^{ls} were required to give sufficient Security to the said def^t to maynteyne & keepe the said house and buildings Vpon the p^{r}miss^s in sufficient repaire during the said Terme And the same sufficently repayred to yeeld and give vp to the said defend^t att the end of the said Terme of Nyne yeares And forasmuchas this Co^{rt} was this day informed by Mr White of Councell wth the said Comp^{lt} [i.e., defendant] That the said [comp^l—CO] def^t hath bene ready to make the said lease accordingly, but the p^{ls} neyther seeke the same nor have hitherto paid the [p^{lt}—CO] def^t any rent since the Commencem^t of the said new Terme, nor have given the def^t Security accordinge to the direccion of the said decree[.] It is therefore ordered that the said Comp^{ls} shall att their perill accept of the said lease in wryting and shall seale a Counterparte thereof to the said def^t and pay vnto him all his rent in arrere, and shall give the Security intended by the said decree by or before Monday next wthout further delay.

31. November 20, 1637. IND.9033. An entry in the indexes to missing affidavit books.

[The month is one page earlier] Nouember
[M, the day] 20

Burbadge versus Brend

32. November 21, 1637. IND.9033. An entry in the indexes to missing affidavit books.[42]

[The month is one page earlier] Nouember
[M, the day] 21

Burbadge versus Brend

33. November 28, 1637. Req.1/160/f.181. An entry in the note book.

[D is one page earlier] Martis xxviij^o die Novembris and the last day of this present Terme

Burbage et al*ii* v^s Brand mil*item* The p^t willing to accept of a lease
sec*undum* decret*um*[;] the improved rent tendred and refused by the
def^t who would rather that the p^{lts} should contynue it at the old rent
then to be pressed to make a new Lease[.] The p^{lts} prayer[,] that they
may be discharged of the encrease of rent for those two yeres[.] The
p^{lts} refused the offer And therevpon the def^t prayes *p*erformance of the
decree for the encrease of rent[.] The p^{lts} to pay it for one of the 2
yeres & [the—CO] to be discharged thereof for the other yere And for
the rem^t [i.e., remnant] of the terme the p^{lts} to accept a new lease at
the improved rent & Mr Lane to consider whether it be fitt that there
be one or two [bonds for security?][.] Herbert[;] in *p*resence of Co[unsel]

NOTES

1. When I allude to documents transcribed at the end of this essay, I give in
   parentheses my number of the document or documents, for example, "They
   framed questions (no. 4) to be put to witnesses."
2. This file of Wallace's papers at the Huntington is in the Wallace Collection,
   Box 5, B III, 3a.
3. See above, pp. 4-7.
4. L.C.5/133/pp.44-51, printed in *Malone Society Collections*, II, pt. 3, 362-73.
5. Chambers, II, 426-27; Bentley, VI, 178-ff.
6. In the bill (no. 1) the date of the document is given as merely February, 1614,
   and Atkins' part is not mentioned; but see Atkins' remarks of September 18,
   1632 (no. 5). For the best description of its contents, see the statement of fact of
   February 5, 1634 (no. 10). Matthew Brend's mother had married a professional horseman, Sir Sigismond Zinzan, and was now Dame Margaret Zinzan;
   Matthew's uncle was her brother, Henry Strelley. See "The Globe: Documents and Ownership" above.
7. See above, pp. 39-43.
8. The father is regularly described as of Courteenhall in Northamptonshire; the
   King's Men's counsel was apprenticed in the Middle Temple in 1605 as son
   and heir of the man of Courteenhall and became a barrister in 1611-12. The
   father was associated with the Court of Requests from about 1571; became
   deputy registrar by November, 1601, when Allen accused him; was still deputy
   registrar and an "attenddant vpon" the court in 1623, when in a lawsuit his
   son was one of his counsel; and died in 1625.
   For the father, see: a letter of his of 1589 (addressed to Richard Oseley, clerk of
   the privy seal and his landlord at Courteenhall), S.P.15/31/#9 (*C.S.P., Dom.,
   Addenda, 1580-1625, p.* 265); the lawsuits, St.Ch.5/A.12/35 and /A.33/32 (see

"A Handlist of Documents" above, D-17, 18), Req.2/410/13 and /394/13 (also C.54/2050/m.24-25); V.C.H., *Northamptonshire*, IV,243; the genealogies in *The Visitations of Northamptonshire Made in 1564 and 1618-19*, ed. Walter C. Metcalfe (London, 1887), p. 107, and *The Visitation of the County of Northampton in the Year 1681*, ed. H. I. Longden (London: Harleian Soc., 1935), pp. 174, 239-40. Though his will is now missing, it is said in the old Calendar of Northamptonshire Wills to have been proved in 1625 (vol. I, first alphabet), Northampton Record Office.

For the son, see: the many entries about him in *Middle Temple Records*, ed. C. H. Hopwood (London, 1904-05), esp. II, 452, 542, 560; Clarendon, *The Life of Edward Earl of Clarendon* (Oxford, 1857), I, 55-56; and his signatures in no. 10 here and in such documents as S.P.16/354/#134, /356/#160, /389/#121, /452/#18, and /539/#44, 45 (*C.S.P., Dom., 1637*, pp. 39, 131; *1637-38*, p. 418; *1640*, pp. 107-08, and *Addenda, 1625-49*, p. 631). There is an account of him in *D.N.B.*

9. See *Middle Temple Records*, I, 408; II, 491, 528, 629, 726, 744, 772, etc.; Clarendon, *History*, I, 264. There is an account of White in *D.N.B.* For Maunsell's personal troubles, see the lawsuits, Req.2/302/3 (and the order, Req.1/27/p.397) and C.2/Chas.I/M.3/7, /M.48/47, M.28/53, M.39/9. He signed, as having drawn up, one of his bills, and his old chamber partner, Francis Keate, signed the others. Maunsell's last recorded appearance in Requests seems to have been on June 25, 1634, and by her next husband his widow had a child baptized May 27, 1636: Req.1/156/f.224ᵛ; George Baker, *The History and Antiquities of the County of Northamptonshire* (London, 1841), II, 132, 134.

Entries in the order, note, and appearance books of the Court of Requests sometimes give the names of counsel appearing before the court. In the order book for the Hilary through Michaelmas terms, 1632, I found twenty-nine appearances by Lane, two by Maunsell, and three by White; and in the note book for the Michaelmas through Trinity terms, 1633-34, thirty-nine by Lane, twelve by Maunsell, and none by White: Req.1/61, /156. I have assumed that "Mʳ Maunsell" is our man, though at least two other Maunsells were barristers at the time: John, who became one at Lincoln's Inn in February, 1632, and Thomas, who became one at the Middle Temple in November, 1633.

10. Beside a great many entries in the order, note, and process books is an abbreviation signifying which of the three attorneys supervised the party who instigated the action reported in the entry. The abbreviations are "La:" for Richard Lane, "Lang:" for Peter Langley, and "Bo:" for Noel Boteler. Only the litigant who had some official connection with the court, an "amicus curiae," did not have to be supervised. The surnames of the attorneys are often spelled out in the marginalia of Req.1/185, and their full names sometimes appear in entries proper, like Req.1/61/9, 25 Oct., 27 Nov., and /156/f.47ᵛ. This Richard Lane could not have been the deputy registrar or his son, the King's Men's counsel, because the deputy registrar died in 1625 and in the hundreds of contemporary allusions to him the counsel is never called attorney; besides an attorney by definition could not also be counsel, and one never finds the other attorneys acting so. The Richard Lane who tried to have Maunsell imprisoned in 1614-15 was not the deputy registrar or his son, either, since in the laswuit he brought against Maunsell and in another of 1613 he gave himself

as "the younger," not the holder of Courteenhall, and of the New Inn, not the Middle Temple. He could well have been the attorney, however, because he was probably associated with Peter Langley in some way. In lawsuits Langley brought in July, 1614, and November, 1615, Langley too gave himself as of the New Inn (he was still so more than thirty years later), adding once that he was also attorney. Moreover, all Lane's and Langley's bills of complaint are not only in the same bundle, a remarkable coincidence, but in it virtually consecutively, Lane's two then Langley's two, and there is no apparent legal reason that they should be so. They bear dates scattered over nearly two and a half years, and the defendants are all different people. Coincidentally, a lawyer who signed one of Langley's bills, hence was his counsel, was Richard Lane the King's Men's counsel. See Req.2/302/3,4,6,7; Req.1/27/p.397; *Middle Temple Records*, II, 936.

11. The case concerned Worcester's Men and the Boar's Head. The court reacted similarly to a case of 1626 concerning the Queen's Men. See C.33/149/f.844^v (A book) or /150/f.953^v (B book), and Chambers, II, 238.

12. Lowin and Taylor are supposed to have acquired two shares each c.1631, and, according to the protesting players in the sharers papers, they had that many in 1635. But they are given in the bill of complaint here (no. 1) as only the "assignees of...William Hemings Executor of...John Hemings," and their names disappear from the case after the events of 1632. William Hemings must have temporarily assigned one or more of his shares to them and late in 1632 or in 1633 done something else with that share or those shares. Perhaps they had half each of the one share Shanks reported buying from Hemings at about that time (in the sharers papers). How, from whom, and when Lowin and Taylor eventually got shares we do not know. See Chambers, II, 425, and Bentley, II, 502-3.

13. See above, pp. 97-98, 104, and C.54/2985/#6; /2594/#15.

14. Maunsell, apparently mistakenly, dated the original lease as January, rather than February, 21, 1599.

15. This information about Hudson comes not from the records of the Carpenters' Company but from remarks by him and others in the law courts, in which he is first described (1592) as a bricklayer but always thereafter as a carpenter: my "Handlist" above, C-17, D-7, D-17; Wallace, *The First London Theatre*, pp. 77, 226-29, 281, 289-90; and nos. 5, 21 here. Hudson signed four of these documents, C-17, D-7, and 5, 21, and the signatures obviously belong to the same man. At least two Richard Hudsons appear in the records of the Carpenters' Company. One (not our man) was apprenticed to Edmund Buckley in February, 1594, for seven years. Another (who could be our man) does not appear as either apprenticed or made free, but he does appear as a carpenter who in 1594-95 took over an apprentice from another man, the apprentice having been bound to serve for seven years from October, 1594, and duly becoming free in 1601-02. Ellam was apprenticed for seven years in 1561 and made free in 1569. See *Records of the Worshipful Company of Carpenters*, comp. by Bower Marsh (Oxford, 1915, 1916), III, 200; IV, 123; comp. by Marsh, ed. John Ainsworth (London, 1939), VI, 314; comp. by A. M. Millard (London, 1968), VII, 25, 38, 44, 136, 137, 155, 156.

16. Archer's memory failed him a little: Nicholas Brend died on October 12, 1601,

when Matthew was one year, eight months, and six days old. See above pp. 87-88. The printed *Registers of St. Mary the Virgin, Aldermanbury, London* (London: Harleian Soc., 1931), p. 67, confirm the date of Brend's baptism.

17. *Scriveners' Company Common Paper 1357-1628*, ed. Francis W. Steer (London: London Record Soc., 1968), p. 115.

18. Withers may have been father of a contemporary of Brend's, the contemporary being a Henry Withers of Chigwell and Little Thurrock in Essex who, it seems, was born in 1608, was a King's servant in 1629, married in 1636, remarried not long after, drew his will in 1643 remembering a sister married to a man named Mease, and died by 1645. Brend's sister, Mercy, was married to Robert Meese by 1622. The signatures of Henry Withers on documents nos. 21 and 22 are of a man considerably older than the man who signed the will in 1643. For Withers see *Allegations for Marriage Licences Issued by the Bishop of London, 1611 to 1828*, ed. G. J. Armytage (London: Harleian Soc., 1887), p. 225; *C.S.P., Dom., 1628-29*, p. 591; the original will, PROB.10/653/Henry Withers/1 Nov. 1635; and above, p. 95. For Bingley, Mainwaringe, and Daniel, see *C.S.P., Dom., 1631-33*, p. 187; *1633-34*, p. 360; *1634-35*, p. 11; *1635*, pp. 278, 282, 295, 315; *Students Admitted to the Inner Temple, 1547-1660* (London, 1877), p. 217; and E.125/27/f.199^v.

19. *Hollands Leaguer* (London, 1632), f.2^v. See Bentley, VI, 251-52.

20. William Hemings was John Hemings' son and heir and also his executor. John dated his will Oct. 9, 1630, three days before he was buried (PROB.11/158/f.176^v-177^v), partly quoted, partly paraphrased by Bentley, II, 643-45). In it, all his debts and legacies of money were to be paid out of the income of his shares in the playhouses. Then all his property was to be shared equally among his unmarried and "vnadvaunced" children, presumably his portionless daughters and his sons who had not received some means of making a livelihood. He had had at least fourteen children. He did not mention the house adjoining the Globe, in which he may have been living at the end of his life, nor did he specifically give William anything. William must have been advanced. He could have passed his father's interest in the house to the King's Men either because it was his advancement and he needed the money (Shanks said he was in prison for a time) or because, having paid debts and legacies, he was sharing the value of his father's property among some of his brothers and sisters as he was bound to do. The ages of three people who testified in both 1632 and 1634 (nos. 5, 8, 21, 22), incidentally, are represented curiously: Atkins was fifty in both years; Archer was seventy in 1632 and seventy-four in 1634 (he had given his age as sixty on Feb. 1, 1623—see above, p. 119); Hudson was sixty-one in 1632 (a mistake for seventy-one, which he probably was) and seventy-three in 1634; he had given himself as thirty-one on February 25, 1592, but as thirty-eight on May 15, 1600. Segood's name is also spelled, and was no doubt pronounced, "Seagood" (no. 22).

21. See Prof. William Ingram's articles, " 'Neere the Playe Howse': The Swan Theater and Community Blight," *Renaissance Drama*, IV (1971), 53-68, and "The Globe Playhouse and its Neighbors in 1600," *Essays in Theatre*, II, no. 2 (May 1984), 63-72.

22. One of the commissioners' accomplishments must have been to cause publication to be granted after they took the examinations on October 1 (nos. 21, 22),

according to a provision in the order of May 12, 1634, but not in their commission (nos. 14, 18). Decisive hearings were not supposed to take place until publication had been granted, but there is no indication in the order book that it was ever granted in this case.

23. Both the note and order books record, alongside the date, which of the five judges of the court sat on a particular day.

24. Clarendon, *History*, V, 169; *Life*, I, 184; *D.N.B.* He is given as one of the lawyers in the lawsuit of the next item and as a lawyer occasionally elsewhere in the papers of the court (for example, Req.1/159/f.141).

25. The word, "then," in the part of Brend's answer (no. 2) where he describes the King's Men's right to pull down buildings may suggest that they could pull down only the buildings that were on the property when they took possession. But the lawyers' agreement leaves no doubt that the King's Men could pull down buildings erected at any time.

26. The original of the paraphrase is in K.B./27/1454/m.692. Wallace published a translation of the whole lawsuit of 1616 in *The Times*, Oct. 4, 1909, p. 9, then a transcription of the original Latin in *Advance Sheets from Shakespeare, the Globe, and Blackfriars* (Stratford-upon-Avon, 1909). *Shakespeare Jahrbuch* reprinted the transcription, XLVI (1910), 235-40. He announced the lawsuit of 1619 in *The Century*, Aug., 1910, p. 508, and transcribed it in *University of Nebraska Studies*, X (1910). See also Bentley, VI, 180.

27. T. W. Baldwin for example, argued in a tidy circle. He acknowledged that the current lease expired at Christmas, 1635, then added, "The lease drawn up in 1635, but not yet confirmed at the time of the [players'] complaint, was for nine years from March 25, 1635," because Brend pulled the Globe down on April 15, 1644: *The Organization and Personnel of the Shakespearean Company* (Princeton, 1927), pp. 108-9. The players may have been deceived by the month and day of the original lease, February 21 (1599) or by those of the document of 1614, February 15.

28. Chambers at first concluded that the cost of the Globe and house was about £1680. He was calculating from charges levied on shares, mentioned in one of the lawsuits Wallace printed, Witter v. Hemings and Condell. In the end, however, he settled on Shanks' figure partly because of another of Wallace's uncited remarks. In *The Times*, October 2, 1909, p. 9, Wallace wrote that Shanks' figure for the Globe alone "is excessive....I have other contemporary documents showing the cost was far less than £1400." Wallace was probably alluding to the present documents, which he had not considered very carefully, or, perhaps, fully. See Chambers, II, 423; Bentley, VI, 182, 185-86.

29. Bentley quoted only the draft and used a version printed in 1885 rather than Rendle's or Chambers', but except for some spelling, punctuation, and omission, his version is identical to Chambers'. Rendle mentioned not only the parish response to the Earl Marshal's committee but another response, of 1637, to the justices of Surrey about "divided houses," and Chambers confused the two. Rendle quoted the latter as alluding to houses in "Globe Alley, Sir Mathew Brand, Knight, of Moulsey, owner." Many papers of this response survive but not, so far as I can find, the one Rendle quoted. For Rendle, see William Harrison, *Description of England*, ed. F. J. Furnivall (London, 1877), pt. II, the first appendix, p. xvii. The documents are kept in the following

order: tax assessment; warrant, draft, and report of 1635; and papers of 1637 (P.92/SAV/1324, 1325-27, 1328-39).

30. The two proclamations of Charles' time are S.T.C. 8771 (May 2, 1625) and 8958 (from which the remark about governing and feeding the multitude comes). See also the many allusions to the commissioners' work in the calendars of state papers, for example: *C.S.P., Dom., 1629-31*, pp. 7, 220-21, 321-22, 479; *1633-34*, pp. 285, 408, 424, 428, 434; *1634-35*, pp. 197-98, 291; *1635*, pp. 352, 595, 608-09; *1635-36*, pp. 267, 522; *1636-37*, p. 2.

31. No entries in the draft have a sum of money beside them, but many in the report do: all thirty for the Clink liberty, eight (of twenty-eight) for Paris Garden, and all thirty for the main part of boroughside but none (of sixteen) for a prosperous part of it called Montague Close. Many of the sums are half the yearly value mentioned in the entry but some rather less or more. A few are the same amount as the yearly value. They could represent fines for illegal buildings allowed to stand, except that they do not seem to relate to the foundation of the building, or what the building was made of (brick or timber), or when it was built. Those for the Clink liberty add up to £87.16s.8d., and a tax assessment of the whole liberty in 1635 came to only £40.16s.8d.

32. E.351/3267/m.7^d, 9^d, 14^d, and /3269/m.4^d (I am indebted to Prof. John Astington for leading me to these documents). See also L. F. Salzman, *Building in England down to 1540* (Oxford, 1952), pp. 197 (the plate), 305 & n.; *Records of the Worshipful Company of Carpenters*, comp. by Bower Marsh (Oxford, 1914), II, 92, 153, and comp. by Marsh, ed. John Ainsworth (London, 1937), V, 29, 197.

33. Oliver Rackham, *Trees and Woodland in the British Landscape* (London, 1976), pp. 22-23, 26, and *Ancient Woodland* (London, 1980), pp. 5, 187, 226; C.2/Chas.I/B.126/62, the bill (Dec., 1624) and answer (Feb. 4, 1625), and above, p. 101.

34. See above, pp. 3, 14. The figures for both the Theatre and the Globe are complicated by sums arising from and spent on other buildings on the properties.

35. ''Bodley'' was regularly written as what seems to be ''Bodlone'' and regularly corrected.

36. Richard Fisher signed his deposition by writing merely ''R''; someone else wrote his name.

37. The two copies are the same except that the other has ''John'' for ''Joseph'' and ''Berwicken'' for ''Barwicken'' and omits ''last'' after ''November.'' By ''Barwicken'' Bell may have meant Barbican. He should have been living with his master, Atkins, who gave himself in both 1632 and 1634 (nos. 5, 21) as of the parish of St. Botolph's Aldersgate, in which the western end of Barbican Street was.

38. The crossed out ''bo'' was the writer's attempt to write ''bond'' before catching his mistake. See the entry just above this one in the note book.

39. The ''et al*ios*'' in the margin (which could be ''et al*ium*'' or, for Brend's wife, ''et al*iam*'') is probably a mistake, because elsewhere Brend is always sole defendant. The remark about the mistaken name of a commissioner must refer to the lawyers' names in no. 12, which were mistaken and were ''amended.''

40. The two people who signed the document were William Lane, deputy registrar of the Court of Requests, and James Milles, a lesser official of the court: Req.1/61/7 Feb. and *C.S.P., Dom., 1635*, p. 445. Richard Lane, the King's Men's counsel, had a brother William alive in 1638 who might have succeeded their father as deputy registrar: see their mother's will at the Northampton Record Office, Northamptonshire Wills, A, Series II, f.75.

41. The document is an undated sheet of paper on which are fifty-one rough entries of commissions, injunctions, and privy seals issued and fees charged. I take "10" to mean the year of the reign, and if I am right, the term would be Michaelmas. The "6-6" is perhaps the fee, which would be 6s.6d. Presumably the renewal would have been taken out and paid for by the King's Men, since it was they who took out, and no doubt paid for, the original document (no. 18) on July 12, 1634.

42. Another affidavit appeared that day in a lawsuit given as "Burbadge v⁵ Oates."

Select Bibliography
Of Items for Which Abbreviations Have Been Used

Acts of the Privy Council of England, 1629-30. Ed. P. A. Penfold. London, 1961.

Adams, J. C. *The Globe Playhouse.* New York, 1942.

Alumni Oxoniensis. 4 vols. Ed. Joseph Foster. Oxford, 1891-92.

Bentley, G. E. *The Jacobean and Caroline Stage*, Vols. III, VI. Oxford, 1968.

Berry, Herbert. *The Boar's Head Playhouse.* Washington, D. C., 1986.

Braines, W. W. *The Site of the Globe Playhouse Southwark.* London, 1921, 1924.

_____ ."The Site of 'the Theatre,' Shoreditch." *London Topographical Record*, Vol. XI. 1917.

_____ ."Shoreditch." *Survey of London.* Vol. VIII. London, 1922.

Calendar of State Papers, Domestic...1591-94, Preserved in the...Public Record Office. Ed. Mary Anne Everett Green. London, 1867.

Calendar of State Papers, Domestic...1595-97, Preserved in the...Public Record Office. Ed. Mary Anne Everett Green. London, 1869.

Calendar of State Papers, Domestic...1598-1601, Preserved in the...Public Record Office. Ed. Mary Anne Everett Green. London, 1869.

Calendar of State Papers, Domestic...1603-10, Preserved in the...Public Record Office. Ed. Mary Anne Everett Green. London, 1869.

Calendar of State Papers, Domestic...1611-18, Preserved in the...Public Record Office. Ed. Mary Anne Everett Green. London, 1858.

Calendar of State Papers, Domestic...1619-23, Preserved in the...Public Record Office. Ed. Mary Anne Everett Green. London, 1858.

Calendar of State Papers, Domestic...1623-25, with Addenda 1603-1625, Preserved in the...Public Record Office. Ed. Mary Anne Everett Green. London, 1859.

Calendar of State Papers, Domestic...1625-26, Preserved in the...Public Record Office. Ed. John Bruce. London, 1858.

Calendar of State Papers, Domestic...1628-29, Preserved in the...Public Record Office. Ed.

John Bruce. London, 1859.

Calendar of State Papers, Domestic...1631-33, Preserved in the...Public Record Office. Ed. John Bruce. London, 1862.

Calendar of State Papers, Domestic...1633-34, Preserved in the...Public Record Office. Ed. John Bruce. London, 1863.

Calendar of State Papers, Domestic...1634-35, Preserved in the...Public Record Office. Ed. John Bruce. London, 1864.

Calendar of State Papers, Domestic...1635, Preserved in the...Public Record Office. Ed. John Bruce. London, 1865.

Calendar of State Papers, Domestic...1635-36, Preserved in the...Public Record Office. Ed. John Bruce. London, 1866.

Calendar of State Papers, Domestic...1636-37, Preserved in the...Public Record Office. Ed. John Bruce. London, 1867.

Calendar of State Papers, Domestic...1637, Preserved in the...Public Record Office. Ed. John Bruce. London, 1868.

Calendar of State Papers, Domestic...1637-38, Preserved in the...Public Record Office. Ed. John Bruce. London, 1869.

Calendar of State Papers, Domestic...1639, Preserved in the...Public Record Office. Ed. W. D. Hamilton. London, 1873.

Calendar of State Papers, Domestic...1640, Preserved in the...Public Record Office. Ed. W. D. Hamilton. London, 1880.

Calendar of State Papers, Domestic...1640-41, Preserved in the...Public Record Office. Ed. W. D. Hamilton. London, 1882.

Calendar of State Papers, Domestic...1641-43, Preserved in the...Public Record Office. Ed. W. D. Hamilton. London, 1887.

Calendar of State Papers, Domestic...1655-56, Preserved in the...Public Record Office. Ed. Mary Anne Everett Green. London, 1882.

Calendar of State Papers, Domestic...1659-60, Preserved in the...Public Record Office. Ed. Mary Anne Everett Green. London, 1886.

Calendar of State Papers, Domestic...Addenda, 1580-1625, Preserved in the...Public Record Office. Ed. Mary Anne Everett Green. London, 1872.

Calendar of State Papers, Domestic...Addenda, 1625-49, Preserved in the...Public Record Office. Ed. W. D. Hamilton. London. 1897.

Calendar of State Papers, Ireland, 1647-60 and Addenda, 1625-60, Preserved in the...Public Record Office. Ed. R. P. Mahaffy. London, 1904.

Calendar of State Papers, Venetian, 1628-29, Preserved in the...Public Record Office. Ed. A. B. Hinds. London, 1916.

Calendar of State Papers, Venetian, 1629-32, Preserved in the...Public Record Office. Ed. A. B. Hinds. London, 1919.

Calendar of the Patent Rolls Preserved in the Public Record Office...1569-72. London, 1966.

Carte, Thomas. *An History of the Life of James Duke of Ormonde.* Vol. I. London, 1736.

Chamberlain, John. *The Letters of John Chamberlain.* Ed. N. E. McClure. Philadelphia, 1939.

Chambers, E. K. *The Elizabethan Stage.* Vols. II, III, IV. Oxford, 1923.

Clarendon, Edward Hyde, first earl of. *History of the Rebellion*. Vols. I, V, VI, VII. Ed. W. Dunn Macray. Oxford, 1888.

_____ . *The Life of Edward Earl of Clarendon*. Vol. I. Oxford, 1857.

Clark, Arthur M. *Thomas Heywood*. Oxford, 1931.

Coates, Charles. *The History and Antiquities of Reading*. London, 1802.

Commons Journal. See *Journals of the House of Commons*.

Darlington, Ida and James Howgego. *Printed Maps of London*. London, 1978.

Dictionary of National Biography. 21 volumes. Ed. Leslie Stephen and Sidney Lee. London, 1885-1900.

The Four Visitations of Berkshire. 2 vols. Ed. W. Harry Rylands. London: Harleian Soc., 1907-8.

Halliwell-Phillipps, J. O. *Outlines of the Life of Shakespeare*. London, 1882.

Historical Manuscripts Commission. *First Report*. London, 1870.

Historical Manuscripts Commission. *Third Report*. London, 1872.

Historical Manuscripts Commission. *Fifth Report*. London, 1876.

Historical Manuscripts Commission. *Sixth Report*. London, 1877.

Historical Manuscripts Commission. *Tenth Report*. Vol. IV. London, 1906.

Historical Manuscripts Commission. *Eleventh Report*. London, 1887.

Historical Manuscripts Commission. *The Manuscripts of Earl Cowper, K. G., Preserved at Melbourne Hall*. Vol. I. London, 1888.

Historical Manuscripts Commission. *Report on the Manuscripts of the Marquess of Downshire, Preserved at Easthampstead Park, Berkshire*. Vol. II. London, 1936.

Historical Manuscripts Commission. *Report on the Manuscripts of the Family of Gawdy, Formerly of Norfolk*. London, 1885.

Historical Manuscripts Commission. *Calendar of the Manuscripts of the Marquess of Ormonde, Preserved at the Castle, Kilkenny*. Vol. I. London, 1895.

Historical Manuscripts Commission. *The Manuscripts of his Grace the Duke of Rutland...Preserved at Belvoir Castle*. Vol. IV. London, 1905.

Historical Manuscripts Commission. *Calendar of the Manuscripts of the Most Hon. The Marquis of Salisbury, K.G., &c. Preserved at Hatfield House,*. Vols. V, XI, XIII, XVII. London, 1894, 1906, 1915.

Hosley, Richard. "Was There a Music-Room at Shakespeare's Globe?" *Shakespeare Survey* 13 (1960).

Hotson, Leslie. *Shakespeare's Wooden O*. London, 1959.

Jonson, Ben. *A Challenge at Tilt*. London, 1614. In *The Complete Masques*. Ed. Stephen Orgel. New Haven, 1969.

_____ . *Hymenaei*. In *The Complete Masques*. Ed. Stephen Orgel. New Haven, 1969.

_____ . *Prince Henry's Barriers*. In *The Complete Masques*. Ed. Stephen Orgel. New Haven, 1969.

Journals of the House of Commons. Vols. I, II, III, IV. London: Printed by order of the House of Commons, n.d.

Laud, William. *The Works of the Most Reverend Father in God, William Laud, D. D.* Vols. III, VI. Oxford, 1853.

Memorials and Affairs of State. Vols. II, III. Ed. Edmund Sawyer. London, 1725.

Middle Temple Records. Vols. I, II. Ed. C. H. Hopwood. London: Middle Temple, 1904-05.

A New English Dictionary on Historical Principles. 10 vols. Ed. James A. H. Murray et al. Oxford, 1888-1928.

Nichols, John. *The Progresses...of King James the First*. 4 vols. London, 1828.

Rushworth, John. *Historical Collections*. Vol. II. London, 1692.

Sharers Papers. In *Malone Society Collections*. Vol. II, pt. 3. Oxford, 1931.

Shaw, W. A. *Knights of England*. Vol. II. London, 1906.

Smith, Irwin. *Shakespeare's Blackfriars Playhouse*. New York, 1964.

Southern, Richard. "On Reconstructing a Practicable Elizabethan Public Playhouse." *Shakespeare Survey* 12 (1959).

Survey of London. Vol. XXII. Eds. Sir Howard Roberts, Walter H. Godfrey. London, 1950.

Victoria County Histories. *The Victoria History of the County of Hampshire*. Vol. V. Ed. William Page. London, 1912.

Victoria County Histories. *The Victoria History of the County of Hertfordshire*. Vol. III. Ed. William Page. London, 1912.

Victoria County Histories. *The Victoria History of the County of Northamptonshire*. Vol. IV. Ed. L. F. Salzman. Oxford, 1937.

Victoria County Histories. *The Victoria History of the County of Somerset*. Vol. III. Ed. R. B. Pugh. London, 1974.

Visitations of Surrey in 1530, 1572, and 1623. Ed. W. Bruce Bannerman. London: Harleian Soc., 1899.

Wallace, C. W. *The Children of the Chapel at Blackfriars 1597-1603*. Lincoln, Nebraska, 1908.

————. *The First London Theatre: Materials for a History*. Lincoln, Nebraska, 1913.

Wickham, Glynne. *Early English Stages*. Vols. I, II. London, 1959, 1963.

Wood, Anthony. *Athenae Oxoniensis*. Vol. I. London, 1721.

INDEX

251